LEST WE FORGIVE

DETECTIVE LIZ MOORLAND BOOK 1

PHILLIPA NEFRI CLARK

LEST WE FORGIVE

Book Cover by Steam Power Studios

Editing by Loiuse Guy

1st Edition 2023

CONTENTS

A QUICK NOTE

The Detective Liz Moorland books are set in Australia and written in Australian English for any authentic experience. Some spelling and word use may differ from that of other English speaking countries.

Despite many rounds of editing and proofing, sneaky errors sometimes get in so should you find a typo please email hello@ phillipaclark.com with the full sentence or paragraph and if you are the first to find it you will be sent another of Phillipa's ebooks as thanks.

Stay in touch through Phillipa's newsletter.
Free short book when you subscribe.

ONE

There's no room along this narrow street to park so I back the van into the driveway of a darkened house. No lights come on. Nobody peers from the window. I turn the motor off.

These new estates are rubbish. Dead ends everywhere. Speed humps. Tiny roundabouts. Oversized houses with front lawns smaller than my handkerchief. Scrawny baby trees replace the old oaks or gums bulldozed to make way for families to cram into boxes. They all look the same to me.

But only one matters.

Number ten.

I'm two doors down and across the road so it's easy to see the occupants inside as they make their way to the door. Their car is in the driveway. Red. Mid-sized. Won't take much to nudge it off a road… if it comes to that.

I light a cigarette and draw in the filthy tar until it hurts my lungs then blow out the smoke. It doesn't help the visibility, so I open the window a crack. The air is bitterly cold already and it is only early evening.

The kid rushes out of the house to the car. She's wearing a short *dress, tights, and a puffer jacket. Makes no sense. Pants would keep her warmer.*

'Hurry up, Dad! I'm freezing to death!'

Like I said. Pants would keep you warmer.

She's eight. Blonde like her mum. She jumps up and down in a circle, puffing out white air. Part way around, she stops and stares in my direction.

I lower the cigarette and stub it out in an empty soft drink can.

There's no way she can see me. Not through the condensation and window tinting. Stare all you want, little girl.

'Melanie, you forgot your backpack.'

Susie Weaver unlocks the car with a remote, handbag over her shoulder and the kid's backpack in her other hand.

Melanie drags the door open and throws herself inside. 'I was almost a snowman, Mum.'

'Might need some snow first.'

'I've never seen snow.'

'Yes you have. We took you to Switzerland when you were three.'

'I was a baby then. Can we go there now?'

Regular little chatterbox.

Her father is fussing with the front door. Checking it's locked. Patting his coat for whatever he thinks he's forgotten.

'We'd better go, David.' *Susie is halfway into the front passenger seat.*

Yes. You'll be late if you don't leave. Wouldn't want you hurrying on the slippery roads. Not yet.

A minute later the sedan backs out carrying the perfect little family.

Soon to face the consequences of a bad decision.

When their taillights disappear around a curve, I turn the ignition.

TWO

'I want to see you eat a whole bowl of linguine *and* dessert, Melanie Weaver!'

Melanie giggled as Carla Pickering tried her best to look serious. It didn't work and she ended up laughing as well. Susie loved that about her best friend. Since Melanie was born, Carla had been more than her godmother. She'd been like a second mum.

'Mummy, when the waiter comes, may I order my own meal please?'

'You can, and even mine if you really want to.'

Spironi's was always busy on Friday nights, and they sat at their regular table near the window. David had stepped outside to take a phone call so they were waiting for him. And for Carla's husband.

'Where is Bradley, hon?'

Carla shrugged. 'You know what they're like, both of them. Always something coming up at work at short notice. He promised he'd only run into the warehouse for a minute. And he'd better turn up because I don't want to get a taxi home.'

'We'll take you if it comes to that.'

'Comes to what? Sorry I'm late.' Bradley Pickering leaned over Carla's shoulder to kiss her cheek. 'You should have started without me.'

'Next time we'll make it a girl's night out,' Susie said. Through the window, David—his back turned—wasn't happy with whoever was on the other end of the phone. His shoulders were tense, and his spare hand ran through his hair. It wasn't the first time this week he'd stood like that during a phone call.

Who is upsetting you so much?

'Hello, baby girl.' Bradley grinned at Melanie as he sat beside her.

'Oh, you're here!' Melanie sat up straight. 'I'm going to order my dinner. And Mummy's.'

'Rightly so. I should look at the menu. Starving.' Bradley leaned back to catch the eye of a waiter. 'Missed lunch.'

'Then let's order. I'll guess for David,' Susie said.

She didn't have to. David came back in as their waiter arrived, sliding into the seat between Bradley and Susie. He made a show of turning his phone off and pocketing it and winked at Melanie. She tried to wink back but both eyes kept opening and closing. As soon as the waiter asked if they were ready to order, she stopped practicing and raised her hand.

'I'd like to place an order please.'

Everyone laughed. It was impossible not to, but Melanie frowned at them until they stopped. Once she had the quiet she wanted, she precisely and politely ordered and then crossed her arms.

Carla whispered something to her, and Melanie's lips flicked up in a smile.

David topped up glasses with red wine.

'Not for me.' Carla covered her glass with a hand.

Bradley was quick to fill her glass with water from a bottle in the middle of the table and she lifted the glass with a quick glance and murmured 'thanks.'

The men began a quiet conversation. Melanie had the notebook she took everywhere and was doodling. Susie leaned closer to Carla. 'No wine? Are you...?'

'I don't know. Maybe. I'll do a home test tomorrow.'

'It will happen. And you will be the best mother ever.' Susie squeezed her arm.

'I just wish...'

'What, hon?'

'Bradley and I waited too long. I always thought... expected...'

'You're not too old, Carla.'

Carla smiled. A sad smile which tugged at Susie's heart. There were a few years between them and when Susie had fallen pregnant within a year of marrying David, Carla had teased her about being a young mum. But Carla never once wavered in her support of Susie and fell in love with Melanie on sight.

'Aunty Carla, would you please smile at me and I will draw you.'

By the time mains arrived, Melanie was satisfied with the portrait but refused to show anyone until she coloured it in at home.

Despite the food in front of him, Bradley had his phone out, showing something to David. Their heads were close together, but the body language was strange. The more Bradley leaned in, the further David pulled back in his seat until his neck was craning to view the screen.

'How about we eat? You know, rather than do business? David?' Susie held her fork aloft to make the point that she wasn't about to start her meal until they stopped dealing with work problems at the table. Both men offered a sorry, and the table settled into a comfortable quiet as they enjoyed what was always a delicious meal. They'd been eating out together almost every Friday or Saturday night for years, often here where the food was great, and the ambience suited them all.

On the other side of the table, Melanie was trying to copy her father as he rolled spaghetti around his fork against a spoon. Flecks of tomato peppered her fingers, but she persevered until a small ribbon wrapped around the prongs and she hastily slid it into her mouth.

'You're so lucky, Susie. You have everything.' Carla said.

Sure, if you mean a husband who is keeping secrets all of a sudden.

Susie glanced at David with a frown and picked up her wine.

Eyes back on Susie, Carla nodded. 'You *do*, honey. Such a perfect family and now, with the new deals the boys are brokering for the business, you'll be in a position to move closer to us. Something bigger. For Mel.'

'I like our house.'

'Well, Mel likes our garden. She loves our fruit trees and the pool. A bit more space.'

Like I once had.

Space to run and be loud and silly and lie on her back to stare at the sky. No fruit trees or pool, but better than that. A pony. Her pony. And a father who was her world...

She grabbed her wine and swallowed more than she intended.

'Mummy? I need to use the ladies room.'

Melanie had left her seat and was beside Susie.

'Oh. Okay, we'll go——.'

'Mother. I know where it is. I'm a big girl.'

Susie smiled and kissed Melanie's forehead. 'You sure are. But you only get to be out of my sight for two minutes or else I'll think you are playing hide and seek, so don't be long.'

Melanie rolled her eyes and darted off toward the back of the restaurant. She was safe here. The staff all knew her, and she'd be fine on her own for a few minutes.

————

She loved the lemony scent of the hand wash so Melanie washed her hands twice, singing. One day she'd be a singer, travelling the world. Or a famous artist. Maybe both.

About to hit the big button on the hand dryer, a noise on the other side of the door stopped her. Was that Daddy? She listened. It was. And Uncle Bradley sounded cross. Really cross.

'Last chance, David. I mean it.'

'And for the last time, I'm not agreeing to this.'

'That's your final word?'

'Final word, Brad.'

'You idiot!'

Melanie slammed her hand onto the dryer button and stood close to it, drowning out the angry voices. She counted to fifty, turning the dryer back on twice.

But when she finally peeked through the door, they were just down the hallway a bit. Not just Uncle Brad and Daddy but another man with an angry face. She closed the door and raised herself up on her toes to look in the mirror.

Her fingers touched the glass, tapping them in time. 'Best. Friends. Shouldn't. Argue.'

————

Susie checked the time since Melanie left. Too long. Just as she was about to go to find her, Melanie slipped back into her seat, eyes down.

'Sweetie pie? You look upset.'

'Maybe a bit.'

'Feel like telling me why?'

Melanie glanced back the way she'd come.

David and Bradley had disappeared in the same direction

just after Melanie left the table. Susie was close to the end of her patience with this cloak and dagger crap, particularly when it impacted their evening out.

'Did you see Daddy?'

With a nod, Melanie turned sad eyes to Susie. 'Uncle Bradley is cross with him.'

Susie exchanged a glance with Carla, whose brow was creased. Obviously she had no idea what was going on either.

'I'm sure it is just about business, so I'll go and remind them they need to order dessert.'

After kicking them up their backsides.

Carla reached for a menu. 'What are you having for dessert, Mel? I thought I'd try...'

Grateful for her friend's automatic response of distracting Melanie, Susie headed for the back of the restaurant. She turned into the hallway to the bathrooms almost running into their waiter.

'Sorry, Marco. Not looking. Do you know where David is?'

'Talking with Mr Bradley. Near the back exit.'

'Ta.'

She heard their argument before she could see them.

'Mate, we both have to sign that contract. If you don't, then I'm stuffed. You're making the mistake of your life. Of all our lives.'

What the hell is Brad going on about?

Behind the men—who were face to face—the exit door clicked shut. David's face was set. Bradley's hands flew everywhere around himself as he waffled on until he noticed Susie. His arms dropped.

'Congratulations to you both. Melanie is upset and thinks you hate each other, and I can see why. This is a social dinner. Not fucking business. Okay?'

———

After dessert, Bradley announced he had to go back to work for a while and before Carla had a chance to object, David insisted on dropping her home.

At Carla's house, Susie climbed out to give her a hug.

'I don't know what's up with those two,' Carla whispered. 'Silly boys.'

Susie rolled her eyes. 'Very.' She pulled back with a smile. 'But thank you for always being there for me. I don't know what I'd do without you.'

'Love you.'

'Always and forever, Carla.'

Within minutes of heading home, Melanie was asleep. When they turned onto the long stretch of open road they used as a shortcut between the two homes, Susie turned to David. 'What was that all about? You and Bradley?'

He glanced in the rear vision mirror at Melanie.

'I'm so sorry. I didn't mean for her to overhear us.'

'Well she did. What is Bradley so angry about?'

'We have different opinions on the direction of the business. You know how much money matters to him and I've knocked back an arrangement I think would land us in trouble. He disagrees.'

'I heard him say you needed to sign a contract.'

'First step on a slippery slope.'

'Something illegal?'

'Let's just say I don't trust the people he wanted to work with.'

Susie frowned. 'Should I be worried?'

David reached across and squeezed her hand. 'Of course not. Anyway, I'm looking forward to our drive tomorrow. Can't wait to show you what I found and perhaps we can stop along the coast for lunch.'

'Oh, I would love that! Melanie will love it!'

A blinding flash of light filled the interior as headlights—on high—appeared from nowhere behind them.

Susie swung around to look. Some idiot was right on their tail.

'David?'

'What the hell? Can't see the road.'

Susie faced forward again, reaching for the grab handle above the door as their car drifted across the middle line.

The headlights disappeared.

They were in the wrong lane.

Thank god the road is empty.

Before David could get back into his lane, an engine roared and something large—a van—matched their speed, hard up against Susie's window.

'David!'

He slammed his foot onto the brake.

The van moved ahead.

They were sliding.

Spinning.

Tyres screaming.

Melanie. Oh my god, Melanie.

THREE

'There are two coffees going cold on a counter back at the food truck thanks to you dragging me away. Another two minutes wouldn't have hurt.' Detective Pete McNamara scowled from the passenger seat.

Detective Liz Moorland didn't answer as she navigated along the icy road. Her partner's first-world complaint wasn't helping. She gripped the steering wheel until her knuckles were white.

It can't be true.

'From the sound of it this was just an accident. Not like we can do anything either.'

She shot him a look which she hoped would shut him up. Pete was an excellent police officer but a royal pain.

Flashing blue and red lights signalled an ambulance approaching and she slowed and moved over as far as she dared on this narrow road. It flew past and she muttered a small prayer for the occupant. She didn't need to believe in a god to offer up her internal cry for help. Pete kept his thoughts to himself. Perhaps the gravity of a speeding ambulance kept his tongue in check.

The scene ahead was sheer carnage.

Patrol cars blocked the road on either end of a fifty metre or so stretch with uniformed officers acting as traffic controllers. A small line-up of cars were stationary at the far end and a couple of people had climbed out to take photographs. An ambulance and two fire trucks parked at angles closer to the crash.

Portable floodlights shone on emergency workers using the jaws of life on the passenger door of a mangled red sedan. Its bonnet was wrapped around the trunk of a large gum tree on the wide, overgrown grass verge.

Liz pulled over out of the way, forcing aside the thought that nobody could survive that impact. The ambulance had had its sirens on. Someone was alive.

Pete was out of the car first. 'I'll go and have a word with that officer. Get him to do his job. Bloody parasites photographing this.'

His absence gave Liz the chance to gather herself. Put her feelings aside. Deal with what was going on around her without letting it get into her head.

Fat chance.

'Liz. Sorry to see you under the circumstances.' Senior Constable Annette Benski met her halfway. They'd worked together on a recent case.

'Is there any chance you're wrong, Annette?'

'Wouldn't have called you if I was. Damned shame.'

An iron band tightened around her chest as they approached the car.

Stay professional.

'Any early ideas on what caused it? Single car accident?'

'No sign of another vehicle. Accident Investigation will be here soon and that's what it looks like on the surface. Road is freezing. Driver might have been going a bit too fast and lost it. Could be drug or alcohol related... sorry. No point speculating.'

With a groan, the machinery forced the metal apart and the passenger door fell away with a thud.

The windscreen was inches from the front seat passenger. A deflated air bag sagged.

And Susie Weaver was dead.

Liz gulped down the lump in her throat.

She peered past Susie to David and recoiled at the damage to his face.

'Melanie? Was she with them?'

'Ambulance just took her. In a bit of pain mostly from a busted arm from the look of it. But Liz. She saw her parents. The paramedics gave her a green whistle, but I know she understood they're deceased.'

Liz touched Susie's arm.

I'll look out for Melanie. And your dad.

'Liz? Maybe don't hang around while they recover the... bodies.'

'Who is telling Vince?'

'Couple of uniforms. Thought it best he knew straight away.'

With a final look at Susie, Liz went in search of Pete. He was laying down the law to curious bystanders. When he noticed her he came over. 'You alright?'

Her heart wasn't even beating anymore. She was sure of it.

'It's not fair. Not again.'

———

Vince Carter worked on a small piece of timber, a turning knife carving out the features of a bird in rapid, expert moves. He liked this one. An Indian Mynah bird, something of a pest in real life but an interesting bird to carve. His stomach rested on the top of his legs as he hunched over the bench to get the most from the narrow beam of light from a desk lamp, the only light in the room other than the muted television.

Headlights arced across the wall Vince faced and he jumped and cut too deeply into the neck of the bird. Tossing it aside, he pushed himself to his feet with a grunt, taking a minute to straighten.

'What the hell.'

Nobody ever visited. Especially not in the dead of night.

He glanced at the clock on the mantelpiece, lit up by the headlights of a car which had pulled up. It was close to midnight.

The light caught the photographs beside the clock. Him in a police uniform, broad shouldered and flat stomached. His wedding day with a sweet-faced woman gripping his hand and smiling up at him. Marion. And another, them both seated with her holding a little girl resembling Melanie. Except it was years ago. Susie.

His stomach churned as he headed for the front door and swung it open.

Two uniformed police were climbing the couple of steps to the porch. Kids. Their nerves showing with quick puffs of misty breath.

'Constables?'

'Um... Sergeant Vincent Carter?'

'Ex. Ex Sergeant Carter. What's happened?'

'Sir, I'm Constable McNeill. This is Constable Lovett. We're here about your... your daughter. Susan Weaver.'

As his legs began to buckle, Vince grabbed the door frame to hold himself up.

'Sir. We regret to inform you there was a fatal car accident this evening. Susan Weaver and her husband David Weaver were travelling home with their daughter—'

'Melanie... please, no.'

'Melanie Weaver has been taken to the hospital. We understand she's in a stable condition. We're so sorry about your daughter and son-in-law.' They stood there. Too young to be tasked with this terrible job. Caught between duty and compassion.

Vince slumped forward, only his grip on the door frame keeping him on his feet.

I never got the chance to put things right. Now I never will.

Constable McNeill put a hand out. A firm touch to his shoulder. Vince raised his head.

'We'll take you to the hospital, sir.'

'I can drive myself.' He stepped back inside to get his keys and wallet from the hall stand.

'We'll get you there faster.'

Hands shaking so hard he could barely pick up his keys, he nodded.

———

There were no more tears left. Just a dull ache behind her eyes and a lump of ice where her heart should be. Carla imagined her face was a mess of mascara and puffiness and she didn't care. Nothing mattered.

How do I get through this, Susie?

Her fingers worked the rosary beads handed down from her grandmother, but no prayer formed on her lips.

She sat with Bradley in a small waiting room more an alcove with a row of seats—in sight of a central nurses' station. Someone had called Brad... a friend on the force, he'd told her. Since arriving they'd heard almost nothing, but Melanie was alive and tonight, that was a blessing.

If only David and Susie hadn't driven her home. If only Bradley hadn't gone back to work. Carla shifted in her seat, putting some air between the two of them.

He didn't notice. Yet again, he was on his phone but texting, not speaking.

The lift doors opened and Vince Carter burst out, pausing to look around before stalking to the central station. It wasn't attended and he gazed around the area until his eyes met hers. If he recognised her, he didn't show it, spinning back to speak to a nurse who stepped behind the counter.

You didn't care about your daughter so why are you here?

An orderly pushed a bed past, and Vince followed.

'She's back.' Carla was on her feet, reaching for her handbag.

'That's good news.' Bradley took her hand. 'We need to wait for permission to see her, baby.'

'He shouldn't be here.'

'Carter? He's her grandpa but yeah. Probably not.' Bradley got to his feet and gently pulled Carla against him. 'This isn't the place or time. We'll wait for as long as it takes. Okay?'

She leaned against him as the grief bubbled up again.

———

Vince waited in the hallway until the orderly left.

Inside the room, a nurse finished adjusting the blankets and looked up as he entered. He stopped at the sight of the small body in the bed. Tiny. Alone.

Melanie's eyes were closed. An IV was in one arm and some gadget on one of her fingers. Monitoring something. The forearm of her left arm was in some kind of brace. She was so little. So vulnerable.

'Only next of kin, dear.' The nurse checked a clipboard at the foot of the bed.

'I'm her grandfather. Vince Carter. Is she going to be... is she alright?'

'The break in her forearm hasn't been set yet. She's sedated but you can sit with her. I'll be back in a few minutes. But let her rest.'

'Thank you.' There was a chair in the corner, and he moved it between the bed and the window.

The nurse hurried out, but her progress was halted by Carla and Bradley. Whatever they thought they were doing here, it wasn't their place. Vince didn't sit but folded his arms and stared at them.

'Can we go in?' Bradley wore a suit and tie and not a hair on his head was out of place.

'I'm afraid not. One visitor at a time and only family—'

'We are family. Her godparents.' Carla tried to slide past the nurse who took a small step to close the gap. 'Please. Please, can't I see her?'

'Why not go back to the waiting room, dear. There's a coffee machine just around the corner.' The nurse closed the door behind herself and whatever else Carla had to say became a muffled noise in the background.

Vince sank onto the chair. He brushed the hair from Melanie's forehead, exposing a bruise. His hand lifted and clenched.

'Grandad?'

Her voice was so quiet. So frail.

She gazed at him.

He took her hand. 'Hello, Melly-belly.'

A tear slipped from the corner of the little girl's eye. 'Mummy? Daddy?'

He gave her hand a little squeeze. 'I'm here, sweetie. I'll always be here for you.'

A flicker of relief crossed her features before her eyes fluttered closed again.

———

The waiting room was occupied but Vince no longer cared if he had to share with two people he had no time for. His need to be here for Melanie outweighed his need to avoid her godparents.

Carla stared at him without a word. He'd never seen her look anything less than perfect, but her face was streaked with makeup, mascara and eyeshadow mixed together by tears and tissues. She'd been Susie's best friend for a long time, as different as they were from each other.

'How is she? Really,' Bradley said.

Vince shrugged.

'Please. We've sat here for hours and haven't had any news.'

He found some words through a throat thick with grief. 'She's comfortable, considering. She woke for a minute and knew I was there.'

'I should be with her,' Carla snapped. 'Susie would want it.'

Not now.

'You know she'd want me there with Melanie. She would hate that you're here after what you said that day. Susie didn't want you in her life anymore so why do you think she'd want you near her daughter?'

Her words stabbed into him. Vince closed his eyes and leaned back in his seat.

———

'Mr Carter?'

Vince lurched out of a half-dream, blinking his eyes to focus them.

Hospital.

Melanie.

Susie.

'Sorry. Just wanted to update you.' A man dropped onto the seat beside him. White coat. Tag. Weary. 'I'm Doctor Lennard.'

'Is she okay?'

'Melanie is doing well, all things considered. She has a fair bit of bruising from the car restraints. A bump on the head. And a simple fracture of her left forearm.'

'She'll recover alright?'

The doctor nodded. 'Physically.'

'Does she know? About... Susie. And David?'

'She was conscious at the scene of the accident and worked it out.' Doctor Lennard said. 'We'll have a counsellor spend some time with her in the morning once she's alert. And arrange ongoing appointments with whoever gets custody of her—'

'Me.'

'Oh. You will take her in?'

'There's nobody else. And she's my grandchild.'

'No family on either side?'

'David's mother is alive but is unwell. Susie and Mel were the only ones left on my side.'

Everyone has gone.

The doctor got to his feet. 'Well, that little girl is very lucky to have you. We'll talk before Melanie is discharged. She's a brave youngster.'

Watching the man hurry away, Vince's hands gripped his knees and he had to remember to breathe.

Of course he was taking Melanie in.

FOUR

As dawn made a dismal attempt to break through the misty darkness of mid-winter, Vince stood on the doorstep of Susie's house, a set of keys in one hand and a small suitcase in the other. For the longest time he stared at the door, his shoulders slumped. He leaned forward until his forehead touched the timber and drew in a long, ragged breath. The air came out white and wispy and floated around his head. A veil of sorrow.

A car passed and he jolted upright.

Among the tangle of keys he found the right one. As long as Susie hadn't changed the locks.

The entry light was on, but the rest of the house was dark apart from a glow at the top of the stairs in the direction of Susie and David's bedroom.

Vince turned abruptly and grabbed the handle of the door he'd just closed behind himself.

'Damn. Dammit.'

But leaving wasn't going to change anything. There were things to collect for Melanie.

He pulled a handwritten note from a pocket and checked it.

More focused, he climbed the stairs. Melanie's room was exactly like Melanie. Pretty—with its cute furnishings and touches; clever—with a shelf of books beyond her years; and neat as a pin apart from a brown teddy bear on the floor beside an unfinished jigsaw puzzle. He dropped the suitcase on the bed and systematically opened drawers and cupboard doors to collect a selection of clothing, socks, slippers, and her dressing gown. A book and a couple of toys. Just what would fit in the suitcase. There'd be time to collect the rest later.

The ensuite light was on at the far side of Susie and David's bedroom and he forced himself to walk in to turn it off.

Past her bed.

Past her jewellery and clothes.

Past her reading chair with her current book open, pages down.

Keeping his eyes on the floor he turned the light off and fled the room. Downstairs he passed the living room and stepped back, drawn to the large family photograph on the feature wall. David. Melanie. Susie.

His little girl.

With her little girl.

The suitcase slipped from his fingers and fell, with a soft thud, onto thick carpet. Vince stumbled to the hallway then beyond the stairs to the kitchen, to the cupboard where Susie kept drinking glasses. One hand on the sink, he turned on the tap and held the glass under, then gulped the contents and refilled it.

As his heart rate came down he glanced in the fridge and pantry. Could he even take snacks into the hospital? Putting the glass down, he pulled the list out again and wrote on it.

Go shopping. Food. Pillows. Sheets.

He didn't have it in him to take anything more from the house. Not today.

The phone on the counter blinked red with a message.

He pressed play and Susie's cheerful voice drifted through the kitchen.

You've reached David, Susie, and Mel! Leave us a message.

Vince put his hands over his ears as his stomach contracted. He threw himself at the sink and vomited. No matter how tightly he squeezed his eyelids together they wouldn't hold back the tears and he let them flow until the gagging stopped. Cleaning up the disgusting evidence of grief forced him to pull his act together.

The end of the message had beeped. He'd missed it.

His hands shook as he picked up the glass and drank until it was empty. Then he pressed play again.

You've reached David, Susie, and Mel! Leave us a message.

Message received at seven pm.

A male voice. Angry.

Pick up, for god sake.

A short silence.

First you ignore my messages on your mobile. Now this. You've made your bed, sunshine. Time's up, Weaver.

'What the hell?' Vince slammed the glass down and it shattered.

He pressed play again, fury blinding him to the shards and when he reached for a notepad near the phone he cut his hand. Before blood could pool on the counter, Vince grabbed a handful of tissues from a box and applied pressure.

Then he pressed play again.

———

Liz dragged herself into the regular morning briefing. The room was almost full, with some detectives perched on desks or chairs, and others standing chatting. Without fail, they all looked at her with varying degrees of sympathy... or pity. Someone shoved a chair her way and she wasn't about to refuse.

I never want a night like that again.

Pete followed a minute later with two takeaway coffees—large ones. 'I told them you needed an extra shot.' He handed her one and leaned against the wall nearby. 'Did you sleep at all?'

'Of course I did.'

She hadn't.

Their shift had only two hours left—hours intended to use on the Hardy case but when the call had come about the car crash she'd yelled at him to get in. Despite Pete's initial protest and continuing complaints, he'd made himself useful and been supportive without any further smart-arsed comments. They'd left the scene when the coroner arrived.

After dropping Pete home she'd driven to Vince's cottage in the middle of nowhere. He wasn't there and she kicked herself. He'd have been at the hospital with little Melanie. And her fronting up there probably wouldn't be what he'd want. He'd never want sympathy.

For an hour she'd sat in the car in his driveway and shed more tears than she knew she had inside.

The tears fell for Vince. He'd been her partner before Homicide Squad, when she was just starting out and he was ten years from retirement. She'd been there and seen what he'd experienced through losing his wife the same day he'd saved innocent people from a shooter at an Anzac parade. His grief and guilt never left him even though he could not have been in two places at one time. He wasn't one to do counselling, apart from the department generated visits.

And Liz had wept for Susie. For the little girl who'd lost her mother and been raised by a father who loved her but probably never said it. Susie used to come in to the station back then, finishing homework while she waited for Vince. Everyone loved the kid.

But mostly, it was for Melanie.

'Liz? All okay?'

She jolted back into the moment. It was unreal being here in the briefing room, which really, was an oversized office where detectives crammed together while renovations were underway. Once again, everyone was staring. She sipped her coffee rather than reply.

'She's good, Terry,' Pete said.

Detective Senior Sergeant Terry Hall didn't look convinced, but he turned to the whiteboard. 'No major updates overnight of any active cases.' He circled a name with a marker and faced the room again. 'And a distinct lack of progress on the recapture of Malcolm Hardy. He's been on the run for two days, people. Two days. A convicted murderer. A violent and intelligent criminal. And nobody knows where he is.'

Pete tossed the coffee cup he'd speed-drunk into an open rubbish bin. 'Thing is, boss, we didn't lose him. Idiots moving him to his new court hearing did so why is it our job to find him?'

There was a murmur of agreement. Every detective without an active case had been looking for Hardy or his accomplices.

'You offering to take lead when he kills again? Explain to his victim's family?' Terry asked.

'He only kills if he has a message to send.'

'Shut up, Pete,' Liz whispered. She didn't need more on her plate.

'Good advice, Liz. Too late though. McNamara? Get yourself down to Footscray and revisit his old haunts.'

Even as Pete groaned, the rest of the room laughed.

'Me too, boss?' Liz asked.

'Go home for a bit. Get some sleep.'

'Thought we might put some money into something for

Vince. Or for Melanie.' Liz got to her feet. 'I don't know what.'

Terry nodded. 'We'll come up with something.' He glanced around the room. 'For anyone who hasn't heard, a car accident last night claimed the lives of Vince Carter's daughter and son-in-law. Their small daughter survived.'

The door from the hallway opened abruptly and Vince stalked in. With all eyes on him, he stopped a few feet in, eyes roaming the room until resting on Liz. He seemed relieved to find her.

'Burning ears, mate?' Terry extended his hand to Vince, who looked at it then shook it. 'We want to offer our deepest condolences. We'll all miss Susie.'

'Yeah. Um, thanks.'

'You shouldn't be in here though.'

'Couldn't find Liz. Or you.'

'I'm here. Let's take a walk.' Liz reached his side. Up close, his skin was almost grey and the lines in his face deeply etched. He looked hollow.

'Where are you with the investigation, Terry?' Vince demanded.

With a surprised look, Terry shook his head. 'Accident Investigation, mate. Their area, not ours.'

'You're joking.' He almost spat the words.

'Icy conditions on the road. No preliminary signs of anything other than an accident, Vince. Not foul play.'

'Go back to the farm.' Pete sniggered at his own comment until Liz shot him a warning glance.

Before Vince had a chance to go and pummel Pete, which he probably deserved, Liz touched his arm. 'It was an accident.'

'You so sure?' Vince pulled a folded piece of paper from his top pocket and pressed it into her hand. As fast as he'd come in, he left.

Liz unfolded and read the few lines of Vince's handwriting

and her heart sank.

'What is it?' Terry asked.

'He may be right.' She handed the paper to Terry. 'I'll be back.'

———

He should have known better than to come here. A phone call would have done. An anonymous tip. He could have claimed he'd overheard someone making a threatening phone call to the Weaver house. This station wasn't his stamping ground anymore. Long gone were the days where he'd be greeted with warmth. Needed for his experience. Appreciated for his knowledge.

'Vince, wait up!'

Liz was the only one who still gave a damn. She'd been like a second daughter to him when they were partners. And Terry might care. But Terry had to toe the line. Be neutral.

He stopped in the middle of the hallway as she caught up.

'The note?' Her words came out like she was puffing.

'Since when does jogging a hundred metres get you out of breath?'

In the twenty plus years he'd known Liz she'd been lean and all muscle thanks to her obsession with running. Half marathons were her gig and she'd won her share.

'I'm not. What's with the note?'

'That was word for word from a message on Susie's answering machine. There was a threat to David which he clearly ignored.'

'A business threat, Vince? Or personal?'

'Either. Both. Since he went into partnership with Pickering he was always just this side of the law, but I could never catch him out. Someone wanted him dead and took Susie with him.'

'Any someone in particular?' Liz asked.

'If you hadn't noticed I don't work here. It's your job to find out.'

'Are you sure it was directed at David?'

His mouth opened to refute the implication. Then closed.

Susie would never be in trouble. Never attract the attention of the wrong people.

Except he didn't believe in never.

'I came to find you. At the cottage,' Liz said.

'You did?'

'And realised where you'd be. Didn't want to intrude at the hospital.'

A ridiculous prickle behind his eyes threatened to undo his resolve to stay strong. This wasn't the place or time to fall apart. But he couldn't look her in the eye.

'How's Melanie? I heard she's not critical, thank god.'

'Broken arm. Bruises. Shock.'

Liz touched his arm again. 'What's going to happen to her?'

'She'll be alright in time. Doctor thinks she can leave hospital soon. I'm going home to shower and change and then I'll head back. She needs me there.'

Pete McNamara sauntered in their direction. Someone needed to wipe that perpetual smirk off his face.

'Is she coming to live with you?' Liz asked.

Something about the way she asked riled him. 'Don't sound so surprised.'

'Vince, I'm not. I'm just worried about you.'

He started walking again. Too many people staring. Judging. Pointing fingers.

Liz caught up. 'What if I drop by later. Once she's home with you?'

'I raised Susie pretty much alone.'

'Yeah I know and that's why... Vince?'

He'd had enough. He increased the length of his stride.

Liz must have stopped. Her voice followed him. 'Vince, come on.'

Thanks for the bloody vote of confidence.

———

'Why are you still here?'

'I'm going in a min.' Liz flopped onto the seat opposite Terry. 'I wanted to write up what I saw last night... early this morning. Get it down while I still remember.'

Terry raised both eyebrows. 'You think there's more to it than an accident.'

'Maybe. When I was at the scene it felt like an odd place to lose control. The road is straight for a kilometre. Open paddocks on either side and no other roads or driveways near the scene. Yet the car spun and ended up on the wrong side of the road buried in a tree trunk.'

'Kangaroos? Some other animal on the road?'

'Always a possibility but still...' She was too tired to figure it out.

'Vince coping?' Terry asked.

'No. Thinks he is. But how much does one person need to bear in their life, Terry? I think that little girl is all he has left.'

'Feel for him. Really do. Look, Liz? Accident Investigation won't get to the car today so go home and sleep. I need you on the Hardy case but go and talk to Jim as well. See what he has to say about the crash. Tomorrow.'

She pushed herself to her feet. 'And the message from the answering machine?'

'Yeah, not really much of a threat. Could be a prank call or anything. Let's see what Jim reports first. I doubt the answering machine is going anywhere.'

FIVE

All Vince wanted was sleep. Proper sleep in his own bed instead of restless naps on a hospital chair and the jolting of his heart every time he remembered. But it wasn't happening anytime soon. He drove up his long driveway and turned the car to face back out. This wouldn't be a long stop.

Someone had left flowers near the front door. A beautiful posy of winter blooms in a jar of water. A white ribbon tied around the jar had a card tucked into it.

No words. Here for you. L.

He climbed down the steps, went around the corner and looked up the hill to his neighbour's house. There was no movement up there.

Word had got around fast.

Lyndall had known him long enough to put the flowers in water or he'd forget. And that he'd hate anything fancy. But this selection from her garden was Lyndall's way of letting him know she knew. And she cared. She always had as his wife's close friend. The one who was there when Vince wasn't.

Vince pushed down gut-wrenching nausea. He couldn't

replay that day. Not now. Losing his wife was the worst thing in his life.

Until now.

He unlocked the door, swept the jar up, and went in. The cottage was almost as cold as outside. He'd never noticed it before but for some reason it mattered. As he passed the living room he glanced at the fireplace. Almost never used. The flowers went onto the kitchen table and he put the kettle on. Perhaps his stomach would settle with some tea and toast.

First though, he showered and shaved.

The tea scorched his throat, and he burnt the toast. But he ate it, slathered with butter to hide the taste. It helped a bit and he left the cottage feeling more level headed than he had in hours.

Back at the hospital he spent a few minutes with Melanie before she was taken to set her forearm. She still was drowsy from painkillers but managed a small smile when he kissed her forehead. When she was wheeled out, he stood by the window, lost.

'Mr Carter?'

A nurse popped her head in.

'Doctor Raju has asked if you'd have a few minutes. He's one of our psychologists here and has already been in to see Melanie. I'll show you the way.'

Vince had vowed never to set foot inside a psych's door again, but this wasn't about him. He was ushered straight into the office by a receptionist.

'Ah, Mr Carter. I'm Doctor Raju, please come and have a seat.' Tall and much older than Vince expected—from his limited exposure to shrinks—the psychologist shook his hand and then gestured to one of three tub chairs set around a coffee table. A woman rose from her seat, mid-forties, unsmiling. 'This is Ms Dawn Burrows and she asked to sit in.'

'Mr Carter, I'm a social worker with Child Services.'

The act of settling into the chair gave Vince a much-needed moment to collect himself. Of course there'd be questions over Melanie's future, both short and long term. He'd dealt with enough situations in the course of his career where different agencies came together for the welfare of a child or family.

'I hear Melanie is having that break set?' The doctor asked.

'She is. One of the nurses said you'd been to see her earlier.'

'I spent a few minutes with her. Her pain medications were making her drowsy, but she spoke to me briefly. She's a brave and intelligent young lady.'

'What did she... um, did she speak of the accident?' He didn't really want to know.

'No. But she said her grandad came to see her.' Doctor Raju smiled.

A small warm glow began somewhere deep in Vince's heart.

And was extinguished when Ms Burrows spoke. 'I understand this is early days and all a terrible shock, but my concern is around the next steps with Melanie. Once she is ready to be released.'

'She'll come home with me,' Vince said.

'I see. What about other family?'

Looking for a better option?

He took his time, forcing his hands to flatten against his legs rather than curl into fists like they wanted to.

'I'm her last relative on Susie's side. Both my wife and I were only children and Susie was also an only child. No cousins and the like. David is similar. No family I'm aware of apart from his mum who had a bad accident years ago and has a full-time carer. There might be a cousin in England. Not sure.'

Ms Burrows wrote on a tablet as he spoke, glancing up as he finished.

'And are you aware of an existing will or other legal documents regarding Melanie?'

'A will was drawn up after she was born. But I also remember an off the cuff comment from Susie about it needing updating.'

'How long ago was that?'

'Couple of years.'

'I see.' She stared at Vince. 'And what were the wishes for Melanie... in case of the current circumstances?'

Who plans for that? Who really does?

He had no answer and she pressed on.

'Was there an expectation you would step in?'

'Children are supposed to outlive their parents.' He regretted the harshness of his tone the minute the words left his mouth. 'Sorry. I'm exhausted.'

Doctor Raju leaned forward a little. 'Please take your time, Mr Carter. Nobody will rush you into making decisions about Melanie.'

The social worker didn't seem to share his opinion. 'If no other family, then godparents?'

Over my dead body.

'There are godparents, but you'd know better than anyone they don't automatically have a claim on the custody of a child. Melanie is coming home with me. I have a spare bedroom which I will do up for her.' Vince wanted to go. This was too much on top of everything else.

'Of course, but if you feel unable to provide a proper home environment—' she started.

'I didn't say that.'

Doctor Raju shuffled in his seat. 'It is natural to feel reluctant to take a young child into your life.'

'I'm not reluctant.'

'Mr Carter, if I may... I believe you live alone, some distance from everything Melanie is familiar with. You have no public transport close by. And an eight-year-old is a lot of work. Primary school. Extra curricula activities. Friends.' Ms Burrows said.

How did she already assume so much about him? What did she want him to say? He stared at his hands which now gripped his knees.

'Melanie needs familiarity right now.' Doctor Raju had a soothing voice. Easy to listen to.

Vince raised his eyes to meet the doctor's. 'She'll have it. Mel knows me. Loves me.'

Ms Burrows stood. 'We'll talk further regarding the next steps, but I agree at this stage Melanie is best coming home with you. But there's a lot of water to pass under the bridge before this becomes permanent so I would suggest you give this thought. A great deal of thought for what is best in the long term for you, and for Melanie.'

After she'd left, Doctor Raju suddenly smiled. 'Melanie is lucky to have you.'

No response came to mind.

'A difficult time for her. But also for you.'

'I don't need a shrink.' Vince managed to keep his voice neutral.

'You lost your wife when Melanie's mother was young.'

'And I don't need a history lesson.'

'Grief has a way of coming back to us. Grief and self-recrimination. If you feel the need to talk...'

'Nah, I'm good. What do I tell Mel about it all?'

'That you love her.'

'I can do that.' Vince got to his feet.

'May I offer some advice?'

The doctor stood but made no move toward the door. 'Think about getting yourself some grief counselling.'

'That's it?' Vince asked.

'I don't bite.'

He might not, but old hurts did and were best kept buried.

———

Carla was slumped against the back of a fashionable leather sofa, a home pregnancy test dangling from her fingers and dried tears again leaving trails through her makeup. Her attention was on a large window facing the street and framed by curtains she'd had made to her exacting specifications. Bradley paced up and down the driveway coming in and out of view as he talked on his phone. His arm waved around. More and more often he wouldn't take calls in the house and Carla had no idea why not.

He stopped dead and held the phone out to look at then swore. She raised her eyebrows lip-reading the expletive but as he shoved it into his pocket and headed for the front door, Carla grabbed a handful of tissues and cleaned up her face. By the time he joined her, throwing himself at the other end of the sofa with a grunt, she was sitting upright, the bunch of tissues hidden in a pocket.

'What's wrong, Brad?'

'Work. Just work.'

'You're upset with someone.'

'Damned right I am. If people just did their job...' he looked at her for the first time. 'Have you been crying?'

She held up the pregnancy test and he slid across to wrap his arms around her.

'It'll happen, Carla. We'll keep trying.'

'I'm getting too old for a miracle.'

'We won't give up.'

'But why is it so unfair? Melanie is all alone with no parents.' She pulled herself out of his embrace and took one of his hands. 'And we're all alone with no children. Where's the sense in that?'

'There is none.'

'I wasn't just crying about the test. I mean, yes, it is upsetting but then I remembered Susie asking me if I was pregnant last night. And if I were then I'd never be able to tell her...' she drew in a long, shuddering sigh. 'And I'm so worried about where Melanie will go once she is released. I couldn't bear for him to get custody.'

'Vince Carter?' Bradley asked.

'Yes, him. Surely whoever makes these decisions will see past his one heroic moment to all the harm he's done? He was a terrible father to Susie, and I shudder to think how Melanie's life would be with him.'

Bradley nodded. Which meant what exactly? Did he agree with her or just want her to calm down?

'I know I sound upset, honey. What do you think we should do to help our little girl?' She said.

His phone rang and he scowled.

Carla released his hand. 'Answer it.'

'I'll get rid of them. What if we go to church for a bit?' He stood, reaching for the phone. 'Spend some time praying for Melanie.'

'I'd like that.'

But he'd already answered the call and was halfway to the door.

'And praying for Susie and David,' she murmured.

SIX

It was late. Vince slumped on the timber floor of the cottage's porch, a half empty bottle of scotch in one hand and an empty glass in the other. He stared into the dark. Little stirred in the cold but in the distance, the mournful howl of a lonely dog periodically echoed.

In the couple of hours he'd sat here there'd been a handful of cars go by and each time, he'd jumped. Except there was no more bad news to be had. Melanie was safe and recovering. Her physical injures would heal. And in hospital she'd come to no harm. He'd wanted to stay all night but was ushered out by nurses who rightly told him Melanie would need him in the morning as the drugs wore off.

He'd identified Susie and David's bodies after leaving the police station. Then spoken to the funeral home.

And he'd kept his head. Not shown as much as a bit of emotion, because he felt none.

Until he got home tonight.

Another sound drifted on the still air. The whinny of a pony.

Did I put her rug on? Did I feed her?

With a groan, he rolled onto his knees and used the wall to push himself upright. He was fine. Nothing that another drink wouldn't fix. He gripped the neck of the bottle. The steps were slippery, and he grabbed the rail, letting go just as fast. It was like an icicle.

'No need for ice for my drink.'

He chuckled at his clever comment.

Another whinny.

'On my way.'

He opened the gate and went through, careful to close it. Not that Apple would stray. She was at his pockets, nuzzling them for treats. Her rug was on. Maybe he forgot to take it off this morning. No matter in the cold weather. She had fresh hay. Lyndall must have checked on her.

'Wanna drink, old girl?'

Vince took a long swig and belched, wiping his hand across his mouth.

''Scuse me.'

He offered the pony the open end of the bottle, and she mouthed it, almost immediately snorting her displeasure and releasing it.

'No? No matter... nobody drinks with me anyway.'

There was a tree stump, and he sank onto it.

'You know we're both past it? At least people love you.'

The pony wandered off and he gazed up at the sky. It had the perfect clarity of mid-winter nights complete with clusters of brilliant stars. Somewhere up there was a star with Susie's name on it. Too soon. Taken long before her time.

She's gone. My baby is gone.

He got to his feet and pointed at the brightest star, jabbing in time with his words.

'You. Fucking. Bastard.'

Someone had to pay for this. Someone should have stopped this happening.

'Happy now?' He screamed at the sky. 'Fucking bastard!'

The earth rolled and rose and he fell onto his knees. The bottle spun away and he pounded the freezing ground with his fists until pain shot through his arms. With a cry, Vince fell onto his side and pulled his legs up, arms around them.

He closed his eyes and whispered, 'You should have protected her. Fucking bastard.'

Nobody heard him. Nobody cared.

———

There was nothing more Liz could do tonight around the Hardy case. She'd just dropped Pete back at the station so he could grab his own car and go home and now she wished she'd gone inside to do paperwork. Taking those couple of hours late this morning to sleep had reduced her level of tiredness but wrecked any chance of settling down this early.

Her car clock taunted her. After ten. Not so early.

One more hour and then I'll go home.

The hunt for Malcolm Hardy had shifted from an all-out, all-cop search of the general area he'd last been seen. Although there wasn't an officer in the state who wasn't going to look twice at every fifty-something, thickset man they passed, there simply weren't enough police to continue at the level they'd begun with, particularly as the criminal had vanished so easily. Now it was about focusing on his contacts. Pete thrived on that kind of policing and hadn't really cared he'd been sent to the most unlikely people in Hardy's old suburb of Footscray. Not that he'd found much yet, but he was like a bloodhound when something got his interest.

She wanted to see Vince. Sit with him. Let him talk if he

wanted. Odds on though, he was at the hospital or sleeping and driving all the way out there again would probably be a waste of a trip. Instead, Liz turned onto the road to Laverton.

At this time of night the suburb was relatively quiet. A couple of freight forwarding companies were as busy as in daytime, trucks being unloaded and workers shouting to each other. Most businesses were closed and kept normal business hours. One of them was Bradley Pickering and David Weaver's warehouse.

It occupied a narrow block part way along a dead-end street. Surrounded by similar buildings, its office was a few steps from the pavement with the rest of the building behind it. Two gates —locked together with a heavy chain and padlock—stretched from the side of the office to the fence of the next building, just wide enough for a semi-trailer to back down.

She drove past at a crawl. Nothing moved and the place was in darkness as she parked a little further down the road. The only street light working was up near the corner, and few of the buildings had exterior lighting. She knew the area well. The proximity of the suburb to Melbourne's docks made it popular for freight forwarding and associated businesses and she'd worked cases here more than once.

Flashlight on, she wandered to the front of the warehouse. The light picked up the name of the business above the office door.

PickerPack Holdings Pty Ltd.

'Cute. Bet you loved sliding your name in there.'

She'd never been inside but she knew Bradley from way back. Judging from his house at the time, and his tailored suits and expensive car, she'd expected his business was booming and would be housed in a more impressive property.

Instead, there was a dreary frontage with no passing traffic. What exactly went on in here?

Cobwebs covered the single window beside the front door,

and it was so grimy the flashlight made almost no inroads. The door itself was unused and had a sign telling people to go around the side. Nobody was around. She checked, glancing each way along the road before holding the flashlight hard against the glass. Her nose almost touched the window.

Eyes stared back at her.

Liz stumbled backwards as her heart pounded.

Had it been a face? Or a trick of the light?

She unholstered her gun.

Back at the window she moved the flashlight around but if anyone were there a moment ago, they'd gone.

This wasn't an office anymore but a makeshift staff room with chairs, tables, sink, and fridge. Beyond was an archway leading to the darkened warehouse. Shadows of shipping containers loomed at the back.

She tried the door. Locked.

Something felt off. The hair was raised on the back of her neck.

At the gate, she rattled the chain. The padlock was heavy and wouldn't give. The outline of a delivery van was at the very end of the driveway but there were no other vehicles in sight. She took out her phone and although the detail was poor thanks to the distance and lack of light, she spent a few minutes taking photographs then returned to the window and did the same.

Back in the car she locked the doors and exhaled slowly.

SEVEN

I'm miles from nowhere. Stupid cop nosing around where she isn't welcome. If only she could see the video footage of her face through the window. Hilarious.

There's no choice but to dump this thing —it will serve a new purpose.

It's exhausting bailing out other people. If they did their jobs then my life would be easier. And I like easier.

The GPS on my phone says there's a turn ahead. With no street lights it's nearly impossible to see. I passed the railway station a few minutes ago. No train until dawn but the walk back to it will fill the time. I turn onto a dirt road.

By the time I'm finished, nobody should find the vehicle but if someone stumbles upon it, the location will misdirect the cops. Unless you're controlling the game, there's no point playing. What has to happen next is co-operation. Unlike stupid David Weaver. That's a lesson for the others to heed.

A kangaroo bounds across the track and I brake. This is their territory, not mine.

The GPS is useless now. Connecting and dropping out thanks to crappy rural networks. But I've memorised the rest of the way. The van doesn't like the terrain. Not built for country roads.

Better not break down.

I let out a breath when we reach the top of the hill. The worst of the drive is over.

The road is little more than a single track now. I'm crawling to avoid potholes and not end up in the ditch. When there is nothing ahead but a dead-end, I drop into first gear and nudge my way into a gap between bushes. Branches scrape along the roof and sides. The squeal as they scratch the paint is music to my ears.

I turn off the motor and begin to clean. Once the interior is spotless I climb out and kill the headlights. I wipe the switch, close the door, and clean that.

With barely any space to exit, I manage to cut my arm on thorns. Once free of the bushes I clean the wound. Nothing more than a couple of grazes. From the track there is no sign of the vehicle.

Satisfying.

I light a cigarette and begin the long walk to the train station.

EIGHT

How he'd got back into the cottage, locked the front door, and climbed into his own bed was anyone's guess. But when Vince had woken not long after dawn, he was warm and had only a vague memory of lying in the paddock.

'Idiot.' His hands hurt.

Showered and dressed, he went outside and fed the pony. The bottle of scotch was empty, the remaining contents spilling out when he'd dropped it. Probably just as well. With a bit of luck Melanie would be home today and he wasn't about to repeat his actions of the previous night with her in the house.

Over coffee and toast, thankfully not burnt, he listened to the news.

Police continue to be baffled by the disappearance of convicted killer, Malcolm Hardy. Fifty-year-old Hardy escaped police custody on the way to a hearing, sparking a manhunt across Melbourne. This has been scaled down overnight.

'Can't keep everyone on it.'

Hardy's legal team have declined to make a statement, but there is growing speculation that police will interview Richard Roscoe to determine if the lawyer can assist with locating the violent offender.

'He's not going to give up his client.'

Vince doubted Hardy's lead lawyer had anything to do with the man escaping. Hardy had taken advantage of a lapse in security, an error which gave him the smallest of opportunities to break free of his guards. What was more likely was Roscoe's knowledge of Hardy's whereabouts. The man had escaped in handcuffs and was doing a good job of evading recapture. Media was having a field day with the police force.

An advertisement came on for a funeral home and Vince pulled the radio's plug from the wall. Yesterday afternoon he'd arranged his daughter's funeral—at least set it in motion until the coroner released her. The funeral home had treated him with sympathy and respect. They'd shown him caskets. Flower arrangements. Music suggestions. He didn't know what to do for the most part and let the kind woman guide his choices. He'd buried his wife so many years ago and things had changed. Some things. Not the agony.

He got to his feet, shaking his head as if shaking away the pain. Today was a new start. A wonderful little girl was about to move in, and he had a lot of work ahead.

By late morning the cottage was as good as he could make it under the circumstances.

Melanie's bed was freshly made with brand new sheets and pillow and on top of the blankets, he'd laid a patchwork quilt. He'd forgotten it was there, folded on the top shelf of the hallway cupboard and still as beautiful as when Susie used to have it on her own bed. Marion had made the quilt for their daughter.

He'd dug up a dusty lamp, cleaned it and put in a new light bulb. Now it was on her bedside table. She had a pretty pink one in her other bedroom and he'd see if she'd like that brought here, or prefer to choose a new one.

When she was recovered and ready, they'd go shopping for more modern furniture.

The sole bathroom had a clean from top to bottom. Not that it was in bad shape but not good enough for a young lady used to having one all to herself. He'd put the best towels out. Even added a flower in a glass from the posy Lyndall had left.

Is it okay? Have I missed anything?

Everything was as clean and inviting as he knew how to make it. He walked from room to room, ending up in the living room, hoping he'd done enough but all he could see was worn carpet and old curtains.

If she hated it here then he'd sell. Find something for them near her school.

What about Apple? She'd have to be agisted somewhere.

He closed his eyes. Leaving here wasn't something he could think about. Not on top of everything... if only he could rewind the last few days. Tell Susie to stay home with Melanie. Stay away from whoever wanted her husband dead and didn't care who went with him.

Forcing his eyes to open, he picked up his phone and dialled.

It went to Liz's voicemail and he didn't leave a message. She was probably knee-deep in finding Hardy.

Terry's mobile number was still in his contacts

'Vince? Everything okay?'

'Hoping to get Mel home today.'

'That is good news. She's doing okay?'

He dropped onto the sofa. 'What's happening with the case?'

Terry's sigh was audible through the phone. 'Still looks like an accident, mate. Report isn't back on the car but—'

'But what, Terry? The message on the answering machine was a threat.'

'Or some business contact of David's feeling frustrated.'

'You didn't hear the tone of voice,' Vince said. 'I'll go and record it for you. Or bring the machine in.'

Why didn't I do that in the first place?

He pushed himself to his feet.

'Make a copy on your phone and send it over. I'm not disregarding you, Vince. Just got a lot on my plate.'

'Malcolm Hardy,' Vince said.

'Yup. Shouldn't be our problem, yet it is. Send me the message, okay?'

After hanging up, Vince collected his wallet and keys. He took one more look around. Next time he was here, Melanie would be with him. Everything was about to change. Again.

———

Back at Susie's house, Vince hesitated at the front door. But this time it was because something felt off. On the surface nothing had changed in just over a day except the doormat had moved a bit. He stepped back and took photographs on his phone. The corner was a few inches away from the doorstep, leaving a faint trace of powdery dirt around it as though it had been lifted and dropped.

There were potted plants on either side of the door. Both had fancy-coloured pebbles as a mulch and both had been scuffed up. Susie was meticulous about the plants but there was dirt through the pebbles.

Someone had searched for a house key.

He reached for a holster which was no longer there.

Hadn't been in years.

Force of habit.

He should call the local cops but what would he say?

Send a unit over with sirens. I have a gut instinct. Things are slightly moved.

Vince unlocked the door and pushed it open. He peered in, then careful not to disturb the doormat, stepped inside. It was cold. As if a window was open somewhere.

The living room looked fine. And the kitchen. Dining room good.

But what he found in the laundry was enough to make him call the local police. And then send a message to Terry.

Laundry door is open. Window smashed.

It was worse than a simple break-in.

Knowing better than to touch anything with bare hands, Vince found a plastic bag in a cupboard and through it, pressed 'play' on the answering machine.

There are no new messages. There are no saved messages.

He'd slammed his fist onto the counter.

If he'd made a copy yesterday... if he'd have picked up the machine and taken it...

Terry arrived before the uniforms. Vince was outside after taking more photographs of anything he considered relevant. Forty minutes and no sign of local law for a break and enter at the home of a murder victim.

'Am I the cavalry?' Terry looked exhausted.

He was only a few years younger than Vince but had done everything right with his job and made a decent career for himself. He must be overdue to retire but still had that passion for the job Vince lost long ago.

'I requested lights and sirens,' Vince said.

'Shall I put mine on?' Terry grinned.

'Save them for catching Hardy. Someone deleted the message.'

'On the answering machine? Crap.'

'I've had a careful walk through and on the surface nothing is missing or disturbed in the house.' Vince pointed at the garage. 'Haven't been in there. Regardless, whoever broke in did it to remove the evidence.'

'Of the voice mail? Bit extreme.'

'If whoever called that night was responsible for the... crash, then they might have had a serious case of message regret. They want to destroy anything linking them to it.'

A patrol car pulled up across the driveway.

'We'll get it looked at.' Terry tapped on his phone. 'I'll see if someone smarter than me can recover the message.'

While Terry made the phone call, Vince walked back to the house. Relief was an odd thing to feel but Terry's support, even if just to pacify him, helped. The uniformed officers caught up with him and he pointed out the doormat and pot plants, then led them to the laundry. He'd need to secure the broken window before leaving. No time to have it replaced today when he had to meet with Melanie's doctor soon.

'Let's check that machine.' Terry tracked him down. 'Meg at Missing Persons is a brilliant cyber forensics person. She'll take a look but is backlogged.'

Nothing's changed from my day.

The message hadn't magically returned, and Terry commandeered it in a large evidence bag. 'Gotta go, mate. I'll bring Liz in on this and let her update you. Have you seen her? I mean since the station yesterday.'

Not ready for that.

'Paths haven't crossed.'

'Then make them cross.' Terry stared at him. 'She broke her heart the other night at the scene, and I'm not comparing it to your loss, so don't give me that look, but Liz is on your side. Always. If there is any evidence that the crash was engineered, then she'll find it.'

'So it is a Homicide investigation?'

'No. But you are still one of us and everyone loved Susie. What Liz does in her own time is her choice.' Terry patted Vince's shoulder. 'Give us a few days with this.' He slightly raised the answering machine. 'Get out of here as soon as you can.'

———

The ride home from the hospital was quiet and Vince took his time, ever so careful going around corners and over speed bumps. Melanie sat beside him staring out of the window. She looked so fragile and small.

The doctor had said she was doing well. She needed rest and her medication and lots of love. He'd arranged a visit to the shrink the next day and suggested it was worth continuing with the visits for a while. The break of her forearm was expected to heal over the coming weeks, as would the bruises and bumps. It was her heart and mind which would take longer to find a way forward.

'Do you remember my house, Mel?'

She nodded, her eyes somewhere out on the passing landscape.

'How's the arm?'

Geez, Vince. Is that the best you can do?

She didn't answer.

'Not far now.'

There was a quick glance his way and Vince's heart dropped at the uncertainty in her eyes, but he smiled until she looked away again.

The rest of the trip was in silence, and he was relieved to turn into the driveway. She sat up a bit to better see ahead.

Are you seeing this like I am?

Years of living on his own had acclimatised him to the decay.

The driveway was a long dirt track between sparsely grassed

space which was neither paddock nor garden. There was a garden—or had been years ago—around the cottage but little more than the sad remains struggled on their own. The cottage itself needed more than paint and a hammer. It was old but not in a heritage listed way. Some had said a bulldozer would have been a kinder death than the tortuous rotting of weatherboards and awnings.

To one side of the cottage was a slightly tilted carport and Vince pulled in underneath. Just ahead was a series of sheds and a lean-to where his stock of winter firewood lived.

He climbed out and opened the passenger door, but Melanie didn't move. Her eyes were wide. Worried. He unclipped the seatbelt. 'I went shopping yesterday. Got lots of food and stuff.'

Her lips quivered.

'Can't remember the last time you visited. I mean, I remember coming to your house but it must be three years since you were here. You were little, not a big girl like now. And I'm very happy you are here with me. Are you hungry?'

She nodded and let him help her out. Her arm was in a sling until she was confident to go without. She waited while he collected the suitcase with her things then took her good hand and led the way.

Halfway to the front door, a cow in the paddock next door bellowed and Melanie squealed and jumped.

'Mamma cow is just calling for her baby.' After putting the suitcase down, Vince hoisted Melanie up with one arm and pointed with the other. 'See. Over there?' A calf ran to its mother in the distance. 'And can you see the big house way up there? That belongs to Lyndall who is much scarier than the cows. She has donkeys as well. Do you like donkeys? Long ears. Noisy.'

The little girl shoved her face against his coat.

———

Raindrops pattered against the metal roof. The temperature dropped.

Melanie lay on the sofa in the living room, a blanket covering everything but her head as she watched some kids show on the television. Every so often, her lips curled up in response to something on the screen. Vince didn't want to intrude on her escape from reality but she noticed him standing in the doorway.

'I have some lunch for you.' He carried a tray and she sat up, arranging the blanket to make space. 'Sorry it is so late. I hope you like strawberry jam. I made one sandwich with that and one with peanut butter.'

'Jam is bad for my teeth. Mummy doesn't like me having it...'

'Well, um, just as a special treat? You can brush your teeth afterwards and look, there's a glass of milk which is good for them. Calcium.'

She picked up the peanut butter sandwich and bit into it as her eyes returned to the television.

It was too cold in here. Vince dug around in the fireplace with a poker at the remnants of a fire long gone.

'Might go chop up a bit of wood to get the fire going. Warm things up. You be okay for a few minutes?'

She made some noise through a full mouthful which he took as a yes.

Lumps of hardwood were stacked beneath the lean-to. Grabbing a long-handled axe from the shed, Vince set to work. Splinters of wood flew as he smashed blow after blow into the blocks. Every so often he stopped long enough to wipe the handle and his eyes from the intensifying rain, then he'd begin again, uncaring that his shirt was clinging to his skin.

Melanie needed warmth. The cottage was too cold for a little girl.

How could I let the place fall apart like this? Marion would hate it. She'd hate more than that.

Chop. The axe sliced into the wood.

I destroyed my relationship with Susie.

Chop. Pieces splintered and flew off.

I can never make amends now.

Marion long gone. Susie gone.

When he wiped the rain away from his eyes again he realised.

Those were tears.

NINE

Bradley stared at the screen of his laptop. He'd read the same sentence twenty times and didn't remember a word. His back hurt from sitting in the same spot for half an hour without moving. Being here, in his office in the warehouse, was just an excuse to take a break from Carla's outpouring of emotion. He loved her to the moon and back but since the car accident she was either crying or drinking. Sometimes both. And he got it. She'd never experienced a loss like Susie and grieving took time and all that, but he just needed his own space for a bit.

'Boss?'

'Mother of...' Bradley almost jumped out of his seat. 'What the hell are you doing here?'

'Warehouse is normally deserted on Sundays. Thought I'd keep working on the container fit-out.'

Tall and bony with white, short-cropped hair, Abel Farrelly was Bradley's foreman. More than that, really. He oversaw the employees and ensured a smooth running of the floor and didn't mind the odd side job if Bradley had something extra for him.

Like working on a shipping container to prepare for special freight.

Pushing his chair back, Bradley stood and stretched. 'Do you need a hand?'

'Thanks. No. You look busy, anyway.'

'Not really. Might head off though.'

'I'll lock up when I leave.' Abel turned to go.

'That reminds me. The gate was open.'

Abel spun back. 'What? The place was broken into?'

'Warehouse was still locked.'

'Yeah, but did you check the padlock on the gate?'

Abel disappeared and with a sigh, Bradley followed him across the semi dark warehouse floor to the side entry. By the time Bradley caught up, Abel was holding the heavy chain in one hand and the padlock in the other.

'Bolt cutters,' Abel said in disgust.

'Didn't even notice.'

'There's enough chain for me to secure it tonight. Tomorrow I'll find a more permanent solution.' Abel stared at Bradley. 'How did you not see that?'

Bradley gazed up the driveway to his car, now joined by a flatbed ute. Abel rotated between it and the van. 'Lot on my mind. Where's the van?'

'Don't you have it?' Abel dropped the chain into a coil near the side of the gate. 'Figured you'd taken it home when I saw your car here.'

'Nobody else has borrowed it? Please tell me nobody had access to the keys?'

Without waiting for an answer, Bradley stormed back inside. This was a joke. Where the hell was his van? There were spare, emergency keys for everything in the safe in his office. He tapped in the code and opened it. All were there. Along with a bundle of cash and a handgun.

'Have you got your personal set, boss?' Abel had followed him in and was staring into the safe.

Bradley closed it with a click. 'On the desk. Yours?'

Abel reached into a pocket and pulled a few sets out. 'Yeah. Van is on this one.'

'You report it. I'm going home.' Bradley closed his laptop.

'Sure. Have you heard from Duncan Chandler lately? Like, since David died?' Abel leaned against the door frame. 'There's an opportunity going to waste.'

About to snap at Abel that there was more to life than facilitating the transport of cheap toys, Bradley bit his lip. It wasn't Abel's fault. An arrangement with the man dubbed a 'discount toy king' would change all their lives. Pity David hadn't lived to benefit from it.

He picked up his keys and wallet. 'Tell you what. You take care of that container and talk to the police. I'll reach out to Duncan. Oh, and maybe lock the container up before you let any cops in?'

———

In a police underground compound, David's mangled car rested awkwardly on a raised tray. The front was smashed in, and the roof crushed from the middle of the car forward.

'How did you survive, Melanie?' Liz murmured.

'The little girl? Mystery to me too.' Jim Joyce carried a folder from an office to one side of the compound. 'Been half-expecting one of you to visit.'

'One of us?'

Jim crossed his arms. 'Terry. You. Someone who still cares for Vince.'

'He's a good man. Was a good cop.'

'Never believed anything else, Lizzie.'

They both turned to contemplate the wreck.

The front—more on the driver's side—of the car had borne the full brunt of the impact with the tree, air bags deployed but no match for the force of the crash. In comparison the back seat was barely damaged.

At least Melanie survived.

'I can't tell you much,' Jim said.

'Can't? Or haven't started?'

'The latter. Only had a quick look but there are questions. I'm trying to push it up the line to get to sooner.'

'Vince is seeing something sinister where it possibly doesn't exist.' Liz gazed at the passenger side with its door missing. 'Oh, Susie. Shit.'

'It was quick.'

'What has been confirmed?' Liz asked, tearing her eyes from the car.

'All the road measurements are done. They were travelling at seventy-eight kilometres an hour in an eighty zone. No traffic about that we can find. Certainly none that stopped to help. Something made David leave his lane.'

'A dog on the road?'

Jim shook his head and opened the folder. 'Be one hell of a big dog.' He went through a series of photographs from the scene, stopping on one with clear tyre tracks and police markers.

'If it was something like a stray animal or some obstacle in the middle of the road, David would have applied his brakes while in his lane. And when the tyre grip failed, and the car skidded to the other side of the road, there'd be more evidence of heavy braking.' He traced the tyre tracks in the photo. 'In this case, the car moved to the other side of the road, the wrong side of the road but at the same speed. No brakes until presumably David was losing control of the car.'

Liz looked more closely at the photo. 'He was driving into oncoming traffic?'

'The car was on a trajectory toward the shoulder of the opposite side. Doubt he'd been in the wrong lane for more than a few seconds when he braked.'

The next photo was a close up of Susie in the wreck and Liz recoiled.

'Sorry.' Jim snapped the folder shut.

She took a deep breath to force the image away. The shock away. 'Are you saying something forced David onto the other side of the road?'

Jim shrugged. 'Let us keep working. The report will be upstairs in the next twenty-four hours.'

Liz knew what Jim really meant. There was more to it than a driver who might have had a bit too much to drink and had forgotten which side of the road he was on.

———

Her next stop was back in the station. She had a meeting soon with Pete and Terry, but first hurried into Missing Persons to find Meg. The forensic analyst was working on two laptops—a hand on either —and flicked a glance Liz's way with a 'Nope. I'll take a look later. When I can.'

Liz had rarely seen the young woman without a device, or two. She was a workaholic and exceptional at what she did. Terry had brought her up to speed about the break-in at Susie's house, but she shouldn't have expected an answer, or even a start, when it came to the deleted message.

'Thank you.' She left Meg in peace and made her way back to Homicide.

It was still circumstantial. Dependent upon Vince's accuracy. Until somebody came up with some evidence, it would remain a theory from a wounded party. On the surface the crash was a tragedy caused by an icy road and possibly a driver over the alcohol limit. That was speculation until the coroner's report came in. But it was also far too common in car accident drivers who'd spent the evening at a restaurant.

And David liked his wine.

She pushed the elevator button and leaned against the wall as she waited.

There'd been a party at Vince's place. Goodness knows how many years ago... twelve? Susie had just finished university. It was her birthday and somehow she'd talked her reclusive father into letting her host a get together. She'd chosen the music, the food, and most of the guests. The party was set up outside and Vince had hired a marquee and even outdoor toilets. The food was vegan and served by one of Susie's friends who'd gone into catering. And it was exceptional.

But two men had ended up in the cottage kitchen cooking themselves frozen hamburger patties to add to their meals. Vince, and David, who'd seemed like a kid back then. Not really a kid, but Susie's age and obviously in love with her. He and Vince had hung out a bit that night, from what Liz could recall. She'd thought it strategic on both their parts as each tried to work out the other. They'd started drinking different wines until a bit too 'happy' and Susie got annoyed with them both.

The elevator doors opened. It was full. She waved it on, then went in search of stairs. Better for her cardio anyway.

Pete was in Terry's office when she tapped.

'Grab a seat, Liz. Any luck with Accident Investigation?' Terry asked.

'Too soon to tell.'

'Because there's nothing to tell,' Pete said. 'Driver couldn't cope with icy conditions and lost control. Simple.'

Rather than give him the satisfaction of debating the point,

Liz looked at Terry. 'It is all over the news that we have blown the chance to catch Malcolm Hardy. What do we do to prove them wrong?'

Terry grimaced. 'I'm going into a meeting soon to discuss this. Hardy isn't out there on his own. He's got enough friends to hide until it hots up for him too much, which is our job to make happen. I'd like you both to start visiting his top ten or so known contacts again. Rattle some cages. Make the suggestion that anyone caught with him will go down hard... unless they play nice and help.'

Pete cracked his knuckles with a wide grin.

'Keep me in the loop.' Terry glanced at his watch. 'I'm going. Do you have an updated list of Hardy's contacts?'

'Know them off by heart.' Pete stood. 'Almost friendly enough to exchange Christmas cards.'

––––––––

The Christmas cards would have to wait. After only one stop—a dead end—Terry had called and told them to go home. A briefing was set for first thing tomorrow and he wanted everyone fresh. Pete had jumped at the chance and got Liz to drop him off near a tram stop in Carlton after he arranged a last-minute date.

Hunger and opportunity saw Liz seated at a table in Spironi's just before eight.

The table was for two and tucked against the window. Despite the cold outside, the footpath was busy enough. All the way along the restaurant precinct of Lygon Street, potential diners were regaled by spruikers competing for customers.

She played with the stem of a glass of red wine, her eyes moving from table to table. She was the only single diner. There were one or two couples, but the rest were parties of four to eight. White aproned servers wound between chairs with large trays of food. The smell of tomatoes and bread and herbs made her stomach rumble.

Her server—a forty-something man with a ready smile—brought her gnocchi and placed it in front of her with a flourish.

'Thank you... Mike?' she read the embroidered top pocket of his apron.

'My pleasure. Would you care for another glass of wine?'

'No, but thanks. I wondered if you work on Fridays?'

Mike gave her a wary look. Liz flashed her badge.

'Oh. Officer. I'm one of the owners. Any particular Friday?'

'Last one. Do you remember a group of two couples and a young girl?'

His face dropped. 'The Weavers and Pickerings. Here most weeks. Terrible what happened. Not what you expect.'

Never was.

'Did you notice anything out of the ordinary?'

'I only seated them. Marco was their waiter but he's off tonight. Did you want me to leave a message?'

'Not necessary. I can always swing by if I need to.'

'I do remember Marco saying the men—Mr Pickering and Mr Weaver—were arguing. Up near the back door, past the restrooms.'

'Did he hear what it was about?'

'Better to ask him.'

'By any chance are there cameras in that part of the building?'

'Afraid not.'

'Thanks, Mike.'

What were they arguing about? And had anyone else overheard it?

Something was out of kilter. Two friends arguing the same night one of them received a cryptic message. Warning or threat? Either way, she needed to find out.

TEN

'Mummy!'

Vince sat bolt upright, dragged from a dream.

'Where *are* you, Mummy?'

'Coming, Susie. Oh. Shit. Melanie.' He rolled out of bed, reaching for a dressing gown which didn't want to be worn. His arm went through the wrong hole, and he had to start over.

'Mummy! Daddy!'

Melanie was standing on her bed, tears streaming down her face. Vince put on the light. Arm outstretched, she pointed at him and shouted, 'I want to go home. I want them back.'

'Melly...'

Her face crumbled into despair, and she plonked onto her bottom. He sat beside her, at a loss. Nothing he could do or say made this better.

'I don't want them dead,' she said with a whimper.

'I know, sweetie. I don't want them dead either.'

She threw herself into his arms and for the longest time he let her cry, rocking them both and stroking her hair. His heart was empty. Stone cold.

The sobs turned into sniffles.

'Hang on. Let me reach for a tissue.' He got some from the bedside table and she let him dab at the tears before taking over and blowing her nose.

'Where's Raymond?' she asked.

'Who's Raymond?'

'Raymond Bear. He always sleeps in the bed with me.'

The teddy in your old bedroom? Why didn't I bring him instead of leaving him on your other bed? Idiot.

'I'll find him in the morning. Okay?'

'But...' she put her hand over her mouth as her eyes glistened again.

'Hang on, Mel. I have an idea if you can give me a minute? Jump back into bed and I'll see if I have a stand in for tonight.'

She climbed in and he tuned on the lamp.

On his way out, he switched the main light off.

In the hall closet he dug around in the furthest corner, extricating a dusty old box. Under the lid was a worn, pink teddy bear resting on photo albums and papers and memorabilia. He left the box and took the teddy to Mel's room. She half-sat up, her eyes curious.

'This is Topsy, and she's been in a box in the cupboard for a long time. I think she needs a lot of cuddles.'

Melanie took the bear and scrutinised it, turning it around. 'Was this your bear?'

'Topsy belonged to your mum.'

Her mouth formed an 'o' and she looked from the bear to Vince and back again. Was the truth too much? He could have lied about it but lying didn't help anyone.

'Do you think Topsy could be a stand-in for Raymond Bear tonight?'

Melanie slid back into bed, clutching the teddy against her. The tears might be gone, but how her little heart must be aching. Vince pulled the blankets higher and straightened them.

'I'll sit here for a bit if that's okay?'

With the smallest of nods, Melanie squeezed her eyes shut.

He'd forgotten this. The middle of the night tears and panic. Susie waking and calling for her mother. Nights he'd sat here hating himself over and over for not getting home in time that day to save Marion's life. Or at least save Susie from seeing her die.

And then he'd sing to Susie. It always calmed her and sometimes it calmed him too.

'The moon is watching...' he began, as softly as he could. 'The stars are dancing...'

Melanie's eyes opened a bit.

'And way up high someone special is thinking of you...'

I can't believe I remember the words.

'They love you always... you are their precious gift...'

Mel's hand reached out for his and she gave him a faint smile.

'And the moon and the stars are adoring you, too...'

She'd drifted off to sleep and he'd kissed her forehead.

He found himself in the living room. He'd collected the box from the cupboard and didn't know what to do with it so dropped it onto the sofa. His heart wasn't empty or cold now. It thudded heavily as he tried to force the terrible sadness down. It was the same nightmare all over again.

They'd got through it, him and Susie.

I can't do this again.

————

He stared at the bench he used for wood carving. The bird was there where he'd left it, the one he'd cut too deeply with the arrival of the police. He picked it up and with a quick motion snapped the neck and tossed the pieces into a waste bin beneath the bench.

At the back of the bench was a finished carving of an exquisite lyrebird, its tail curved upwards, and every feather perfectly defined. Vince grabbed it, held it over the bin.

Then he drew in a shuddering breath and carried it to the mantlepiece. Between photographs and other birds, he found a space for it.

His legs shook. There was a roaring in his ears.

Picking up the photograph of him with Susie and Marion, he held it against his chest and stumbled to the sofa. He rocked back and forth as he stared at the image of his daughter and wife.

Tears welled in his eyes until they spilled over, running down his cheeks as he reached into the box and pulled out a baby book. On the first page was Marion, heavily pregnant with a radiant smile competing with a mild expression of panic.

On the next page was newly arrived Susie. Susan Marie.

A pink teddy bear was in the corner of the crib.

Page after page of memories.

A lock of Susie's hair.

Images of her crawling, then walking.

Her first word. 'Dad-da.'

Vince closed it abruptly and wiped the tears from his face.

Framed in dark timber was their marriage certificate. Vincent John Carter and Marion Leigh McLean. His finger traced Marion's signature. It had never changed over the years, the way she wrote so neatly, unlike his messy scrawl.

There were a handful of letters Marion had kept when they'd been engaged and he'd had to be away for weeks at a time. Both to and from her and one day he'd read them again, but he didn't have the courage yet.

At the bottom was a small box and within it was a gold

medal with entwined 'V' and 'A' in its centre. The Police Valour Award for bravery. He snapped the case shut.

His bravery meant nothing.

Yellowed and folded, a newspaper article caught his eye. He had forgotten he had it. Why he'd kept it... perhaps somebody gave it to him, and he'd shoved it in here with the other reminders. The main photograph showed a uniformed police officer helping an elderly lady to her feet. They were on a road where people milled about and crowd control barriers lined either side. She wore an armed services uniform and medals.

Another photo of a sheet over a body at the top of steps overlooking the same road.

And one of a paramedic attending to another police officer, her face bleeding.

Liz.

A headline.

Tragedy Averted at Regional Anzac Day March.

His eyes closed as memories hammered him.

A shaven-headed young man lurking behind a statue at the top of the steps. The glint of something in his hand sent Vince flying up the steps even as a gun was pointed at the crowd below. A warning screamed over his shoulder might have alerted the crowd but also the gunman who squeezed off an ill-aimed shot which grazed Liz's face.

He'd positioned himself in the line of fire and took down the man in two shots.

Nobody else was seriously injured. The man had left a note behind. He intended to kill as many people that day as he could. It was the half-baked plan of someone on bail on charges of threatening his estranged grandfather, a veteran who was one of only a handful in this march in a town two hours from the city.

Vince opened his eyes, refolded the newspaper, and returned it to the box. He'd been there that day on short notice, driving up with Liz. He couldn't remember why them. Or why the local police wanted a stronger presence.

'It was my day off.'

The medal box dropped onto the newspaper clipping.

Marion had been unwell with asthma overnight. But he'd left her alone anyway. Her and Susie.

He added the baby book to the box.

As the panic of the shooting had subsided, as his own adrenalin had finally crashed, a call came. He was told to get home.

The ambulance was still at his house when, sirens screaming, he'd turned into his driveway. Lyndall had Susie in the kitchen. Marion was on the sofa in the living room. He was too late.

He held a large envelope against his chest for a while, eyes far away. It had been a long time since anyone touched this. With a sigh which came from his soul, he opened the envelope. Two wedding bands. His. And Marion's. And her death certificate.

ELEVEN

Vince carried a cup of coffee outside, quietly closing the front door with the intention of sitting on the porch to watch the sun rise. It was too cold to stay still so he wandered around to check on the pony. She nickered a welcome and nudged him until he set the cup down and gave her an early breakfast. The pony was ageing. Susie's, from twenty or so years ago. Nevertheless, she was fit and if Melanie was so inclined, would probably be willing to wear a bridle again.

'Morning, Vincent.'

He'd noticed Lyndall was moving livestock in one of her paddocks but hadn't seen her cross her driveway. His first reaction was to grunt and go back inside but manners took over. Manners and a sudden thought.

He joined her at the fence. 'Thanks for the flowers. It was nice of you.'

She rested her arms on the top rail and gazed at him from under the wide-brimmed, oilskin hat she almost always wore. 'Your little grandchild has come to live with you.'

Do you miss anything?

'I remember meeting Melanie a couple of years ago. Susie brought her up to the house.'

'She's a good girl.' He didn't know what else to say.

'Of course she is. Look at her mother. And grandfather.'

A silence stretched out between them. They'd been neighbours for decades. She'd been friends with Marion. Helped out when Susie was growing up. But they'd barely acknowledged each other since his estrangement with his daughter. She'd drawn some line in silent disapproval.

Lyndall straightened. 'Anyway, the cows won't move themselves.'

Ask her.

'Okay. Well, thanks again,' he said.

Lyndall took a few steps away before looking back. 'If you ever need anything. Or a babysitter, then—'

'Um, yeah. Are you sure?'

Her smile was suspiciously knowing. 'When?'

'Need to collect some of her things from Susie's house. I can't bring myself to take her there yet.'

'Ten o'clock? I'll bring Melanie something for morning tea.'

'Appreciate it.'

She waved as she walked back across the driveway and climbed through the fence to her paddock.

He hated asking.

But just this once.

He'd find someone local who he could pay to help out if it came to that. Anything was better than making demands of a woman who had seen him at his worst. Who probably still judged him for Marion's death.

He already regretted the conversation.

———

The fridge doors were open in the Weaver kitchen. Bradley leaned against a kitchen bench drinking orange juice—made by Susie from Carla's beloved orange tree—straight from a jug. He'd already demolished half a plate of homemade cupcakes. Everything was still fresh. Delicious. Good thing Susie had given Carla keys in case she was helping with Melanie after school and the like.

Something had happened here. Fingerprint residue marked surfaces from the potted plants near the front door to the counters. It made no sense. Why would the police dust the place when the car accident was exactly that? An accident.

The fridge beeped in protest of being left open so long and he returned the jug and closed the doors. There were cooler bags in the walk-in pantry, and he put them on the bench to remind him to fill them before he left. No point the contents of the fridge and freezer going to waste.

He eyed the coffee machine but a quick glance at his watch was enough for him to head up to David's office. In an hour he had a meeting and if there was any chance of salvaging this wreck of a week he needed to collect some ammunition.

As expected the desk was immaculate. Its drawers were orderly and disappointingly it was too modern to have secret compartments. A timber filing cabinet was locked which presented no problem. David kept the important stuff in a wall safe inside the walk-in-robe in the master bedroom. Good thing they shared each other's combinations in case of emergency. Yeah, well this qualified.

He brushed against one of David's suits and he paused, touching the lapel. The times he'd straightened David's tie over the years. Smartened him up for meetings.

'I miss you, mate.'

Losing David was a blow on many levels. Friend. Business partner. Confidante. But he would grieve in his own time. For now he had to make sure the business forged ahead because Melanie needed what was fairly hers.

The filing cabinet keys were in the safe and went into his pocket. He systematically searched through the remaining contents. Passports. Birth certificates and the like. A wad of cash. There was a thick, sealed envelope. Interesting. He reached for it.

Click.

He jumped at a sound from downstairs and grabbed the one thing he'd come for—a folder.

Afraid to be caught in here, Bradley closed the safe and reset the combination to something unlikely to be guessed by anyone else. He'd come back later.

From the top of the stairs the house was quiet. Nobody moved around. Clearly, all this cloak and dagger stuff was messing with his nerves.

The key to the filing cabinet did its job and Bradley helped himself to an armful of folders, sliding them into a briefcase he'd brought with him. He opened David's laptop and searched its history, writing down an account number on a piece of paper he tore from a notepad. He'd take the laptop anyway but needed this number for the meeting.

Bradley folded the paper to put in his pocket.

'What the hell are you doing here?'

The paper dropped out of his fingers as he started.

'You scared the crap out of me, Vince!'

Vince carried a small suitcase.

'Why are you in the house, Pickering? This is private property.'

'Gonna call the police, ex Officer Carter?' He couldn't keep the disdain from his voice but didn't care. Vince Carter was a waste of space back when he was a cop and nowadays was little more than an obstacle to his and Carla's access to Melanie. When Vince moved toward him he raised both hands to diffuse the situation. 'Take it easy. You startled me. All I'm doing is collecting company paperwork David was bringing back to the office. I need it.'

He scooped up the fallen paper then reached for the laptop.

'Leave it,' Vince snapped.

'Belongs to the business.'

'Somebody broke in yesterday. Any idea what they were after?'

'Ah, that explains the residue. Broke in here?' Bradley gazed around the office. Nothing looked out of place. 'Was anything stolen?'

'Not stolen. Not that we can find yet. But the police have taken copious amounts of fingerprints and other trace.'

With a smile, Bradley closed the briefcase. 'Mine will be everywhere. Carla's as well.'

'I'll show you out.'

I need that laptop.

It didn't matter for now. He had to get to the meeting and stalked past Vince, who followed. 'Where's Melanie? You didn't leave her in the car alone?'

'Where she is isn't your business.' Vince was right behind him coming down the stairs.

'We're her godparents, Vince.' He opened the front door and turned to face the other man. 'Carla's going crazy wanting to see her. We want her to visit.'

Vince put the suitcase down and for an instant, Bradley's heart raced in anticipation of being physically pushed out of the house. But Vince crossed his arms and stared. 'What was David into?'

'I don't under—'

'Maybe you're as far in the shit as David was.'

'Our business is above board.'

'That crash was no accident,' Vince said.

'Well, the police said the road was icy.'

'And what do you say, Bradley?'

Nothing which wouldn't get him punched.

'I'll take the house keys. There's no reason for you to have them.'

Bradley handed them over. 'Still need the laptop and a lot more files.'

'Then arrange it through David and Susie's solicitor.'

'Maybe Melanie should move in with us for a while. You obviously need time to grieve.'

Vince's arms dropped and he stepped toward Bradley. 'Maybe you should get out of here.'

As soon as Bradley was outside, the door shut behind him.

———

Vince waited until Bradley drove away before moving from the front door. He didn't trust the other man not to have a second set of keys. He had no reason to dislike Bradley so much, but he always had. The fact he was married to Susie's best friend had made for discomfort at the events they'd all been at, but he'd always stayed civil. For her sake.

Liz had dealings with them.

Why that popped into his mind was a mystery, but his old partner had been involved in a case surrounding Carla years ago and he couldn't remember why or the outcome. He needed to ask her. Which meant dealing with a hundred worried questions from her.

With a shake of his head, Vince headed up to Melanie's bedroom.

Raymond Bear was first into the suitcase, followed by more of her clothes. He'd asked her what she wanted him to bring this time and all she could think of was Raymond. She'd gone very quiet, and he didn't press her for more ideas.

He found slippers, more shoes and pyjamas, a couple of jumpers and other warmer items. There was a cute, knitted hat and some little jars of hand cream or something, so those went in with a couple of books. All he could hope was he had enough for her for a little while. Until after the funeral.

Room by room he checked the house. Every window was locked. Back door locked. The laundry door had a sheet of timber nailed in place of glass and would be hard to get through.

He stopped at the sight of the cooler bags in the kitchen. They'd not been there the previous day. Bradley must have been planning to clean out the place.

'Little shit.'

The fridge was well stocked. He packed what he could use into one cooler bag. Cheese. Cupcakes. Fruit. Yoghurt. He should give the rest away. Or throw away what was getting too old. Or something.

It had to wait. He had to meet with Susie's solicitor, a last-minute appointment thanks to Lyndall's availability this morning.

At the front door he put the suitcase and cooler bag down to find the keys.

He'd stood here another time. A bit more than a year ago. With his daughter.

'Susie, you don't understand what he's doing to you both.'

'I said to leave, Dad.'

She was furious. Her hands were on her hips and her face was red with anger. Vince had just found out David had been questioned about the immigration status of some of his employees. It wasn't for the first time.

'Sweetie, you need to think of Melanie.'

'I am.'

'Her being exposed to that kind of—'

'Kind of what?' Susie shook her head. 'If there is an issue with the staff then David will fix it. He's above board and always has been. The person I need to protect Melanie from is you.'

As if he'd been kicked in the gut, Vince had recoiled.

'You live in the past, Dad. What I want is for you to get some help. Deal with Mum's death and all the other crap. Start being the grandfather Melanie deserves.'

'I don't need help.'

All the anger had drained away from her, replaced by sadness. Her tone had flattened. 'See? Just go, Dad. Come back once you're ready to step up.'

Those were the last words they'd exchanged.

He'd gone away and sulked instead of changing and fixing their relationship.

Now he was forced to step up.

Too late.

TWELVE

Lyndall was nice. Not at all scary like Grandad said. She had wrinkly smiley eyes and interesting lines on her face, and she liked drawing.

Melanie loved to draw and hoped Grandad would bring her art book from home. Lyndall had brought one with her and coloured pencils and they'd taken turns drawing different things.

Flowers in the jar which Lyndall said were from her own garden.

One of Grandad's wooden birds he carved.

A drawing of each other.

And then some from imagination.

When Grandad came home he looked sad again. But he put the suitcase on her bed and said to look inside and there was Raymond Bear. And after she cuddled Raymond she cuddled Grandad and then he smiled.

One of her art books was there but no pencils.

'What's up, darlin'? Lyndall was putting on her coat to leave.

She didn't want Grandad to look sad again in case he felt bad about forgetting the pencils. 'Oh, nothing really.'

'You know, I'd like you to hang on to those pencils and sketch book until we have another drawing session. And use them in the meantime if you feel like it. Okay?'

It was! Melanie set to work on a new drawing. She'd use her imagination again.

'Mind if I walk to the fence with Lyndall?' Grandad asked. 'Won't be long.'

'Hm mm.'

She was going to create something beautiful.

———

'Sorry I was a bit longer than expected.'

Vince and Lyndall wandered from the cottage in the direction of her driveway.

'Melanie is very special. She's a bit quiet which is to be expected but that bubbly little personality I remember is just under the surface, waiting for the sun to shine again.'

Arriving home to colourful sketches all over the living room floor wasn't what he'd expected. And there'd even been a couple of smiles from Mel.

'She's taken to you, Lyndall. Thank you.'

'I like her too. You looked glum when you got back. Bad news?'

'I found Bradley Pickering going through things in David's home office.'

'Threw him out on his ear, I hope?'

He smiled. It was a pleasant thought.

'Didn't come to that but I've taken his set of keys. Carla had them when she used to help out with Melanie.'

'Worth telling the police?'

'Thinking about it.'

They stopped at the fence and Lyndall had an odd expression. Odd, even for her.

'What?' Vince would rather know.

'Mel mentioned she misses Carla.'

This was a problem for another day. He glanced at the fence. 'Why are we here and not near my car? I can drive you back up.'

She rolled her eyes and in one fluid motion climbed the rails and was on the other side. 'Not bad for an old bird. What did the solicitor say?'

He gazed back at the cottage. 'Susie and David have a will but it's old, from just after Mel was born. Since then David bought into the business with Bradley and there is nothing about how to manage his share. While it should go to Melanie, there are always complications and Bradley might have some agreement in place which impacts it. They owned their house outright and I have to say Lyndall,' he turned back to her, she hadn't moved, her eyes were on him, 'that surprised me. They're young... they *were* young... to have paid off a mortgage so soon.'

It had him stumped. Susie hadn't worked in a couple of years although involved in charity organisations. The income, as far as he knew, was from David's business. Must be doing better than the impression the badly maintained warehouse gave out.

And that was a dumpster fire.

'They never changed the will about Melanie... where they wished her to go in such circumstances?' Her voice was the gentlest he'd ever heard.

'Never changed. It was always understood she'd come to me. But the solicitor warned me it won't happen automatically— legal custody. I have some hoops to jump through.'

With a grin, Lyndall patted his shoulder. 'Better start getting fit then. You just saw a sixty-five-year-old climb a fence in half a second. Imagine what you could do if you tried.' Before he could answer she was off at a jog. Then she raised her arm to wave without a backward glance.

'Show-off,' he muttered.

'Hearing is still good, Vincent,' she called.

He patted his gut. Losing a bit of weight wouldn't hurt. Hoops or no hoops.

———

Carla stood near the living room window; curtain held aside as she stared out at the street.

Bradley tapped on a laptop from the sofa, glancing at her every so often. It worried him seeing her so hopeful. She needed to keep her expectations low. At least for now. 'Baby, I'm not sure this is the best move.'

She didn't turn. 'She needs to know the truth. How can Child Services make proper decisions without it? Oh, she's here!'

Bradley closed the laptop. He'd made the mistake of telling Carla too much about his encounter with Vince and she'd been straight on the phone. The odd thing was that she'd liked Vince well enough until Susie excommunicated him. Loyalty for Susie ran deep in his wife.

Carla hurried to the front door and a moment later returned with the other woman, a frumpy female public servant with a briefcase. He stood and extended his hand to shake. 'I'm Bradley.'

'Dawn Burrows. Nice to meet you both.'

'Coffee?' Carla asked.

'No, thank you. I'm a bit short on time but your call sounded urgent.'

'Please take a seat.' Bradley gestured to an armchair opposite the sofa, where he and Carla then sat.

'Ms Burrows, this is concerning Melanie Weaver.' Carla

started. 'She's our godchild and we love her very much. We've been in her life since she was born, and she has spent a lot of time with us. Susie was my best friend. From our university days.'

'I'm very sorry for your loss, Mrs Pickering.'

'Thank you. It is hard to imagine Susie is gone. And just as hard not knowing what is to become of Melanie.'

'I don't quite understand.'

Not the brightest spark, are you?

'We're worried about Melanie,' Bradley said. 'We've asked Vince Carter to let us see her, but he flatly refused.'

'It is still early days. She's just out of hospital and he and Melanie have a lot to work though. A lot of adjusting. I'm sure she is in good hands.'

Carla glanced at Bradley then back at the other woman. 'The thing is that Vince and Susie had a big falling out a while ago and he pretty much cut all ties with her. *And* with his own grand-child. But our house is like a second home to her. She feels safe here. Ideally, we'd love Melanie to live with us.'

The social worker frowned. 'Visits are one thing. Custody is quite another.'

'Even if the custodian is unsuitable?' The panic in Carla's voice tugged at Bradley's heart.

'How is Vince Carter unsuitable?' Dawn narrowed her eyes.

'He had something against David. Accused him more than once of being a criminal and it just broke Susie's heart. She told him he wasn't welcome until he got help.'

'What kind of help, Mrs Pickering? Do you know?'

Carla nodded. 'He has anger issues. And the violence. He's a killer.'

That seemed to shock Ms Burrows, who touched the handle of her briefcase as if about to pick it up, then crossed her hands on her lap. 'I'm aware he took a life in the line of duty. And potentially saved several at the same time. Is that what you mean?'

There were tears forming in Carla's eyes. She was getting frustrated. Bradley took her hand and squeezed it and her shoulders seemed to relax a little. He'd speak for her. Take the pressure away.

'Everyone knows Vince saved lives that day but what most people don't know is that he never dealt with the fallout. I mean, his own wife passed away that day because he couldn't be in two places at one time, and it messed with his head. Carla and I are genuinely worried about Melanie's long-term welfare if she stays with him. It was hard enough for Susie being raised out there, all alone except a bitter old man.'

'And Susie said she wanted me to always be part of Melanie's life,' Carla whispered as a single tear slid down her cheek.

After checking her watch, Ms Burrows picked up her briefcase and stood. 'I can assure you all aspects will be considered before any recommendations are made. Until the will is read and other factors taken into account, the status quo remains. Now, please excuse me.'

Bradley led her out of the living room, but she stopped in the doorway with what might have been an attempted smile at Carla. 'Let me speak to Mr Carter about a visit. I'll be in touch.'

Carla nodded but when Bradley returned a minute later, she was wiping more tears away.

'She said she'll talk to him. Focus on that.'

'We need to do something, Brad. She's going to miss out on all the things Susie wanted. And I miss her.' Her lips quivered. 'I really miss her.'

'Me too. Let's see if this Burrows person gets anywhere and if not, we might have to step things up a bit.' There were more ways to win this war than Dawn Burrows could even dream about.

———

While Melanie watched television in the living room, Vince opened his laptop in the kitchen. Weeks usually went by without him using it, but it booted up okay. He ignored its request for an update.

Pen and notebook close by, Vince searched for the business registration.

PickerPack Holdings Pty Ltd.

He wrote down the Australian Business Number and registered address, which was Bradley's. It was originally set up as a private company close to ten years ago. Going through the historical record of its existence, he found when David bought in and became a co-director. Four years ago.

It was a surprise at the time, to Vince anyway. David was a senior manager at a leading logistics company on the other side of the city. He'd complained often enough about the daily commute, but Susie didn't want to move to the Eastern suburbs. His job was secure, well-paying, and offered him potential to advance his career, whereas buying into a struggling business sent alarm bells ringing.

And Susie was worried.

Vince opened his emails and mumbled a swear word as ding after ding heralded the arrival of several weeks' worth of correspondence. Much of it was rubbish. Junk from cold-callers and accounts he'd already paid. He got up to check Melanie.

She was cuddled up with both Raymond and Topsy on the sofa, a throw blanket covering her back and shoulders. The fire was going but she was accustomed to central heating, and he'd need to consider how to do a better job of keeping her warm. She didn't notice him, and he left before he could disturb her.

The emails had all loaded and he typed in 'Susie' to begin a search.

The most recent ones were commiserations for her death from old colleagues and he changed his search to her actual email address. This brought up hundreds of emails from her over a long period, right back to her university days when she'd lived on campus.

His heart thumped uncomfortably.

He scrolled back four years and found the one he remembered. David was about to leave his old job.

I trust him completely, of course. David doesn't make decisions lightly, but I guess he really has had enough of driving across town five days a week and working for someone else. He and Bradley are such good friends and they'll be partners. David is brimming with ideas to use his logistics background to bring in more clients. I'm sure he knows what he's doing.

'And yet, he didn't.'

There was another, a couple of months further on.

David's a bit disappointed in Bradley who wants any changes to come slowly. He doesn't want to move the warehouse to facilitate more clients so for now, David is trying to learn all aspects of the business so he has a stronger case for development. He mentioned there was some kind of issue with an employee. Something about their immigration status. But otherwise, all is well. I'll come up on the weekend with Melly-belly if you like?

She had visited and they'd argued. It was the beginning of the real decline of their relationship, and she'd only brought Melanie out a couple more times. Vince had done some quiet checking and was less than impressed that Bradley was being investigated for hiring illegal immigrants. Not only that, but underpaying them for long hours of work. Susie denied that David knew anything of it but refused to accept Vince's opinion that Bradley's poor practices would reflect on his new partner.

He copied both emails to a file. Then added the link to the business registration.

Sitting on his hands was impossible. Someone had targeted David and his gut screamed it was related to the business. But why that someone decided to murder an innocent woman and injure a child wasn't something his brain could get around. Being a police officer had exposed him to the worst of human nature and this was right up there with the most evil actions he'd come across. If he couldn't investigate it as a member of the force, and if they wouldn't investigate it, then he'd take matters into his own hands. And heaven help who he found at the end of this.

THIRTEEN

Pete was driving. Liz's head pounded from lack of sleep and too much worry and she figured giving him the wheel would keep Pete too busy to bother her. It didn't, and she swallowed more painkillers before they reached their next stop. After an early briefing, they'd spent the day working through their share of a list of Hardy's known associates. Not all were criminals, but none, so far, had been forthcoming with any information.

'Two more, Lizzie. Do you reckon phones are ringing hot around the city right now? Might even be arranging a meeting to discuss the annoying police who won't give them peace.'

I could use some peace.

Wishing she could close her eyes wasn't helping. She tapped on her phone which was loaded with the information they were managing.

'You've met this one before... Ginny Makos.'

He grinned.

'What?'

'She likes me.'

It wasn't the first time Pete had said something similar about a person of interest. He'd been undercover for a long time in a covert unit and there were few people he didn't know, or know of.

'Then you stay in the car.'

He laughed as he pulled the car into a parking spot. 'She won't even talk to you. Not a woman's woman, if you get my drift. Men? Whole different thing.'

When the door of the fifth-floor apartment opened, Liz understood.

The woman didn't even glance her way, but almost purred as she welcomed Pete like a long-lost friend. She let them in as far as a small living room but didn't offer them a seat. All the curtains and internal doors were closed, and the air was overly warm and filled with soft classical music. Ginny wore a satin dressing gown open enough to display the top of a lacy red bra, and six-inch red stilettos.

'Detective Pete... too long between hellos. But you should have called first. I already have a friend arriving soon.'

'A minute will do. Someone we both know is playing hide and seek with me and I thought... who better to give me a clue or two than sweet Ginny.'

I'm seriously going to vomit.

Ginny's smile widened even as her eyes hardened. 'You know I love games, Petey. But I don't think I can help.'

'Ms Makos, do you know the whereabouts of Malcolm Hardy?' Liz asked.

She might as well not have spoken. She was ignored.

'I have to prepare for my visitor.' Ginny put her hand on Pete's cheek. 'But none of my friends are hiding.'

Pete took out his card and slowly slid it into the top of her bra. 'If you hear anything, any rumours, or happen to see Malcolm... I'd be most grateful to hear from you.' He gently removed her hand from his face. 'We'll let ourselves out.'

They reached the elevator without speaking and Liz hit the 'down' button hard.

'Was that Ginny you just imagined hitting?' Pete asked innocently.

'Or you.'

The doors opened and they stepped into the empty lift.

'Just how exactly do you know her so well? Actually, don't answer.'

'I arrested her.'

'For?'

'Let's just say she was in something over her head and after she co-operated, walked away with a misdemeanour. If any of Hardy's contacts are going to spill the beans about him, I reckon she's the one.'

Liz didn't share his confidence but so far they'd hit brick walls at every turn, so she was happy to be proven wrong.

The last person they wanted to speak with wasn't home. They'd driven across to Wyndham Vale in the western suburbs and waited for half an hour before heading back. Liz had napped while Pete followed up leads on his phone and when she woke, the headache was almost gone. There was little point waiting any longer.

'Fancy a short side trip?'

'Where?' Pete asked.

'I was at Bradley Pickering's warehouse the other night.'

'Why?'

'Curiosity.' She had expected some smart-arsed comment. 'Place looked deserted, but someone was there. A man I think, staring back at me through the window.'

'You were creeping around their property?'

'More or less.'

Pete turned onto the road to Laverton. 'And why are we going there again?'

'Terry was at Susie's house yesterday in Caroline Springs. There's been a break in but nothing taken from what anyone could see. Then Vince walked in on Pickering going through the office—he messaged me a bit earlier to say he'd taken a set of keys off Pickering.'

'Not connecting the dots, Liz. He had keys.'

'Yeah. But no permission to take anything from the house yet he was about to remove a computer. He's bad news. And he was overheard arguing with David the night of the accident.'

There was no reply. Liz glanced at Pete and he turned to meet her eyes, eyebrows raised.

'Thought you'd have something to say about Vince,' she said.

'My beef is with him, Liz. Not you. If you want to dig around and stir up Pickering then I'm happy to help.'

Are you mellowing? Or just enjoying the prospect of an argument?

Regardless, she appreciated him coming with her. Not much spooked Liz, but there was something about the warehouse—and the man who owned it—which bothered her.

———

Today couldn't end fast enough. Bradley's meeting earlier in the day had resulted in more work for him—only some of which he'd covered at home waiting for the blasted social worker to visit.

The outcome of months of planning hung in the balance thanks to David's accident. If he had to start over and find a new transport company to fit the bill it would add an unacceptable delay to other parts of the process. David had set the deal up, and with him gone the other party was getting cold feet. They'd never dealt with Bradley and questioned his ability to manage the logistic side of the arrangement.

If only they knew how much money is on the line with this deal.

He'd come back to the warehouse to complete a new

proposal and had just emailed it to them. Now began the wait. The workers were all traipsing out as he locked his office door. Abel was at the side door checking their bags as usual. Since he'd begun doing that each day, theft had dropped right off. And a couple of employees had left which suited him. Bad workers made his life hell.

'I'm having dinner with Duncan.' Bradley was last out apart from Abel and stopped to talk. 'Should get a yes from the transport company soon.'

'Be a short dinner otherwise.'

Maybe he should make Abel a partner. The man had a knack for sniffing out where the money was and enjoyed getting his hands dirty.

Outside the wind had picked up, blowing bits of rubbish around the concrete. Bradley checked his phone as he walked away, almost dropping it at the sight of two cops heading up the driveway. At least, he knew one was a cop. The last one he wanted to engage with. He slid the phone away.

'Well, if it isn't Constable Moorland.'

How satisfying that a flash of irritation crossed her face. She'd not aged well. Lines which makeup couldn't disguise. Not that she wore much. Probably didn't like men.

'Detective Sergeant Moorland,' she said.

'I'm on my way home.' He made a show of checking his Rolex.

'Not going to keep you long, Mr Pickering.' Her eyes roamed up and down the driveway. 'No van?'

'Impressive that two detectives check up on stolen vehicles.'

The cops glanced at each other. They hadn't heard. So why were they here?

'We don't, but for the sake of the conversation, when was it stolen?' The other detective had found his voice. He was scruffy. Longish hair like a surfer but way too old.

'And who are you?' Bradley asked.

'Detective Sergeant Pete McNamara. What exactly does your business do?'

'Resell goods. And we noticed the van missing yesterday. Someone had taken bolt cutters to the padlock on the gate and helped themselves to my property. We reported it.'

'We?'

'My foreman did. He drives it. Or whoever needs to do deliveries.'

'And you also drive it?' The female asked.

He almost spluttered at the idea. 'Never. Not my type.'

'Where is your foreman?'

'Why?' What did they think they knew?

Surfer-cop stepped forward. 'Is he here?'

'Sure he is.'

Bradley went back to the door, which had closed. And was locked. He unlocked it and glanced inside. 'Sorry. He must have left for the day.'

Where the hell are you, Abel?

'I can get him to call you. Or would you like his number? Anything to help us get it back.'

With a strong gust of wind, the door slammed back against the wall.

Surfer-cop stuck his head inside. 'Lots of tables. Are those toys? You said you are a reseller. Of toys?'

'Among other things. We buy rejected imported items. Stuff the original buyer changes their mind about when they see it and that happens a lot more than you'd expect. Most times there's nothing wrong with the products except the importer's expectations and we've made a thriving business from buying on the cheap, repackaging, and on-selling. David had a way of finding a market for anything.'

'Anything?'

'Anything legal, Detective McNamara.'

'What were you and David Weaver arguing about at Spironi's the night of the car crash?'

This was the last thing he'd expected from Moorland's mouth. 'What? Who said we were arguing?'

'Were you?' She pressed.

'Course not. We were as close as brothers. Now, I'm sorry to hurry you but I really do have to leave.' He closed the door. 'You know, David was my friend and my business partner. Susie was Carla's best friend, and she cries herself to sleep every night. And we've not even been allowed to see Melanie.'

'What were you doing in their house?'

It took a lot of control not to snap at the woman with her boring face and knowing eyes. Always had thought she was better than him. Better than Carla. But blowing up wasn't going to get him out of here any quicker and he wasn't about to hand her any ammunition.

'I had keys. They are back with Carter now. And I still have a business to run. David had files in his home office that I needed today. And there's a laptop. Carter refused to let me collect but I own it.'

'Thank you for your time, Mr Pickering.' Surfer-cop nodded and then they were leaving. Not a word about how he could recover the laptop. Nor any sympathy for their loss. And now there was a bigger problem. Who had overheard him talking to David that night?

FOURTEEN

Another freezing night and here I am, outside yet again.

I light another smoke.

The back door of Spironi's finally swings open and the one I want to see comes out. He doesn't notice me at first until I blow some smoke his way and he jumps.

'Who's there?'

He's carrying a garbage bag.

'Chuck that away, kid. I have an offer for you.'

But he backs toward the door so I step where he can see me.

His face relaxes. 'Didn't see your face in the dark, Mr—'

'Chuck it away, kid.'

He tosses it in a dumpster and gives me his attention.

'Young bloke like you needs a few dollars. Right?'

'Sure, but—'

'Just listen.' I toss the cigarette onto the filthy ground. 'You might get someone asking about a certain disagreement you overheard.'

His mouth drops open.

I pull a wad of notes from a pocket and start peeling some off.

'Thing is. That was a private conversation, and it needs to remain private. You need to forget anything you think you heard.'

The kid's eyes don't leave my hands. Probably counting. There's a thousand there. Not bad just for not saying something.

'Heard what?'

'Good boy.' I curl his notes into a cylinder and slide them into his apron pocket. 'Keep that up and you'll get another grand.'

'When.'

'Never know when I might drop in. Come around to check up on you.'

He has the money in his hand, counting rapidly.

'Mind you, one word out of place and that'll be paying for your funeral.'

The kid shoves the cash into his pocket and almost trips over his own feet getting back inside. He's got my message loud and clear.

FIFTEEN

Carla had woken to an empty house and lay in bed for a while going over the stupid argument with Bradley last night. They rarely disagreed and it hurt that they'd not settled things before bed. He hadn't come to the bedroom and she wasn't convinced he'd even stayed in the house for long. His obsession with work at the moment wasn't the reason but it didn't make anything easier.

The need for coffee drove her downstairs, not bothering to shower and still wearing her dressing gown. Another day stretched ahead with this heaviness in her heart the only constant.

There was a note on the counter.

Sorry about last night, baby. Let's go out for dinner tonight. Have some us time. Love you.

Her lips curled up and some of the sadness lifted.

Going out for dinner didn't appeal. It would be a long time before she could sit in a restaurant and not think of that night.

But she could make something nice for them to eat here. Go shopping. Set the dining room table and buy nice wine.

She set about planning a menu and then wrote a shopping list.

After washing her coffee cup she wiped over the sink with a paper towel and opened the bin to dispose of it.

Really, Brad?

The reason they'd argued last night was in the bin. An empty cigarette packet she'd found in his jacket pocket. She'd smelt the smoke on the jacket when he'd taken it off and wanted to dry clean it. He often smelled of smoke after being at one of his dinners with clients. But there'd been the packet and he'd shrugged and blamed stress.

This was a small betrayal. They wanted a baby and he'd promised not to start smoking again after giving up twice. She pushed it down and slammed the bin shut.

———

Vince sat in the waiting room outside Doctor Raju's office.

Melanie had already had a physical check up with Doctor Lennard who was happy with her progress. He'd drawn a kitten on her cast which made her giggle. The next stop was a session with the therapist, one of several Vince had booked after the original visit. He might not like shrinks but Mel was too young to navigate the loss of her parents with only him to help. As if he could help anyone.

He sent a message to Liz.

Morning. Any updates?

The answering machine was as close to a dead end as he could imagine and would be a low priority with the workload on the Melbourne team. But the car. The coroner's report. Those were due soon. The funeral home had called early to advise the funeral was scheduled now. He had yet to talk to Melanie about it and dreaded doing so.

He leaned back in his seat, eyes closed, fingers curling into his palms. If his heart beat any louder the receptionist would hear it. Years ago he'd been given a list of ways to manage stress, none of which he'd taken notice of apart from buying a stress ball. It was still in its plastic wrapping in a drawer somewhere.

Carving the birds helped. Tending to the pony did as well.

His phone vibrated and he opened his eyes to a message from Liz.

> Should have some news today and will call when I do. Could we meet up later?

Not yet. He loved Liz but wasn't ready. The phone went into his pocket, the message unanswered. But he'd have to deal with it soon, once he had a bit more information and needed her help.

The door to the office opened and Melanie rushed out to show Vince another drawing on her cast. 'It's a lion! To give me courage when I feel afraid.'

'A lion and a kitten. Is there a theme here?'

'Maybe.' She puzzled over it, touching one then the other.

'Mr Carter, may I have a moment?' Doctor Raju asked.

'Are you fine to sit here for a little bit, Mel?'

The receptionist glanced over. 'Hi Melanie, would you like to come here with me and draw some pictures? I've got some new coloured pencils waiting to be used.'

Apparently that was an invitation worth accepting. Vince followed the doctor into his office.

'Please, take a seat.'

At least the social worker was absent this time. Vince sat in one of the tub chairs.

'How are you doing, Mr Carter?'

'Please, it's Vince. I'm more interested in how Melanie is.'

'She's where I'd expect about now, not that grief and shock can be measured. Her understanding of the changes in her life are overwhelming so I've given her some little tricks to help her manage one at a time. I've got copies of everything I've suggested so will get you a copy.'

'Okay. Do I need to do anything special?'

What if I stuff it up?

'No. Familiarise yourself with the techniques I'm teaching her, so you understand her process. She might, for example, ask for you to sit with her so she feels secure. Or want to be alone, which is fine in small doses.'

I can do that.

'What do I say about her mother?'

'The truth. But filter everything and let her ask questions. Has she settled in at home? How is she on a day-to-day basis?'

'Fine,' Vince said.

'Would you like me to arrange some home visits by someone who can—'

'I don't mean to sound rude, Doctor, but Melanie is my grandchild and we're doing okay. She's a bit scared and misses her parents. I'm doing my best.'

'And she's lucky to have you,' Doctor Raju said.

Lucky was the last thing he felt and knew Mel would swap him for her parents in a heartbeat. So would he.

'She misses her Auntie Carla.'

'She's not her aunt,' Vince said.

'To Melanie she is. And familiar. Think about taking her to visit them if she asks.'

Vince got to his feet. 'I think she likes kittens.'

'Next she'll be wanting one.' The doctor grinned.

'Yeah. Not sure about that.' Vince managed a smile in return.

'Might not be fair to give her something to love which might be left behind. Should she move again.'

Vince's smile dropped. 'She's not going anywhere.'

The doctor gazed at him for a moment then nodded. 'Good for you. Good for you.'

————

Melanie was quiet all the way home and the second Vince parked, she opened the door and took off to the cottage. By the time he caught up she was hopping from foot to foot outside the front door. 'I'm cold, Grandad!'

'Are you too cold to be outside for a couple more minutes? I'd like to introduce you to someone very, very special? We won't be long.'

'Well, I guess so.'

She took Vince's hand, and he led her around the other side of the cottage where the grass was a bit long and there was a clear view of Lyndall's house higher up the hill. But it was the paddock behind the cottage where he headed.

The pony was grazing at the far end and when Vince whistled, her head shot up. She trotted across with a welcoming nicker.

Melanie hid behind Vince and his heart sank.

'She's come to meet you, so how about...' he grunted as he lifted Mel so her legs wrapped around him, 'you say hello. Do you remember Apple?'

Apple leaned over the fence, her ears flicking back and forward as she tried to reach Melanie's feet. Melanie shrieked and pulled them up and Apple snorted.

'She is curious about you. Do you think she's a red apple or a green one? Grannie Smith or Red Delicious?'

Melanie giggled. 'She's a horse. Not an apple.'

'She's a pony. And she's an old girl.'

Apple tried again to snuffle against Melanie, who buried her head against Vince. 'I want to go inside. Please can we go now?'

After rubbing Apple between her eyes, Vince trudged away from the paddock. 'You know, your mum used to ride Apple everywhere. Every day when she was your age.'

'She did? Mummy rode *that* pony?'

'Not only rode Apple, but groomed her, fed her, and was her best friend.'

Although there was no reply, Melanie peeped over Vince's shoulder to take another look.

Little steps. Next time they'd take some carrots.

———

Vince was sitting on the front steps when a car drove up. Thanks to her phoning first, he was expecting the visit from the social worker. She'd assured him it was nothing but a follow up to their meeting in the hospital, but he'd had a million thoughts run through his mind since she'd rung and was prepared to stand his ground if she wanted to move Melanie.

She climbed out of her car, opened the back door, and extracted a heavy coat. After putting this on, she collected a briefcase and locked the car.

He went to greet her.

'Ms Burrows. You found the place okay?'

'Mr Carter, please call me Dawn. And yes, your directions were easy to follow.' She gazed at the front of the property with its sparse grass and struggling plants, then turned her attention to the cottage. Her expression barely changed but how could she not find it run down and wanting?

'Would you like a cup of tea or coffee? Bit cold out here.'

'I wouldn't mind some tea, thank you.'

'Melanie is doing drawings in her room.' Vince led the way up the steps and opened the door, gesturing for the woman to go first. 'Kitchen's at the end of the hallway. As long as you don't mind sitting in there?'

As he boiled the kettle, he told Dawn about the visit to the hospital earlier in the day.

'And I've made some appointments for her. Just until Doctor Raju thinks she doesn't need to see him. How do you like your tea?'

'White with three sugars. He is a kind man. Excellent with difficult situations.'

She didn't need to add 'like this.' He knew what she was thinking. Little girl left with nobody other than a grandfather well past his prime, living in a shack in the middle of nowhere.

Vince brought the tea to the table and sat opposite. 'I met with Susie's lawyer and he's sorting out the will and stuff. The house is owned outright... was owned outright. Imagine it will be sold and I'll set up a trust for Mel. There's a lot of unknowns at the moment.'

'Is it worth considering moving into that house? Closer to Melanie's school and friends and activities. It would keep her life a bit more normal.'

Never happening.

'Anything is possible but as I mentioned, there's a lot to be done by the legal people first.'

'I did a search before I drove up. Public transport is a fair distance away and almost impossible for an eight-year-old going to an Eastern suburbs school and back. I understand she's doing well there so moving her might not be the best option.'

He sipped some tea to give himself a chance to think of a reply. He'd been through this with Susie after her mother died. Visits by social workers. Well-meaning but asking questions he had no answers to. Same as now.

'We'll work through it all. Melanie and me.'

'There will be some resources made available to you both. I can see how much you care for her. Just one thing. I spoke with Carla and Bradley Pickering.'

What the hell for?

'They mentioned how much they would like to see her. I understand Melanie is close to them.'

'Hmm.'

She titled her head in question.

'I'll think about it. But after the funeral.'

He must have used the appropriate tone of voice to convince her it was the end of the discussion because she smiled and changed the conversation to the weather.

SIXTEEN

'Liz, a minute?' Terry called from the doorway of his office.

She was in the midst of making a list of secondary contacts of Hardy. Pete was getting them lunch and then they'd head out.

Terry was back in his chair when she joined him. The palms of his hands rested on a file on his desk. 'Grab a seat. What came of your visit to Pickering?'

'He was a bit hostile but trying to cover it. But it may be due to our past dealings.'

'Heard a rumour you'd had prior contact. What was that about?'

'Oh gosh, it was years ago. I was in uniform but not partnered with Vince yet so I had no idea of the relationship between the two families until much later. They wanted to bring charges against the son of a new neighbour. He'd done nothing wrong, but they accused him of loitering outside their house and suggested... well, that's the nice word, he was hanging around the front in order to case their house with a view to breaking in.'

'Was this a kid?'

'Young teen.'

'So why was he there?'

She laughed. 'The school bus stopped there for morning pick up. Same as it had since the Pickerings moved in. Funny thing was they'd never complained about any of the other kids who did precisely the same thing.'

Terry raised both eyebrows. 'Wrong colour or faith?'

'Both.'

'Nice people. Not.'

'They made a fuss. Tried to turn it into something it wasn't, and I pushed back. Explained a few facts of life. A few laws. Bradley threatened to have me fired. I suggested he try.'

'Go you.' Terry grinned. 'And the outcome?'

'Given the situation, a house went on the market. People moved. Problem solved.'

'What? Not the kid's family?'

'Nope. Bradley and Carla found a house in a suburb they felt suited their 'needs' more. And what made it all the better was they took a hit on the sale. Below market value because Carla couldn't bear living there anymore.'

Liz had gone to the auction out of interest. The house was already empty and when the reserve wasn't met, there'd been a hurried phone call between agent and vendors who immediately approved the highest bid.

'And Bradley recognised you?'

'Almost dropped his phone.'

She was pleased Pete was with her. Gave him a chance to see the kind of person Vince was dealing with. He'd been uncomplimentary about Bradley on the way back, calling him a loser in typical Pete-speak.

'The warehouse is a dive. They resell toys rejected by importers. Apparently. His reasons for being in Susie's house seem legit. But here's something interesting, boss. The van I saw the other night? Stolen.'

'Well, isn't that convenient.' Terry pushed the file across the desk. 'It's from Jim. Traces of black paint were found on the front passenger door of the Weaver vehicle. More on the same side but rear. And traces on the road mixed up with some from the other car.'

Vince was right. Instincts never fail him.

'I'd like you to take a look at the scene of the crash with this new information in mind.'

'So... this is official?'

'More a fishing expedition.'

'And Vince?' Liz asked.

'In the dark until something nibbles on your hook.'

———

Pete took the list of contacts to make a start after groaning when Liz said where she was going. She was good with being on her own to revisit the site of the accident.

She followed the route David had most likely taken that night. From Lygon Street to his house in the western suburb of Caroline Springs was about thirty minutes at that time of night if he'd used the main roads. A bit longer using back roads.

But it didn't make sense why he was on *that* road.

By sticking to the GPS route from the restaurant to the Weaver house, she'd miss the accident site by several kilometres.

'So where did you detour to first?'

Maybe one of the recovered mobile phones would provide some data. The car had no built in navigation nor a fitting for any. Another job for the understaffed, backed-up Forensic Services Department.

After a detour she turned onto the right road. There were no street lights and few homes so not many driveways. Lots of open paddocks with cattle or sheep. A few side roads turned off to goodness knows where. Under normal circumstances there was nothing to indicate this was a dangerous stretch.

The air was cool as she climbed out after parking on a grassy shoulder twenty or so metres from the scene and she glanced at the sky. Rain was on its way.

It was eerie being here again. This time there was no crumpled car, just deep indentations in the lower part of the gum tree. Pieces of bark and glass littered a radius around it. On closer inspection, fragments of metal pierced the trunk. She shuddered. This was a place of death.

Forcing away the urge to throw up, she walked slowly around the tree, taking a lot of photos with her phone and adding voice notes. Accident Investigation would already have done this and more, but she needed to make her own records.

The next step was to follow the barbed wire fence of a neighbouring property, zig-zagging from it to the road and back through the thick grass and weeds of the wide verge. She kept her eyes down searching for who-knew-what and after fifty or so metres, crossed the road and did the same. Halfway back to the tree, she saw it.

A half-smoked cigarette had clearly been dropped or tossed, not scrunched beneath a shoe.

Probably some dropkick litterbug.

But what if it wasn't?

Once she'd taken photos of it and of the location, it went into an evidence bag.

She gazed in the direction of the tree. The car had faced this way, smashed and broken, its front seat occupants dead or dying. Had a passing car stopped, its driver tossing away their smoke before running to see if they could assist? Who had called in the accident? She made more notes.

Rain began to spit as she continued her search in the other direction and she pulled the hood up from her jacket. Nowhere along this stretch—a hundred metres or more—were any gates or driveways. Roaming livestock might be responsible for David changing lanes. She'd visit the closest farmhouses next.

But that didn't explain the trace of black paint on two parts of his car. Nor the combination of black and red paint on the road a bit before he'd begun to brake and almost in the wrong lane.

Another vehicle had hit the Weavers. Now she had to find the driver.

As the rain intensified she returned to the tree and put her hand on the trunk. 'I'll find out the truth, Susie.'

———

After dropping the cigarette back to the station, Liz had one more stop before meeting with Pete. They still had a crap-load to cover before the end of the day.

She was back at Lygon Street and had driven via Williamstown where Carla and Bradley lived which was a straight run across country from the accident site. Had the couples headed back there after dinner? Or had the Weaver's picked up and dropped off the Pickerings?

Spironi's was at the tail end of its lunch service and although still open, had no customers. Two servers were preparing the tables for the dinner service and when Liz stepped inside, one of them immediately approached her. A young man with the name 'Marco' on his apron. Perfect.

'My apologies, ma'am. We are now closed for lunch.'

'That's fine. I'm here to speak with Marco... and I can see from your name tag that I have the right person.'

Marco returned to the table. 'I have to keep working. Are you the police officer? Mike said you'd be back.'

The man kept his eyes on his job, which he attended to with speed and precision.

'I won't keep you long. I understand that you overheard an argument. The night the Pickering and Weaver party was here.'

Moving to the next table, Marco shook his head. 'Don't remember.'

'They are regulars. And there was a car accident which killed David and Susie Weaver on their way home that night. Funny you'd not know because when I was here yesterday, Mike knew all about it and said you looked after their table.'

'I remember them. They were regular guests. Doesn't mean I heard an argument.'

'Yet you told your workmate about it.'

Marco glanced up. 'He's mistaken.'

'So there was no argument? Two customers near the toilets?' This was both annoying and interesting. 'You heard no raised voices?'

'Nothing. I'm sorry I can't help you.'

'Another question then I'll leave you to your work. Did the guests all arrive at the same time?'

He straightened. 'I didn't seat them, but they were all present when I went to take them water a couple of minutes later.'

Liz handed her card to Marco. 'Give me a call if you remember David Weaver—who died soon after, arguing with Bradley Pickering. It matters.'

She let herself out.

SEVENTEEN

The warehouse was noisy and busy. Abel and three other men unloaded boxes onto pallets from the flatbed ute which was backed in thanks to the rain. A forklift moved the pallets as soon as they were loaded, depositing them at the end of the long work benches. A small delivery truck idled outside waiting its turn.

In the middle of this, a black luxury SUV edged past and found a parking spot at the back of the driveway.

Bradley grabbed an umbrella and shot out into the weather, hurrying to get to the visitor before he got out.

He held it over the driver's door, water trickling down his neck as he lost coverage.

'Day for ducks, not people.' Duncan Chandler sounded cheery as he climbed out after checking where his feet—clad in crocodile leather shoes—would land. 'I look forward to an early retirement in a place of perpetual warmth and rare downpours.'

Don't we all.

Not yet forty, the man's paunch and red nose and cheeks reflected his lifestyle. He'd been heard saying it often enough—

work hard, play harder. And Bradley admired him. Kind of. Certainly enough to want to work with him.

'Let's get out of the weather.'

The rain battered the roof of the warehouse, adding to people yelling to each other and the beeping of the forklift.

'Coffee, Duncan?'

'Actually, I'd like to see how this all works, if you don't mind?'

'That's right, you've not been here before.'

'Walk me through.'

Bradley caught Abel's eye and in a moment, he joined them.

'This is Abel Farrelly. He keeps things on track, and you can always speak with him if I'm unavailable.'

'Looks busy. Are those all toys?' Duncan gazed at the tables where boxes were being opened and tipped out.

'Every last one. There's a container-load coming through here over the next week thanks to the importer going belly-up while the boat was on its way. It sat on the wharves for a bit longer than hoped. Been hard, losing David,' Abel said.

'And now you want to change direction.' Duncan turned his back on Abel.

Bradley nodded for Abel to go back to work and led the visitor to the first table. 'As I said at our dinner, I've secured a new arrangement with the freight company pending signing of a contract.'

Duncan glanced at him with a frown. 'Pending isn't signed.'

'It will be though.' Time to get off the subject. 'The first thing we do is check the product. Sometimes several are stuffed inside a large bag and other times, like this box, each is wrapped.' Bradley picked up a purple dragon inside a cheap clear bag. 'All the packaging is removed, and the product inspected for integrity. They might be dirt cheap, but they need to pass muster.' He ripped the bag open and passed the toy to Duncan. 'What do you think of this?'

The toy dragon was large enough for a little kid to cuddle and the fabric was soft. The stitching was good enough and it was cute.

'Assuming it made it through customs and doesn't contain drugs, it is exactly the type of thing I'd buy.' Duncan tossed it back onto the table. 'Yet you've only offered me a transport and distribution arrangement. Why?'

Not keen for their conversation to be overheard by employees, Bradley guided Duncan toward the back end of the warehouse to the shipping containers. The doors of one were padlocked but the other was open and workers were packing it with large colourful boxes.

'Once a toy passes inspection it is repackaged. That usually means in a thick clear plastic bag with a cardboard header. Those big boxes are ours and the brand changes depending on the items. We've got half a dozen brands registered.'

Duncan smiled but not in a nice way. His earlier cheeriness was long gone. 'Why am I here?'

Time for coffee.

'Let's go to the office. Bit quieter in there.'

Once he got them both a coffee and closed the door to keep the noise out, Bradley turned on the charm. 'Duncan's Discount Toys is a rock star business. You built an empire from the ground up in less than a decade and are a masterclass in entrepreneurial enterprises.'

'Don't blow smoke up my arse, mate. Just answer the question.'

'Fair enough. Look, we've been slowly increasing market share in other states and some remote regional hubs. But sending half-empty containers interstate is a waste of money. We deal with a handful of two buck shops in Queensland and less in Darwin and Adelaide. Not enough to service weekly unless—'

'Unless you can fill the container. Thing is... I didn't make a fortune by helping my competition.' Duncan leaned back in his chair and crossed an ankle over his knee. He stared at Bradley; his lips pressed together.

This was do or die time. If Duncan pulled the pin on negotiations they'd be stuffed.

'When David Weaver came on board a few years ago, your empire was moving fast. Our business was growing as well, and we'd made a few connections in China and on the docks, so we'd get wind of unwanted shipments. Even back then it made sense to reach out to you. See if we could fit into your supply chain somewhere.'

'But?'

Bradley shrugged. 'David said no. He wanted to keep doing what we've always done with the mixed loads. But a few months ago when we did the sums for expanding and sending our boxes interstate, I knew we needed to offer regular container space to another business. To you.'

'Which you raised with me months ago. Then nothing until yesterday.'

'There's more. I can offer you first look at any toys now. My business model is for the dirt cheap stuff so it makes sense for you to buy the better quality shipments. Then we jointly transport them.'

'Where was this offer last time we spoke?'

'My hands were tied.'

The phone began to ring. Bradley lifted and replaced the receiver.

'What changed, Bradley?'

On the top of the filing cabinet was a photograph of Bradley and David shaking hands, taken the day their partnership became official. Bradley dragged his eyes from it.

'I'll tell you what changed, Duncan. The person who had

stopped me from going forward with you died. As tragic as it is, David is gone. That's what changed.'

———

Melanie insisted on helping clear the kitchen table after dinner. Since her session with Doctor Raju this morning, she'd seemed a bit less withdrawn and more interested in being active rather than curled up in front of the television.

'That was a big help, Melanie. Are you going to read for a bit now?'

'I've read all the books in my room.'

'Already? Have you checked the bookcase in the living room? I'm pretty sure there's a few your mum used to read.'

She nodded.

'You have checked?'

'May I borrow them?'

His heart hurt a little at her polite request. Did she not yet understand she would live here now and that everything his, was hers?

He pulled up a chair and motioned for her to sit near him. 'Melanie, you have lovely manners. But you don't need to ask to read the books because they are yours now. Same as you can help yourself to anything in the fridge. Everything here is yours as well. Probably prefer you leave the grown-up books for when you are older and ask if you need anything that is high up, but otherwise, help yourself.'

'What about the rest of my clothes and toys and books and stuff. At home.'

Wide, serious, eyes regarded him.

When Marion died, he'd tried to shield Susie from the realities of life without her mother. Avoided being honest if it would hurt her too much.

Hurt me too much.

'Grandad? I heard you talking with the lady before. I didn't mean to hear but was going to go to the bathroom and she was talking about my school.'

'You should have come and said hello, Mel. Ms Burrows is a social worker who looks out for people who might need a hand sometimes.' He shifted in his seat as he cast his mind back to the conversation. 'Was it about how far we are from your school?'

'She said the public transport is a long way away. But I can walk a long way, Grandad. So I can keep going there. Can't I?' Her lips quivered and Vince quickly nodded and smiled.

'Going to do my best to make that happen. And you won't need to walk.'

'I have homework I haven't done yet. In my room at home. Can we go and get it?'

He'd not given school or school holidays a thought. 'When do you go back?'

'Um... not next week. The one after. So when can we get my homework?'

'Well, it depends if you want to come with me. I can see if Lyndall can stop by for a bit tomorrow to spend time with you if you prefer I go alone.'

Melanie hopped off the chair. 'May I come with you?'

What could he do but agree? She had to go back sometime.

EIGHTEEN

Breakfast was done and a load of washing was hung out in the hope there'd be no rain until later in the day. The fire was ready to light. There were no more excuses to put off the inevitable.

Going back to Susie's house was the last thing Vince wanted. Taking Mel there was even worse. How would Mel cope being back where she'd grown up, where every room held memories of her parents and her sweet little heart might break into pieces?

'Why are you breathing funny?' Melanie took his hand, and he drew in air slowly, concentrating on the feel of her fingers. Small and attached to the one person he had left in the world. Her needs outranked his.

Pull yourself together, Carter.

'Must have carried a bit too much wood in the last time.'

'Then I shall help you next time.'

'Let's make a deal,' he said. 'You write a list of everything you need from the house, and we'll go and get those things. But if you don't feel up to going inside, you sit in the car, and I'll be quick getting them. Okay?'

'I'll be quicker.'

Vince laughed and she did too... for a moment. Then she ran out.

'Mel?'

'I need paper to make a list.'

Of course you do. And when you have, please tell me how to be resilient like you?

———

They sat in the driveway for a few minutes. Melanie had made her list and when Vince suggested bringing a suitcase she'd told him there were plenty in the upstairs hallway closet.

'Would you like to stay here in the car?'

'I wrote two lists. One for each of us.' She handed him a neatly written list of five items. 'I'll find my homework first.'

He glanced at his list.

• Pink suitcase in upstairs hall closet
• Sheets with unicorns on the shelf above the suitcases
• Board games in cupboard in living room
• Herb box on kitchen window
• Bean bag in living room

Locations and all.

'I'll get the suitcase first and bring it to your bedroom, okay? So you can pack whatever you need from your room.'

She nodded and unclipped her seatbelt.

'What is the herb box, Mel?'

'We grow fresh herbs in it.' She screwed up her face as if trying to find the words to describe it and held her hands about a foot apart. 'The bottom bit is wood and there are little pots inside with the herbs. It's my job to water them every day.' With that, she pushed the door open and jumped out.

Shit. No water for how long now?

Mel waited for him to unlock the door, her eyes darting to his face a couple of times. He squeezed her shoulder and opened the door, and she ran straight up the stairs.

The air in the house was stale and Vince mentally kicked himself. Ignoring the problem didn't make it go away. It was only a house. Only furniture. Belongings. Things. He'd make a start on the legal stuff. Work out what he needed to attend to. Speak to the lawyer again.

'Grandad, can I have my suitcase?' Mel was at the top of the stairs staring down.

'On my way.'

The pink suitcase was stored inside a much larger black one. Vince found the unicorn sheets and took them as well, opening the suitcase on Mel's bed and placing them in the bottom. She had already located her homework and was piling books on her small desk. 'Need a hand?'

She shook her head.

Back downstairs, he grabbed the beanbag and took it straight to the boot of the car.

Then a dozen or so board games.

An elderly woman shuffled up the driveway with a handful of mail.

'Letterbox full. Keeps falling out. You're Susan's poppa, eh?'

'Yes, Mrs Rionetti, it's Vince. We've met. And thanks for keeping these.'

'Bad. Very bad news.' She shook her head and switched to a few words of Italian as she went back the way she'd come.

Mel emerged with an armful of stuffed toys. 'I can't close the suitcase.'

'Here, those can sit on the bean bag.' He moved the board games to make space for the suitcase. 'Is there a key to the letterbox?'

'It has a code thing. Eleven-twelve.'

His breath caught. That was his birthday.

'Grandad, what about the herb box? You get the mail and my suitcase, and I'll find that.' She ran inside.

It only took a minute to open the letterbox which was stuffed full with mail and junk mail. He'd go through everything later. Pay any bills. For now, they were added to the boot, and he headed upstairs again. She was right about the suitcase. Vince muttered and grunted as he squashed the lid down enough to zip it. What on earth was in here? He lugged it downstairs and repacked the boot because the beanbag made it impossible to fit the suitcase in. He stood holding the beanbag.

Mel wasn't back.

It landed on the ground with a soft thump as he took off for the house. 'Melanie?'

She was standing on a step she must have carried from somewhere, staring at the wooden box on the windowsill in the kitchen.

'Shall I reach it for you?' Not waiting for a reply, he picked up the box. The soil was dry and all but one plant was withered to the point of no return. The other didn't look flash but might bounce back.

'Bit of water, Mel—'

She whispered something he didn't catch and ran a hand across her eyes leaving a trail of tears on her skin. 'It was my job to water them. My... fault.'

The herb box found itself in the sink as he swept Mel up into his arms. Her tears flowed unchecked, and rage scorched his gut. If Susie and Mel hadn't gone to dinner that night... if David hadn't put his family in danger... if a killer hadn't murdered his child...

If I hadn't ruined everything with Susie.

There were a million words to say and none at all.

———

The rain began on the trip home.

After a lot of crying curled on her mother's side of the bed, and then a long walk through the house gripping Vince's hand as if she'd never release him, Melanie had quietly announced it was time to go. She'd reluctantly agreed to take the herb box with them. Vince knew stuff all about growing herbs, but he was about to learn. There was so much unused space around the cottage and as he drove, ideas rushed through his head. How hard could it be to create a real vegetable garden? Something they could tend together.

He hauled her suitcase into the cottage and left Mel unpacking it. She'd need the little desk from her old bedroom. And her bed was newer and nicer than the one in this room. They should fit in the old trailer out the back on a less-rainy day.

Once he'd brought the remainder of the list in, he set to work getting the fire going in the living room and found a spot for the beanbag. That done, he tossed the mail onto the kitchen table to worry about later.

For now, he needed to feed them. He rummaged around the pantry for ideas.

———

She wasn't in her room, but the suitcase was empty, rezipped, and left against a wall. Her stuffed toys lined up in a row on the bed. The sheets were folded on the end. Her shoes were neatly placed near the wardrobe. Susie at this age was a tornado of mess.

Melanie had found the beanbag and was curled up in it with Raymond and a book.

'Hungry? I am.'

She didn't reply or look up.

'Any fancies for lunch?'

Her head shook.

'What about soup and some crusty bread. Being such a dull old day now, it'll warm us both up. Tomato or chicken noodle?'

'Don't mind.'

'Tomato it is.'

———

The rain intensified, pouring from the edge of the roof to cascade from the front of the verandah like a waterfall. Melanie took Raymond to the window to watch. The torrent formed sludgy pools in the dirt and grass, and she could barely see the road in the distance. Not like at home where her room was high and overlooked the back garden.

A tiny, bedraggled kitten ran past the verandah.

Dropping Raymond, Melanie bolted for the front door.

She shivered, rubbing her arms once she pulled the door closed behind herself. There was no time for a jacket. Somewhere out here, all alone, was a little lost kitten. Taking a quick breath, she jumped off the verandah through the sheet of water, gasping as it soaked her hair and top.

But where had the kitten gone?

Melanie padded around the side of the house in soggy socks.

'Kitty?'

Past the cottage was another building with pieces of metal stuck out to one side covering Grandad's wood he used for the fireplace. He'd left a big block out in the rain with an axe stuck into it.

There was a sound from under the shelter.

Melanie climbed under, stooping because of the low roof.

'Kitty?'

There was a pitiful meow.

Trembling from the cold and wet from nose to tail, it sat upon a piece of wood.

'Oh... it's okay little one. I'm here now. I'm Melanie Weaver.'

She knelt and the kitten—tail high—pranced across, shaking one paw after another. When it was close, she gently lifted the tiny creature and tucked it beneath her wet top. She giggled when a purr resonated against her chest.

'We'll go find Grandad and get you dry.'

But somebody was striding toward her. Somebody in huge black boots, wearing a long, flapping, brown coat and wide-brimmed hat hiding most of their face. They stopped at the block of wood and yanked the axe out.

Had the angry man found her?

Melanie backed as far in as she could, but those boots stomped through the puddles until reaching the edge of the shelter, blocking the way to freedom.

The axe swung from side to side.

Melanie couldn't breathe. Her chest hurt from holding herself so still.

Why hadn't she told Grandad before she came out?

She clamped a hand over her mouth in case she made a noise.

The kitten popped its head up and meowed.

The figure crouched, peering into the piles of wood. They slid the axe onto its side out of the rain and took off their hat.

'Hello there. I see you've found my lost baby.'

Melanie had never been so happy to see someone in her life. It wasn't the angry man. 'It's you, Lyndall!'

'Who else would it be? Come on out, darlin'.' Lyndall offered a hand and Melanie slid forward and took it, keeping her grip on the kitten as she climbed out. 'Well, well, well. Look at you both. As bedraggled as each other!'

'Melanie! Melanie, where are you?' Grandad shouted in the distance.

'Uh-oh, here comes the spoil-sport.'

Melanie giggled.

'Nothing wrong with a bit of a walk in the rain, huh?'

'Thank God, Mel!'

Grandad's hair looked funny all plastered to his head from the rain, but his face was serious and worried. He wore a raincoat and was puffing.

'Afternoon, Vincent.'

'*Lyndall?* Mel, what are you doing out here in this downpour?'

'This downpour fills up my dam so let it rain.'

Melanie extricated the kitten from inside her top and offered it to Lyndall, who gave it a kiss on its head.

'This clever grandchild of yours found my lost kitten. His mother's been searching everywhere. Mind you, she'll be happy to see the back of them soon enough. Vincent, you should get this child inside before she gets a chill.' Lyndall squashed the big hat back on her head and winked at Mel. 'Next visit you come to my place and spend some time with these cats, little miss.'

A moment later she disappeared around the back of the building and Mel's hand was tightly inside Grandad's as they headed to the front door.

'Told you Lyndall was scary,' he said.

'She's nice. Can I go and see the kittens?'

'Maybe. Right now you're going to get dry and have some soup. Soup! Oh no...'

He let go of her hand. She hadn't known he could run so fast.

———

Soup dripped over the edge of the stove to form blood-like pools on the floor. The boiling liquid had extinguished the flame. Vince turned off the element and opened the window.

'Ew. That smells terrible.'

Melanie held her nose with her finger and thumb.

'It's what happens when the gas is still going and meets up with burnt soup. How about you jump in and have a shower and I'll start cleaning up.'

'I can help first.'

With such a water-logged child in front of him, Vince couldn't help himself. He chuckled.

Crossing her arms, Melanie lifted her chin.

'You are dripping all over the floor, Melly-belly. Your clothes are drenched, and I think you collected some cobwebs in your hair.'

With a small shriek, she swatted at her head.

'No spiders. None I can see.'

'This isn't funny, Grand*father*.'

'It is. A little bit.'

'I have decided to have a shower and put on dry clothes.' Melanie trounced out of the room. 'And I'm really hungry.'

Atta girl.

He dropped the saucepan into the sink to fix later and used copious amounts of paper towel to sop up the soup on the stove. The floor was a mop and bucket job, but he waited for the shower to turn off before fetching them. Two taps at the same time would mean cold water for both, thanks to his antiquated hot water system and Melanie would think he'd done it to annoy her further.

He found another saucepan and heated the other can of soup, staring into it as he stirred. He had to do better. Melanie had disappeared without a word, leaving her beloved Raymond behind, and he'd run halfway to the road before thinking it through. If she'd left the property, getting the car to search for her was a better option. He'd been almost back at the cottage for the car keys when he thought he heard voices. Finding Lyndall with his granddaughter was like a gift. But he had to do better.

'Shall I cut up the bread?'

Vince jumped. He'd not heard Mel come back in. Her hair was damp, but she wore dry clothes and had slippers on her feet. And a smile on her face.

'Um... er, the knife is pretty sharp.'

'I won't cut myself.'

She cut two thick slices and buttered them. Generously. After putting them on side plates, she collected bowls and soup spoons. These all went onto the kitchen table, and she located salt and pepper from the small pantry.

'Do you have any baking soda?' She peered into the pantry.

'Dunno. Why?'

'To clean the saucepan. Oh, goodie.' She dug out an unopened packet Vince could not recall buying. 'After lunch I'll fix that saucepan up. Good as new!'

Susie used to say that.

'Daddy? You know the tear in my school uniform... well, I practiced sewing until I made it look as good as new.'

'Don't worry about making the stain on the carpet, Daddy. Its only red wine and I found out how to get it so it will be as good as new.'

'Oh dear... but don't worry, Dad. The bouquet is so fragile and you weren't to know so let me just get one of the bridesmaids to loan me a couple of their flowers. Promise, it will be as good as new.'

'Earth to Grandad. I've turned the soup off.'

With a sickening thud, Vince was back in the here and now. His hands shook as he poured soup into the bowls. He carried them to the table caught between the need to run out and find somewhere private to vomit... or cry.

NINETEEN

'You go and talk to him. If you're going to insist on believing Vince's ramblings then feel free but I want to eat now we've come to a stop for a few minutes.' As if to reinforce his words, Pete leaned into the back seat and grabbed a plastic wrapped roll of some kind. 'You wouldn't like me when I'm hungry.'

'I don't like you full stop. Not when you're mean about Vince.' Liz glanced at the sky as she climbed out, then stuck her head back in. 'Paint trace doesn't lie. Particularly when the car shouldn't even have been on that road. Enjoy whatever that is.'

She hadn't meant to snap at Pete but some days he pushed a bit too much. Before the rain could return, she hurried across and down the road.

This part of North Melbourne was on its way up in market value as people renovated and sold for huge amounts of money. Terrace houses lined both sides of the road and every one she passed was a work of beauty. Except for Abel Farrelly's home.

His gate was rusted and squealed as she pushed it open. The short path to the door was uneven and where a small ornamental tree might have once thrived in the middle of the handkerchief sized garden was a dry shell of branches. Long dead. The front door needed painting yet there was one of those fancy schmancy talking cameras near the front door.

She didn't ring the doorbell, curious to see how long it would take for him to answer the door if she stared into the camera. The flatbed ute was parked out the front so odds were he was home.

It took exactly two minutes.

He said nothing, just stood there staring at her.

'Abel Farrelly?'

'What of it.'

'I'm Detective Sergeant Liz Moorland.' She flashed her badge. 'Would you mind answering a couple of questions?'

'Not much of a talker.'

Nevertheless, Abel stepped back and nodded for her to enter. Once inside, he turned one of several locks on the door and led the way to a kitchen. Not just any kitchen, but one straight out of a lifestyle magazine. For that matter, the little she could see of the rest of the narrow house matched it perfectly. Nothing at all like the outside.

Abel put a marble counter between them and crossed his arms.

'I understand you recently reported a stolen vehicle. The property of PickerPack Holdings?' Liz asked.

'I did.'

'When was the last time you saw the vehicle?'

'Friday night. Locked up at the back of the driveway of the warehouse when I closed the place up.'

'I saw it on Saturday night at the warehouse.'

His eyes didn't waver, but one side of his lips flicked up for an instant. 'I don't work Saturdays. If you saw it, then it was stolen afterwards.'

'You have a beautiful home, Mr Farrelly. Lived here for long?'

'Why is a detective asking about a stolen van?' His arms dropped and he placed both palms onto the counter.

'I'm not at liberty to say but appreciate any assistance you can provide. Who had access to the van?'

'Me. Bradley. Anyone who gets their hands on one of the sets of keys for it.'

'So a set of keys is missing?'

'Didn't say that.'

She forced a smile. 'Are any of the keys to the stolen van missing?'

'Best to ask the boss, but not that I know of.'

'Do other employees drive it? Mr Pickering mentioned it is used for pickups and deliveries.'

'I've said what I know. Anyone could have got the keys, stolen the van, and who knows what. I drive it. Half a dozen of the others might drive it if I'm busy and need something done. Bradley drives it.'

You two need to get your stories straight.

She took out a card and dropped it on the counter. 'Get in touch if you think of anything.'

'Bradley told you somebody cut the chain on the gates the night it went missing? We found the gates open.'

'He did,' she said.

'Hope you find it.'

'I'll see myself out.'

He didn't argue and she didn't waste any time leaving. He'd been perfectly civil, but her senses were on high alert.

Raindrops fell as she returned to the car and the temperature was dropping fast.

Pete gave her an odd look.

'What?'

'Tell you in a minute. What did he say?'

'That he knows nothing about the theft. That he last saw it on Friday night. And that Bradley is one of the people who drives it.'

Pete's lips curled up. 'Lie. Lie. Lie. Let me show you something.' He tapped his phone and started a video.

He'd taken it while she'd waited at Abel's front door. A white Lexus coupe had pulled up on the same side as Abel's house but a bit further along the road. The driver's door opened, stayed open for about ten seconds before closing again. And the car drove off.

'Nice car,' Liz said.

'Not many in the state.'

'Should I know who owns it?'

'I've been reviewing footage around the Hardy case. The day he escaped there were press all over the front of the courthouse and they tried to get an interview with Richard Roscoe. He bundled himself into a white Lexus coupe and I reckon if we do a check that this car,' he pointed at the screen of the phone, 'is his.'

Liz gazed over to Farrelly's house and back to Pete, who had a ridiculously pleased expression on his face. 'So what does Hardy's lawyer have to do with our mate over there?'

Dropping his phone into the centre console, Pete started the car. 'That, my colleague, is your job to find out.'

———

Following an afternoon of playing board games and making and eating macaroni cheese for dinner, they went their separate ways —Melanie taking a book to the living room and Vince cleaning up.

She'd talked a lot during the afternoon and mostly about the kitten and Lyndall. But one thing she said had stuck in the back of his mind.

'I was *so* happy it was Lyndall and *not* the angry man.'

By then he'd heard about every detail of her following the cat and how she'd climbed into the woodpile to retrieve the little creature. He was waiting for her to ask—again—when she could visit Lyndall's house and her throwaway comment took a minute to digest.

'So, can I?'

'Can you... oh, visit Lyndall. Yes, we'll arrange something. But, Mel, who is the angry man?'

Her eyes had dropped, and she'd put a forkful of macaroni onto her fork and shoved it in her mouth.

Had he misheard? Perhaps she meant she was relieved it wasn't an angry person ... a stranger. From underneath the shelter in the pouring rain, the sight of Lyndall with that hat of hers pulled down and her oilskin coat flapping around was enough to frighten anyone.

He let it go but filed it away.

The rain was back after a late afternoon break, during which he'd restocked the wood supply, and for once he'd got the cottage warm. When Melanie was settled back at school and his time free again, he'd arrange a new hot water system and look at better heating options.

Vince gathered the mail he'd brought from Susie's house and began sorting it on the kitchen table. Most of it was junk mail, which was something he didn't get out here. Mail was delivered three times a week but never a free paper or retail catalogues, which suited him fine.

There were half a dozen bills. Power. Insurance on the house. Insurance on the cars.

He'd forgotten Susie and David had a second car and hadn't ventured into the garage.

A letter from Melanie's school was addressed only to David. He was vaguely familiar with the school by reputation and remembered Susie raving about the quality of the staff and advantages for Melanie to attend. How she'd been on some waiting list since birth.

Fancy school at a fancy price.

The letter was from the principal, Joyce McCoy, and again, was directed to David. There were only two relevant paragraphs.

As we approach term three with no sign of this year's payments, we request an urgent meeting to discuss Melanie's future with us. As much as we'd like her to stay as one of our students, the arrangements we accepted in term one have not been honoured by you.

We appreciate the difficult situation you are in with your business but remind you that fees are compulsory for our school. We cannot offer the range of options for a student without your contribution. Please contact me at your earliest convenience, but definitely before the next term begins.

He read it twice.

'What difficult situation?'

Susie always said the business was going well. How long had David been missing school fee payments?

There was a second page.

An invoice.

'Holy mother of...'

There was no way anyone should pay so much for schooling! What did they do there... three course meals? Excursions to the moon?

He ran his eyes down the list.

This was just for fees. Two terms unpaid this year.

Before his blood pressure hit the roof he returned the letter and invoice to the envelope. In the morning he'd phone the school and arrange a meeting and he had some thinking to do because those fees were out of his budget.

The rest of the bills were paltry by comparison. He made a list of who to contact tomorrow, who to pay, and which services to cancel or adjust. That done, he put everything into a folder and took it into his bedroom. There was no way he wanted Melanie seeing any of it.

She was in the living room, fast asleep. She'd changed into her pyjamas and her book was closed on the coffee table and Raymond cuddled under her arm. Ever so carefully, he lifted her into his arms and carried her to her bedroom.

After tucking her in and kissing her forehead, he closed the door and returned to the living room. His intention to check the fireplace and go to bed was interrupted by headlights on the wall and his heart jolted. The last time that happened he had got the worst news.

He looked through the worn curtains and grunted.

Liz ran to the steps with a jacket held over her head. He held the door open as she shook the jacket and hung it on a hook outside.

'Not the best night to be out.'

'Needed a beer.' She grinned and showed him the six-pack in her other hand.

'She's just gone to bed, so head for the living room.'

They sat opposite each other. The remnants of the fire were the only light, flickering and casting shadows. Liz pulled two beers out and handed one to Vince.

'You look exhausted,' she said.

'You don't exactly look like someone ready to party all night.'

Two beers were opened. Two mouthfuls were drunk.

'How's Melanie?'

'Yeah. Asleep.'

Another mouthful. Or two.

The beer was good. He might be tired, but he'd been far from relaxed. This helped a bit.

Liz settled back in the chair and crossed her legs. 'I'm sorry I've taken so long to visit.'

'You doing okay, Lizzie? Seems a long time between drinks.' He raised the beer.

'Too long. Still love my job. Still have no interest in climbing the corporate ladder. Not home enough. The usual. And chasing my tail thanks to Malcolm Hardy being invisible. We're struggling to pin down where he is.' She tapped the side of her beer with her fingers then leaned forward. 'How much do you know about PickerPack Holdings?'

What have you been up to?

'Pickering is a criminal,' he said.

'Quite possibly. Do you know any of his staff?'

Now, he snorted.

Liz smiled. 'Shall I rephrase?'

'No need. He has a poor track record with employees. I warned Susie about it when he got fined last time.'

'Illegals?'

'Yup and underpaid. Far as I know only one person has stayed with the business. His right-hand man, Abel Farrelly.'

'Impression of him?' Liz was watching him closely, so it meant something to her.

'He looks squeaky clean. Gut feeling is he's dirty. Susie wasn't a big fan. Why?'

'I'm trying to make the connection between Farrelly and Richard Roscoe.'

'Roscoe?' A spark of excitement, almost unsettling, fluttered in his gut. Just like police days when he was close to an arrest. He'd not felt this in years. 'Roscoe is Hardy's lawyer.'

'Well, yes. I know. And Farrelly might be his client as well. Or a friend. The other thing is... the report came back on the vehicle. David's.'

With a sense of dread he put down the beer.

'There's some evidence a second vehicle was involved in the crash.'

'What evidence?'

'Paint transference. We're working to identify paint from what kind of vehicle, exactly. It still might have been accidental.'

It wasn't.

Rain pattered on the roof. Liz's eyes moved to the mantle-piece, to the photograph of Vince's wedding day. 'She'd have been proud of you taking in Melanie. Marion would.'

'She'd be here if not for me.'

'You were saving lives. Possibly mine. Innocent bystanders. You couldn't be in two places at one time so think about forgiving yourself, Vince.'

Not so easy.

He gestured toward the back of the cottage. 'That little girl down the hallway? She disappeared for a few minutes today. Ran out of the cottage in the rain. I thought... I thought the world had stopped.' He finished his beer with a couple of big mouthfuls.

'Where did she go?'

'She rescued a god-damned kitten, Lizzie. Then she helped clean up the mess I'd made running out to look for her. Soup everywhere. And she even let me tease her.' A ridiculous lump filled his throat and he reached for a fresh bottle, unwilling to meet the eyes of his friend. 'Melanie deserves better.'

'Than?'

'Have you taken a good look at this place? Hardly the best environment for a little girl to grow up in and before you say it, I know Susie did. But Susie should have had a nice house and been closer to other kids and the like. I was wrong to make her live that way.'

'Yet she turned out just fine. And so will Melanie. She's lucky to have you.'

Later, after Liz had driven away and the fire had died down,

Vince found himself holding that photograph. Marion's smile still lit his heart. She would have been proud of him. He touched her face and put the photograph back where it belonged.

TWENTY

Turning into the Pickering's street, Vince almost stopped the car and backed out, but Melanie was already peering through the window with a broad smile lighting her face.

Her happiness meant more than his misgivings.

But if anything went wrong... if Carla or Bradley upset her...

His knuckles were white on the steering wheel, and he made an effort to loosen his fingers. At this rate he'd end up having to see Doctor Raju or one of his colleagues before he blew a gasket.

'We went past their house!'

'Just turning around.' He drove to the end of their cul-de-sac and circled, sliding the car into a spot near their driveway. Bradley's car was parked in front of the garage.

'I can see Carla!'

Carla was on the footpath, waving.

'Wait a sec. Are you sure you're okay here for a couple of hours?'

He might as well have saved his breath for the minute the motor was off, Melanie was out of her seat belt and pushing the door open.

'Melanie... okay, off you go.'

In a minute she was in Carla's arms, who picked her right up as if greeting her own long-lost child. She squeezed Melanie so tightly she squealed and wiggled her way back to the ground.

Vince collected Melanie's backpack from the back seat.

'Here you go, Mel. I'll be back in two hours, okay?'

She nodded and shrugged it on, then grabbed Carla's hand. 'Are we going to cook?'

'Cook and play and make some jewellery if you like, honey. Let's go inside.' Carla led the way up the driveway.

Bradley wandered toward them from the house.

'Hi, Uncle Brad.' Melanie's voice was barely a whisper.

'Hi there, baby girl. You ladies go in and I'll be right behind you both.'

He stopped on the other side of the footpath from Vince. 'She's welcome to stay all day.'

'I'll be back in two hours. Call me if there are any issues.'

'Why would there be issues, mate? She's safe here with her godparents. And she loves us.'

Don't poke the beast. Mate.

'Once Melanie goes back to school I'd like a meeting to discuss David's share of your business. Our lawyers can sort out the details, but I want you to talk me through whatever arrangements you both had.'

'Why wait? Come to the warehouse now and I'll answer your questions.'

'Not today. I'll arrange something after the funeral

'Sure. Text me a time and I'll make sure I'm there,' Bradley said. 'I've got some pictures of David in my office which Melanie might like. Can I ask a favour? The laptop in the house really does belong to the business and has files on it I need. Any chance I can collect it?'

'None. But I'll check with the lawyer and think about bringing it to you.'

Bradley's mouth opened and then he changed his mind and closed it.

Carla was at the window watching. She turned away when Vince caught her eye. Her obvious disapproval of him was odd. She'd been Susie's friend since university and visited his house with her more than once. Over the years, particularly since the two husbands became business partners, she'd become standoff-ish, but never so angry with him as she'd been since the night of the accident.

'Was something wrong the other night? Was David upset. When he left... was something bothering him?'

'No. Nothing. We had a nice night.'

The other man stared at the footpath, the tip of his shoe moving a pebble about.

'Would you tell me about the dinner? Susie...'

Bradley looked up. 'Of course, mate. Of course you'd want to know. Just not much to tell. The four of us spoiling Melanie. David and I talked shop and sports. Carla and Susie were talking babies, I think?'

'Babies?'

'Ours, not Susie. Carla was hopeful that night. But she isn't.'

'Sorry.'

'God's will. Our time will come when He's ready.'

'And nothing out of the ordinary happened? David was fine. Susie was fine? Even when they got in the car?'

Bradley stared him in the eye. 'They drove off with a wave. Melanie was sleepy. Nothing out of the ordinary, Vince.'

'Honey, you coming in?' Carla called from the doorway.

'Better go. Three hours?'

'Two.'

With a shrug, Bradley headed back to the house.

———

Two hours later to a minute, Vince tapped on the door. Bradley's car was gone, and it was Melanie who opened the door with a smile. 'I'm almost ready, Grandad.'

'Good girl. Did you have fun?'

She nodded and then, leaving the door open, ran into one of the rooms. 'Be right back!'

There was muffled words and Melanie returned, this time with her backpack on and carrying a clothes bag.

She struggled to hold it up and Vince took it. 'What's this?'

'Um, Auntie Carla got me a special dress for... the thing... you know.' Her smile vanished and her eyes were huge. 'And tights and shoes.'

His eyelids squeezed tight of their own volition as a roaring sound filled his ears. How dare she! In what world would someone outside a family, unwanted and unasked, take it upon herself to dress his grandchild for the funeral? She had no right.

'Vince... I'm her godmother. Doing what Susie would have expected.'

The words were so softly spoken he barely heard them but as the sound in his ears subsided, he opened his eyes. Carla stood right in front of him, her hand on his arm. She wasn't angry. Just sad.

'Melanie is fetching you a glass of water. Do you want to sit?'

He gulped in oxygen. Had he said those things aloud?

'Vince?'

'No... thank you. Why? Why do that?'

Carla glanced over her shoulder.

'For my friend. To honour her. Is that so wrong?'

'Here, Grandad. Did you get too thirsty?' Melanie carried an over-full glass, careful not to spill any water.

'I did get too thirsty.' And although his throat was tight, he forced the water down. 'Much better.'

'I'll take the glass back.'

As soon as Melanie was out of sight, Carla picked up the clothes bag which he must have dropped without realising. '*You* think I overstepped. *I* think I was looking out for Melanie and for you. Letting other people help isn't a crime.' She held it out. 'It's okay if you don't want her to have it.'

But Melanie expects to wear this now.

'Thank you.' He accepted the clothes bag. 'And... sorry.'

Her lips flickered up for a second.

Melanie ran back. 'Are you better now?'

'All better. Say bye to Auntie Carla.'

There was a hug and more quiet words and then he had Melanie's hand in his. At the car, he opened her door for her to get in, and then the boot, laying down the clothes bag.

Next to the Target bag with its own Melanie-sized black dress inside he'd just bought.

TWENTY-ONE

'I saw Vince last night.'

Liz and Terry had settled with coffee in his office with the door closed. The main office was abuzz with detectives and support staff brainstorming the Hardy case. Pete was running things—allegedly—and the noise level was blissfully less in here.

'How's Melanie?' Terry asked.

'I was there a bit late, and she was asleep, but from the sound of things, she's doing alright. Gave him a scare by following a kitten in the rain but I think he's more worried she'll ask to adopt it than anything.'

Terry laughed at that. 'I can see him with a tiny kitten. He just doesn't know yet how much he'll love it.'

'I'll reserve judgement on that. Look, I know you said to keep him in the dark, but I did mention the paint transfer—with a strong reminder of the possibility it was an accident.'

'How'd he take it?'

'Was quiet. But at least he knows I'm digging around. Pity

FSD is so backed up. Would have liked a result on the cigarette I found near the scene, but they reckon weeks, not days.'

'Anything on the answering machine?' Terry asked.

Liz checked her phone as if hopeful of a message. 'Sadly, not yet. Want your opinion, boss. Spoke to Abel Farrelly who works for Bradley Pickering as his foreman. He reported the van missing and when I asked who had access, he pretty much named everyone. Said he drives it, as do some of the employees, and Bradley.'

'And?'

'And Bradley told me he never drives it. Pete was present when he said it. I don't know.' She swirled the remaining coffee around. 'I might have this all wrong, but something isn't sitting right. People are lying. Even the server at the restaurant says he's been misquoted and never heard or mentioned an argument. And then there's the sighting of Richard Roscoe... well, at least his car because we can't tell from the video, outside Farrelly's place when I was waiting for the door to open.'

Terry sat forward. 'Explain.'

She did. And showed him the video Pete took.

'We're planning on visiting Roscoe but he's out of the city today, according to his office. We'll go and see him after the funeral.'

There were no words for a moment or two. Everybody she knew wanted to say goodbye to Susie, some of the cops she'd grown up around, some who were retired and coming to pay their respects and others who had swapped shifts to be available. She was too young to die and there were too many people who remembered her from the days she'd be at the station waiting for her dad to finish a shift.

There was a tap on the door and Pete stuck his head in. 'We're about done here and have all got our to-do-lists.' He grinned. 'I made one for you, Liz.'

'Jeez, thanks.'

'Pleasure. Main thing is there's been a possible sighting of Hardy in Ballarat and two cars are leaving to head up there now.'

Terry stood and grabbed his jacket. 'Count me in. Need to get some air and catching Hardy would be a good way to end the day.'

Pete had gone again.

'If you don't need me, boss, I'll do some digging on Farrelly. And see if I can find that van,' Liz said.

'Still curious how Farrelly and Roscoe fit together. Give me a call when you find out.'

'Will do. Go catch the bad guy.'

———

Abel Farrelly had no record.

No trouble with the police. Not even a parking ticket.

No time in the armed forces.

He had no social media footprint, at least not under his real name.

'A rare bird these days,' Liz muttered.

She reviewed what she did know. He was born in the small Gippsland town of Moe. An only child. Parents deceased. After high school he moved to Melbourne. If he'd gone to university she couldn't find any trail and his next appearance was completing a police check for a job in a morgue, of all places.

There was much she couldn't access without due cause, but Farrelly appeared to be an ordinary person living an ordinary life. Records of his address gave a date of the last purchase some eight years earlier for more than one million dollars. Compared to similar properties selling at the time in that area, a million was on the high side.

So how did you afford your house?

Inheritance?

Short of asking him, it would have to stay a mystery for the moment.

After getting her third coffee since Terry and Pete left—for that matter everyone was gone apart from her—Liz stared at the screen while she thought about the video.

The car belonged to Richard Roscoe, owner of the legal firm which represented Malcolm Hardy. He was also Hardy's personal lawyer. Sadly, the footage didn't show the driver, but the car had moved very slowly past Farrelly's house and parked a couple of houses down. The driver's door had opened but nobody stepped out. There was ten seconds or so until the door closed again, and the car pulled out onto the road. All of that time, Liz had waited at Farrelly's door, oblivious.

Did you phone Farrelly? Ask who was visiting? And he could see me through the camera.

Or was this purely coincidental. Someone pulling over to answer the phone?

Liz didn't believe in coincidences.

She started looking into Richard Roscoe. Now here was a person who knew how to make his digital footprint large. He had social media accounts everywhere. Personal and for the firm. Liz went to the firm's website and clicked on his 'about Richard' page. Mostly a whole lot of preening and posturing. Places he'd donated to. His university.

LinkedIn provided more.

After graduating at the top of his class, Richard Roscoe began his illustrious career at the bottom—as should all good lawyers. He quickly rose to the top, becoming a partner within a few years and then buying the firm. Not bad for a boy from Moe.

'Is that right? Moe.'

She checked the date of birth for both men. It was within

months of each other. They both attended the same high school. Same year of graduation.

Liz leaned back in her seat, lacing her fingers behind her head.

She'd found the connection but now, what to do with it?

TWENTY-TWO

Two open graves.

Side by side.

Resting together. Forever.

Melanie's fingers were enclosed in Vince's hand. Her eyes hadn't left Susie's grave since the priest made his final blessing but she'd neither spoken nor wept. She wore the ridiculous frilled black dress Carla had bought which she'd told him in secret wasn't very comfortable. Liz had been close by during the ceremony and he'd felt her hand on his arm a few times.

Close to one hundred people were here and as they began to break up into smaller groups to quietly talk, Melanie released his hand and ran to Carla. He almost stopped her, but this wasn't the place or time to make a stand of some sort.

For a few minutes he spoke to the priest and to David's mother, a frail woman who barely understood why she was there and was accompanied by a carer. She was wheeled away, and he didn't know what to do with himself. There were people he'd not seen in years who were here for Susie, not him. He'd burned a whole city of bridges before retiring.

The sun was out. The storm long gone. Not a cloud in the sky.

A clear path to heaven, my little one.

'Saddest of days, mate.' Terry appeared from nowhere and shook his hand. 'If there's anything I can do. You know I'm only a call away.'

'You know what I need.'

Terry grimaced and nodded. 'Liz is investigating. We can talk about it another day.'

Vince grunted. Terry was right. Not here.

Liz came across from where she'd been talking to a group of cops. 'Melanie is so brave.'

'Yeah. We're going home now. Let her rest.'

Liz leaned close and whispered. 'Are you going to be able to extricate her? Carla doesn't look ready to hand her back.'

There was no chance Carla had heard Liz from the distance, but she swung around to glare. Black smudging around her eyes gave her a slightly sinister look.

'Need help?' Liz hadn't taken her eyes off Carla, who pursed her lips at the scrutiny.

'You can remind me what happened back then. Between you and Carla.'

'Happy to. Give me a call.'

He would.

'You didn't need to be here. Either of you. But thank you.'

'We did,' Terry said with a half-smile. 'You're family.'

It wasn't true. Terry and Liz said all the right things and meant well but his time as part of the force was long gone. But he nodded and went to get Mel.

Carla squatted and hugged Melanie, whispering in her ear. Bradley stood nearby with a blank look on his face. Probably realising it was his problems with David which killed Susie.

Vince knew it in his bones.

'Melanie? How about we get you home?'

The little girl peeked at him.

'Carla. It's time.'

A tear dripped down Carla's face at his quiet words and she lifted her chin a fraction and if anything, tightened the arm around Melanie.

Bradley stepped in, picking up Melanie and giving her a hug. 'Auntie Carla and I love you lots, poppet. Okay?' He passed Melanie to Vince, and she transferred her arms to his neck.

'You be a good girl, and we'll see you very soon.' Carla's voice broke at the end and Bradley led her away.

There was no reason to remain here. The priest was gone. Most of the mourners had left or were leaving.

This was it.

His daughter was now a memory.

'I need Mummy and Daddy.'

The shaft of pain stabbing through his heart was too much to bear. They'd lost everything. Tears filled his eyes as he forced out the words. 'Me too, Melly. Me too.'

She buried her head against his neck and wept until her body shook with the strength of her grief and he held her close and slowly walked away from the graves.

TWENTY-THREE

It felt wrong to be at work. Everyone who'd attended the funeral was quieter than normal and Liz understood. The gravity of the morning had come back to the office with them. She'd arranged for a basket of fruit and chocolates to be delivered to Vince and Melanie and it wasn't nearly enough.

What else can I do?

Terry had a similar air about him, but he was also intent on catching Malcolm Hardy and was at a clean whiteboard with a marker.

'Let's start afresh, boys and girls.' He tapped the end of the marker on the board. 'Yesterday was a waste of resources with no sign of Hardy in Ballarat nor of the place where he was allegedly seen. We want to catch the little shit, but we need to be alert to false alarms.'

'Probably in another state by now.' One of the younger detectives said and there was a murmur of agreement by a couple of others.

Pete shook his head.

'Why not, Pete? It's been ten days since he escaped. Plenty of time to hitch a ride out of Victoria,' Terry said.

'He had a few minutes jump on us when he took off which meant we had all major exits covered before he could do more than fall into a hole to hide in until some of the heat came off. By then his face was plastered everywhere in the state. Freight companies and public transport authorities are on alert as well as police throughout the state.'

It was solid logic but with every passing day and no sign of the criminal, the chance of finding him lessened.

'And I agree with Pete,' Terry continued and began scrawling on the whiteboard. 'We can't keep surveillance on all his old haunts nor his main contacts. What if we draw him out of wherever he's hiding?'

He'd written a name. *Betty Hardy.*

'Boss, we've had his mum under watch since the first day,' Liz said. 'She can't shop without a shadow let alone meet with her son.'

'Time to have another chat with her. See if we can give her a reason to help us locate him. Or plant a seed in her head. Let him think he has a window of opportunity to leave town.'

Pete was grinning. 'Her place or ours?'

'Hers. Make it obvious we're there. Take a unit and let them sit over the road to get the neighbours talking.'

———

Betty Hardy had claimed from the time her son was arrested the first time that she had cut him out of her life. She'd lived in the same house for most of her adult life and at close to eighty maintained she wasn't interested in leaving it.

Liz had met her once or twice in the course of past interviews and the woman remembered her when she opened the door, staring up at her through thick glasses.

'I suppose you'll both be wanting coffee.'

'Not necessary, Mrs Hardy,' Pete said. 'Just a quick chat if you don't mind.'

'Does it matter if I do?' The elderly woman used a cane as she limped away from the front door and disappeared into another room. 'Close that, young man.'

Pete had a silly grin on his face and Liz shook her head at him.

They joined Mrs Hardy in the living room, a small and gloomy part of a small and gloomy house. She was lowering herself onto a chair and grunted when she sat. The curtains were drawn and a couple of lamps cast weird shadows on old wallpaper.

'Sit down and ask your questions. But don't bother to ask if I've seen Malcolm or know where he is because I haven't, and I don't. Same as always.'

Pete sat on a sofa, his eyes darting around the room.

Liz stayed on her feet. 'You've been clear about not having contact with your son for a number of years, but we wondered if you know a man called Abel Farrelly?' She almost held her breath. She wanted to find a connection so much it hurt.

'Name doesn't ring a bell. Do you have a photograph?'

Pete opened his phone and showed her Farrelly's drivers licence photo.

She peered at it for a long time then leaned back. 'Can't say I know him. Is he helping my son?'

It was never going to be that easy.

'We don't know. But thank you for looking. Have you heard from Richard Roscoe recently?'

Mrs Hardy scoffed. 'Him? Useless man with more money than sense. He still phones me once a week to make sure I'm alive. Probably wants to be ready to snatch this prime real estate to sell to cover his fees the minute I go to God.'

Liz exchanged a glance with Pete, and he took over.

'Bit of an odd thing to call you each week? Has he always done that?'

She nodded so vigorously that her glasses slid down her nose. 'Ever since Malcolm went to prison. Once a week without fail, apart from a few times when he was overseas and then he'd get that Mr Black to ring instead. His assistant. Always the same.' Her voice changed to a gruff, 'How are you, Betty? Malcolm sends his love. Anything you'd like me to pass on?'

'And was there?'

Mrs Hardy stared at Pete over the top of her glasses then pushed them back up. 'Wouldn't know what to say to him if he was sitting here with us right now.'

Pete took out his phone. 'Sorry, message.' He made a show of reading it then jumped to his feet. 'We need to go, I'm afraid. Thank you for being so helpful.'

'What's wrong?' Mrs Hardy touched a button on her chair which began to lift her to her feet. 'Have you found Malcolm?'

'No... but... I shouldn't say.'

He showed Liz the 'message' which was a blank screen.

'Oh! Perhaps you should tell Mrs Hardy. Just to keep her up to date.'

Phone back in his pocket, Pete took his time making a decision. By then, Mrs Hardy was upright and leaned on her cane, waiting.

'The message was from our boss, who is overseeing the search for your son. He wants all available police to concentrate on an area on the Mornington Peninsula. Sounds like a big search planned with most of our units heading down. Anyway, thanks again. We'll lock the door on our way out.'

A minute later, Liz and Pete hurried to their car.

'She's not a stupid woman,' Pete said as he climbed in.

'Not at all. But if she cares at all for her son she might just let something slip to Roscoe.'

'And if she knows where Malcolm is, it might make him feel confident enough to make a mistake.'

———

Bradley nosed his car up the warehouse driveway and turned it around to face the road again, parking alongside the side fence. The flatbed ute wasn't here, nor was the hire van Abel had organised to manage deliveries and pickups until theirs was located. The theft was disturbing. Abel was particular about keeping the place locked up and having the heavy chain cut and the van stolen had sent a ripple of worry through the staff.

'Still there, Brad?'

He was on a phone call with his solicitor, who had a list of issues to address thanks to David's death, but their subject for the past few minutes was every bit as important.

'Sorry, Gary.'

Gary continued. 'As I was saying, with Vince Carter in the picture as Melanie's only viable relative, and being willing and able to become her custodian, it makes things tricky.'

'Tricky? Or impossible?' There was silence and Bradley tapped his fingers on the steering wheel. 'Are you telling me we have no way to ensure Melanie has a better life? No way to bring her home to a place she loves and will thrive in?'

'Anything's possible. I'm laying it on the table so you can manage your expectations. And Carla's. On the surface, Vince Carter is a hero, a decorated, retired police officer. He strikes a sympathetic figure by losing his daughter. And he has the widower card. His wife died the same day he was saving lives in a highly publicised shooting. Who wouldn't want him to have his grandchild in his life?'

'Jesus. *I'm* almost rooting for him when you say it like that.'

Gary laughed. 'I'm good at my job.'

'Then tell me what to do instead of adding glowing testimonies to our enemy.' Bradley spat the words.

'Chill. He's not your enemy, he's just a man standing in the way of what you want. You need compelling evidence to counteract the sympathy vote.'

'Compelling? How.'

'Incompetency. Abuse. Substance or otherwise. History of neglect. Unaddressed mental illness. Anger issues. Dig up some dark secret.'

Abel drove past in the flatbed ute.

Bradley smiled. 'Thanks.'

'For the record, that wasn't legal advice.'

'Sure. Yep. Talk to you soon.'

'But we need to cover the—'

Bradley terminated the call. He sent a message to a number in his phone then opened the door as Abel headed toward the warehouse. 'Abel. A word?'

That word turned into twenty minutes of debate about how far behind they were. Not debate. Full on yelling. At least from Bradley's side because Abel didn't as much as raise his voice.

'Dunno what you're so riled up about, boss.' Clearly tired of standing in the middle of the warehouse being told off, Abel stalked toward the containers at the back. 'Have you even looked at the fit out?'

Although his temper still had things to say, Bradley's brain figured nothing was coming of the discussion other than an increased risk of heart attack. The workers had slowed down as well during the conversation, casting curious looks at him.

'Back to work, you lot.'

He followed Abel, who opened the back of the first container with a loud clang. Bradley waited until the door was propped securely before stepping foot inside.

'This is almost ready to pack up and put on the truck.' Abel brushed past. 'See those tracks...' He gestured upwards. Several rows of tracks—an industrial equivalent of the kind found in windows for vertical blinds—criss-crossed the roof. Within them were multiple hooks able to slide into a range of positions. 'Lets us configure nets or straps to contain whatever is packed. We can mix and match boxes with small machinery. Or send part loads if our brands aren't needing transport.'

'Bit of a waste not to fill the thing.'

'Not at the rates Duncan will pay. He just wants a no-nonsense solution to getting his products interstate now that he can see how easy expanding will be and this is by far the cheapest option,' Abel said. 'If he takes you up on the offer to buy some of our toys then that solidifies the working arrangement.'

Bradley touched the sides. 'Why add interior walls?'

'Insulated. Better for sensitive cargo.'

'Like?'

Abel shrugged. 'Alcohol. Bottled water.' He grinned. 'People.'

Moron.

He looked outside to make sure nobody overheard that.

'How much did this cost?'

'Within budget.' Abel ran a hand over the wall at the front of the container.

'When was this done, Abel? I've been here every day for weeks and—'

'Night time, boss. Easier without working around the staff considering how noisy a job it was. One done. Another ready to start when you say.'

Bradley had had enough of the confined space and stepped out.

'Before you go.' Abel closed the container doors then leaned against them. 'Those cops here the other day... I heard everything.'

'About that night at the restaurant?'

Abel nodded.

'Trouble is I don't remember seeing anyone around while he and I were talking. Susie came and had words with us but she's dead, so she doesn't count. The waiter was in and out of the door but never long enough to overhear anything.'

'Think. Were you facing the back door or the dining area?'

'Dining. But around the corner, near the toilets... oh, shit.'

How had he forgotten Melanie?

Bradley's phone rang. It was the number he'd texted after speaking to Gary. 'Hold that thought, Abel. I have to answer this.'

———

Carla finished clearing the dining room table and took a bottle of wine from the fridge. Dinner had been quiet with both of them preoccupied. It was partly the after effects of the funeral and on top of that, whatever was bothering Bradley, he was keeping to himself.

It didn't matter. Sooner or later he'd talk to her, and she had enough on her mind.

Going through her phone after the funeral, she'd found a forgotten photo of herself with Susie a few weeks after they'd met. Carla was in her final year of university at an open day, talking to prospective students and parents. Susie was half interested in the course Carla was finishing and after they'd spoken for a while they discovered a mutual interest in musical theatre. They went to a play together and then it became a regular thing. That photograph was taken outside Her Majesty's Theatre.

'And then we were best friends. Forever.' Carla had wept

anew, holding the phone against her chest until there were no more tears to cry. She'd kissed the image of Susie. How many beautiful memories they'd shared, and she'd never let her be forgotten.

She was still exhausted from grief and seeing Melanie without being able to bring her home. Picking up the bottle, she collected two glasses and went in search of her husband. He sat in the living room, turning his phone in his fingers, frowning.

'Good thinking.' He took the glasses and held them while she poured.

'You look worried, honey,' she said.

'Hm? Oh, no, just work stuff.' He patted the sofa. 'To us, baby.'

Joining him, she tapped her glass to his. 'Are there lots of problems now David's gone? Are you doing his work as well as yours?'

'Kinda. The pressing issue is he hadn't signed off on a transport deal and I'm scrambling to get up to speed and make it happen. Our business is on the cusp of booming and this new supply chain contract was key.'

'I thought your supply chain was local.'

'We've had the chance to put containers onto interstate trucks each week. Duncan wants to expand, and this is a cheapish option to do regular runs to places like Far North Queensland and the Northern Territory.'

'Still transporting toys and stuff? And ours as well as his?' she asked.

'Yeah. Will open some new markets.'

'So what needs doing to make it happen? Was it just changes on the contract?'

'They got cold feet. Said with David dying they were worried about the stability of our company—losing one of two partners, and the one who was the logistics expert. I've sent them a new proposal and they just returned an amended version. They want a guarantee of three months of shipments paid up front.'

'Then what are you waiting for?' Carla frowned.

Bradley took a long drink from his glass.

Melanie had a stake in this. The legal people on all sides would work out what would happen with David's share of the company, but their success meant more for the little girl's future.

'Brad don't wait. If Duncan is ready to commit then do the same. Three months up front is nothing compared to the long-term benefit and anyway, just pass it on.'

He almost spluttered his wine out. 'To Duncan?'

She nodded. 'Tell him their quote came in a bit higher. Up your price to him to cover the cost. Do whatever you must to ensure the future of this company!'

Bradley chuckled, put down his glass, and took her hand. 'You are sensational, baby. I'd forgotten how passionate you are about business.'

'I do have a degree in business management, Brad. It just never gets put to good use anymore.'

Because you chose a man to be your partner instead of your wife.

Not knowing where that thought came from, or why it suddenly mattered, Carla took a sip of her wine. She didn't want to fight. Or look too closely at what was going on at the warehouse. Better to think about Melanie. 'I was considering a soft lilac with some yellow accents.'

'Sorry?' Bradley obviously had no idea what she was talking about.

'And I know she wants a kitten, but we might have to persuade her a fish tank is better. I can't abide the idea of litter trays and a cat scratching our furniture, can you?'

'Whatever are you talking about?'

'I've been thinking of how to redecorate the second bedroom for Melanie. Soft colours. A double bed with a canopy... like a princess's bed. Lots of beautiful toys. I'm so pleased that bedroom has its own ensuite otherwise we'd need to renovate. But I think I can turn the existing one into a beautiful little room for her.'

'Slow down.' Bradley kissed her fingers. 'There's a lot of water under the bridge ahead.'

'Susie would want her living with us. Why else make us her godparents? Why else cut Vince out of their lives?'

Bradley held his arm out and she moved closer to lean against him.

'Melanie is going to be our little girl. Isn't she?'

What did the lawyer say? Get dirt on him?

'Yes, Carla. I'll make it happen. One way or another, I promise Melanie will come to live with us.'

TWENTY-FOUR

There's no movement at the dump he calls home. How anyone can live like that, let alone force a child to endure it is beyond me. And such a sweet kid.

My binoculars sweep across the front of the cottage. No external cameras. The curtains are flimsy. There's no screen door, just a plain wooden one with no deadlock. Excellent. Smoke curls out of a chimney. A fireplace. Even better. House fires are common.

Only one way off the property unless there's a gate at the back.

Too far to see.

But I need to know.

There's a long driveway going to the next house which runs alongside Carter's property. Plenty of bushes line it. Nobody will see me if a car happens along. My watch says it's almost two in the morning and I almost laugh at the idea any of these hicks would be out and about this late.

Every few metres along the other driveway I stop and listen and watch. If either property have dogs they're inside. Not another house is in sight of here. Just the two and they couldn't be more different from each other.

Carter's land goes back a long way. Narrow but long and it gets steep at the back. There's a pony asleep in a shed with three sides. That paddock shares a gate with the driveway. Does Carter sneak up there sometimes to visit the old lady? Yuk. There's a padlock on the gate. Not so easy for a quick escape. Not for Vince.

Looking back to the road it's obvious how this will go down.

When the time is right.

A place so unsecured? Asking for trouble.

TWENTY-FIVE

There was so much to do. All the things Vince had put off prior to the funeral were on a long list to take care of today and he didn't mind.

Stay busy.

He began making pancakes. Flour. Eggs. Milk. Measure. Mix. Rest.

Melanie had already showered and was in her room. Good little girl getting herself up each day, showering, keeping her room tidy. He'd been forever reminding Susie to do the same until she'd gone to high school and suddenly cared about how she looked.

He stuck his head out of the kitchen. 'Breakfast in ten, Melly.'

There was a muffled response which he hoped was acknowledgement.

Yesterday they'd played board games and watched television and eaten fruit and chocolate from baskets sent by Liz and other people. There'd been a lasagne on the doorstep when they'd got home after the funeral with a note from Lyndall.

Susie's old favourite.

Lyndall didn't do funerals. Hadn't attended Marion's, who was her friend. Told him once she couldn't face them anymore. Not after everything she'd lost. He hadn't asked what she meant, and she hadn't volunteered any further information. Despite being neighbours for years, her background was a mystery. For the first time, he was curious.

'Ooh, pancakes!' Melanie peered into the bowl. 'Can I help?'

'Um... sure. What do you want to do?'

'Flip them.'

About to say no, he'd do the cooking part, he stopped himself. Marion always encouraged Susie to help whether with cooking or stacking timber. She'd been a pragmatic woman who wanted her daughter to have a range of skills. After she died and Vince tried to take on every aspect of life without her, it was Susie who stubbornly kept doing her chores and adding to them so there was equity in the house. It wasn't how he'd been raised and sometimes he still heard his father's voice in his head reminding him to protect his women. Not that he'd ever considered anyone in his life to be 'his.' Different times.

'May I?' Melanie asked.

'Have you flipped them before?'

'Mm. Yes and no. Mummy helped. I might need a little bit of help still.'

He smiled. 'I'm right here if so. Do you know how much butter needs to go in first?'

With a nod, Melanie went to the sink and washed her hands.

After a couple of minor mishaps, they each settled at the table with plates of pancakes with fresh cream and more of the fruit from Liz.

'Is she your friend?' Melanie finally stopped eating after

somehow fitting in more pancakes than Vince. 'The lady police officer?'

'Lizzie? I guess she is.'

'Then why doesn't she visit you?'

'She did the other night. You were fast asleep.'

'Oh.' Melanie tilted her head. 'Lyndall is nice. Is she your friend?'

He bought himself a minute to think about the answer by collecting the plates. 'Another hot chocolate?'

'I'm full to the brim.' She patted her stomach. 'So is she?'

Curious little thing, aren't you?

'We've been neighbours for a long time. She and your grandmother were close friends and she even used to look after your mum sometimes, when she was your age.'

'Can we visit her soon?'

'Sure. Maybe not today though. I have to do some paperwork and we might go food shopping a bit later.'

Melanie jumped to her feet and started putting the remaining fruit into the fridge. 'I'm going to do some more drawings and give them to Lyndall when we see her. Maybe one of the little kitten.'

'Great idea, Mel.'

Anything to distract her from asking more questions about Lyndall. He'd have no idea how to answer.

————

After paying a stack of bills which would keep Susie's house insured and with power for a bit longer, Vince turned to the bigger problem at hand.

He reread the letter from the principal at Melanie's school.

Two points stood out.

The length of time the account had been left unpaid, and the mention of David's business being in trouble.

After checking Melanie was nowhere in earshot, he phoned the school. It went through to a voicemail, and he left his number. School holidays were on for another week or so. He found the email address on the letter and began to type a message, interrupted when the phone rang.

'Mr Carter? This is Mrs Joyce McCoy from Melanie's school, returning your call.' The voice on the other end was crisp and polite.

'Thanks for the call. I forgot it was holidays.'

'I'm working in my office and normally let the messages go but given the situation... what a dreadful shock about Susan and David. I'm terribly sorry for your loss.'

'Yeah. Thanks.'

'And how is Melanie faring?'

'One day at a time. Her broken arm isn't giving her any trouble. The reason for the call is that I've collected the mail and have your letter and invoice.'

There was silence.

'It was a bit of a shock to see how much is owing to the school,' he said.

'Under normal circumstances it wouldn't have got this far,' she said. 'But the family had been very generous in the past helping another student stay in the school... David was adamant he'd be able to pay the full invoice no later than a fortnight ago.'

'Did he tell you what was wrong in his business?'

'I shouldn't be speaking about our confidential conversations.'

Vince rolled his eyes.

'Mrs McCoy, I'm Susie's father. I have Melanie living with me and am trying to piece together why David would say his business was in trouble because there is no sign of that being the case.'

She drew her breathe in audibly. 'How very odd.'

Why the lies, David?

'Mr Carter, I'd rather speak about this in person. Are you able to meet with me?'

'Of course. Melanie loves the school. I want to make sure she can continue.'

'We'll talk about your options. It will need to be tomorrow or the day after.'

They arranged a time and terminated the call.

Vince deleted the email he'd been writing. David and Susie had paid off the mortgage on their house at the beginning of the year. No more repayments. More disposable income each pay period and there was a solid record of a decent salary being drawn. So why tell a school that the business was struggling? Where was the extra money going?

While he had the emails open he searched David's name. Lots of mentions in Susie's emails and he couldn't bear to read them. Not just yet.

'Can we go shopping now?'

He jumped. How had Melanie snuck up so quietly?

'I'm sorry to frighten you.' She put her hand on his arm and her smile faded. 'I've only got socks on my feet so you mustn't have heard.'

'You could never frighten me, sweetie. My mind was elsewhere, and you walk very softly. And yes, we can go shopping now. If I can arrange it, would you like to visit Lyndall after lunch?'

Her smile came back in full force and she jumped up and down.

'All right. You find some shoes and I'll phone her now and ask.'

———

Vince sat at David's desk in the office in Susie's house. He only ever thought about it in terms of belonging to Susie, but it had been their joint home. No point pretending otherwise. He was waiting on the phone while his lawyer spoke to theirs. He knew he could look through anything here and nobody would find out but taking David's business property home with him might create a problem later on.

'Vince? Sorry to keep you. Look, as long as you keep a record of what you take from the house then there's nothing to stop you. Pickering hasn't presented proof of ownership of the laptop. It was worth checking but as we've applied for you to administer the estate all you are doing is planning ahead.'

'Thanks, Sally. After the break-in here it worried me there might be another go.'

'Fair call. While I've got you, their lawyer mentioned they've received a letter from Pickering's lawyer about the company. He wants to buy out David's share.'

'No,' Vince snapped.

Sally chuckled. 'Once the dust settles and Melanie is permanently in your care, they can't do anything without your approval. But in my opinion as your legal counsel, let them make an offer. If it's fair then Melanie will have money in a trust fund for her future use and more importantly for you, I imagine, is breaking off all contact with them.'

'They're her godparents.'

'Which will be the only role they'll be able to play in Melanie's life. Nothing legal to bind her to them. You'll decide if there is any further contact.'

That appealed to Vince. After the call finished, he opened the suitcase he'd already collected from the hallway cupboard and began to fill it. Files, the laptop, speed sticks, a tape recorder, phone, and a leather-bound diary. There was plenty of space left so he collected more clothes from Melanie's room.

Before he left he went into Susie's bedroom.

Somehow it was easier than before. Easier, since he'd told himself he was only here for Melanie's benefit rather than intruding in his daughter's home. Any flutters of grief got stomped on the minute they appeared.

There were precious photographs on her bedside table of Melanie at different ages and he took those. On the chance there might be something Melanie needed from the safe, he tapped in the combination Susie always used. It didn't work. He tried others—his birthdate, hers, David's, Melanie's. Nothing.

Had Pickering been in here the other day?

He sent a text to Liz.

> At Susie's house. Think Pickering has changed combo on her safe. Can we get it dusted?

Back in the office Vince gazed at the filing cabinet. In the past, David was anal about locking it. He once joked that he locked up his keys.

But the filing cabinet wasn't locked.

And there were gaps where whole files were missing.

His phone beeped with a message.

> Can I drop around tonight? Things to discuss.
> Should be able to get it dusted.

He frowned. Liz reminded him of better days. And the worst days. But she was the only one taking him seriously, apart from Terry to a degree.

> Come for dinner?

Melanie wanted to get to know her.

Love to. What shall I bring?

A way to trap a killer.

Dessert. Melanie loves anything lemony.

Done. :-)

Thank goodness they'd shopped earlier. Plenty of options to throw in the oven. Vince realised he was smiling.

TWENTY-SIX

The offices of Roscoe & Henderson were in Balwyn North in the eastern suburbs, on the second floor of an old brick building near the main drag.

Liz and Pete settled in uncomfortable seats opposite Richard Roscoe in a huge corner office with tiny windows and expensive furniture. The carpet though was threadbare and there were cracks in the walls.

She'd met Roscoe a dozen or so times. Met wasn't the right word. Observed him. Listened to him defend killers in the courtroom—Malcolm Hardy being the first of many almost a decade ago. The Hardy case got him other clients because he'd managed to reduce the sentence using voodoo or something. Liz had no idea how he'd done it. But the lawyer had some talent which was wasted on defending criminals of the worst type.

A middle-aged woman with very high heels crept in with a tray, lowered it onto the desk, and hurried out.

'Help yourselves.' Roscoe waved an arm.

Pete wasted no time doing so. There was coffee and a plate of biscuits, and he grabbed a couple of those. How the man kept fit the way he ate and drank was one of life's great mysteries.

'Mr Roscoe, we're here to ask about your recent visit to the home of Abel Farrelly,' Liz said. 'How do you know him?'

Roscoe's eyes widened and his mouth opened a fraction. Was he going to lie about being outside Farrelly's house? She had the video ready to show him if so.

'Abel? He's been a friend since school days. If you mean the day before yesterday, actually, the one prior to that, then I was in the area and planned to drop in to grab a coffee with him.'

'Planned to?'

'Phone rang before I could get out of the car.'

He was confident of himself. Once he knew this was about Abel he'd relaxed.

'Important enough to stop you visiting your old friend?'

'It was a client on the phone. Anyway, Abel wasn't expecting me and for all I know, might have been out. What's this about?'

'Is Abel your client as well as an old friend?'

Roscoe smirked. 'I'm not going to discuss my relationship with Abel unless you explain why you are asking.'

Mouth half-full of biscuit, Pete waved his spare hand around. 'And Hardy?'

'And Hardy... what?' Roscoe frowned.

Pete swallowed and drank some coffee, wrinkling his face up at the taste. He returned the cup to the tray. 'I can see why your secretary rushed out again. When did you last see him?'

Roscoe grabbed a cup and took his time sipping.

'Last week? Today?' Pete pressed.

'Been weeks. Told your lot the other day I'd met with him in prison to talk about his next court appearance. That was it. Now, if there's nothing else?' Roscoe pushed himself out of the chair.

'It would be in your best interests to assist us with locating Hardy.'

It was fascinating how a glow of redness grew around the man's ears. He crossed his arms and said nothing.

'Rightio.' Pete stood and brushed crumbs off his front, grinning at the obvious disapproval on Roscoe's face. 'We'll take that as confirmation that you're in communication with Hardy. Keep in mind that he's a cold-blooded killer. And not above sending a strong message to anyone who isn't playing by his rules.'

He spoke the truth. Hardy was convicted for killing two colleagues who'd let him down. Being anywhere in his circle was a risk. Even for his lawyer.

———

Outside the building, Pete took a phone call and Liz caught up with messages. Vince was on about Pickering again and she was happy to explore the possibility the man was somehow involved in the deaths of Susie and David. It surprised her he not only agreed to her visiting later but asked her to come for dinner.

'Why are you smiling?' Pete was off his call. 'Special date?'

'Yes and no. Right to go?'

'Not quite. Look who's heading our way.'

Jerry Black hadn't seen them as he crossed the road, waiting part way for a tram to pass. He was Roscoe's right-hand man but his role was hard to define. Part lawyer, part investigator, part errand boy. He had sat in on all of Hardy's appearances over the years and Pete had testified in several cases he'd been involved in. When he made it to their side of the road he scowled and went to pass them.

Pete stepped in front of the door. '*Mate*. Jerry—been too long.'

'I'm busy.'

'Been to see Hardy?' Pete asked.

'Idiot.'

'My feelings are hurt. So no sign of Hardy lately?'

'God sake, just said that. Is there a point to you stopping me or is it entertainment?'

Black went to push past Pete, who moved with him, putting an arm around the man's shoulders as if they were just talking. Liz grabbed her phone out.

'Mr Black, would you mind looking at something for us, and then we will leave you in peace?' Before he could respond she played the video of Roscoe's car near Farrelly's house. 'Do you know who owns this house?'

'No. But that's Richard's car so you need to ask him.'

'We did,' Pete hadn't loosened his hold.

To a casual observer it would look like a couple of friends catching up, having a chat and sharing a video. Up close, Black's hands were clenched, and they were one false move away from him taking a swing at Pete.

This man knew a lot more than he was prepared to tell them and Liz watched his face closely. 'See how I'm at the door? When it opens you'll get a look at the occupant.'

The instant that Farrelly appeared, Black's eyes widened and he twisted out of Pete's grip. 'I'll make a complaint if you ever touch me again, McNamara.' He wrenched the door open and was gone.

'Something I said?'

As she put the phone away, a curious sensation ran down Liz's spine. She wasn't big on the theory of knowing when you're being watched, but... she took a moment to scan the opposite side of the road. Shops, people, cars. Nobody looking at her.

'Do you reckon he knows Abel?' Pete asked.

'Mm? Yeah.' She gave up looking and nodded. 'And not in a friendly way.'

'Between him and Roscoe, hopefully we rattled something loose.'

———

Back at the station, Terry was at the whiteboard again but this time he had a series of photographs held in place with magnets. No other detectives were in the office. Pete had somewhere to be and had dropped Liz and driven off.

'What am I looking at?' She dropped her keys and phone onto her desk and joined him.

'Aerials of where Hardy escaped and likely routes he took.' Terry tapped the central image which was the largest and was an overview of about four city blocks. 'When he took off he had maybe thirty seconds head start. He should have been in ankle cuffs but was still wearing a brace after an injury a week prior. If anything, he shouldn't have been able to run.'

'Maybe he faked it.'

Terry shook his head. 'Nah. X-rays showed two broken bones in his foot. One of a series of reasons his escorts slacked off but that's for someone else to deal with. What we know is he headed in this direction...' He pointed north, 'with the last sighting being here.'

'Close to Queen Vic Markets. We've looked for footage there?'

'Yeah. But he'd have stood out with handcuffs on, so I reckon he skirted around some of these side streets until he found someone to help him.' Stepping back from the board, Terry crossed his arms and stared at it. 'Reason I'm doing this all over again is we found something. His cuffs.'

'Where?'

'Tossed them into a dumpster and a friendly informant who lives on the streets found them. Hardy had got more than a kilometre across town if they were removed close to where they were found.'

Liz squinted at the overhead image of the block where a circled dumpster was just visible in an alley. 'Isn't that close to...

hang on a sec, boss.' She grabbed her phone and scrolled through notes. 'Ginny Makos. Pete has history with her—I think as an informant of sorts. We questioned her the other day.'

'And she lives?'

'A block away from that alley.'

Terry headed for his office. 'We might have another chat with her.' He was dialling his phone as he collected his keys. 'Mate, any chance of rushing the prints on those cuffs? Yeah. This number. Thanks.'

'Should I call Pete?' Liz joined Terry on his way out.

'Let's see what we come up with first.'

———

Ginny was surprisingly nice. She still ignored Liz but invited them both in and asked where Pete was.

'Miss Makos—'

'Mrs. I might be a widow, but I still wear his ring.' Ginny wiggled her ring finger with its plain gold band to prove her point. 'But I only answer to Ginny.'

'Sorry for your loss,' Terry said.

Unlike the first time Liz had met her, Ginny was dressed, wearing jeans and a pink jumper. The doors to the other rooms were open and a news channel played on the radio in place of classical music.

'We have some new information about Malcolm Hardy,' Terry said. 'Do you happen to own bolt cutters?'

With a nervous giggle, Ginny plonked onto the arm of a chair. She hadn't suggested they sit so they didn't. She might be laughing but her eyes were hard. 'My dear policeman, what on earth would I do with such an item? My... visitors, might enjoy a little pain but nothing which would permanently scar them.'

'Don't you ever accidentally lock someone into cuffs and lose the key?' Liz couldn't help herself and from the corner of her eye she got the impression Terry was struggling not to chuckle. 'I'd think it would pay to keep bolt cutters around for such situations.'

Although Ginny's smile changed into a glare, she still didn't speak to Liz.

'Do you mind if we take a look around?' Terry asked.

'Actually, I do mind.'

'When did you last see Malcolm Hardy?'

Ginny stood. 'I told Pete the other day and I'll say the same to you that Malcolm hasn't dropped by in years. I went to visit him once in prison and it was so awful in there I never went back.'

'And prison was the last time you spoke to or saw him?' Terry asked.

'Well, yes. That's what I said.'

At the front door Terry glanced back. 'Ginny? If you thought prison was awful as a visitor, think about how much you'd hate it as a resident. Easily avoided if you help us.'

Her face changed. She wavered. And then she shrugged and turned away.

TWENTY-SEVEN

The warehouse was finally quiet. The workers were gone and the tables cleared ready for the next day. Next to the remodelled shipping container wooden pallets were loaded with large, sealed cardboard boxes. Bradley stood outside his office with a well-earned scotch. Things were falling into place and for the first time in weeks, the cloud was lifting off the horizon.

Abel came in through the passenger door, a duffle bag slung over a shoulder. 'You're still here, boss?'

'Want a drink?'

'Thanks, no. I want to double check the container.' He dropped the bag at his feet when he joined Bradley. 'So this is finally happening.'

'Signed the paperwork with the transport company. Hated giving them the money guarantee but if this works out...'

With a rare smile, Abel nodded. 'It will work out. This time next year you'll be ready to upgrade your car. Your house. Buy that yacht.'

A yacht sounded good.

'First pick up?' Abel asked.

'Yeah, well, that is the only hitch. First available spot is four days out—'

'That won't work.'

'I know, if you'd let me finish, I've asked them to consider helping out with this first haul and with a bonus to them if they can do it within two days. Offered double for the one time. They'll let me know first thing tomorrow.' More upfront money which had better be worth it. 'Duncan Chandler has his people delivering four pallets at eight a.m. so get a team organised to pack the container so we're ready.'

'I'll pack our boxes tonight.' Abel picked up his bag.

'We pay people good money to do that crap.'

'You pay them *money*. I want to work out the best configuration so let me do my job.' Abel's phoned beeped and he scowled as he read the message. 'Wants an update.'

'I already told Duncan—'

'Not Duncan.'

'Oh. Tell him there'll be one in the morning.' Bradley's glass was empty. 'I'm going home. Any issues give me a call.'

Briefcase packed, glass washed and back in the cupboard, he went to turn off the office light and just about had a heart attack as a shadow loomed from outside the door.

'Shit, Vince,' he muttered.

'I messaged you. Said I was outside.'

Bradley checked his phone. 'Oh, okay. Didn't hear it. Why are you here?'

'We talked about this the other day.'

With some vague recollection of a conversation outside his house, he waved Vince into the office. 'Grab a seat then. I can't stay long.'

'Me either. Have to collect Melanie.' Vince stared at the photograph of David on the cabinet.

'She's with Carla?'

'No. A friend.'

You don't have friends.

'Are you going to sit?'

'I understand you want to buy David's share of the business?' Vince leaned against the wall; arms crossed. 'Why would that be in Melanie's best interests?'

Dropping into his own chair, Bradley sighed. 'Vince, I'm trying to navigate the changes ahead. Melanie can't help run this place. She can't invest or consult or work for the business. All the things her dad brought with him, the skills and talent and time —I need to replace those. A silent partner isn't on the cards for a small business.'

'Are you in a position to buy her out?'

'That's not a problem.'

Vince had the audacity to raise his eyebrows. 'I hear that David was struggling financially.'

In the distance, a loud clang rang out.

'Something you need to check?'

'We're doing work on a container preparing for a load to go out thanks to a big new contract with Duncan Chandler to facilitate transport of his products interstate. Which is why I will have the money to buy David's share and why your suggestion about his finances is ludicrous. Both of us draw a decent wage from the business and he's never once asked for more.'

What was Vince really here for? This could have been discussed by phone or even better, by their respective lawyers. And what crap was he going on about? David had no money issues. He pushed his chair back and stood. 'No laptop for me?'

'What files did you take from his house the other day?'

'Actually, they were the contracts for this new deal. He had them to go over before signing them but of course that didn't happen. And there's a whole filing cabinet of work-related folders I need so how do we come to an arrangement, Vince? I'm happy to go there with you if you think I'm likely to steal the silver.'

'David's safe. What is the combination?'

'What?'

Rather than answering, Vince straightened and went to the photograph, picking it up. 'You said you had some more photos of David. For Melanie.'

'Sure. I want to keep that one though. I'll collect them and drop them to your house.'

'Just message me and I'll pick them up.' He replaced the photograph. 'The combination, please.'

Try as he might to control it, his neck and face were heating up. 'What safe?'

Vince headed to the door, pausing as he reached it. 'Let me know once you remember and I'll get those other files to you. Maybe even the laptop.'

Then he was gone.

Bradley shot around the desk. Vince better not try to snoop around the warehouse. But he didn't, slamming the warehouse door behind himself as he left.

————

'And the teeny weeny kitten remembered me, Grandad, and followed me everywhere!' Like the kitten, Melanie followed Vince around the kitchen. 'Lyndall showed me how to make a bo.. um.. bo thingy of flowers.'

'Bouquet?'

'That's it. Bouquet.'

'How about you set the table and that way we aren't tripping over each other?'

'Okay. When is the lady coming?'

'Lizzie? Anytime now. Did you go to see the donkeys?'

Hands in the cutlery drawer, Melanie gave him a funny look and shook her head.

'Didn't have time?'

'They're kind of big.'

'Ah. But they are very gentle. Like Apple is.'

She nibbled on her bottom lip. How could Susie's child be so afraid of animals? Let alone change so much in three years? It made no sense. Melanie had been here plenty of times when she was younger, and he was sure he had a photo somewhere of her sitting on Apple with Susie holding onto her. Perhaps in those photo albums.

Melanie finished setting the table and ran off to look out of the living room window.

She hadn't stopped chatting since he'd picked her up earlier, heaps later than he'd planned. Lyndall hadn't seemed bothered —if anything she was smiling more than he remembered. They might be good for each other. Even if there were cats involved.

'She's here!'

'Open the door, Mel.' He turned the oven down a bit and caught up with Melanie as she waited inside the front door. 'It's okay.'

'I just thought... what if it was someone else's car? I don't know her.' Like earlier, Melanie nibbled her bottom lip, and the excitement and earlier brightness was overshadowed by caution. She'd been coming back out of the shell that the accident created so why the sudden concern? And which 'someone else'?

He leaned down to whisper, 'Liz is nervous about seeing you.'

Her mouth opened and her eyes widened in surprise.

'I'm counting on you to help her remember you because you used to know her.'

With a quick nod, Melanie opened the door wide, just as Liz reached the top of the steps. 'Hello. I'm Melanie Weaver and you are welcome to visit us.' She extended her right hand.

Liz shot a surprised look at Vince and then shook Melanie's hand. 'What a lovely welcome, Melanie Weaver. My name is Liz Moorland. But I think we have met before.'

'You *do* remember me! Grandad thought you'd forgotten.'

'It has been a long time, but I could never forget you. Oh, and I have something for dessert so may I come in?'

Taking a dramatic step back to make way for Liz, Melanie spoke with such seriousness that Vince almost burst into laughter. 'A person with dessert is always allowed to come inside.'

———

Why had he put off having Liz over for dinner for so long? They'd been friends for more than two decades as well as partners in the force and he'd missed her dry sense of humour and kindness. And the bonus was seeing Melanie smile so much. She'd regaled Liz with the story about the kitten in the rain then the kitten remembering her today.

'So you enjoyed visiting Lyndall?' Liz scooped up the last of her lemon gelato.

'Uh huh. She is really nice and not at all scary.'

'Scary?' Liz asked through a mouthful.

'Grandad said—'

'How about we clear the table, young lady.' Vince was already on his feet. No need to have his opinions repeated. Liz grinned as she helped take plates to the sink.

Melanie asked if she could finish watching a movie on Vince's old DVD player. She'd been going through an old collection he still had from a few years ago. Things he'd bought when she and Susie still visited.

'Like a glass of wine, Liz?'

'Better not. Pete's doing surveillance tonight and I might need to go back to work.'

With a disapproving humph, which was directed purely at Pete, Vince sat at the kitchen table again, joining Liz.

'He really isn't that bad,' she said. 'Even gave me a hand when I began investigating...'

'The accident? No need to sweet coat it. Not unless Mel's around.'

Melanie's laughter from the other room was right on cue.

'She's grown up so much, Vince. Must be two years since I saw her last, apart from the other day. She's just a gem of a kid. And obviously she adores you.'

Something felt warm around his heart. A little bit of happiness. 'Goes both ways.'

The silence dragged. Maybe Liz was embarrassed by his small show of emotion, not something she'd been exposed to a lot. Well, not mushy feelings. She'd seen too much anger and too much blame, for sure.

'Has Melanie said anything about the accident?' Liz asked quietly, one eye on the doorway. 'Anything at all?'

'Why?'

'Don't get defensive. I'm trying to piece the world's most difficult jigsaw puzzle together and could use some help.'

'Sorry. Terry wanted to talk to her early in the piece and I said no. I figured if she had anything to say then she will. When she's ready. But,' he lowered his voice as well, 'there's a couple of things. When you drove up I told her to go open the front door and she went all quiet and said something about not knowing if it was really you. That it might be somebody else. Actually, somebody else's car.'

Liz leaned her elbows on the table and gazed at him.

'And the other day she made some odd comment about when Lyndall was out in the rain. Gave her a bit of a scare as she was right under the shelter and could only see part of Lyndall.'

'What did she say?'

'That she was happy it was Lyndall and not the angry man.'

He had to explore this. Why would she think there was an angry man and what did she even mean by it?

'Vince. You need to—'

'I will. I'll talk to her shrink first. Tell me what you know about the killer.'

'Might have been accidental. Okay, I had to say that. What we know is there was paint transference on the back and the front passenger side of the car, that it was black paint, and that it came from one of three types of vehicle. David had moved into the oncoming lane but there was no sign of braking or skidding for several second's worth of driving. I also found a half-smoked cigarette up the road from the scene. Within sight. Being tested now.'

Breathe.

She sat back. 'Nothing yet on the answering machine. No unexpected prints from the break in of their house... and I will arrange for the safe to be dusted.'

'That's it?'

He knew the expression on her face. She was keeping something from him.

'Tell me what happened with the Pickerings all those years ago.'

She almost visibly relaxed and told him about the strange demands of the Pickerings with the new neighbour's kid. He remembered bits of it as she spoke.

'Always knew he was bad news. Didn't think Carla was though,' he said. 'Bet they weren't thrilled to see you again and in Homicide.'

'When I walked up the driveway of the warehouse, Bradley just about keeled over.'

Wait...

'Why were you there?'

She looked away.

'Lizzie?'

Eyes back on him, she chose her words carefully. He hated that. 'I wanted to know why he was in Susie's house.'

'And?'

'Told me what he told you. Retrieving files belonging to the business. And... I asked what he and David were arguing about at the restaurant that night. They were overheard by a waiter.'

'Why wasn't I told this? I've let Melanie go to their house. Have I put her in danger?' Aware his voice was rising he clamped him lips shut. But his heart pounded, and he wanted to drive to Pickering's house and confront him.

'Doubt she is at risk with them. They're her godparents and Susie trusted Carla with her, so take a breath. The waiter denies saying anything and so does Bradley. I shouldn't have told you.'

'Yeah. You should.'

Her phone beeped and as she read the message her shoulders dropped.

'Damn. Dammit. Sorry, I have to go.'

She was on her feet.

'What's wrong?'

'There's been a murder. Someone I spoke to about Malcolm Hardy.' She was clearly angry with herself. 'I've had a feeling... dammit.'

'Go. Say goodbye to Melanie and stay safe.'

He wanted to hug her but didn't know how.

'Let me handle things, Vince. I'll find out what happened.'

A hug for Melanie and Liz was driving off. The minute she turned onto the road, her lights and siren went on.

TWENTY-EIGHT

Patrol car lights flashed along the street turning buildings blue and red. People stopped on the footpath and were moved along, most crossing to the other side of the road and getting their phones out. A media van rocked up. Probably the first of many.

Liz showed her badge to get past the police tape and then into the building. The lift was taped up so she ran up the five flights of stairs.

Outside the door she was handed slip on shoe coverings and put them on.

Pete was inside the apartment, barking orders to a uniform, who hurried past her.

The body was in the bedroom.

'Crime Scene are on their way. Touch nothing.' He barely glanced at Liz.

'Seriously, Peter? You're not speaking to a rookie.'

Ginny might have been sleeping, other than the black stocking around her throat. She wore only a lacy black bra, matching panties, and the other black stocking.

'A john?'

Pete began scanning the room. 'Hardy.'

'Hardy?'

'Strangulation. She put up no fight from the look of things so knew her killer. He probably liked it rough, and she'd have thought it was part of the game until she passed out.'

'He cuts throats.'

'He also has only ever killed men that we're aware of. This is a woman who he once cared about. Different version of the same crime.' Pete stalked out of the room. 'You were here with Terry.'

Liz followed. 'Handcuffs were found a block over which belonged to the officer who put them onto Hardy so we came to have a chat.'

They were in the kitchen, away from any other police.

'Why didn't you get me to meet you here?' Pete demanded.

'Terry's decision.'

'Liz... shit.' He ran a hand through his hair, his eyes furious. 'We should have kept an eye on her. He's found out you visited and shut her up.'

'Or he found out you and I were here the other day.'

The anger on her partner's face told her he knew that was possible.

'Tell me what happened.'

Liz ran him through the conversation leaving out the bit about her suggestion that Ginny might accidentally lock her clients in cuffs and need to cut them out. No point adding to his frustration. 'Terry asked to have a look around and she said no. He decided to wait for the prints from the cuffs to come back before trying for a warrant.'

'And have they?'

'Not that I know of. But we can search now.' Leaving Pete to sort himself out, Liz donned gloves and found the laundry. With barely room to turn, there was a combined washer/dryer, sink, and narrow broom cupboard, which she opened. 'Pete?'

They should have got the warrant earlier.

A pair of bolt cutters nestled behind an ironing board and a broom.

———

'This changes things.' Terry poured coffee for Liz and Pete as well as himself.

They were the only ones in the room. Those who'd been available were already back on the search for Hardy.

'I've asked for a warrant to access Richard Roscoe's communications and I want you two on his trail. If Hardy feels safe enough to kill one of his old contacts then he might slip up and make contact with his lawyer. Or strike again. I've sent someone to keep an eye on Roscoe but you both take over tonight please.'

Pete had had words with Terry earlier over Ginny. Liz had left them to it and gone to the locker room to change into her usual pants and jacket and on return they were back to normal and planning ahead.

'The other thing is the media are getting themselves in a twist so be careful they don't follow you. They're speculating Hardy is behind this and stirring up outrage that he's on the loose.'

'Where's Roscoe now?' Pete finished his coffee.

'I'll check and message you by the time you get downstairs.'

———

Vince knew he wouldn't sleep yet so turned on the television, keeping the sound down. There was nothing of interest to watch, but he wanted some kind of company and this would do. Melanie had been asleep for a couple of hours, exhausted in a content way by her afternoon with Lyndall and dinner with Liz.

It was Liz's revelations which unsettled him.

There'd been some kind of disagreement at the restaurant. If a waiter overheard it, then presumably it wasn't in the dining area... so where? Outside? Along a corridor? He knew Spironi's from a couple of lunches there with Susie. There was a vague recollection of a long corridor leading to both the kitchen and the restrooms. And perhaps the back exit.

The person who'd left the message on Susie's answering machine was threatening David and had enough of waiting for him to agree to something. It hadn't been Bradley's voice so who was David mixed up with? Or what?

I need to find the waiter and have a quiet word.

If they'd told one person there'd been an argument then changed their story it was likely a third party was involved. More threats? Or a nice payout?

A newsflash caught his eye and he turned the sound up enough to hear.

'The death of Ginny Makos, rumoured to be a high-end escort, is being treated as suspicious.'

Overhead footage from a helicopter showed the scene. An apartment building in the north-west of the city with police cars, ambulance, and a crowd despite the late hour.

'A police spokesperson has assured reporters on the scene that the killer poses no threat to the general public. We believe they know who the killer is. There will be a full report on our regular newscast and we will ask the question: Did Malcolm Hardy kill Ginny Makos?'

'Crap.'

He turned the television off and started to dial Liz on his phone. This Ginny was the person she'd spoken to about Hardy. Liz would be knee-deep in it. He sent a message instead.

Malcolm Hardy behind it?

The man was a menace. Vince had been at the end of his career when Hardy went to prison and had nothing to do with the arrest but knew enough to want him back behind bars. If it was him then where was he hiding? The heat this killing would generate would be enough for any of his old contacts to refuse to help him. Unless it was a warning —*don't mess with me.*

A message flashed up.

We think so.

He put the phone away. She was busy enough. Hardy had done well to stay out of sight for so long but staying in a city where every police officer had you in their sights would change that. He'd need a way out. By sea was one option. Get someone with a small boat to take a risk moving him along the coast. Airports would be impossible unless he had a friend on the inside and a small plane, but it wasn't as easy as it looked in the movies. Same with bus and rail. Lots of cameras. Lots of people watching out.

Either Malcolm Hardy was bunkered down somewhere invisible or would make a move to get out of the state. Which only left road transport. A private car might get through unseen, but the risk was high. Cars needed fuel and petrol stations had cameras.

With a yawn, Vince got to his feet. His mind wasn't going to rest just yet, but his body was exhausted and he could think just as well in bed as in here.

———

Altona Beach was almost deserted. The shopping strip—usually buzzing even this late—was quiet, most likely thanks to the cold tonight.

Richard Roscoe had led Liz and Pete here and now they waited.

He'd parked his fancy car along the waterfront and walked to the half-kilometre long pier where he'd stayed for the past half hour. He didn't follow its length or make any calls. Just stood staring back at the shops.

'Does he not feel the cold?' Liz was freezing. She should have kept a jumper on instead of the jacket which did little to keep her warm.

Pete didn't answer. He'd been quiet since they'd taken over trailing Roscoe and was either still angry or mourning Ginny. He didn't want to talk about it and Liz wasn't about to pry into whatever odd connection he'd had with the woman.

Someone walked along the beach toward the pier. Liz found binoculars but it was too dark to see who the person was. 'Pete?'

'Yeah, I can see him. He's meeting Roscoe.'

The man stepped onto the pier and the overhead light gave Liz what she'd wanted. Pete began taking photos with the camera he favoured and its giant lens.

A conversation ensued. Mostly from Roscoe's side but with the occasional comment from the other man. Roscoe waved his arms around and got into the other man's personal space. There was a quick shove and Roscoe backed off. More words spoken and then a tentative handshake before both went their separate ways.

Pete kept snapping images of the other man until he climbed into a flatbed ute.

'What the hell was that about?' Liz kept her eyes on Roscoe. 'Why is Roscoe meeting Abel Farrelly in the dead of the night?'

TWENTY-NINE

True to her word, Liz had arranged for someone to dust the safe in spite of her long night. She'd called Vince not long after dawn with a time and a brief update that she'd followed Richard Roscoe for the past few hours. She hesitated at one point, considering her words, then said to give Melanie her love.

There was something else there that she was keeping to herself which meant it concerned David or Pickering.

He'd given in to Melanie's request to visit Carla and dropped her off after making sure Bradley wasn't around. What Liz had said last night was true. Susie loved and trusted Carla and the woman had never shown anything but care for Melanie. Hopefully, as Melanie got older and made friends closer to her new home, she'd gradually need Carla less.

While he waited for the young officer to work on the safe, Vince found himself back in David's office. On the wall above the desk were photos of the family mixed in with framed certificates —a business degree specialising in logistics was completed at the same time as Susie finished her own, although she'd changed from the business course where they'd first met to one in tourism.

And never used it the way she wanted.

After they'd married, both wanted to save for a house and while David found his perfect position, Susie had taken a government job out of the field thanks to a downturn in her chosen profession. Once Melanie was a few months old she settled for part time in a travel agency chain. She'd once told Vince it was little more than a glorified data entry position with no room to advance. But it paid well enough to help them with the deposit on the house.

They'd lived here since Melanie was a couple of years old. She'd never known another home and it was a credit to her fortitude how quickly she'd adapted to living with him.

'Mr Carter?'

The officer, who looked more like a high school kid, hesitated outside the office.

'Finished?'

'Yes, sir. Sorry about the mess. There are some products which work better to clean the dust than others if you'd like some ideas?'

'All good. Done it before.'

'Oh, of course. Sorry. I'll get this back then.'

Vince locked the front door behind him and collected the ammonia mix he'd prepared and some cleaning rags. He'd already moved most of David's hanging clothes onto the bed earlier so had clear access to the safe without risking getting dust or ammonia on them. Putting on a mask, he set to work, first taking photographs of the prints with his phone. Just in case.

Once he'd done as good a job as he could, Vince opened the bedroom window to let some fresh air in, wishing he'd done it earlier. The early signs of a headache were forming.

Not knowing what to do long term with David's clothes, and nowhere near ready to think about Susie's, he began to sort them in piles. The man had more outfits than Vince had owned in a lifetime and that was just the ones on hangers. Pants for every occasion. Lots of business shirts long and short sleeved. Work jackets. A couple of wool winter jackets which were almost new by the look of them.

'Not cheap. But no money to pay school fees?'

It wasn't adding up.

Several suits. A tuxedo. And a well-worn puffer jacket. Vince had seen him in it plenty of times and was probably why Melanie loved wearing them. He lifted it to place on the pile of other jackets and an envelope slipped from the pocket. Vince had read books where something like that had occurred and scoffed at the convenience.

'Better write my own book.'

A message beeped on his phone as he started opening the envelope. A glance was all it took to make him drop it.

> Vince, Melanie's broken arm is hurting a bit. I think she might need to get it checked and I can run her over to the hospital if you are busy?

His breath caught.

> Is she in a lot of pain?

Grabbing the envelope he shoved it into a pocket and hurried from the room. Then turned back and rushed to close the window. Another message.

> Just some discomfort but I don't know much about broken arms.

He tried to text as he went down the stairs and almost fell so stopped.

> On my way. Tell her to sit quietly and I'll be there soon.

Not if he broke his neck first. He checked the house was locked and told himself, all the way to the car, to focus. This wasn't an emergency. Just discomfort. Melanie was okay.

———

While Melanie was being checked at outpatients, Vince went upstairs. He had to wait a few minutes but was able to see Doctor Raju between his patients.

'I appreciate this, doc. Melanie is seeing you in a few days but with her being downstairs unexpectedly...'

'Please, sit with me. How is she?'

Vince settled on a tub chair. This time though, he wasn't as stressed. Melanie was in a bit of pain but still bright and happy. And disappointed to cut her visit short. Carla was more worried than Melanie although her little face screwed up a few times on the drive down.

'Melanie is smart and funny and kind. And grieving, although the funeral was a turning point. We've had some sad moments. But I'm seeing more smiles. And she's working on me to bring a kitten into the family.'

'A kitten?'

'Yep. She found the little mite out in the wet the other day and since reuniting it with the owner has harped on about it so much.'

'I understand Melanie has some discomfort in her arm today. Is there another reason you are here?'

He must be short on time being so direct. It was decent of him to fit an unexpected visitor in on no notice.

'A couple of times, Mel has mentioned someone she calls an angry man. Nothing specific. But she's said it twice and also got worried about opening our front door last night to a friend—in case it wasn't our friend.'

'Have you asked her about this?'

Vince shook his head. 'First time she'd had a bit of a scare out in the rain chasing the kitten and I put it down to that. But now I'm worried she's carrying a fear around and I don't know if I should encourage her to talk about it.'

Doctor Raju leaned forward. 'Encourage her to talk but don't press her. Let her guide the conversation. She draws... I'm sure she told me.'

'Lots,' Vince laughed. 'Artwork all over the house.'

'Excellent. Be aware of what she's drawing. For some victims, art is a way to express what they can't or won't verbalise.'

'Victim?'

'She's been in a terrible accident. Her parents died in front of her. Don't mistake her smiles for healing... although they are a part of it.' Doctor Raju stood. 'I'm sorry I can't give you more time.'

Vince got to his feet. 'No, no, thank you. You aren't like any other shrinks I've met and you're making a difference for Melanie.'

With a smile, the other man opened the door. 'And you also, I hope.'

————

The wait for Melanie gave Vince a chance to open the envelope from David's jacket. He sat in the café on the hospital's ground floor. Coffee pushed to one side; he slid the letter out. It was from a business broker and none of it made sense. Dated two weeks earlier, it had the usual pleasantries then launched into an acceptance of an offer from David to purchase a business.

There was a date when the remainder of the deposit was due. An amount was already being held by the broker subject to the acceptance on both sides. Vince had no idea if that was normal. He'd only ever bought a house.

He read it twice and came to the same conclusion. David was buying his own company, a small freight forwarding outfit based in the outer western suburbs. Only his name was on the letter. No mention of Susie.

Vince googled the business.

A small outfit, it covered metro Melbourne and specialised in fast turnaround deliveries. There was a slick website and a booking portal. The gallery showed off a modern building and fleet of five vans, each with a smiling, uniformed driver.

The letter went back in his pocket and Vince slid a small, folded piece of paper from his wallet. It was the original copy of the note he'd written from the answering machine message. All along his gut had told him there was something in the phone call connected to the car crash.

First you ignore my messages on your mobile. Now this. You've made your bed, sunshine. Time's up, Weaver

It was a threat—but who made it? What deadline had David failed to meet?

He felt sick to the stomach and had to force himself not to crumple the note in his hand. David had been targeted for failing to do something the caller expected done. Surely not signing the papers for the new business venture? The deadline for the deposit had only just expired a day ago. Where did Bradley fit into this? Did he even know?

There'd been no mail or any other paperwork at the house regarding this purchase so where was he collecting his mail? Taking the envelope back out he found the answer with a post office box in Laverton.

'You've been keeping secrets.'

He thought he'd said it quietly but a woman with a pram shot him an odd look from the next table.

What else might be waiting at the post office box?

Vince needed help with this. But Liz was busy now. Too busy with catching that bastard Hardy to be available and he wasn't about to put her under any more pressure. Terry wasn't convinced yet that the crash was deliberate. And there was nobody else serving who had the time of day for him.

His phone beeped. Melanie was ready.

If the police weren't able or willing to view Susie's death as homicide in need of urgent investigation, then somebody else had to step up. Take charge of the growing list of anomalies and events. Talk to people in the know. Uncover the secrets.

Vince took a deep breath as Susie's words that he needed to step up suddenly filled his thoughts. She was right. He'd failed her then, but he wouldn't fail her now. It was time to step up.

THIRTY

Abel and Bradley were inside the container again but this time it was almost full, with cardboard boxes on pallets secured by straps. A narrow, twisting path led to the back. Bradley hated small spaces but their conversation couldn't be overheard here so he sucked up the tightness in his chest and aimed to keep it short.

'I dunno what Roscoe's problem is, boss,' Abel said. His eyes were bloodshot, and he lacked the usual energy Bradley was accustomed to. Late night.

'Explain.'

'He's looking over his shoulder all the time. Cops visited him and then bailed up one of his men outside the building insisting that Hardy is in communication with them,' Abel said.

'Good luck with that. He's not going to tell them if he is and anyway, Malcolm Hardy has to be master of the disappearing act. Who else could take advantage of the smallest lapse in security and escape custody with handcuffs and an injured foot in the middle of a busy city and still be in hiding?'

'Almost sounds like you admire him.'

Bradley shrugged.

'Anyway, Roscoe has his knickers in a knot over last night's killing,' Abel said.

'The call girl?'

'She was Hardy's go-to before prison.'

He'd not known that. The air was getting harder to breathe. If Abel felt it, he didn't show it, but there was a smirk on his lips. Probably could see how uncomfortable it was in this enclosed space and thought it funny.

'Still have no idea why that affects us, Abel.'

'He's terrified that Hardy was sending one of his famous messages by killing her. A message for Roscoe that his patience is running out and he wants to leave the state.'

'And what did you tell him?' Bradley started back out.

'Same thing as before.' Abel hadn't moved. 'And boss?'

Bradley stopped halfway through the container and waited.

'Got the feeling Hardy has the upper hand. Let's hope we don't fall on his wrong side.'

———

'I haven't stopped thinking about you. And my heart... it hurts. Do you know how often I've dialled your number just to hear your voicemail?'

Carla gripped an oversized bouquet of lilies and roses. She gazed at the new headstone.

Susan Marie Weaver.

Beloved daughter of Vince and Marion.

Adored mother of Melanie.

Soulmate of David.

Your light guides our hearts.

'It really does, Susie. You shone so brightly and even through the darkest moments I feel you are with me, telling me it will get better.' She sighed deeply and laid the flowers near the head-stone. 'But why didn't you make a new will? One which would have shown the world you wanted Melanie to come to me and Brad? We're going to fight for her, of course we will, but every day she's with Vince, Melanie gets closer to him.'

Under any other circumstances that would be a good thing.

But Vince Carter wasn't a typical grandparent. He'd fooled plenty of people into putting him on some pedestal as a hero. Not Carla though. Not even Susie, although she loved him despite his true nature and had struggled with the sadness of making him stay away for the past year.

Her eyes roamed to the church in the distance. A place of comfort and forgiveness. A pang of guilt touched her. Was she being too hard on Vince? She shouldn't speak ill of him... not here.

'Melanie came to visit earlier. We were making a batch of brownies and she said her arm hurt a bit. I made her sit and gave her some orange juice, but she wasn't comfortable. Anyway, Vince took her to the hospital to check her and she's fine, she really is. They did an x-ray, and the bones are healing but her cast needed adjusting. Anyway, the point is that Vince phoned me to say she was fine. I never thought he'd do that.'

A group of people wandered past and she said a prayer until they were out of earshot.

'I am keeping her as safe as I can, Susie. Brad is going to meet with Vince in the next day or two and see if we can arrange at least partial custody, so Melanie gets to spend some time with him and most with us. We're closer to her school so she could go to him on the weekends. Do you think that is okay?'

She and Bradley had talked it through last night for several hours. It was unlikely Vince would entertain the idea of them having full custody of Melanie, so this was a compromise. If the two parties were able to arrange something privately, then surely social services or whoever made final decisions about these things would look favourably on it. They had a lovely home and security. A long history with Melanie. Stable people.

'And I promise I'll make sure Melanie never forgets you. She's been so brave and today I showed her the photograph of you and me at Her Majesty's Theatre and told her a bit about how we met. She had a small cry... we both did. But then she said that mummy is always here...' Carla touched her chest. 'I almost lost it. But then I looked at her sweet face and decided I'm going to be like Melanie and be brave.'

The weak winter sun disappeared behind a cloud and Carla shivered. She had to do grocery shopping on the way home and would rather not end up soaking wet getting back to the car.

'I might go past that furniture store near the mall. See if there's anything for Melanie's new room. And I'll tell you all about it next visit.' She stepped forward and touched the head-stone. 'Love you, Susie. Always and forever.'

As hard as it was to walk away from the grave, the idea of choosing furniture for Melanie was enough to take the heaviest of the pain away. God willing, Melanie would be living with them soon.

———

'I want him in for an interview. Time to rattle some cages and see if he bites.' Terry fastened several photographs of Abel and Roscoe to the whiteboard.

'More likely one of Hardy's old contacts will be bitten. Like Ginny.'

Pete had been in a better frame of mind since they'd spotted the duo on the pier, but Ginny's death obviously still stung. He'd finally told Liz that Ginny had been an informant before Hardy went on his killing spree and she'd talked of leaving her life behind for a family. Liz had rarely seen Pete upset over an informant or criminal so Ginny's tough exterior must have had a softer side which had got under his skin.

'Always a risk, Pete. I've got people collecting footage from all directions, so we'll find out who killed her.'

'Boss, what about Mrs Hardy? Is her watch aware she might be in danger?' Liz asked.

Both Pete and Terry looked at her as if she was mad.

She wasn't. 'Think about it. We spent some time there the other day and she was quite happy to tell us Roscoe keeps in touch. So what if she's on Hardy's hit list?'

Terry shook his head. 'His own mother?'

'Liz, did you notice her living room?' Pete perched on the edge of a desk.

'It was gloomy in the house. Curtains closed. Only a lamp or two on.'

'Figured you'd overlooked the brand new television, expensive artwork, and top of the line lifting chair.'

How did I miss those first two?

'I saw the chair.'

He grinned. 'See what I mean? One out of several.'

'So you think Hardy is funding her fancy gadgets? If he is, why would he take out his own mum?' Terry asked.

'Because he's a lunatic. A sociopath who only cares for his own freedom and if he believed Ginny had betrayed him then he might very well work his way through anyone he gets the shits with.'

'Fair point. I'll touch base with the uniforms keeping an eye on Mrs Hardy. Tell them to be more visible.' Terry made a note on his phone. 'Anyone else I need to babysit?'

Liz glanced at Pete. He must be thinking the same as she was and neither spoke.

If Jerry Black was a target now, from their brief conversation, it would shock her. Unless he had a pipeline to Hardy—or told someone who did—and then was considered a threat.... Nothing had occurred to put the man in jeopardy.

Apart from that weird feeling of being watched.

She mentally shook the thought—and the feeling—away.

'So we'll invite Farrelly in for a chat?' She asked.

'Worth it, I reckon.' Terry tapped one of the photos. 'Exactly why was he meeting Roscoe in the dead of the night at a deserted pier?'

———

'A better question might be what you lot were doing following Richard?' Abel had said little since the patrol car brought him in, apparently more interested in listening to questions and gazing around the room or at his fingernails. Liz sat watching as one by one, Pete had placed a collection of the photographs he'd taken in front of Abel.

'Maybe we were following you,' Pete said.

'I'm boring. Go to work. Go home. Shop sometimes.'

'Yet you were out on a freezing night meeting a man who was going to drop in to visit you the other day... until he noticed the police were already there.'

'We both work odd hours. Mine are around the needs of my boss so sometimes it is eight to five and others it is of an evening. Not much rhyme nor reason to how the docks work, and we have to fit in with them.'

'And Roscoe?'

'He is at the beck and call of his clients. We've been meaning to catch up for weeks.'

Pete leaned his arms on the table. 'You both went to the same school. And then what? You kept in touch? Do a bit of work on the side for your old mate?'

'I work for Bradley. Imagine you've done your research on my background which might highlight the lack of legal qualifications.'

'Nah, I was thinking more along the lines of activities where the law is a hindrance. Those little jobs a lawyer couldn't do without landing themselves in the very place they aim to keep their clients out of.'

Abel's face barely changed. He was clever—sly, Liz had no doubt, and would be hard to get an admission out of. Certainly not without proof.

'So, how does Malcolm Hardy fit into this?' Pete asked.

'Into this what?'

'Relationship of yours. You, Roscoe, and Hardy.'

With a shake of his head, Abel leaned back in his chair. 'Only ever seen Hardy on television. Richard and I never talk business. Not his. Not mine.'

'What do you talk about?' Liz decided to join the conversation.

He didn't even look her way. 'We support opposing football teams. That makes for lively discussions and is why we only catch up every so often. Why am I here?'

'Wait on... you only talk football?' Pete grinned. 'Must have been an important round to mean meeting up when it is stupid degrees cold, *and* he got you riled up enough to push him. Whose team won?'

'You're wasting my time.'

Pete kept smiling and moved his chair to look at Liz. 'Is it a waste?'

'Depends on which footie team won.'

Abel almost smiled.

The silence dragged for a couple of minutes. Liz had to hand it to Pete—he loved this. He was a natural with interviews and the dirtier the person, the better. Having a quiet room often led to the blurting of useful information or tripping over facts. But Abel relaxed and closed his eyes. This wasn't a typical response.

'Roscoe and your boss, Pickering. Good mates?'

Eyes opening slowly, Abel gave off a vibe of not caring. He probably didn't.

'You'd need to ask them. Why am I here? Have you found the van yet? It's a pain with the one we've hired. Never starts properly.'

'My heart is breaking for you. What do you know about the argument between Pickering and Weaver the night of the crash, and don't tell me you know nothing.'

'I know nothing.'

'See, I don't believe you. I reckon you know everything going on in that warehouse and good for you. It's your job to know. So do yourself a favour and throw us a crumb. In the long run, it will be better for you.'

Except he believes he's untouchable.

'Can't tell what I don't know.' Abel pushed his chair back and stood. 'We're done.'

'And that van, mate? Reckon when we find it there'll be evidence of it hitting another vehicle.'

On his way out, Abel stopped long enough to sniff loudly. 'I smell a set-up.'

The door closed behind him.

'Surprised he can smell anything he's so deep in shit.' Pete stood and pushed his chair over.

THIRTY-ONE

'I knew I still had this photo! Look at this, Mel, and tell me you don't like Apple.'

The fireplace was crackling and despite a frost warning tonight, the living room was warm. Vince and Melanie shared the sofa with a platter of finger food on the coffee table within easy reach. He'd elected for an early dinner after Mel's trip to the hospital, cutting up cheese, fruit, crusty bread, tomatoes, onions, and a few other bits and pieces from the fridge. It was easy for Mel to fill a small plate and nibble as she pleased without putting any stress on the broken arm.

'Apple is a computer. And a phone. Also an iPad. Hmm, and a fruit!'

'And a pony,' Vince said.

Melanie popped a grape into her mouth and chewed, her eyes darting to the open photo album in Vince's hands.

'Before I show this to you let me tell you a bit about Apple. When your mum was a bit older than you, all she wanted was a pony. Those books you love reading... the horsey adventure ones?'

She nodded; her eyes wide as she listened.

'Susie longed to find adventures on the back of a big chestnut stallion. Off to find bad guys or defeat an army. But instead, one day she and I were riding our bikes—'

'*You* ride a bike?'

Jeez, kid. Thanks.

'Still have two bikes in the shed. Do *you* ride one?'

Melanie pouted. 'No.'

'Well we can fix that.'

He had no idea if he could even fit on his bike now. Once he would think nothing of riding for hours and Susie and he would discover creeks and valleys and all kinds of places.

'Grandad?'

'Melanie?'

She giggled. 'You were just smiling. Such a big happy smile.'

'I was thinking about your mum. How we used to ride bikes together. But anyway, I digress. One day, we were on our way home, cycling down a narrow track, and we came upon a young pony who was lost. Your mum jumped off her bike, pulled an apple out of her pocket and held out a hand and the pony came straight to her.'

Those eyes of Melanie's were even bigger, and she leaned closer.

'It turns out that the pony kept escaping. She was the last of her family and it seemed she really wanted more attention than her owners could give her. Their kids were grown and moved away, and the pony was lonely.'

'And that was Apple?'

'It sure was.'

Melanie's mouth formed a wide 'o'.

'And your mum and Apple were inseparable. By the time she grew up and left home, Apple was getting on in years and not so lonely. Still had me to hang around with. Sometimes visits with the donkeys. And every time Susie came to visit she'd take an apple or a carrot out to her pony, who never forgot her.'

Melanie sidled closer and peered at the photographs. There were four, all of Apple with Susie and Melanie petting her, and the last one with Mel sitting on her back. There was no saddle or even a halter thanks to how gentle the pony was.

'Are you sure that's me?'

'I sure am sure. Guess you were about four years old.' He moved the album onto her lap. 'See how gentle Apple is? She loves people a lot and when you are ready, I'm sure she'd enjoy taking you for a proper ride.'

There was no response as Melanie traced Susie's face with her finger.

'Would you like to see some pictures of your mum when she was little?'

Am I rushing her?

With a beautiful smile, and a hint of a tear in her eyes, Melanie looked up and nodded.

'Alrighty then,' Vince said. 'In that case, shall we start with her baby book?'

———

'Did I tell you how much Melanie enjoyed cooking today?' Carla called from the kitchen. 'At least until her arm played up.'

Bradley selected a bottle of white wine from the fridge near the bar. 'You did. Would you care for a glass of wine, baby?'

'Now, what sort of silly question is that?' Carla, aproned and hands covered in flour, gave him one of those smiles he lived for. 'I couldn't stop cooking after she left so have some delicious little pastries for you to take for lunch tomorrow. And I just rolled some pastry for tartlets for dessert.'

He kissed her, staying clear of her hands. 'You look after me so well.'

'Better believe it.' She pretended to reach for him with floury hands and laughed as he ducked around the counter. 'What? Don't want pretty white handprints on your nice jumper?'

'If you want wine then you'll keep your hands to yourself.' He busied himself pouring two glasses as she washed her hands. When she checked the oven, opening it a crack, his mouth watered. Something smelled very good.

'Time for a sip or two then I'll get that out.'

They sat at the counter on stools after tapping their glasses together.

'You didn't say why you came home early?'

He'd left the warehouse not long after Carter stormed out, bringing home a pile of files and shutting himself in his office for a few hours. At least he had pulled together paperwork for the future. An altered, printed, and photocopied email from David expressing his firm intention to sell his share to Bradley. Didn't matter who really wrote it.

David was gone. Susie was gone.

Melanie would benefit.

'Brad?'

'Sorry, baby. Was miles away.'

'I can see that. Would you like to eat in here or the dining room?'

'Here is fine.'

She left her half-finished glass to collect placemats and cutlery. He refilled it, not offering to help because Carla always refused. She said she loved being able to look after him with home cooked meals and a happy house because he made her happy.

'*You* make me happy.'

He spoke without thinking and her head shot up. Her face lit up with love and if she wasn't about to take dinner out of the oven, he'd have suggested another activity right here and now.

'Thank you, honey. It goes both ways.'

Sometimes he wondered if they needed a child. They had the best relationship he'd ever seen. Not like his own parents who each had remarried twice. And his friends were as bad... apart from David who was committed to Susie.

Except he'd lied to her.

And to me.

Dinner was delicious, as always. Carla insisted on cleaning up and Bradley wandered to the living room to put on some music. He'd missed seeing Melanie today but on her last visit she had been a bit distant with him. Not for the first time. Ever since her parents died, she barely looked at him. It had to be more than grief because around Carla, the little girl laughed and chattered away like she'd always done. How had he upset her? He picked up a stuffed bunny Melanie had left on the sofa, stroking its ears. They'd always got along so well. Even David used to joke about Bradley being her substitute dad. What changed?

That night... at the restaurant. Two happy couples doting on one happy child. Their regular Friday night dinner at least twice a month for years.

He'd been late and Carla had caught an Uber to get there. But once dinner started there was laughter and talk. Melanie was so excited about school holidays, which just began. But later, she'd barely looked at him when he'd left before anyone else. He'd said goodbye and gone to kiss her cheek as usual, but she'd turned away.

So what happened between entrée and leaving?

She'd come out of the ladies restroom when he and David were arguing. How much had she heard?

'Shall we have some more wine?' Carla settled next to him.

'Sure thing.'

'What are you doing to that poor bunny, Brad?'

His hand gripped its neck.

'Craving rabbit stew?' He laughed and plopped it onto her lap. 'Does this need to go back to Mel, or stay here?'

'Here. I'm getting a cute collection for her. Anyway, she was telling me about Vince's farm.'

He snorted. 'Farm?' He filled up their glasses. 'I suppose to a little girl who isn't used to the country it must feel like one.'

'I guess. He has Susie's old pony. Apple. The name amuses Mel but I get the feeling she's a bit scared of it so she must have no memories of being out there. And the neighbour has cows and donkeys.'

Bradley handed Carla her glass then leaned back. 'Actually, the place next door is nice. Big house high up the hill. Reckon it is architect built. Paddocks with post and rail fences. Whoever owns it looks after it, unlike Carter's dump.' He swallowed some wine. Then some more.

'Unless she sold it, that Lyndall woman would still be there. Susie just adored her, but I found her odd, always wearing an old hat and rescuing donkeys and the like.'

'I forgot you'd been out there so often. Of course you'd know.'

Carla cuddled the bunny against herself. 'Mel said she has her own room but likes being in the living room because of the fireplace. Sounds a bit dangerous having her near an open fire. Anyway, she likes looking at the birds that Vince carves and the photos of her grandmother and mother on the mantlepiece. Nice that she gets some comfort from those.'

'It is. What else?'

'Oh, that's right. And this is a bit of a concern. She saw a little kitten out in the rain and followed it. Once she caught the creature, a scary person in a big hat—those are her words—stomped through all the puddles and found Mel underneath a wood shelter. It was Lyndall who owned the kitten and Melanie wants to adopt it.'

'A kitten?'

She nodded. Her eyes were sad. 'Apparently the kitten isn't quite ready to leave home but Mel hopes she might be allowed to have it later on.'

'Carter won't let her.'

'But how can you be sure? Mel wants this kitten so much which I get. I really do. She needs something to love. But if he relents then what will happen when she moves here? I don't want a cat. They smell and ruin things.'

Bradley took another mouthful to give him time to come up with something as she spoke again.

'But I'd put up with it to have Mel.' Her bottom lip quivered.

Don't cry, baby. God. Enough crying.

He took her hand. 'We will cross that bridge later. Our lawyer is investigating options about Melanie coming to live here. Until we get the lowdown there's no point speculating and imagining the worst, is there?'

'I didn't know, honey. Not about the lawyer. She will be our girl, won't she?' Carla leaned against him.

'Going to do everything I can to make it happen.'

Even if it means killing Vince Carter to get him out of my way.

———

Vince closed a book he'd been reading to Melanie. 'And that is enough for tonight.'

'One more chapter?'

'There's only two left so let's keep them for tomorrow and I'll read both.'

The book went on the nightstand, and he turned off the lamp.

'I like this room.' Mel's eyes were closed and she cuddled Raymond and Topsy.

'That's good.' Vince kissed her forehead.

'Even if Carla makes me a pretty room in her house, I think I will like this one more.'

The phone began to ring from the kitchen.

'I'd better answer that. 'Nite, Melly-belly.'

''Nite, Grandad.'

As he closed the door, she mustered a sleepy smile, and he blew her a kiss. What rubbish was Carla going on about?

His mind raced as he grabbed the phone. 'Vince Carter.'

'Lyndall here. Is that sweet little one asleep?'

He leaned against the table. 'Almost. Just finished reading her a story.'

The soft chuckle at the other end made him smile. She wasn't laughing at him as such. But of everyone in his life, she would appreciate the irony.

'She's one of the reasons I'm phoning, Vince.'

'One?'

'I think it's time she had that kitten... if you agree. Don't decide now. Come up tomorrow and see for yourself.'

'Not big on cats.'

'Not about you. Is it?'

Until he got left doing everything for it.

'Anyway, need to chat about some other stuff. Early as you like.'

'What other stuff, Lyn—'

But she'd disconnected the call.

THIRTY-TWO

Melanie skipped her way up the driveway to Lyndall's house, staying a safe distance from the curious donkeys which wandered to the fence line. Vince trudged behind.

Closer to the top the paddocks changed to manicured gardens and Melanie paused several times to smell this flower or that. Lyndall's home was a masterpiece of architecture, designed by some award-winning Melbourne firm which still won awards. Every bit of it was environmentally friendly and fitted into the landscape. And it was huge, yet Vince had never seen family visiting. No adult children or grandkids.

When he caught up with Melanie she reached for his hand and led the way. This was more like the little girl he knew. Curious and naturally friendly. The sadness was there beneath the surface and would be for a long time to come, but it lifted his spirits seeing her emerge a little from the fog.

At the top of the driveway was a garage with four open doors side by side. Lyndall's Range Rover was inside one and a quad bike in another. The other two were empty. Parked behind the garage, just showing on one side, was an old cattle truck. Lyndall had once said it was in case she needed to move all the donkeys and her handful of cows in one if there was a fire threat.

I can imagine you driving it.

'Oh! Here you are, little kitty!' Melanie squealed as the kitten hurtled toward her from around the corner of the house. She dropped to her knees and gently picked it up. Close behind was another kitten and an adult, presumably the mother, who inspected Melanie at a distance.

It was infectious, the joy on Melanie's face. Vince almost squatted down beside her.

'He remembers you.' Lyndall followed the cats.

The mother cat padded around Melanie and rubbed her head against her leg.

'Yep. Mum approves. Now you've only got to deal with Grandad.' Lyndall leaned down to tickle the kitten's chin. 'Leave him to me. The kitten is as good as yours.'

Vince spluttered.

'Are you good to sit here and watch these creatures while I have a chat to him?' Lyndall asked. 'Else you know where the kitchen is and there's some freshly made lemonade on the table.'

Melanie nodded with a smile that looked permanent.

I think I've lost this battle.

Lyndall joined him. 'Walk with me? Your girl is fine here.' She headed toward the paddock in front of the house.

'Be okay for a minute, Mel?'

She'd already adjusted herself to sit on the ground and the three felines curled around her.

He caught up with Lyndall, who dropped her arms on the top rail of the fence. The donkeys noticed her and began to wander up.

She gave him a long look. 'Your decision about the kitten, but it seems to me that little girl needs something to hold onto. Something new to love.'

They gazed out over the paddock, which was several acres in size and just one of a dozen or so on the property. Lyndall's animals were all rescued and she spent most of her waking hours making their lives good. Vince had no idea where her money had come from or what her story was. There'd never been a reason to ask.

'Came home yesterday and there was some fellow parked in your driveway,' Lyndall said.

'Parked?'

'Car was parked. He came from around the side of your house, busy taking photographs. Big lens on the camera.'

Vince's gut churned.

'I challenged him, of course,' she added. 'Asked who he was and what he was doing.'

'Did he say?'

'Pointed the camera at me and I gave him something worth photographing.' There was a touch of anger in her tone. 'The gall of him.'

The first of the donkeys arrived and poked its muzzle through the fence searching for Lyndall's pockets. 'Hello darlin.' I figured he might be a real estate agent. But he was too rude. You annoy someone?'

'Lots.'

'But seriously, anyone checking up on you?'

'Maybe. Dunno. Mel said...'

'What?'

He shook his head and reached over to pet the donkey. 'Probably nothing. Mel's godmother, Carla, said something to her about making a special bedroom at their house. For Mel.'

'I remember her.' Lyndall's expression made it clear she wasn't a fan.

'She does love Mel. And Susie trusted her.'

'I'd be watching Melanie pretty closely. Just in case.'

There was such gravity in her last three words that Vince shot her a look.

'Just in case what?'

She wanted to say something. Her eyes were serious.

'What, Lyndall? What are you thinking?'

'Out there are some bad people who will—'

'Grandad!'

Both of them jumped as Melanie, kitten tucked up in her unplastered arm, appeared from nowhere. Lyndall bit her bottom lip. Vince wasn't going to let that go, but with Melanie present, it would need to wait.

'What's up, Mel?'

'Please, please, please may I have this little kitten?' She stopped between the adults, eyes going from one to the other as a frown formed between her eyes. 'I don't like arguments.'

Vince squatted down in front of her. 'I don't like them either. Nor does Lyndall. We are only talking about you having the kitten and we were petting the donkeys.'

She looked at the donkey which was still trying to find a treat in Lyndall's jacket, and then back to Vince. Some of the worry left her face. 'Did you decide?'

'You know a kitten takes a bit of work. Feeding. Cleaning the litter tray. Playing. Are you up for that?'

Melanie nodded.

'And not just for a week. For a lifetime. And cats live a long time.'

'I promise I will take such good care and do everything for Robbie.'

Lyndall made a funny sound which she quickly muffled.

'Well, in that case, yes, you may have Robbie,' Vince said.

With shining eyes, Melanie hugged Vince until the kitten protested. He got himself upright again after a failed first attempt. Squatting wasn't a good decision. 'Um... we'll need to go shopping for... Robbie. And we have the appointment first at your school.'

'Leave him here for now and I'll bring him down the minute you call.' Lyndall held a hand out and after kissing his nose, Melanie handed him over. 'Good girl. I'll text Grandad a little list so he can get the same food and stuff.'

'Come on, Grandad. Let's go!' Melanie started off without a backward look.

When Vince went to follow, Lyndall touched his arm with her free hand. 'Wait a sec.' She found a piece of paper in her pocket. 'Rego of the intruder. The photographer. Run it past your police friends.'

'Thank you.'

'Hey, Melanie,' Lyndall called before the little girl disappeared down the driveway. 'I'll bring him down later and you can call me anytime if you have any questions.'

'Okay, thanks, Lyndall.' She turned and waved with a big smile.

Lyndall's voice softened. 'My pleasure, darlin'.'

Vince followed Melanie.

'Goes for you, too,' Lyndall said as he passed.

He gave her a sideways glance but managed to avoid smiling until she couldn't see his face.

———

It was weird being at a school with no pupils. Melanie led the way to Mrs McCoy's office where they were ushered inside with a smile by a tall, thin woman with a furrowed brow.

For a few minutes, Melanie and the principal chatted about the coming term and which subject Melanie was most excited about. It was art. Mrs McCoy suggested Melanie head to her usual classroom where her teacher was setting up the room.

As soon as the door closed again, her smile vanished. 'I am so very sorry about Melanie's parents, Mr Carter. Susie was active here, more than just as part of the requirements of parents to volunteer their time. She really loved helping with the students.'

He'd expected mention of the loss but it still gripped his guts. 'Thank you.' Sympathy wasn't bringing his daughter back. Social manners kicked in a lot at the moment.

'Will Melanie be ready to be back at school, Mr Carter?'

'Her arm will be in plaster for a while but she's managing well.'

'I mean... emotionally. She's had a terrible experience between being in the car accident and losing her parents. There's been a big change in her life.'

'Which makes having some normalcy important,' Vince said. 'Her psychologist said it helps.'

'Ah. She is seeing someone then. And of course we have support here. Our chaplaincy system is excellent. Are you familiar with our school? I don't recall seeing you here for any of Melanie's open nights or concerts, not that I meet every grand-parent of course.'

You're judging me.

Deciding if he was worthy of having custody. Or good enough for the school.

She pursed her lips as she opened a folder on the desk.

'Was it a long drive for you? To bring Melanie?'

'Forty minutes.'

'In the middle of the morning. It might be as much as an hour each way during rush hour, which is when you'd drop her off. There's no easy public transport route I can find so unless you have someone closer who—'

'Nobody.' His fingers tensed and he flattened them against his legs. 'I'll bring her each day. Pick her up each afternoon.'

'I see.'

No. You don't.

'Will there be a list of what Mel needs this term? So I can begin arranging things.'

'Perhaps.'

'Mrs McCoy... is there an issue with Melanie? Or me?'

With a quick nod, the woman turned the open folder. 'Nothing personal. We love Melanie. She's a good student. Kind and inquisitive. But as we briefly discussed on the phone, there's the matter of payment. And I think it best this be addressed now.' She gestured at the sheet of paper facing Vince.

It was a copy of what he had in his top pocket.

'Aren't these things normally paid in advance?'

'This is Melanie's third year with us, and her father always paid at the beginning of each year. Not for a term, but a whole year which was more than expected. And often there'd be a bit extra as well, to help out if another family struggled. In fact, David paid for a full term for another child at one point which made the difference for that family.'

'Why?'

Her mouth dropped open and she blinked.

'I mean, why would David pay for the child of a stranger, but not pay for his own daughter?' Vince clarified.

'Oh, I see.'

'I don't.'

'It was before his company went into financial distress, Mr Carter. In the previous two years, money was not an issue. The family was like almost every other family here. Financially stable. Engaged in the education of their child. And because he'd been so generous in the past, we extended a grace period for him until the middle of the year.'

What financial distress? Did Susie know?

He opened his mouth to ask what proof she'd been given and closed it. This meeting was about Melanie. Not David.

She offered a smile. 'Nobody expected this tragedy. And of course, Melanie is welcome here and so are you, Mr Carter, as a volunteer, which is normally twenty hours a month, but we could increase that to help with the cost... as long as you are willing to get a working with children card and have the usual police checks?'

If he wasn't gripping his knees so hard now, he'd throw back his head in hysterical laughter. Instead, he smiled in return.

'I can provide those. I have to ask if you are assuming I can't afford Melanie's fees. There's also assets to be realised. Melanie is all that matters and if she wishes to stay in this school, then the fees will be kept up to date.'

The principle looked uncomfortable now, fidgeting in her seat.

He stood. 'Would you point me in the direction of where Melanie is?'

'Of course.'

At the door, she gave him brief instructions and then touched his arm. 'Before you leave... I hope I didn't sound... well, anyway, I'm happy you wish your granddaughter to stay with us. And I am here to answer any questions, although her teacher is best placed to give you information about the next term. It's just... although I knew Susie best, it was David who paid the accounts and he once said... well, he mentioned you. Said you weren't in a good situation. My apologies.'

There was only one response which came to mind. 'I see.'

With that, he stepped into the hallway and went in search of Melanie.

THIRTY-THREE

Tonight was important. One of those pivotal moments in a man's life. Bradley had worked hard all his life, from paperboy at ten to pulling all night shifts in fast food outlets to pay his way through university. Then at the age of twenty-one he'd got a taste for money after success at the casino one incredible day. While his mates lost all their money, somehow he went home with twenty grand. And he was smart enough never to gamble again. Not that kind of gambling. He studied calculated risks and loved the rush when a plan worked out against the odds.

We're so close.

Everything was ready.

Bradley walked through the warehouse for the third time in the hour since the workers left. The hired van was locked inside the building and the roller door down. Abel was checking something on the roof of the shipping container, tapping away at some part he wasn't quite satisfied with but that was how the man rolled. Always a perfectionist.

He fancied an early drink to celebrate and poured a double in his office. On his desk, he'd piled up several framed photos of David to give to Melanie.

'Cheers, mate. If only you were here to see this day.' He raised the glass to David's image and drank quickly. He'd kept his grief at bay by staying busy and looking after Carla but sooner or later, it would catch up.

Beside the photos was a large white envelope, part of his to-do-list for later this evening. He had time between now and midnight to visit Vince and be back in plenty of time to oversee their first joint shipment with Duncan Chandler safely leave on its inaugural journey to Far North Queensland. A long road trip to a beautiful part of the country.

'Hey boss. The container is one hundred percent ready to go. All we need now is the final cargo and the truck.' Abel leaned against the door frame. 'I might go and eat. Been a crap day thanks to stupid coppers. Bit of a feed and I'll be back before the truck arrives.'

'You never said what they wanted.'

'No idea except them banging on about me catching up with Richard the other night.' He laughed. 'Idiots have no idea.'

'Well, go eat. I'm heading up to Carter's. Have some stuff to fix.'

His phone rang and when he saw the number, he held his hand up to Abel.

One minute later, he slammed the phone on top of the envelope.

'What?' Abel hadn't moved.

'Their driver is down with a stomach bug. They've pushed it out another twenty-four hours.'

Abel swore.

'I know.' Bradley slumped on his chair and dropped his head onto his hands. 'Damn, damn, dammit.'

'It has to be tonight, boss.'

Bradley's head flew up. 'Then *you* find a truck and drive the container there yourself!' He stood so fast his chair flew back. 'I've knocked myself out making this happen. Extra payments. Bonuses. Pleading. There is no tonight!'

'Don't yell at me. I'm as frustrated as you are.'

Abel hadn't moved but he'd calmed down much faster than Bradley.

Forcing his tone back to normal, Bradley pushed the chair back to its normal spot. 'What the hell are you going to tell him?'

The laugh from Abel sent a shiver down Bradley's spine.

'Me?'

Sweeping up the envelope, phone, and photographs, Bradley stalked to the door. Abel still didn't move.

'You. And make it good. I'm tired of looking incompetent thanks to the actions of other parties. This business funds both our lifestyles and this mess is risking that lifestyle getting a massive, long term, injection of cash.'

Abel raised both eyebrows and stepped aside. 'If this cargo doesn't get moved soon it'll be more than our lifestyle at risk.'

He wasn't wrong.

'Just make the call. Then take the night off.' Not waiting for further debate, Bradley crossed the warehouse. At the side door he glanced back. Abel was at the container, leaning against it as he dialled his phone.

———

Lyndall had arrived with the kitten late in the afternoon, refusing a cup of coffee with an excuse about making sure mother cat wasn't too upset. She'd avoided being drawn back into the earlier conversation when she'd begun to warn Vince about keeping Melanie close, leaving almost as quickly as she came.

Now, as Melanie ran through the laws of the cottage with Robbie, a knock on the front door drew Vince away from the dinner he was preparing.

On his way to open it, he glanced into Melanie's room where she lay on her stomach, solemnly talking in a soft voice to Robbie, who sat listening. He couldn't help smiling.

Until he opened the door.

Bradley stood on the verandah.

'What are you doing here?'

'Got those photographs for Melanie.'

'Said I'd collect them.'

'Well, I need a quick chat so brought them with me. Here.' Bradley handed over a clear bag with loose photographs. The man was cagey. He didn't meet Vince's eyes and moved from one foot to another.

'I'm in the middle of something,' Vince said.

'One question then I'll go. Carla and I would like to make a legal arrangement with you for custody, at least partial, of Melanie.'

'Not a chance.'

'Come on, mate. At least hear me out.'

'Time for you to go.'

Instead of moving, Bradley held out a large envelope and this time, he met Vince's eyes. 'Pity you feel that way. You should take a look.'

Vince glanced over his shoulder and stepped outside, pulling the door closed behind himself. 'What the hell is this, Pickering?'

'Open it.'

Although he knew he should go inside and lock the other man out, Vince couldn't help himself. Within the envelope was a folder about half an inch thick. He flicked through, his stomach churning more with every page.

There were photographs of his property looking desolate and neglected.

A close up of hundreds of empty wine and spirits bottles piled up behind a shed.

Carcasses of dead rabbits near warren entrances, bullet holes riddling them.

'You know these bottles aren't mine.'

'The place is run down. Unsuitable for a child.' Bradley had a tone in his voice. A challenge.

'I don't go around shooting rabbits for fun and I'd never keep a gun near a child.' Beneath the last photograph was a typed letter signed 'Susan Weaver'.

Phrases stood out.

I had to throw Dad out again.

He was drunk and getting violent.

I'd never trust him with my child.

He wasn't a hero at home.

'That's not Susie's signature,' Vince said.

'Near enough.'

'Is this blackmail?'

Bradley grinned, cocky. 'Nothing like it. It is a friendly look at what might happen if you let things continue on. None of it is necessary and that folder and its copies need never be seen by another soul.'

He wanted to grab the slimy bastard by the throat. But Melanie was in the house, and he wasn't about to give the creep the satisfaction.

'What do you want?'

'Only what David and Susie would have expected. For Melanie to live with us. And for David's share of the company to transfer to me without any issues.'

Vince stuffed the folder back into the envelope.

'Melanie loves us. And Carla lives for Mel, would do anything for her. She'll have a good life with every advantage,' Bradley said.

'A good life with a criminal in the house?'

'Well that's just rude. I'm offering a peaceful arrangement. You'll be able to see her, but you need to let the appropriate people know you want us to adopt her.'

'Over my dead body.' Vince held out the envelope.

'Keep it. What's your answer?'

'You have thirty seconds to leave my property. Twenty-nine—'

'You fool.'

'Twenty-eight. Twenty-seven.'

'Stop! For Melanie's sake think this through!'

Vince closed in on Bradley, who shrank back.

'You are destroying her future—'

'Twenty-six. Run.' He followed Bradley who half fell, half slid down the steps. 'You ever step foot on this property again...

Bradley was running.

Vince took half a dozen strides after him, watching to make sure the man was in his car and driving off before turning back.

The living room curtain moved.

————

Melanie was using the bathroom when he got back inside which gave him time to toss the offending envelope into his bedroom. He checked the oven and slid the dish onto a rack. His heart gradually returned to its normal beat, but his head was spinning with thoughts of what he'd like to do to Bradley. Bad thoughts.

Had Melanie overheard any of the conversation or just looked out the window as Bradley left the property? He headed for her bedroom.

She lay on her back on the floor with the kitten on her chest.

'Uncle Brad was so much fun before. He used to tell the funniest stories.'

Vince stayed in the hallway.

'And Auntie Carla is still the same as always and I love doing stuff with her. But Robbie? Uncle Brad got so cross that terrible night at Daddy and now he's cross with Grandad... I hope he never comes here to our house again, Robbie.'

Somehow Vince stopped himself from going in and picking up the little girl and telling her he'd never allow anything bad to happen. Would it help? She didn't sound teary or worried. Matter-of-fact if anything. And if she thought he listened in on her conversations then she might be less willing to air them, even if only to a cat. Anyway, how could he promise such a thing?

He went back to the kitchen and dialled his phone.

'Lizzie? It's Vince. Call me back when you can. And would you check this rego for me...' he pulled the piece of paper out Lyndall gave him earlier and read it off.

————

Bradley let himself into the house, fuming. On the drive back he'd come up with a dozen ways to kill Carter and discarded them all. He wasn't that kind of person.

But I've had a gut-full of high and mighty Carter.

The living room lights were on but Carla was elsewhere in the house, so he poured a brandy and paced, trying to clear his head and dilute the anger. Any other person would have folded with the damning evidence he'd collected. Didn't matter that some of it was fake. There was enough truth to make someone fear their secrets were about to be shown to the world. And Vince Carter had plenty of those. The pile of bottles might not be from his property, but everyone knew the man had a drinking problem. The place was a dump and if child services went visiting they'd surely question its suitability for a child to live in. Which might be worth suggesting to that frumpy woman who'd done nothing to help last time.

'Honey?'

'In the living room.'

He held up a second glass as she came in. 'Brandy?'

'Oh, sure.' She kissed his cheek. 'I didn't hear you drive in but thought I heard a voice.'

'Probably talking to myself. There you go. Cheers.'

'Cheers. To Melanie.'

'Yeah. Always to our little Melanie.'

Carla tilted her head in question.

Damn Vince.

'What's for dinner, baby?'

'Brad... when is Melanie coming?'

He took her spare hand.

'You did see Vince? Explain that we will make sure he gets to see her often and how wonderful her life will be...'

'He refuses to listen, Carla. I'm sorry. I tried so hard.'

'Then I'll go and speak with him.'

'It's worse than him not listening, baby. He said he doesn't want us seeing her anymore.'

Carla gasped and the glass in her hand shook.

'But I have an idea. I'm going to speak to the lawyer again and ask how we report the poor conditions Melanie lives in. This battle has only just begun. I promise.' He kissed her fingers, but her eyes shone with tears and she gently withdrew her hand.

'I... I might check dinner.'

He'd stuffed up. He should have thought this through before coming home so she had hope. The muffled sound of his wife crying from the kitchen stabbed into him.

———

After dinner, Melanie helped wash up and then read for a while on the beanbag with the kitten on her lap. It was still early when she changed for bed. She looked exhausted.

'Seems as if Robbie likes it here.' Vince brought a cup of hot chocolate into her bedroom. 'Do you think he'll sleep all night?'

Melanie took the cup with a soft 'thank you' and sat on the side of her bed. Robbie was curled up in his bed beside hers, his tiny paws twitching in a dream. It was easier to take a good look at him now he was still. He was mostly black with white tips on his nose and feet.

'Do you like him?' She whispered. 'We need to be very quiet and not disturb him.'

'Of course I like him,' he whispered in return. 'He makes you smile. I like that a lot.'

'I love him, Grandad. Thank you.'

And I love you, sweetheart.

'Shall we read?'

'Too noisy. He's a baby and has to sleep.'

'Fair enough. Would you like me to turn off the overhead light then?'

'Yes please. And can you close the door because that way he won't get lost if he wakes up early.'

She let him kiss her forehead and then he made a show of creeping out, hoping for a smile. It eventually came but Melanie's earlier joy had been quelched by whatever she'd seen between Vince and Bradley.

And I'm to blame for that.

There were a hundred ways, or at least a handful, he should have managed the other man's visit. As satisfying as sending him off had been, it wasn't worth fallout.

He collected the envelope from his bedroom and tossed it onto the coffee table in the living room. After turning off most of the lights in the cottage, he got a bottle of whisky from a top cupboard and a glass and wandered back to the sofa. Headlights flicked on the wall and his heart missed a beat. But it was just someone using the driveway to turn in.

For a few minutes he watched to be certain. That car had gone, but another cruised past slowly. His nerves were getting the better of him. He pulled the curtains across and sat by the flickering light from the fireplace.

He poured a drink but didn't touch it, instead, opening the envelope.

His phone beeped.

Liz.

> Can I do rego check in the morning? What's the context?

He tapped back.

> Someone lurking around my place. Have a bit to tell you.

Before he'd put the phone down, another beep.

> Want company?

Vince gazed at the glass. Then replied.

> All good. Talk tomorrow.

He turned the phone off.

THIRTY-FOUR

Liz was ready for an afternoon nap, yet it was just after dawn. She'd worked through to close on two this morning interviewing potential witnesses and speaking to Crime Scene officers as well as first responders.

Thanks to another damned killing.

The call had come in just after she'd heard from Vince last night. Despite asking him if she could chase up the rego later, she'd been intrigued and run a search on the spot. Before she'd done more than take a few notes, Pete was grabbing his gear and telling her to hurry. Some poor late night walker had stumbled upon a body in a public toilet.

Pete's complaints about going back out had ceased the second they'd arrived at the scene. Personality aside, the man was a gun. Hard working, intelligent, and street-smart. He'd put all of those qualities to good use by evaluating the gruesome discovery and instigating the investigation while Liz spoke to the young officer who'd been the first responder.

Alerted to a possible overdose by the member of the public who'd found the body, the constable had gone into the facilities unprepared. He had a greenish pallor and was shaky when she took him aside. One look at the body explained his reaction. A middle-aged male, stabbed in the neck and left to die in the filthy public toilet, was not a pretty sight slumped with his eyes open, against a toilet bowl. Coupled with the stench of urine, blood, and faeces, it was no wonder the constable excused himself twice to vomit behind a tree.

Eventually Liz and Pete left to get some sleep and now, hours later, body gone, the scene was quieter but curious onlookers still peppered the area.

'Liz?' Pete stuck his head out of the doorway to the men's toilet. 'Need your opinion.'

'Air freshener. Lots of air freshener.'

Pete was already back inside and she followed. Crime Scene Investigators had finished, leaving markers and fingerprint residue. There were two stalls and a urinal, a grimy sink, and air-dryer hanging on one hinge. The building was brick, with a tin roof elevated a few inches above the top row for ventilation.

'How long since anyone cleaned?' Liz asked. 'Surely there's a contract for regular servicing.'

'Have you never been in a men's loo?' Pete shook his head. 'Why was our victim here?' Pete crossed his arms. 'Miles away from his home and his workplace.'

The image of the crumbled body loomed in Liz's mind, and she forced it away. She loved Homicide but not the bodies. 'Let's step outside.'

A television crew was setting up on the other side of the tape. Liz and Pete found a spot out of their view, sheltered beneath trees but far enough from the building to lose the stench. It was icy cold though and Liz shoved her hands beneath her armpits.

'Did we contribute to this, Pete?' Liz knew nobody was responsible for a murder other than the murderer but there was a pattern emerging. 'First we speak to Ginny, and she is stran-gled. Then we chat to Jerry Black and Hardy cuts his throat.'

Pete's eyebrows flicked up. 'Haven't proved it was Hardy.'

'It was Hardy.'

'Okay. It was. You and I know that.'

'Which means he's still here in Melbourne. So why the hell can't we find him?' Liz wanted to scream. Malcolm Hardy was playing with them. Sending them on wild goose chases... 'Jerry Black was the person who sent everyone to the airport after Hardy escaped. Do you remember?'

'And his back peddling. We need another chat with Roscoe.' Pete grinned. 'We'll inform him of the death of one of his employees. But I bet you he already knows.'

Liz agreed. 'Reckon it's a warning to Roscoe.'

But a warning about what?

———

Brilliant sunlight through open curtains woke Vince. That and the pounding in his head.

He covered his eyes and sat up carefully, disturbing a blanket over his body. He hadn't put it over himself. He didn't think he had. His feet touched the floor, and he groaned as the headache followed him.

The whisky bottle was on the coffee table, the lid on. The glass was missing.

Beside the bottle were the photographs and letter. No enve-lope. He had a vague memory of ripping the white paper to shreds and tossing them onto the floor. So where were the pieces?

For that matter... who opened the curtains?

Shit.

Vince pushed himself to his feet and waited a few seconds.

The room wasn't swaying or spinning. He turned his phone on and picked up the photographs and letter and took them to the bedroom. Melanie didn't need to see that crap but he had no recollection of leaving them anywhere other than scattered on the floor. The sick feeling in his gut wasn't from a hangover.

In the kitchen, Melanie's back was to the door as she buttered toast. A glass of orange juice and a cup of coffee—its steam rising—were on a tray. The toast done, she added the plate to the tray. When she turned, her eyes widened seeing Vince and no wonder, he must look a sight with his clothes wrinkled from sleep and what was left of his hair uncombed.

'Good morning, Melly. Is that for me?'

She nodded and carried the tray very carefully to the table.

'It looks delicious. Are you having some?'

'I had breakfast earlier.' She glanced at the clock on the wall and his eyes followed. Almost ten.

'Will you sit with me while I eat?'

Another nod and she slipped into a chair.

'Where's Robbie?' Vince asked, taking a sip of coffee. He needed painkillers and a large glass of water but those could wait until Melanie left the kitchen.

'In my room. He likes playing with the spinning top.'

'He slept okay?'

'I think he misses his mother.'

Her head was down, and it wasn't just Robbie she was talking about.

'Sweetie... did you pick up those photographs and papers off the floor?'

'Yes.'

'Thank you. Um... did you look at them? I'm not cross if you did.'

'I think Robbie would like to go outside and play in the

sunshine today.' She fidgeted with her fingers, still not looking up.

Vince jumped when his phone rang. Liz's number came up. 'Sorry, Mel, I need to answer this. I'll be back in a—'

'Robbie needs to visit the litter box.' Melanie jumped up and tore out of the kitchen.

'Dammit, Vince,' he muttered, then tapped accept call. 'Hello, Liz.'

'Sorry it took so long to get back to you. We've had another murder... Chasing Hardy is... well, you know.'

He did.

'Can we meet up? I'd rather talk face to face.' Liz said.

'Melanie has an appointment with her shrink at three. But not long enough for me to leave the hospital.'

'Text me the time and place and I'll come to you.'

'Need to talk to you anyway. Think Melanie overheard Pickering threaten her father, night of the crash.'

There was a pause. Vince thought he heard a soft 'dammit' but wasn't sure.

'I can't leave what I'm doing at the moment,' Liz said.

'You don't need to. See you at three.'

He hung up before she could say anything else. He couldn't deal with Liz's well-meaning sympathy right now. Or anyone's.

———

'We're sorry for your loss,' Pete said. 'When did you last see Mr Black?'

Richard Roscoe's elbows were on his desk and his head was in his hands. To the casual observer he was shocked and distraught by the news of his colleague's death.

'Yesterday. Here, in this office. He came to ask for a few days off.' He mumbled into his palms.

'Was that normal?'

'No. But he'd not had leave for a while so I granted it. Told him to rest up because we'd need him once Hardy is found.'

'And when did Mr Black last see Hardy?' Liz asked.

Roscoe's head shot up. 'Huh? Why would he need to see him? Jerry was taken off Hardy's case after the unfortunate misunderstanding about the airport. He was completely misled by an anonymous caller, as well you know, but I thought it prudent to have him step away.'

Now why did you raise that?

'As I asked, when did the men last see each other? Was Jerry Black meeting Hardy yesterday?'

An interesting rush of colour appeared above Roscoe's collar, travelling quickly to the top of his ears. 'No of course not! Why would he?'

'Where was he going?' Pete asked.

'Going?'

'On leave. Holiday?'

Roscoe shrugged. 'Not my business. He asked for time off. I approved it. End of story.'

Certainly was for Jerry Black.

'Any idea why he was near Hopper's Crossing last night? Long way from home.' Liz asked.

'Told you he was on leave. What people do on their own time isn't my business. And I need to call his wife now, so if there's nothing else?' He made a show of picking up the phone and dialling.

Pete closed the door behind them and held his finger against his lips. There was an odd sound coming from somewhere between the office and the reception desk.

The source was in a kitchen, where behind a partly closed door, the secretary who'd brought coffee the other day was crying.

'Excuse me... ma'am, are you alright?' Liz stepped inside.

The secretary—her back to the door—jumped. She grabbed a handful of tissues from a box and did something to her face. 'I'll be right there. Sorry. Something in my eye.'

'Thanks for the coffee and biscuits the other day.' Pete went to her. 'Why are you crying? We're police officers if you need help.'

She shook her head and sniffed. 'Being silly. Just about Jerry.'

'Very sad. My condolences. Were you close?'

'Not really. We'd have a laugh sometimes. And always chatted at staff functions and the like. It just is such a shock for him to be murdered!'

'Where did you hear that?' Liz asked.

'Oh... Mr Roscoe told me it was him on the telly. They said he was visiting a men's convenience and some junkie attacked him. I can't imagine why he was even in that area because he always refers to himself as an Eastern suburbs man.'

'He'd said nothing about going on leave? Any chance he was on his way somewhere for a break?'

Her face screwed up as she thought. Then she shook her head.

'Didn't know he was on leave. I'm not his assistant but even so, I'd expect he'd have said something. Particularly as I saw him briefly yesterday. He came out of a meeting with the boss and we almost collided around a corner.'

Footsteps headed down the hallway in their direction and Liz quickly gave her card to the woman just as Roscoe stormed in.

'Why are you bothering my staff?'

'Mr Roscoe, how did you know Jerry Black was the person found last night?' Pete asked.

'I didn't. I guessed. Get a warrant if you want to come back.'

The woman shrank back against the wall, her eyes down.

'We're going.' Liz followed Pete out of the kitchen.

'What did you tell them?' Roscoe started.

'I was upset about Jerry and they just asked if I was okay. Nothing else, Mr Roscoe.'

A moment later she rushed from the kitchen going in the opposite direction.

'Hope that little shit doesn't take it out on her.' Pete kept his voice down as they headed for the main door. 'Reckon she might know something, even if she doesn't realise it.'

Liz agreed on both counts. What she didn't yet know was how to connect all the dots together.

THIRTY-FIVE

Thanks to a bit of warmth and a clear sky, Vince and Melanie sat outside to eat lunch. Robbie played close by, making them both laugh at his brave exploration of some bushes, where he hid and then pounced out at their feet.

Vince had dug up a small table and two chairs from a shed, given them a clean and placed them in a sheltered spot out of any wind. He couldn't remember the last time these had seen the light of day, but they would do the job. Mel brought Robbie's lunch out in a bowl so he wouldn't miss out.

'Why isn't there much grass, Grandad?'

'It gets hot here in summer and dries out.'

'But there's been a lot of rain. Shouldn't it be green, like at my house?' Melanie took a bite of her sandwich, her eyes curious. 'Daddy was always complaining about having to mow the garden.'

That tiny piece of lawn?

Vince gazed around, trying to see things through her eyes. They were on the side of the cottage facing Lyndall's driveway, not far from Apple's paddock. Against the cottage were the small bushes where the kitten played but they were hardy little things that nothing could kill. The ground was hard. Grass, yes, but it struggled to grow and was sporadic. The pony paddock had a couple of nice big trees as did other parts of the property, but there was precious little around here. Almost barren.

'You have a point, Melly. Not much to be done in the middle of winter, but come springtime, what if you help me come up with some ideas to make this look nicer? Your mum and I even planted some fruits trees a long time ago and I have no idea if they are even still growing.'

Mel jumped up. 'Let's find them.'

'They're further up the ridge. How about we do that tomorrow, as long as the weather is nice?'

'I guess.' She sat again. 'And I can bring Robbie.'

'Sure thing.'

Robbie decided he'd had enough of playing on his own and meowed at Mel. She scooped him up onto her lap, her lunch finished. Soon she'd want to go inside and the chance to ask her would disappear again.

But how do I not frighten her?

He took a deep breath. 'Melanie? You don't need to answer me, but I have to ask a question. Okay?'

She was tickling Robbie and nodded.

'I accidentally overheard you talking to Robbie last night.'

Melanie glanced up.

'He's a good listener. I wondered if you would feel comfortable telling me about Uncle Brad being cross with your Dad?'

Her eyes widened and she cuddled Robbie against her chest.

'I guess you know Uncle Brad was here last night? He was cross with me but I'm safe. And you are safe, sweetie.'

Her voice wavered. 'And... Robbie?'

'Especially Robbie.' Vince reached over and stroked the kitten's back. It was softer than he expected. Been years since he'd had a small animal in his life. 'Do you remember what Uncle Brad and your Dad were talking about?'

She nibbled on her lip.

'Are we seeing Doctor Raju today?'

'Yes, Mel. In a couple of hours. Would you prefer to speak to him about it?'

'Maybe.'

'Well, maybe is fine. Now, has Robbie run around out here long enough?' Vince got to his feet and collected their plates. 'I wouldn't mind taking a shower before we go.'

'I'll wash up then.' Melanie tried to pick up their empty glasses.

'You have your hands full of kitten.' Vince added the glasses to the plates. 'We'll need to leave Robbie at home when we go out, so how about you go and play with him for a while so he is nice and tired and will sleep the afternoon away?'

'I wonder if he'll like the feathered wand.'

'One way to find out.'

She was smiling again. Well, at least, she wasn't frowning.

———

Liz met Vince in the café on the ground floor.

'You look like crap, Vince.'

'Can always count on you to be honest. Not looking too flash yourself.'

'We think Malcolm Hardy struck again. Was a long night. And longer day.'

'Who's dead? Don't have the news on when Mel's around.'

'Jerry Black. Worked for Richard Roscoe.'

That flutter of interest stirred again in Vince's gut. He'd loved to have worked on this case, once upon a time. Hardy was playing with the police which made him as intriguing as he was dangerous.

Liz laughed. 'I can see it in your eyes. This is right up your alley so tell me again why you never became a detective?'

'Too much risk considering I had Susie to consider. You know, Hardy has a reputation for sending nasty messages to people who aren't co-operating. But you'd already have worked that bit out so tell me, who is he sending the messages to?'

'When Ginny was murdered we figured he thought she'd said too much to us. And to be honest... Pete and I chatted to Jerry in a public place the other day. Possibly as simple as warning off any of his other contacts who might put his freedom at risk, but still.'

'But still, what?' Vince asked.

'No point warning people not to speak to us but making no move to leave the city.'

'Maybe the answer is in the reason why he's still here then.'

Liz gazed at him. He could almost see her mind ticking over.

He checked his watch.

'How is she?' Liz asked.

'She overheard Pickering having a go at David, but she doesn't want to talk about it, at least, not with me. Or not yet. Hoping she will with the shrink. But that server at the restaurant said they know nothing?'

'He did. But Vince, what reason would Pickering have to harm his own business partner? It was probably just a disagreement. Unless you know something more?'

Nothing I want to share yet.

'You said you had some info about those plates.'

Liz took out her phone. 'I do. But you can't do your own investigation. I mean it, Vince. Promise me you won't chase this up.'

'I had a visit from Bradley Pickering last night. Wants to adopt Melanie.'

'Yeah, well, I bet that went well.'

'He handed me a stack of photographs made to look like my place. There were a few taken of the property, but the majority were from god-knows-where and make me look like an alcoholic-rabbit murdering-monster. And there's more. A letter signed by someone pretending to be Susie with a list of my transgressions.'

Liz groaned. 'Oh, Vince.'

'Idiot left them all with me, so I want to get them authenticated. Just in case.'

'Did he say he'll use them because if this is a blackmail attempt—'

'He wants David's share of the company, but he knows he's poked the dragon now. I need to go back upstairs.'

Liz came with him. They didn't speak again until in the elevator.

'Vince? I'd like to talk with Melanie about that night.'

'Yeah. Nah.'

It didn't matter that Vince would have wanted exactly the same thing under different circumstances. This was his grandchild.

'Didn't you just say she doesn't want Bradley in your home?' Liz pressed.

'I'll think about it.' He felt his fingers curling into balls.

'It could shed some—'

'You heard me, Liz.'

The elevator doors opened, and Vince stepped out. Liz held the door open to speak. 'The plates? Car belongs to a private investigator. He's done some work for PickerPack Holdings a few years ago. If you find anything, Vince, anything... you call me.'

The doors closed.

Sure Lizzie. You'll be first to know.

———

Halfway home, Melanie began to talk. She'd been quiet since leaving Doctor Raju's—or at least since saying goodbye to him. The doctor had smiled and raised a hand in acknowledgement to Vince but there'd been no summons to his office.

'Do you think Robbie missed us? He's never been left alone before,' said Melanie.

'I imagine he curled up in that fancy bed you got him and has been asleep. You'll need to spend some time playing with him and burn off some energy.'

She nodded. 'He will want to play a *lot*!'

'You are doing a good job with him, Mel.'

'Doctor Raju says Robbie sounds like a nice cat. I told him he is a nice kitten. And Doctor Raju laughed and said I was right.'

All those visits were doing some good, then.

'Grandad?'

'Melanie.'

'I was feeling a bit funny this morning. When I got up and you were asleep, I went and did some drawings to take to school. I like my art teacher a lot and she likes seeing what I draw over the holidays. Anyway, I drew the cottage. And Robbie. And Apple.'

That was a surprise.

'You drew Apple?'

'Uh huh. But then I felt like I didn't want to go back to school.'

Vince glanced over. Melanie was looking out the window like she did when something upset her.

'Do you know why you felt that way?'

'Not then. But Doctor Raju helped. He always helps.'

'Anything you'd like to share?'

Now, she turned to stare at him. Her eyes were huge.

'Mummy always came to school. She helped out there every week and... I feel funny about it all. Sad. But Doctor Raju said it is okay to feel sad and funny about school because my heart is remembering, and it will take a while to um... something about getting used to?'

'Adjust?'

'Adjust. And that Mummy and Daddy are always here in my mind and heart.'

'Doctor Raju is very wise.'

'And he makes me laugh.'

She told him a bit more about her session, all stuff that sounded sensible and helpful. They arrived home and he parked, expecting her to dive out to see Robbie, but she gave him an earnest look.

'Grandad? Mummy taught me never to read other people's mail without permission. I wanted to help tidy up.'

Relief flooded him.

'And you did a great job, Mel. Thank you. Shall we go let that kitten of yours out for a play?'

THIRTY-SIX

Bradley was tired of waiting for Abel to open his front door and pounded on it with increased intensity. He knew Abel could see him through the front door camera so unless the man was running around naked there was no reason not to answer. The flatbed ute was out the front so where the hell was he?

'Are you trying to disturb my neighbours?'

The gate squealed as Abel pushed it open. He was carrying shopping bags.

'You walk to the shops?'

'You don't?' Abel passed a handful to Bradley and unlocked the front door. 'Give me a sec to disarm the alarm.' He went inside.

'I've been here for ten minutes.'

'Close the door on the way in.'

Bradley did so and followed Abel's voice to the kitchen. He loved this house. Classy furnishings and expensive paintings. Carla had been here once and thought it lacked character, but he'd have happily copied a lot of the ideas if she'd liked them.

Abel was clever to keep the frontage uninviting. Probably kept his rates down as well as deterring burglars.

Abel was unpacking fresh, unwrapped vegetables and fruit, and fish in butcher's paper.

'Queen Vic Markets?'

'Next to growing and catching my own it's the best option.'

After putting the other bags onto the counter, Bradley pulled out a stool. 'Then buy some land and grow your own. Buy Vince's place. Lots of empty space there. Put in a lake.'

'Why are you here, boss?'

'Your phone is turned off.'

'And?' Abel began to fill a sink with water, loading vegetables into it. 'There's nothing more to do until tonight. I talked to all the parties like you told me to. But I don't need to be hassled all day by them. Nor by you.'

'I'm crapping myself if you must know.'

'About our shipment? Then leave it with me to manage later. You stay home with wifey.' Abel scrubbed vegetables with a small wire brush, tossing them onto a drying rack as he finished each one.

How can you be so calm about this? What if it is delayed again?

His heart had been racing for hours. 'My business is at stake.'

'A bit more than just your business. But having a stroke over it isn't the solution.'

'And what about Jerry Black?' Bradley slapped his hands on the counter. It hurt him more than the marble and he winced. 'Look, I'm stressing. Jumping at shadows.'

With a sigh, Abel dried his hands and took a jug of some green concoction from the fridge. He poured two glasses and when Bradley began to protest that he couldn't drink that healthy shit, added a shot of vodka to one and pushed it across.

'Jerry Black isn't our problem. Is he? Roscoe is the one who needs to jump at shadows because it looks like his client has turned on him, but it isn't our problem.' Abel drank half his glass. 'You should drink these daily. Filled with anti-oxidants and vitamins. Helps with mood swings.'

'Don't have mood swings and Carla makes me take vitamins.'

'Not natural ones like this. I'll send her the recipe.'

He was teasing Bradley. One never really knew with Abel but it had to be a joke as he and Carla weren't close. Not by a long shot. If he was any more relaxed he'd be asleep. Somehow it helped, seeing Abel unconcerned.

'Have you spoken to Roscoe?' Bradley asked.

'God no. And I'm not going near him again until Hardy packs up and leaves. He has a police tail, and I don't need any more visits to the station for nice little chats because they don't believe me that Richard and I don't have some illegal business arrangement.'

'Well, you don't.' Bradley tried the green drink and screwed his nose up. But he wanted the vodka so swallowed some anyway. 'Just makes me sick thinking that Hardy is running around killing people again and making every cop in town have an itchy trigger finger.'

'Finish your drink and go home. I meant what I said. You can leave it to me to make sure the shipping container is secure on that truck.' Abel finished his drink and wiped a finger inside the glass to collect the thick goo before sucking it off his skin.

Disgusting.

There was no way Bradley could force any more down. He got off the stool. 'I'll be there. Can't rest until this is done. And bloody Vince Carter is doing my head in. I'll be there at eleven.'

'Shut the door on the way out.' Abel took both glasses to the sink.

'And turn your phone back on.'

Carla hadn't felt like this in years. Not since the career she'd adored had come to an abrupt stop through no fault of her own. One too many inappropriate touches from her direct supervisor and she'd snapped, formally complaining to HR and finding herself out of a job within days.

Bradley had been no help in fighting for her career, discouraging her from taking legal action even as he poured jewellery and love on her to compensate. He loved having her home and probably had always hoped she'd lose interest in work. His mother never worked outside the home, and he'd mentioned that more times than she cared to think about. Of course, he was supportive. Comforting. But not really understanding that she'd just lost everything she'd worked so hard to achieve.

Once, she would have fought tooth and nail to keep her job and see justice done. But something changed. Susie had just had Melanie and her own heart was filled with an aching hunger for a child of her own. But when a year went by and there was no baby, Carla fell into a dark place. She wanted a baby so badly it hurt. Specialists found no reason why she wasn't falling pregnant and told them to just keep trying. After another year of no career and no baby, Carla became depressed.

She hid it for a while, but Susie was the one who worked out her best friend was suffering and talked her into getting some help. Bradley tried to make her happy with pretty baubles and holidays to exotic locations, but it was being able to be part of Melanie's life which eventually helped her into a happier place again. And she'd never given up hope of having her own child one day.

Until now.

'You are too old,' she said to her reflection.

She'd just finished applying makeup after a long shower, hoping the water would wash away her mood. It hadn't.

Downstairs, the front door closed.

'I'm home, baby.' Bradley called.

She hadn't started dinner. Or even thought about it.

Carla finished buttoning up her blouse and sprayed scent onto her wrists. It didn't matter how she felt inside. She had to look nice. It was the only way she'd bluff her way through the evening.

'There you are.' Bradley strode into the bedroom and tossed a jumper onto the bed. 'Remember I'm going back out tonight to oversee the first of our new shipments going out.'

'What time?'

'I'll head off around ten. But don't stay up. Containers are fiddly things to move, and the truck will be in the warehouse for the first time.' He stripped off his top and dropped that onto the jumper before disappearing into the walk-in robe. 'Have you seen my turtleneck skivvy? It'll be freezing later.'

'Third shelf on the right.'

Carla picked up the dropped clothes and deposited them into the laundry hamper tucked inside the robe. Bradley had found what he wanted and pulled the skivvy over his head. 'Sorry. I'd have done that.'

But you didn't. You never do.

And it had never mattered before.

'It's fine, honey. What would you like for dinner?'

He followed her out, catching her near the door in his arms. 'Anything. Something easy. You smell nice.'

She wiggled out of his embrace. 'Well, you don't. Whatever is that odd smell?'

'Hm? Oh, I had one of Abel's green concoctions just now. Tasted awful.'

'Smells awful.'

'He reckons I should drink them every day to increase my health. Says he'll send you some recipes.'

'I hope you're joking, Bradley. Otherwise I see divorce in our near future.'

Bradley chuckled. 'As if you'd ever leave me. We're together forever, baby. I'm going to check my emails and will be right down.' He was gone again.

It was how it was with him. Running from one thing to the next. Days and often nights full of ideas and plans and work. He expected her to be around to remind him where his clothes were or feed him. And he loved her. She loved him too.

But you can't seem to find a way to bring Melanie home to me.

———

Liz drove along a narrow country road. She was close to two hours from the station, and it was getting dark faster than she could get to her destination. The GPS flickered every so often when she went into a dead spot and the risk of having to use a normal map was real.

'Still there, Liz?'

'Yeah, just went under a bridge.'

She'd been on the phone to Pete for a few minutes.

'We've got the communications tap on Roscoe's phone but there's been no calls in or out since we set it up. Terry dropped the daytime tail. Just too stretched to follow him to his office and home again as well as watch Mrs Hardy and half a dozen others.'

'Anything back on trace from the scene of Black's murder?'

'Should get some results in the morning. Liz, where the hell are you going?'

'Told you.'

'No. You sent me some weird message about a drone.'

Maybe she hadn't been clear earlier. The opportunity to follow up this lead came while Pete was at home on a break, thanks to his intention to spend the night watching Roscoe again.

'Someone was flying a drone and noticed what looks like our missing van buried in bushland. They called their local station who have located it,' she said.

'So you're going there instead of letting local cops manage it.'

'Of course I am.'

A car approached at some speed, headlights on full beam. Liz slowed and moved onto the shoulder. There was barely room to pass with the other car barrelling down the centre. Liz looked over her shoulder as it hurtled by.

'You're not going to believe this, but I reckon Roscoe just drove in the other direction. Can't be too many cars like his around so can you check if he owns a property out here?' She gave Pete the address where she was heading.

Was he visiting someone or his own property? He owned a portfolio of investment properties around the country.

Is it too much to hope this is one of them?

She turned onto an even narrower road. There were no lights out here, no houses that she could see. Lots of trees and potholes. She braked as a dozen kangaroos bounded over the road ahead, the largest of them stopping at the verge to watch her.

'Okay, Liz. Looks like he owns five hundred hectares not far from there. Has a big house backing onto a national park where he invites special clients.'

'Oh crap. Do you suppose Hardy is one of them?'

'Wouldn't that be nice for us? Tell me again why you are driving up there alone?' Pete's tone was part amused; part annoyed. He'd hate to miss the chance to catch Hardy.

She went up a steep hill, then down into what looked like a dead end. The headlights picked up a parked patrol car. 'Where the hell is the van?' All around was dense bush and the track went no further. 'I'm there. I'll call you shortly.'

She hung up before Pete could debate it and manoeuvred the vehicle so it was next to the patrol car, headlights shining into the undergrowth. There was the faintest shape of something large hidden from the road and a couple of flashlights headed her way.

Outside, the air was crisp. Another icy night was ahead and already, mist coloured her breath. She turned on a flashlight and flicked it around. A road to nowhere. Trees, dense bushland, rocky ground.

Two constables appeared through the gloom.

'We checked nobody was inside. But haven't disturbed the scene.'

'I'll take a look.'

The van was covered with branches, a mix of long dead ones and others cut from nearby bushes. It was a miracle it was spotted by the drone. The constables helped carefully remove enough foliage to allow access to the front.

Perhaps the person who dumped the vehicle had been clever using branches, for there were scratches and marks over much of the paintwork.

'Someone went to a great deal of trouble to mess this up,' Liz said. She squatted near the front far right. 'Don't think this is from a branch.' She focused the flashlight onto a small series of dents, some with flakes of paint missing. 'Would one of you hold this and concentrate on that spot?' Handing the flashlight to a constable, she took out her phone and opened the camera.

Through the zoom of her phone, there was something else.

Red paint.

'We'll need to advise FSD.'

She didn't need forensic evidence to prove what she saw but the courts would.

Once she'd made a few phone calls, the constables were tasked with watching the van and warned it might be a long night with nobody available from Crime Scene to come up until dawn.

'I'll give your sergeant a call on my way back to make sure you're not stuck here all night.' The youngsters looked glum. 'Do you happen to know who owns the land here?'

'The van's on council land, ma'am. But on the other side of the fence,' she pointed, 'that belongs to the solicitor. The one whose client escaped custody.'

'Richard Roscoe?'

'Yes. Him.'

'Do you see him up here? Around your local town?'

'Now and then. He sometimes hosts big parties. House is a mansion, and he puts money into local businesses. You know, caterers and the like.'

'I might need one of you to show me. Let me make another phone call.'

———

'That's what happens when you stop tailing someone. Roscoe might have been ferrying Hardy back and forward to his own damned property.' Pete was in Liz's car, binoculars trained on the front of Roscoe's house from a nearby hill.

'Are you liking Hardy for the Weaver crash?'

Pete nodded. 'Dumb to dump the van close to Roscoe's property but he probably reckoned it was well hidden. Dump it and walk to the house.'

'There's so many loose ends, Pete. Why would Hardy want David dead? How would he get hold of that van, which belongs to Pickering? Does he want Bradley blamed for it? And why leave it here, where his own lawyer will be implicated?'

'With a bit of luck, the sleazebag is in that house and we'll get to ask him those and other questions before the night is through.'

Liz couldn't wait for the Critical Incident Response Team to arrive and take over. She'd been here for more than two hours, and nothing had moved at the property. Terry was on another boundary along with three other officers.

'The place is huge.' Liz had downloaded a floorplan. Roscoe only purchased it a year earlier and the original sale ad was on a 'past sales' page of the selling agent. 'Seven bedrooms, four bathrooms, cinema room, games room, indoor pool with conservatory, plus staff accommodation.'

'So where are the staff?' Pete lowered the binoculars. 'A place this size would need people to maintain it but apart from the outside lights there isn't a sign of anyone.'

'Unless Roscoe cleared them out. If he has stashed Hardy here then people knowing is a liability.'

Pete snorted. 'Hundreds of acres to bury any bodies on his own land and thousands around him.'

Terry's number came up on the phone.

'You're on speaker, boss,' said Liz.

'Richard Roscoe has been taken in for questioning screaming blue murder about how he will sue us. His fancy car is impounded and I'm not sure if he's more upset about that or being interviewed.'

Liz and Pete grinned at each other. Best news in days.

Terry continued. 'CIRT is a few minutes out. One of you come and meet me on foot back down the hill near the road.'

He hung up.

'Rock, paper, scissors?' Pete suggested.

'I know you can't resist hanging around with the real police.' Liz teased. 'Go. I'll be here making sure not even a mouse shows its face down there.'

'And if it does?' Pete opened the door.

'I'll tell you. And then I'll go and catch it. Or is it the other way around?'

'Funny. Keep your head down.'

'You too.'

Within a minute Pete was out of sight. The house was surrounded by hills with one long driveway winding for half a kilometre from the dirt road Pete was heading to. Through the binoculars the house was still quiet. No vehicles. Darkness surrounded the car.

The phone rang and Liz jumped.

Settle down.

It was Vince and she hesitated. Now wasn't the time to lose her focus. But if it was urgent...

'You okay?' She answered.

'Yeah. Bad time?'

'Stakeout.'

'Damn. Sorry, call me tomorrow,' he said.

'I have a minute.'

'Any chance I can drop into the station tomorrow? I've run into a wall with some of David's paperwork and need to escalate it. Get some official help.'

You're asking for help? What on earth is it?

'You know you can. But I don't know yet when I'll be there.'

'Where are you?'

'On a hill surrounded by bushland outside a town near Maryborough.'

Vince chuckled. 'And you sound thrilled. You're not expecting to come across Hardy out there?'

'Given how slippery he is, probably not.'

A light came on in the house on the upper floor.

'Vince, there's some movement. Can I message you in the morning?' Liz was climbing out of the car.

'Go. Be safe.' He hung up.

She dialled Pete as she popped the boot. 'There's a light on. Left corner, top floor.'

'Heading back now.'

Her vest went over the head, and she prepped the rifle. If Hardy was in that house he wasn't going to get away from them.

THIRTY-SEVEN

Liz and Terry waited back a bit but Pete went with the CIRT team to the house. He'd done enough work with them in the past to know when to get out of the way and thanks to the size of the place, covering all the bases mattered. Other police officers formed a boundary of sorts, like Liz, twenty or so metres from the main building.

All the hours of waiting came to a quick end as the unit moved in. Within a few minutes it was clear for Liz to go inside, and Terry ran around to the back of the house to help with searching the small buildings.

Pete was flicking on internal lights as she went in, muttering expletives to himself.

'Nothing?' Her heart sank. She'd been sure they were on the right path.

'One terrified housekeeper. Reckons she had a nap after Roscoe left and just woke up.'

'And I suppose she knows nothing about Malcolm Hardy.'

Tactical officers moved about the house, revisiting each room. There'd been no need for a warrant based on the belief that Hardy was inside. But unless a visual search turned up some evidence of illegal activity, they'd need to leave soon.

'I'm going to see if Terry had any luck.' Liz left without looking back. She felt sick from tiredness and the crash from the excitement.

Terry looked like she felt. 'Not giving up. We've asked for a warrant to do a full search but doubt if we'll see that before mid-morning. Local uniforms will post a guard here and at the van... unless anything happens, and they need to use them. Small town and all that.'

'I'll stay.'

He shook his head. 'Pete can stay. You and I need to go back.'

'Now?'

'I'll talk in your car. Meet me there in ten?'

Terry disappeared into the night. Liz hurried back to the house to find Pete. He brushed off the fact he was staying. 'Don't mind it. That way I'll nab the little shit if he comes back. You go home and sleep and I'll bring his head in as a trophy.'

She was still grinning at his attitude when Terry got into the car. He was straight on his phone, so she navigated her way back down the almost non-existent track to the main road—such as it was—and followed that to the small town of Talbot. It was a ten-minute drive along dark roads and came out not far from the railway station. She slowed, frowning. Maybe an hour on foot would get someone there.

Terry hung up. 'Why are we going at a snail's pace?'

'Railway station.'

He glanced back. 'Deserted for the night.'

'Just a thought. Since I'm driving, do you mind making a note for me? I'd like to check any footage from the station from the night Susie died to the time the van was reported missing.'

'What are you thinking, Lizzie?' He tapped on his phone. 'Note made.'

'Not sure. But someone dumped that van, and it may be that they went to Roscoe's house. But boss, what if it wasn't Hardy? What if whoever stole the van and ran the Weaver's off the road brought it up here for a reason? Perhaps to target Roscoe.'

Terry was quiet and Liz glanced across. He had his thinking face on. She let him ponder as they reached the open road and she accelerated.

'As in... organised crime? Not sure,' he said. 'Hardy skirted around the outside of it although heaven knows he had contacts inside it. I've spent plenty of time at Keilor and Faulkner cemeteries keeping an eye on gangland funerals.'

'Or blackmail.'

Why didn't I see this earlier?

'Blackmailing who?

'That is the million-dollar question.' Liz overtook a car. 'Why are we going back?'

'Ah. It occurred to me that visiting Bradley Pickering's warehouse might be time well served.'

Liz put her foot down.

———

Vince stared at the screen. He'd mustered the courage to read more of Susie's emails and had a handwritten list of notes to one side. She'd been one to write daily more often than not, from a cheery check in to pictures of Melanie—which he'd copied to a folder—to longer, more reflective emails. There was one he kept returning to, written a few days before she'd cut him out of her life.

We've been talking about buying another house. You know how much I love it here, but I guess David has some valid points. He reminded me how much I miss having more space around me. I miss

Apple. Remembering those days riding her and when you and I used to ride our bikes... I'd love for Melly to have some more nature-based experiences. Maybe not her own pony but at least some space to throw a ball and invent adventures in the garden. It was a good childhood for me.

Every time he read those words his breath had caught. Vince always thought she'd hated her life, not only because of losing her mother but all the things she'd missed out on. She'd only had a couple of school friends and none of the fancy clothes or expensive gadgets kids wanted. He'd forgotten this email. Forgotten reading this at the time she sent it and being shocked her experience was different from his memories.

'What else have I got wrong?'

Melanie is growing up so quickly that I can see why David is wanting this for her. It would mean going out a bit further and that's where my biggest concern is. We'd need to change schools and Melanie loves hers. It is horribly expensive and as she gets into the higher grades there will be even more pressure financially. And although I like going there to help out, they've started asking for more of my time and it already takes so many hours each week. I'd love to get back to having a career. If we moved, I think she'd understand the distance is too great. So there are pluses there.

Little pieces were fitting together. David had wanted to make big life changes for his family. Buy a new business. Move further from town. Change schools. Why?

But Dad? I have the oddest feeling there's more to this than David is saying. He isn't talking about what goes on at work much. Some days I get the impression he'd rather stay home. I know you have

*your opinions about him—and you are wrong —he loves us a lot
and has said he'll never let anything bad happen.*

Vince pushed himself back from the table. 'But you did,
David. You did let something bad happen.' He wiped a hand
across his eyes to brush away the stupid tears.

As much as he wanted to hate David, to blame David, the
man hadn't asked to be run off the road. Just maybe he had done
nothing wrong. He picked up the letter to David about success-
fully buying the other business. Was this all a new start for his
family? Had David had enough of the shady practices that
Bradley undertook?

How does this all connect together?

With a heavy heart, he returned to the emails.

———

'Chances are the place is locked up. But since I got to Roscoe's
property I've had Jerry Black in my head,' Terry said. 'No way to
prove it but he sent us to the airport deliberately that day.'

The roads were quiet at this late hour, even back in the
suburbs. They were only a few minutes from the warehouse, and
she turned onto the main road leading to its street.

'He denied it. Said he'd had a call from someone who saw
Hardy near the airport, and we sent how many officers?' Terry
shook his head. 'Would have made it a bit easier for Hardy to be
moved somewhere.'

'And you think Roscoe just did the same thing?'

A truck approached carrying a shipping container, passing by
in the direction of the docks. That place never stopped working.

Liz was bone weary and longed for her bed. But if Terry was
right...

'Perhaps. It is convenient somebody called in a sighting of

that van. It wouldn't take much to work out one of us would investigate it. And where you saw Roscoe's car? Easy for him to have sat at the top of that hill waiting and make a show of taking up the road to get attention.'

'Lots of moving parts, boss. We might have missed him. Or not connected that he had a house up there.'

'But he's a weasel and it might have been a risk worth taking.'

They rounded the corner to the warehouse.

'Go past slowly, Liz. I'll take a look.'

As usual the dead-end street was devoid of lights and movement. None of the businesses were open and the warehouse was in darkness. Liz turned at the bottom of the road and pulled the car over across the driveway.

'Dammit.' Terry muttered.

'Shall we take a look?'

'Locked up. Chain on the gate. No vehicles. We either missed something or there was nothing to miss.' Terry patted the dashboard. 'Can you drop me at the station so I can grab my car?'

A chill ran down Liz's spine. It was happening again.

'Lizzie?'

She pulled the sleeve up on her arm and held it for Terry to see. All the hairs were raised. 'I think we're being watched.'

Instead of laughing at her like Pete might have, Terry was out of the car in an instant. She followed and grabbed a large flashlight. They stood almost back-to-back on the footpath searching for any sign of movement.

'Any idea from where?' Terry kept his voice low.

'Just a weird feeling. Probably nothing.'

'Trust your instincts. Do you want to take one side of the street and I'll do the other?'

The feeling didn't leave Liz as she checked the frontage of the half dozen businesses. No sign of a person. There were a few work vans behind locked gates. If someone was inside one of the buildings they would be able to see her, and most had tinted windows so her flashlight reflected back on itself.

'Not even a rat heading for a gutter.' Terry met her at the end of the street. 'If we're being observed, they're hiding themselves.'

'Have you checked the warehouse?'

They started back up, Liz continuing to sweep the light from side to side.

'Chains on the gate. Nothing through the windows. No vehicles parked. It looks all locked up and quiet.'

Outside the warehouse, Liz shook her head. 'Sorry, Terry. I'm overtired.' She stepped around the car. 'Hang on.'

In the gutter was a half-smoked cigarette. She picked it up in an evidence bag. 'Still warm.'

'I'll make a request for an urgent comparison to the one you found near the site of the car crash. That's what you're thinking?' Terry took it from her, his eyes intense. 'That whoever smoked this one might have smoked the other?'

'That van we found... it belongs to Pickering and had red paint transference. I know there's a long bow here—'

'I reckon its getting shorter.'

So do I.

She took one final look around, her spine tingling.

THIRTY-EIGHT

The time we bought was well spent but still too close.

If the coppers arrived a bit earlier they'd have ruined everything.

She just can't leave well enough alone.

I watch her snooping around. Flashing her torch. Searching for evidence which doesn't exist. Far too careful to leave anything for them to find. But she needs to take care. Stop digging.

Or I'll stop her.

That is a pleasant thought.

They've walked the street, her and her boss. The van was a bad idea. Told him not to use it as bait. It risks our operation. No chance of pinning the crash on me but there might be questions. Interference for a while.

No matter. Our first cargo is safely away and so begins our brave new business.

She picks something up from the gutter. I can't see... her car blocks my view, but she has a plastic bag from her pocket and shows her boss.

Something startled her.

Stupid woman. Looking around as if she can see in the dark.

She's looking straight at me and doesn't know it.
Just like the kid did.

THIRTY-NINE

Bradley whistled to himself as he poured two cups of coffee and carried them to the breakfast bar. He'd cut up some fruit and had a large bowl of yoghurt and a plate of fresh croissants from the local bakery already waiting. Despite the late night, he was in good spirits and planning a relaxed day with his beautiful wife. Maybe lunch out somewhere nice.

'What are you doing?'

He hadn't heard Carla come downstairs. She stood in the doorway, still in her dressing gown which was so rare that he worried she was ill. Perhaps she'd not slept well with him being out until the early hours of the morning.

'Breakfast. And fresh coffee if you'd like some?' He crossed the floor and gave her a kiss on the cheek. 'Feeling okay?'

'A bit tired. But I should shower and dress first...'

'No. You can be a lady of leisure today and let me fuss over you a bit. Come and have some coffee to start with.'

Carla frowned but sat at the breakfast bar. 'You've gone to so much trouble.'

'Not really. No eggs or fancy crepes like you do but the croissants are straight from the bakery. Would you like butter with them? Or honey?'

With a shake of her head, Carla lifted her cup. 'This first. Thanks.'

He joined her and took a sip of his own coffee, watching her over the rim. Little lines formed around her eyes and there was something else. Sadness.

'Sorry I was so late last night but it is good news. We got the shipment off safely at last,' he said.

'Duncan Chandler's?'

'Yes. His and ours combined. First of many.'

She nodded but her mind was obviously elsewhere. Melanie?

'I was thinking... now I have a bit more time we should have a few days away. What about Bali? Or Fiji?'

'A holiday?' She looked at him as if he'd suggested they go to purgatory. 'I couldn't possibly go anywhere until Melanie's future is sorted out.'

'Four or five days won't make a difference, baby. Vince is a long way from adoption and—'

Carla stood. 'Do you even want Melanie to live with us?'

'Of course I do. You know I love her.' He reached his hand out for hers. 'We don't need to go away. Just thought you might like a break from all the recent upheaval, but I can see how much you are stressing about Mel.'

The doorbell rang and Bradley stood. 'Have your coffee and I'll be right back.'

When he swung the door open, Carter was a few metres away, his back turned. This was the last person he'd expected, and his first instinct was to slam the door closed. But what if this was about Melanie?

'Changed your mind?' After pulling the door shut, Bradley walked partway to the other man. He wasn't game to get too close in case Carter swung at him.

'Password, thanks.'

'Huh?'

Carter turned around. He didn't appear angry. Smug, possibly.

'I want the password to Susie and David's safe in their house.'

'Look, I already told you I have no idea—'

'Yet your fingerprints are on it. Just got the report and you've touched the number pad. So you get one chance to tell me what you changed the password to, or I press charges.'

Even if the police could be bothered dusting the safe, telling Carter that kind of information was illegal. Surely. He was bluffing. Except as an ex-cop he probably still knew people who'd tell him.

The door behind him clicked open.

'Vince?' Carla sounded concerned and Bradley glanced back. She was barely visible, just her face peering through a crack. 'Is Melanie okay?'

'Melanie is fine, Carla,' Carter said.

'I'll be right back in, baby. Give us a minute.'

As soon as the door closed, Carter was in his face. 'And that's the other thing. If you ever want your wife to have any access to Melanie, you'll do what I ask. Last chance. Or do I ask her if she knows it?'

'She doesn't and she's not part of this so leave her alone. I opened the safe to get the contract which David had mentioned was in there.'

Bradley told Carter the combination.

'Wasn't hard, was it?' Carter walked away.

After a second, Bradley hurried after him. 'What about Melanie? You didn't mean what you said the other night? Carla adores her. And Melanie loves Carla so it would be cruel to keep them apart.'

At his car, Carter paused and for a second, Bradley thought he was about to agree. Give him something in return for the combination.

But then he opened his door. 'You should have considered that before trying to blackmail me. I'm never letting either of you near my granddaughter again.'

Bradley's feet were like lead as Carter drove away. How could that man be so evil and selfish? How would he tell Carla? Rage bubbled up until his hands were clenched.

'You've just made the worst mistake of your life, Vince Carter. The worst.'

———

Pickering was like a garden gnome in the rear-vision mirror. Short, red-faced, and angry. But he couldn't underestimate the man and regretted his last words. Carla deserved better than her husband and he had no intention of stopping her seeing Melanie for as long as Mel wanted. Under his supervision though and away from Pickering.

He couldn't believe his bluff worked. Knowing it could be days before official results came through he'd taken a calculated risk. Odds were that Pickering had cleared the safe of anything of interest, but he needed to cross it off his long list for the morning. Mel was spending the day with Lyndall, and he had a lot of ground to cover. From here, he was going to Susie's house.

The GPS guided him the most direct route, out of this suburb and toward the freeway before following a series of increasingly quiet roads. He knew this area well and only used the GPS for its traffic hazard updates. So when the navigator's voice insisted he turn right, when he would have gone straight for a while longer, he followed out of curiosity. Had the road changed to make this a better option?

A couple of kilometres in and his stomach began to churn. He'd not been paying attention. And up until now, he'd gone out of his way to avoid coming here.

On the left was a large gum tree with chunk of its side ripped apart.

He pulled over a bit further along and sat for a while as the car idled, hands gripping the steering wheel and his back and shoulders so tense it hurt. With an abrupt twist he turned off the motor and before he could think it through, pushed the door open and climbed out.

There was no traffic. No houses in sight. Only a few cows dotted around vast paddocks on either side. The tree loomed ahead as he walked along the road. Under feet that felt heavy, the bitumen was in good condition. No potholes or dips which might contribute to a car skidding under icy conditions. It was narrow, yes, but adequate for passing other traffic, oncoming or not and the centre was clearly marked.

He came to a stop a few metres away and without his footsteps, an eerie silence fell. The air was still. Clouds were low and grey. Nothing moved.

There'd have been a terrible screeching of brakes before a sickening thud as metal met wood. Glass shattering. And then a dreadful quiet.

Did Susie know what was happening?

Had she screamed as the tree rushed toward her?

What was her final thought? Melanie?

Was Melanie awake?

How did Melanie survive-.

'No!' His head swung back. 'I want her BACK!' His voice rose into a cry of fury, of loss, of helplessness. And when he had no more breath, all that remained was a sob.

A car approached, slowing until he forced his legs to work and moved out of the way. The driver stared at him as if working out if they needed to stop and help. Vince raised a hand. 'I'm okay.'

At the base of the tree were flowers. Wreaths and bouquets, some fresh, others dying. Handwritten cards, pouring out the sorrow of friends. Lots were from Carla. Did she drive here every day? He touched a lily. Susie loved these. He'd not thought to bring flowers here and why would he? This tree took her life.

Marion used to say, 'flowers are for the living.'

How long since I've visited you, love?

His hands curled into fists, and he raised an arm as if preparing to pummel the tree. Death was everywhere. In the air and the grass and the tree and he could smell it and taste it and feel it. A card had slipped onto the ground and the words jumped out at him. He leaned down and picked it up.

'We'll all miss you Susie, and we'll be there for Melanie.'

It was signed by several people whose names he didn't recognise. Friends... from the school, perhaps.

Melanie was alive and she needed him.

He turned his back on the tree and strode to the car.

————

Vince tapped in the combination Pickering had provided, releasing a breath of relief when the barrels rolled and the door clicked open. He had a small carry bag and emptied everything into it. Passports by three. Melanie's was current. Birth certificates by three. A thick wad of cash. All one-hundred-dollar bills and without counting it, Vince estimated ten thousand dollars. A lot of cash to have sitting in a safe. And interesting that Pickering hadn't absconded with it.

At the bottom was a thick yellow envelope. Sealed. This was important somehow. Vince closed the safe and changed the combination. The robe was still bare and there was no point returning the contents, still strewn on the bed.

He'd ask Carla if she'd help with the clothes. She kept going on about wanting to help and this was too hard for him. He didn't care if she kept them, sold them, or gave them away but unless Melanie particularly wanted an item as a keepsake, then he'd be pleased to have that off his plate. He'd speak to Carla once Mel was back at school. For now, he collected Susie and David's jewellery so Melanie could decide, when she was ready, what she'd like to keep.

Vince packed up almost all the rest of Melanie's room, carefully placing her clothes, shoes, books, toys, and knick-knacks into more suitcases from the cupboard. There was little left in there now. Furniture he'd transport across after school holidays.

Bags packed into the car, he emptied the fridge and freezer. Much of the refrigerated goods went into a bin which he'd leave out for collection. The freezer was packed with homemade meals, and odds and ends such as ice cream and vegetables. He couldn't bear the idea of eating those meals. Every bite would be a reminder too hard to stomach. Sliding them all into a freezer bag, he went to the house next door and tapped.

'Susan's papa, buongiorno.'

'Good morning, Mrs Rionetti. I wondered if you could use these... or know someone who could?' He opened the bag to show her. 'Susie made them all.'

'Not for you and little one?'

He shook his head.

'I take. Share with others. And call me Rosa. Come, carry it in for me.' Mrs Rionetti led the way to her kitchen and Vince helped her stow the meals in her freezer. Then she took several jars from her cupboard and put them in the bag before he could protest. 'I make. Passata. Artichoke. Stuffed peppers. Keep in cupboard. Eat by summer time.'

'You are too kind. Thank you, Rosa.'

At the front door, she pointed diagonally to a house a few doors up. 'Did police find out who had the van?'

'Which van?'

'That sad night. Before family left in car, black van in that driveway. Not belong in street.'

Heart thudding, he took another look at the house. A vehicle parked there would have an excellent view of Susie's house, particularly the front rooms and the driveway.

'Did you see the driver?'

'Too far. Too dark. And windows had ... er, made darker?'

'Tinting?

'Ci. David drove away and van followed.'

Does anyone have security cameras? Please let there be.

'The other day, when the police did the door knock about the break-in... did you tell the officer about it?'

She nodded. 'He wrote it down.'

'One of my friends who is a police detective might come and see you. Is that okay?'

Mrs Rionetti patted his arm. 'Send your friend and I tell again. And kiss Melanie from Rosa.'

Back in the house he texted Liz.

> Have new information. Are you at the station?

He emptied the contents of the pantry into two big boxes and stowed those on the back seat of the car. All the perishables were out of the house. The appliances could be switched off and the house left locked up until he had more time to attend to it.

For now, he had to see Liz. And find whichever idiot in a uniform had vital information they'd not bothered to pass on.

FORTY

Liz's legs were cramping from standing still in front of the whiteboard for so long. Might have been ten minutes or an hour, but since the last update was added, she'd forced her tired brain to make connections and now her body was protesting.

Too much driving, too much sitting in a car, too much running.

And very little to show for it all.

'Coffee?' Terry appeared from nowhere and pushed a cup into her hands. 'What are you thinking?'

'That I'd like more sleep. And a vacation, boss.'

He chuckled. 'You and me both.'

The coffee cup warmed fingers she'd not noticed were cold. Terry had bought it from a café instead of making the crap they usually tolerated, and it was good.

She remembered his question. 'There's a connection between Malcolm Hardy and PickerPack... but what the hell is it?' Her finger stabbed the photograph of Abel and Roscoe on the pier. 'These two aren't friends. Friends don't behave that way so who has a hold over who?'

'What do we know about Farrelly? Beyond what we've previously discussed.'

He's a sleazy little shit?

'Nothing comes up. No odd history or police record.'

'Then look again, Liz. Do a deep dive into the life and times of Abel Farrelly. Pete should be back on board soon so put him onto to it if you want.'

'Nah. I'm really curious. The other thing is where did Farrelly and Pickering meet? What is really going on in that warehouse? What do we know about Pickering?'

'I can help with the last question.'

Both swung around. Vince was inside the door, folder under an arm and his eyes devouring the information on the white-board. Terry put his hand up to turn it.

'Wait a sec, mate.' Vince closed in. 'I have some new informa-tion and letting me take a quick look at what you've got might help. You know I have good instincts.'

'Ten seconds.'

Terry stepped out of the way and took a sip of his coffee.

Vince closed in on the board, a hand hovering just inches from the photos and words. It was his way of focusing on the pieces, at least, he'd told Liz that more than once. He paused at the image of Farrelly and Roscoe and moved on to a shadowy image of the van.

'Who heads up the uniforms these days?'

'Why?'

He turned his back on the whiteboard and gazed at Liz. 'Susie's neighbour saw a black van in the street the night of the crash. It was parked in a nearby driveway and followed their car when they left. Mrs Rionetti gave this information to whoever asked her about the break in. Now, either they didn't think it was important enough to pass on, or you know about it and have done nothing.'

'We didn't know, Vince. But I will tell you—that van there? It is at the garage now and is likely the vehicle involved in the crash.'

His shoulders dropped as if releasing long-held tension. 'Where was it found?'

'Dumped up north. It was stolen.'

'Who owns it?'

Terry must have decided they'd done enough sharing. 'You said you could help with Pickering's background.'

With a slight smile to acknowledge he was being shut out of any more details about the van, Vince nodded. 'Bradley didn't set out to own a business. He had grand plans for his life, but university wasn't kind to him and he failed his final exams. Instead of doing another year and taking another go, he married Carla, who had money behind her. She comes from a decent family. Hard working. Self-made. And when her parents retired and moved to warmer weather, they gifted her the warehouse.'

'She owns it?' Liz asked. She hadn't seen that coming.

'She gave it to her husband. Carla was on her way to being an executive in a major company when she ruffled feathers by daring to call out workplace harassment. By then, Bradley was so involved in building up his tiny empire that she was left out in the cold.'

Still don't like her. Less now if anything for not standing up for herself.

These unkind thoughts bothered Liz and she put it to the back of her mind. 'Vince, you said Pickering failed his tertiary studies. Do you know what they were?'

'You don't? He had dreams of becoming a barrister, eventually. He studied law.'

Her eyes flew to Terry's, and she could imagine his thoughts were the same as hers. Was it possible Pickering knew Roscoe despite protesting he didn't? Was Farrelly acting as a go between and if so, why?

'That's helpful, Vince. How is Melanie?' Terry asked.

'Good. She's at Lyndall's house today to let me cover some ground without her. Hoping she won't come home with another kitten.' He opened the folder. 'I found an envelope in one of David's jackets when I was emptying the closet. He just bought a business.'

'What?' Liz took the letter he offered and scanned it. 'Was he leaving PickerPack?'

'Looks it. But Pickering has said nothing about it, just that he wants to buy David's share in his business and be done with it. My gut says he has no idea... or only found out recently,' Vince said. 'I also found about ten thousand in cash in the safe.'

'You got into the safe?'

She'd not seen a report on the fingerprints.

He grinned. 'I may have lied a bit.'

Terry muffled a laugh.

'What else was in there?' Liz asked. 'That envelope?'

Vince glanced at the large and fat yellow envelope with no writing. 'Haven't opened it yet. What do I do with the cash? What if it is illegally sourced?' He held out a wad of notes. 'All hundreds by the look of them and new.'

After putting down his coffee, Terry located an evidence bag and opened it for Vince to drop the money into. 'Leave it with me. Best to check it's not sus. Do you reckon he'd keep that amount on hand?'

'No idea. But Melanie's school fees haven't been paid this year and David gave the principal some sob story about his business going under. More likely he was pouring everything into buying himself and family a new life. And he'd been talking to Susie last year about moving further out onto a bigger block of land.'

'Speaking of land, don't you have a cow to milk or something?' Pete tossed keys onto his desk then perched on the corner, arms crossed.

'Caught Hardy yet?' Vince countered. 'Or is the body count gonna keep rising on your watch?'

Pete was straight onto his feet and Terry held up a hand.

'Enough already, you two. Vince, I'll let you know about the money.'

Vince glanced at the whiteboard, then at Liz. 'Melanie did a new drawing of you.'

'Tell her I'll come and see it soon.' She couldn't help smiling. But the minute Vince was out of the room the smile faded and she glared at Pete. 'Pull that crap anymore and I'll ditch you, mate.'

Pete's eyebrows almost touched his hairline. 'Rather have that dinosaur back? Be my guest.'

Yes. Yes, I'd have Vince as my partner again in a heartbeat. But I'm stuck with you.

'Just saying... lay off him.'

Terry was ignoring them both and Liz joined him at the whiteboard and touched the image of the van. 'He doesn't know it belongs to Pickering,' she said.

'Which brings me to my question, Liz. Was it stolen, or did Pickering... or one of his associates, use it to run David Weaver off the road?'

———

As annoying as McNamara was, he'd arrived at a good time. Vince had no intention of opening the envelope around anyone else and only carried it into the station to keep it safe. It was probably nothing of importance but might contain personal stuff best kept from other people's eyes.

Next stop would be Lygon Street. Again, he used the GPS.

Although he knew all of these routes, he had a reason for navigating them today. Later, he'd download the data of all the trips and analyse them. Something hadn't sat right with him for days about where the crash occurred and there had to be an answer somewhere beyond assurances that everyone was in the place they were meant to be.

The whiteboard at the station had been interesting. Informative. And confusing.

Back in his time as a sergeant—in charge of a large unit of often young officers—he'd dissected info boards more times than he cared to remember. There was an order to them. A way of connecting details visually or with a few words which trumped written reports or verbal discussions.

Marion used to say he had a talent for seeing beyond the obvious. He'd believed her then and trusted his instincts. Often, a picture would correlate with a report, or a witness statement, and he'd be the first to see a pattern. Or the only one to see it.

Which is why I knew there was a gunman at the top of the stairs at the march that day.

He had to slow down. The speedo said he was ten kilometres above the limit.

'God sake, Vince. Stay on track. Focus on the issues at hand.'

The property owned by Roscoe had something sinister about it. A sprawling parcel of land in the back of nowhere was ideal to hide criminals. Was that where the van was dumped? On Roscoe's land?

The look between Lizzie and Terry hadn't gone unnoticed. His backstory of Pickering had filled in some blanks—possibly made a connection clear. They thought Pickering and Roscoe knew each other and why wouldn't they? Abel Farrelly in that photo on the board, deep in discussion with the lawyer, proved there had to be more than a chance meeting late at night on Altona Beach.

For the first time in a long time, he wished he still carried a badge.

Lygon Street was impossible to park on this early in the day, so Vince left the car in a side street and walked to Spironi's. The 'closed' sign was turned and he checked the time. A bit too early for lunch service although there were signs the chefs were there. He crossed to the other side, letting trams and cars pass before weaving across to get a coffee at a café. From a window seat he'd see any staff arrive. And because he had no idea which one had overheard the argument, he'd stay there until he spoke to every one of them.

———

The staff at Spironi's were less than helpful but Vince admired their solidarity in repeating the same answers to his questions.

'Do you remember Susie Weaver and her family?'

Yes.

'Did you witness an argument between David and Bradley?'

No.

'Did you notice anything out of the ordinary?'

No.

'Was Melanie upset at any stage?'

No idea.

Customers were beginning to come in and a waiter with the tag of 'Mike' on his apron was agitated by Vince's presence. 'If you're not going to have a table and order then you need to leave, sir.'

'If I do that, will you be honest with me?'

'Are you police?' Mike asked, waving his arm at one of the other staff to attend a couple who stood inside the door. 'I've already told them nothing happened.'

'Someone told my ex-partner that another member of the

staff here overheard a heated discussion that night. Are you either of those people she spoke to?'

Mike's face hardened. 'Please leave, sir.'

'I'll use your restroom first.'

'That is for customers only.'

'I've eaten here in the past. Gotta count for something.'

With a shake of his head, Mike walked away.

Vince used the restroom and waited inside the door. The ladies room was next to this so if Melanie had been in there, she might have overheard her father having words with Pickering if they were close by.

He stepped into the hallway. The lights weren't on and even if they were he doubted it would add much to the dingy space which only had two bare lightbulbs for the entire length. To his left and around the corner was the dining area. Diagonally across was the door to the kitchen, complete with raised voices and banging pots. Right was the exit. If he'd wanted to argue with someone, away from curious ears, he'd have been between here and the exit. Vince positioned himself there.

Had someone come out of the kitchen, they'd see him.

Same with the restrooms.

'What did you stumble into, Melly?' He murmured.

Voices approached from the dining area, and he let himself out through the exit, stopping so his eyes could adjust to the relative brightness outside. He was in a narrow alley made smaller by dumpsters and a row of cars parked behind each other. And leaning against the wall, a young man wearing the Spironi's apron had his eyes down concentrating on a game on his phone.

He spoke without looking up. 'Has he gone, Mike?'

Vince made it all the way to him before answering. 'Has he left the restaurant? Yup. I'd like a word, son.'

FORTY-ONE

'Marco? Well, you must be.' Vince rested the palm of his hand on the wall near the waiter's head, effectively blocking him from running thanks to the dumpster on his other side.

The kid shrank back. 'I'm not Marco.'

'Apron says otherwise.'

'Um... not mine. Borrowed.'

'Your colleagues inside have been most helpful, Marco,' Vince said. 'Ran through the events of the evening David Weaver, Bradley Pickering, and their families were here for the final time together.'

'I wasn't working.'

There was panic in the kid's eyes. Someone had threatened him. Or blackmailed him.

'Yes you were. Mike's confirmed it.'

Marco expressed his feelings about that in a string of expletives. Even one Vince had never heard.

'Feel better? Good. Look, I'm not here to arrest you. Not this time. And we can keep this conversation between us? Okay?'

Perhaps his run of bluffing people was at an end. Marco's lips were clamped together. Was it fear? Or fear of losing something if he talked?

'We both know you overheard an argument between David and Bradley. I'm not interested in you... not unless you refuse to help me.'

'Wadda you want?'

'The little girl. Melanie? Did she hear what they said?'

Marco's eyes darted left and right and then back to Vince's. 'How could I know what she heard?'

'Did you see her near them?'

Beads of perspiration formed on Marco's forehead.

Give me something.

'She's a little girl, mate. Whole life ahead of her. Did you know she was in the back seat of the car when a van hit it and forced it into a tree? She saw her parents die. Did you know she is all alone in the world apart from her grandfather? She'll never see her mum again. Never hug her. Or her dad.'

'Then you'd better keep her safe.' Marco ducked under Vince's arm and ran.

'Holy shit.' Vince took off after him.

Marco was gone by the time he reached the end of the alley. As he doubled over, desperately drawing in air, the words ran through his mind over and over.

You'd better keep her safe.

————

Short of a road trip to Gippsland, the best Liz could do was trawl through years' worth of news reports from Abel Farrelly's home town of Moe. She'd been there a couple of times on the way to other destinations and remembered little other than a sense of a town not ageing well despite its pretty aspect. Lots of empty shops.

Statistically, the town had a high crime rate compared to the state average. Almost double. Income was lower. Not unlike many small towns which once flourished but over the decades had failed to grow and thrive.

Beginning the year of Farrelly's birth, she searched for his surname. There was mention of his birth as the first child to his parents. No later children appeared. His father owned a hardware store which burned to the ground in a non-suspicious fire when Farrelly was a young teen. The newspaper article described it as a loss to the town and that it was lucky nobody was hurt.

She found the obituary of his parents only two years on... killed in a house fire.

'Are you serious?'

This had made the front page of the local paper with a disturbing image of the destroyed home and a body in a bag being carried out. Abel was described as an orphan with no remaining family. He was fifteen. Later reports advised the fire was deemed accidental after a fireplace mishap. Six months on was a sports article about promising AFL players Abel Farrelly and Richard Roscoe being suspended from the local football grand final for undisclosed club offences.

Liz cut and pasted all the references and printed off one document, complete with links. As minors, Farrelly or Roscoe would have had any disciplinary action kept quiet but someone would know. It took several phone calls to track down the man who'd coached the team that year.

'My goodness, that was half a lifetime ago, officer.' Bob Kirk now lived in Queensland in his retirement. 'That team suffered with the loss of those two boys but I had no choice. Break the rules, lose your place.'

'What rules in particular?'

'Am I allowed to speak of it? I don't have to make a formal statement do I?'

'Not at all. This is purely to help me piece together the early lives of Abel and Richard. Anything at all you remember will make a difference.'

'Well, in that case, I remember being disappointed in Richard. He came from a good family, a stable family. Both boys were bright, but Richard had the ability to do anything with his life. Abel... well, his background was different.'

'With his parents' dying?' Liz scribbled notes.

'Before then. I don't usually speak ill of the dead, but his father was a nasty piece of work. The kid worked in that hardware shop of his from a young age and was knocked to the ground in front of customers more than once. When they died, Abel went to live with Richard's family and I thought it would help but if anything, he led Richard down a bad path.'

'Mr Kirk, do you recall why they were suspended?'

'After the fuss Richard Roscoe senior made when I made that decision?' He snorted. 'Stuck to my guns despite him telling me boys will be boys. Rubbish. Boys are no different from anyone else and if they blackmail a fellow team member then they get what's coming. Lucky it wasn't escalated to the police.'

'Blackmail?'

'They got photos of another lad kissing a girl—means nothing these days but the kid was from a strict religious family and would have been in a helluva lot of trouble. Never found out how far it went but those two had the lad scared and paying them weekly. Wasn't having that nonsense in my team.'

After finishing the call, Liz returned to the whiteboard.

Farrelly and Roscoe on the pier that night had seemed such an odd pairing. The argument, the push, and then the shaking of hands. Were they even friends or was this adult relationship connected to their past behaviour? A lawyer and a warehouse foreman on opposite ends of the professional and financial world. At least, on the surface.

'What did the coach say?'

Pete joined her to pin up a printed image.

'That Farrelly and Roscoe not only lived in the same house as teens but blackmailed another kid for a while. Farrelly was abused at home. The family business burned down when he was thirteen and the family house two years later and both parents died in it.'

'Shit. That's a whole lot of backstory from one phone call.' He pointed at the image. 'All I have is this shadowy figure at Talbot railway station.'

Liz peered closer. A man waited on the dark platform, hands in the pockets of an overcoat and a hat pulled down. 'Is that the best one?'

'So far. I've asked local police to talk to their local traders who have cameras on the streets he might have taken but I think he'd have kept to back roads.'

Liz patted his shoulder. 'Okay, I'll keep you for a bit longer. Good work.'

'Before you two get too lovey-dovey, Vince just called. He's at Spironi's and is about to get himself into trouble.' Terry waved them out. 'Remind him he's not a cop, please.'

———

'He misrepresented himself as a police officer! Isn't that illegal?' Mike's face was red and he waved his arms around.

Pete nodded solemnly, clearly enjoying the situation they'd walked into. He'd be loving the idea that he could turn the tables and get Vince in trouble as payback for the investigation into Pete which almost ended his career all those years ago. He'd been exonerated but Vince had done the right thing reporting Pete's suspicious behaviour at the time. Not that Pete saw it that way.

They were in the alley behind Spironi's with Mike and Vince, who'd been shouting at each other when they arrived. Liz immediately sent Vince to the opposite side with an 'I'll get to you shortly' before trying to placate the waiter. He was getting more worked up and she'd had enough.

'Mike, do you remember me having a meal here recently? I asked about the night the Weavers were here.'

'No.'

'Sure you do. You told me they were nice people. Good customers. You remembered their little girl.'

He glared across at Vince, who stood, legs apart and arms crossed, staring back. 'He chased off my waiter.'

'Who was hiding out here waiting for you to give him the all clear.'

'Vince, shut up.' Liz turned her back to him. 'Mike, ignore him for the minute please. You told me that Marco had served their table and that he mentioned overhearing an argument. Up past the restrooms, you told me.'

Finally meeting her eyes, Mike nodded. 'I did say that.'

Oh thank heaven!

'When I came back another time and spoke to Marco, he denied it. Said you were mistaken, so if you sent him out here while Vince was inside asking questions about him, there must be a reason.'

'He was scared.'

'Of what?'

'Ask Marco,' Mike said.

'I'll need his address and phone number. Did someone threaten him? Because we can offer protection.'

Mike's mouth opened and closed again.

'Something happened in your restaurant, Mike. We think it led to the car crash which took the life of Vince's daughter.'

'You should have said.' Mike gazed at Vince. 'I did not know you were her father.'

Vince kept his mouth shut for once.

'Marco was told to stay quiet about what he heard or saw, and I have no more details. I'll get his address.' Mike made for the back door, Pete on his heels.

Liz took a deep breath. This was progress.

'I knew he was hiding something.'

'This is time I needed to use elsewhere, Vince.'

He didn't look the least bit ashamed of himself and why would he?

'Lizzie, before your idiot partner comes back, Marco said something which is bugging me. He told me I'd better keep Melanie safe.'

'Context?'

'I'd said she only had her grandfather left in the world now.'

'He didn't tell *you* to be careful?'

'No. To keep her safe.' He looked down for a moment and muttered something she didn't catch.

'Vince?'

'Maybe... okay, you can talk to her. About that night.' His expression, when he raised his head, hurt her to see. This was painful for him.

'Do you want me to come to you... or bring her to the station?'

'Am I right to go? I have ground to cover before I pick her up.'

'Sure. Let me know?'

He nodded and turned on his heel. In a moment he was out of sight. He was on some kind of mission today, focused. Determined.

Just stay out of trouble.

———

Marco wasn't at his apartment and a door knock of his immediate neighbours didn't help. Nobody knew anything.

'Can't sit here waiting for him, Liz.' For someone complaining about waiting in the car, Pete looked comfortable. He took a large bite of the burger he'd just picked up.

'We'll stay until you finish eating. Which smells disgusting.' She wound down a window. 'I'd really like to chat to young Marco and find out who he met with.'

'Pickering.'

'Most obvious choice. But what if Pickering is in the middle of something criminal? Something bigger than we know. All he'd need to do is let slip he had that argument and one of his cronies might step in. I'm not seeing where Hardy fits in. Nor Roscoe and now he and his fancy car are cut loose with no evidence. '

Her phone beeped a message. Vince.

> After dinner is fine if you like.

It was going to be another long day.

> Will do my best. Otherwise tomorrow morning?

'Pete, you've had a bit to do with child witnesses... I have permission to speak to Melanie Weaver about the restaurant, maybe even the car crash.'

He chewed for a while, thinking. Pete's experience was broader than hers thanks to undercover assignments and time working closely with Terry back in organised crime. She always trusted him with serious matters. It was the peripheral stuff which annoyed her.

'She's a smart little cookie, which means she's sensitive as well. For whatever reason—shock, fear, disbelief—she's closed off the normal channels of communication. Trauma. As long as she remembers, you'll find a way if you tiptoe. But don't under-estimate her. If you are direct with your questions, in a gentle way, she'll feel more trusting.'

Crap. How'd did you get so wise?

'I think she likes me so that's a start. The other thing is that she draws a lot. Like, everything.'

'Get her to draw what happened.' Pete shoved the rest of the burger into his mouth.

After another look down and across the road, with no sign of Marco, Liz started the car. She'd ask for someone to watch for him. Sooner or later he'd go back to Spironi's or home. It wasn't as if anyone else was looking for him.

FORTY-TWO

Mistake one. Believing money talks to all people.

Mistake two. Leaving a witness to their own devices.

Mistake three? This one is his. What fool tells me he thinks he needs to talk to the police? What part of paying for his funeral did he not understand?

Little man wants more money to keep quiet and that made me laugh and laugh.

I like this alley.

No cameras.

Almost no foot traffic.

He wants to go back to work so meeting him here suits us both.

He thinks he'll see the inside of that restaurant again.

He's a dead fool walking.

FORTY-THREE

He shouldn't have agreed to let Liz come over later. Melanie didn't need any pressure to talk about the night of the accident. Vince sat in his car a bit down the road from Pickering's warehouse, where he'd been for twenty minutes. He checked the time. Again. No sign of Pickering or Farrelly, their cars, or for that matter, any movement inside. It was a weekday and it made no sense the place was closed.

Unless you're really going under.

Somehow he doubted it. Pickering was too cocky at his house this morning. At least until he found out why Vince was there.

The envelope was on the passenger seat. He could multitask.

He slid a key under the flap and opened it, emptying the contents onto the seat.

Two white, sealed envelopes were inside, along with a set of keys, a mobile phone, and more cash in crisp, one-hundred-dollar notes. Another ten grand or so. The mobile was flat, but his charger fitted so he plugged it in. The keys were a mix, including a post office box key and what might be a house key.

The first envelope was addressed to Mrs McCoy at Melanie's school.

Unsure whether to open it, he put it down.

Lyndall's number came up as his phone rang and he grabbed it.

'That was fast. Before you ask, Melanie is fine. So am I.' There was humour in her tone and Vince's heart began to beat again.

'What's up?'

'My farrier called. He's coming over first thing tomorrow to do the donkeys' feet so bring that pony of yours up when you get home and he'll trim hers. She can go in with them for the night. Bit of company won't hurt her.'

'She isn't lonely but could use a trim. I should be home in a couple of hours.'

'Well we're about to roll pastry for homemade sausage rolls so don't you hurry. We plan to make an apple tart as well, so it is in your best interests to let Melanie stay for another three hours. Or more.'

'Thank you, Lyndall.'

'My pleasure, darlin'.'

She hung up.

Without her this would be harder. Impossible, because he'd never have exposed Melanie to the police station or Spironi's. Hopefully, he wouldn't need to keep asking Lyndall for so much help soon. He just had to put the puzzle together.

The other envelope was not addressed to anyone. Inside were two documents. One letter and a copy of a will. It was in Susie and David's names and dated just three months ago.

His eyes closed. How could he read this knowing it might destroy any chance of him adopting, or even having custody of Melanie? If Susie had decided she'd waited long enough for her father to become a better man...

Melanie needs me.

Was there another copy? Surely they'd lodged it with some-one, but their lawyer only spoke of the original from years ago.

'I won't let you go, Mel. I promise I won't.'

He opened his eyes. Assuming this was the only copy he could keep it hidden. Never let it see the light of day. Go through the motions already underway to secure her future.

Fearing the worst, he held it up to read.

A car turned into the street and then, into the warehouse driveway, stopping at the locked gates. A man stepped out, checked his phone, and sank back inside. Vince shoved every-thing into the glovebox.

What was Richard Roscoe doing here?

The Lexus reversed out and headed back the way it came.

Vince started the motor and followed.

———

It was a subdued group of detectives in the office when Terry called a mid-afternoon meeting. Many had been up at Talbot the previous night while others were tired from too-long hours working on other aspects of the Hardy case. Liz figured she had it better than some, with her five hours or so of sleep, even if it was unsettled.

A platter of deli goods—cheese, meats, crackers and the like —was in the middle of four tables all pushed together, and everyone was nibbling. Terry was a decent boss. One who knew how to regenerate flagging spirits.

He slowly paced back and forth in the space between the tables and the whiteboard, occasionally stopping when one of the detectives spoke. Like now.

Pete had constructed something out of two crackers with a large piece of hard cheese, sundried tomato, salami, and relish wedged between them and he waved it around as he spoke. Liz couldn't take her eyes off it as she waited for it to explode all over him.

'Let me get this straight, Terry. From that whole exercise last night we have nothing. No evidence Hardy has ever visited Roscoe's property. No prints from the van we recovered. And nothing from Roscoe's car, or our interview with him.'

Terry nodded. 'Yup. Yup. Yup, and... yup.'

'Should have let me interrogate him.' Pete finally bit into his creation.

'It isn't a lost cause. What we know is that someone dumped that van close enough to Roscoe's property—maybe to make him a suspect in the crash which killed the Weavers. And another someone—probably the same person—made sure we knew it was there.'

'Yeah, but what nutcase would draw attention to themselves that way?' One of the detectives asked and several others nodded.

Liz got to her feet and went to the whiteboard, grabbing a marker.

Terry glanced at her but kept talking. 'No reason to believe Roscoe had anything to do with this. Whoever dumped it there may very well have done so in order to control him.'

She drew a line between individual pictures of Farrelly and Roscoe and above it wrote 'history of blackmailing others'. Then beneath the line, 'who is being blackmailed now?'.

'Care to share your thoughts, Lizzie?'

Not certain I know what they are.

Nevertheless, she faced the room and everyone, even Pete, gave her their attention.

'A short while ago I spoke to a past coach of the Moe footie club about these men. Back then they were teenagers and Farrelly lived with the Roscoe family after the death of his parents in a house fire. According to the coach, the two of them were blackmailing another team mate and he suspended them from playing in the finals. There'd have to have been a lot of anger and resentment and sometimes that's enough to bond people.'

'Who lit the fire?' Someone asked.

'It was ruled an accident. However...' she tapped on Farrelly's image, 'his father's hardware shop burned to the ground two years earlier *and* he was knocked about as a kid by his dad.'

Pete began creating another cracker sandwich. 'If the powers that be who regulate law firms get wind of Roscoe's past, it might cause some issues for him.' He glanced up with a grin. 'I'd love to chat to him knowing this. See if Farrelly is using their shared history to get something from him.'

'And at the same time, a chat with Farrelly, raising those juvenile incidents, might rattle his cage for once,' Liz said. 'But what are the stakes? Malcolm Hardy has to fit in here some-where, but I'll be damned if I can see where.'

And why were we sent to find the van last night?

'Liz and Pete, you pick up Farrelly. I'll get Roscoe.' Terry surveyed the room with a slight smile. 'If anyone hasn't slept since last night then go home. The rest of you get back to going through the footage from the camera feeds from the areas around the two killings and Talbot.'

'Yeah... but this food won't eat itself.' Pete began loading a napkin with goodies.

———

To Vince's disappointment, Roscoe did nothing more than drive back to his offices.

The trek across town had eaten into his plans—he'd hoped to take a look at the business David had put the deposit on but time was against him and he headed home.

After a stop at the supermarket he got back to the cottage as the light began to change. Leaving the items from Susie's house for later, he took the shopping inside and quickly changed into boots and went to collect Apple.

'I hope you're not lonely, old girl,' he said as he clipped a lead to her headstall. She nuzzled his pockets then snorted when no treat was forthcoming. 'Lyndall says you need some company.'

He unlocked the side gate and she happily followed him out. The gate was Lyndall's idea years ago when Susie was young and used to ride up to see her. It saved going down to the road and back up and there was a track she could access from a bit further leading to countless acres of riding trails. Not far up there was where he and Susie planted those fruit trees. The land was his but thanks to the steep nature of the back of his place, was more accessible from Lyndall's long driveway.

It took him and Apple longer than he expected with the pony stopping every so often to grab a mouthful of the grass which must have been sufficiently different from that in her paddock to get her attention. By the time he went around the back of the house, Lyndall was striding across from a smaller paddock with multiple three-sided shelters and half a dozen donkeys munching on a pile of fresh hay.

'Come on, Apple, they'll leave none for you if we don't get you in there.'

'Hi Grandad!' Melanie waved from a spacious open deck.

He waved back. 'All packed up?'

'Almost.' She ran back into the house.

'She'll sleep well,' Lyndall said. She opened the gate, gently pushing back one of the donkeys who wanted to greet Apple. 'Not much she hasn't done today, other than help me move this lot, but when I did she stayed in sight the whole time.'

Lead unclipped, Apple trotted to the main group, nickering

as they looked up. She occasionally spent time with them and did seem happy about being here again.

'Get everything done?' Lyndall closed and secured the gate.

'Not quite. Was side tracked a couple of times but it's been productive. More information to look at but I think it will be in Melanie's best interests.'

She gave him one of the long, thoughtful looks which always felt like she knew his thoughts. 'Having you as her custodian is the number one best interest she has. Melanie doesn't need fancy. She needs authentic. Speaking of which, there is a home-made apple tart and plenty of sausage rolls to take home and she's helped with every part of making them.' They reached the steps to the deck. 'Like to come in?'

Melanie pushed the back door open, struggling with her good arm to carry an oversized bag.

'Or maybe not this time.' Lyndall chuckled as Vince hurried to take the bag.

'We made the best pie ever!'

'In that case, we should take it home and try it.'

'Grandad, not until after dinner.' Melanie tried to be serious, but her eyes were bright and happy. She threw her arms around Lyndall's waist. 'You're the best, Lyndall.'

If those were tears forming in her eyes, Lyndall made it clear she didn't want them seen, turning her head away and patting Melanie's back. 'You take your grandfather home, darlin' and remember to put the baked goods into the fridge to keep them fresh.'

One day I hope you'll share your story with me.

'Time to go, so say thank you,' Vince said.

Melanie stepped back. 'Thank you for having me.'

'You are most welcome.'

'From me as well.' Vince reached for Melanie's hand with his spare one. 'I'll be up in the morning to pay the farrier and bring Apple home.'

'No rush. She's welcome to visit. Just like you two.' Lyndall headed back to the paddock with a wave.

When they reached the path to the fruit trees, Vince pointed it out. 'What if we go for a walk there tomorrow? See if those trees have anything to pick. Might be something the birds didn't get.'

'Where does the track go?' Melanie peered into the near darkness. 'I can't see far enough.'

'It weaves along the back of the block then up a bit higher so you can look down on our cottage. After that there's a valley behind the ridge where your mum used to ride Apple. She'd sometimes take a little picnic and be gone for hours.'

'On the pony?'

'On the pony.'

'Apple the pony. And now we have swapped her for apple the pie.' She began to giggle, and Vince laughed along with her as they headed home.

FORTY-FOUR

Carla couldn't believe what they'd accomplished in a day. Melanie's new bedroom was taking shape and although there was still a lot to do, this was a great start. All the old furniture was gone and there were drop sheets on the carpet ready for the walls to be painted. They were primed for her to start in the morning. She wasn't half bad at painting and decorating and this was a total labour of love.

Whatever Vince Carter said to Bradley when he visited this morning had galvanised her husband into taking positive action. He wouldn't tell her about the conversation but when he suggested they go furniture shopping... well, it was obvious.

Vince had reconsidered.

Whether Melanie became a permanent part of their family, or a regular visitor didn't matter at this point. Little by little, Carla would work on Vince. She'd prove to him how happy she made Melanie and how much easier his life was playing the important role of grandparent—but on the weekends. Or every other weekend.

Bradley had helped her choose a new bed, a bedside table,

and lovely chair which could turn into a single bed for when her friends stayed over. All of these were a few weeks away from delivery which gave her time to finish all the other touches. Melanie could choose her own manchester and anything else she wanted. Perhaps a small bookcase. And a fish tank.

When they'd got home she was on a high and wasted no time showing her husband exactly how much she loved him for being so supportive. But while he'd have stayed in their bed for the rest of the day, she'd prodded him and made him help her in here.

And now it is becoming a room fit for a little girl.

'Our little girl.'

There was nothing more to do in here tonight, so she closed the door and went into the kitchen to begin dinner. She'd make one of Brad's favourites and they could share a bottle of wine and have an early night.

Red or white?

He wasn't in the living room but from there she could hear him talking to someone and followed the sound. The front door was open a crack and after peeping through to confirm he was on his phone rather than with a visitor, she started back.

'Not at the warehouse. Too many eyes on it.'

Carla froze at the doorway to the living room. Who was watching the business? And why?

'No. Never my house. Not ever. Carla knows nothing of any of this and I'll be damned if she's ever going to.'

A sudden cold swept through her and her body stiffened.

Bradley laughed shortly. 'You've got to be kidding, but yeah, I'll meet you there. But we have to talk about Carter as well as the other matters.'

Vince? What about Vince?

'I'm leaving now.'

She couldn't be caught here, eavesdropping. Carla moved quickly and quietly as the front door closed.

'Baby? I'm going out for an hour.'

Her throat was constricted, and she had to force out a squeaky, 'See you then.'

'You okay?'

Fingers crossed behind her back; she took a deep breath. 'Going to have a shower. Then do dinner.'

'Sure thing. Back soon.'

The second the front door clicked shut, she raced for her handbag and keys.

————

'Pete packed it in?' Terry went past Liz's desk to toss his keys into his office, then wandered back. There was only a couple of other detectives left and both worked on local video footage from the areas of the two different murders.

'No. He's meeting with one of his old informants. Something about Ginny.'

'A break would be nice.' Terry dragged a chair across and sat opposite. 'So far all the footage around her building showed exactly nothing of value. Trouble is it has more than a hundred apartments. Strange there's no internal cameras.'

'Why she lived there, I imagine. The average john wouldn't want to be caught going into her place. We are following up on a couple of deliveries which looked odd, out of normal business hours, but if Pete's information can help, so much the better.' Liz stretched. 'What happened with Roscoe?'

Terry grunted. 'He said if I wasn't arresting him then he wasn't coming in for another interview. Very tempting but I want the case solid before we take that step. We just need one thing. Just one.'

'So you didn't ask about his teenage years?'

'Not yet. Weren't you bringing Farrelly in?'

'Will do, boss, once we find him. Not at home and the ware-house is closed. There's a small sign on the window now, some-thing about having a day off and being open as usual tomorrow. I'd love to know if something happened there last night. It just feels as if it did.'

Terry pushed himself to his feet. 'Go home, Liz. We'll start over in the morning and I'll put a unit onto Roscoe overnight. Might see if one is spare to cover Farrelly's home as well.' He headed to his office.

She didn't want to go home. Didn't want to stop searching through the mountain of paperwork she'd collected on her desk to cross reference everything available since the moment Malcolm Hardy escaped. And with the van now confirmed as the one involved in Susie's death—and belonging to PickerPack Holdings—her gut screamed that there was more to this than a stolen vehicle and an accident.

The detecting part of being a detective isn't working.

Liz closed folders and piled papers. Terry was right. Go home, eat, sleep.

Shrugging on an overcoat, Terry came out of his office. The expression on his face had Liz on her feet in a second.

'There's a body.'

'No going home then?' She reached for her keys.

'Behind Spironi's.'

He was out of the door.

'No going home.'

———

Pete was already on the scene in the alley behind the restaurant. Someone had called an ambulance but one look at the body should have told the caller not to bother.

'Same as Ginny. Strangled. Hardy again,' Pete said.

Not convinced, Liz stood back as a crime scene officer took photographs. It was Marco, his eyes open and the strings from his apron wrapped around his neck. It wasn't surprising nobody had found him until now as his body lay length-wise against the alley wall and he was on his side. From a few metres away he might have been asleep if he'd even been noticed in the dark.

'He didn't die in that position, did he?'

'Signs of a struggle near the dumpster. He has a cut on his arm and there's blood on the metal there. Back of his shoes show scuff marks. Might be from dragging him here, so no, this is a placed scene.'

She walked away, tipping her head for Pete to follow. Terry was near the back door of the restaurant speaking to a distraught woman wearing a Spironi's apron, so Liz stopped far enough away for a private conversation.

'What did your informant say?'

'Reckons Ginny had cut all ties with Hardy when he went to prison, or shortly after. And that she had a boyfriend of sorts. Some dude who didn't care about the johns as long as she was available when he called around,' Pete said.

'Anyone we know?'

'He never met him. Only thing he knows is the dude can fix anything. Handyman kind of thing.'

Mike burst out of the back door and began yelling at Terry.

'Handyman... someone who might own bolt cutters?'

Pete nodded. 'Like the ones we found in Ginny's laundry.'

'Useful for removing hand cuffs and cutting padlocks on gates.'

His eyes widened. 'We might get the bolt cutters revisited. And another full sweep of Ginny's apartment. Do you reckon this is enough to get a warrant for the warehouse? See if that padlock is still on the premises?'

'I guess we could simply ask Pickering... but where would the fun be in that?'

The yelling got louder. 'That man did this! Pretending to be one of you and has a score to settle.'

Pete leaned in a bit. 'Maybe it *was* Vince.'

Liz rolled her eyes.

———

Why on earth are you here?

After second-guessing herself for following Bradley, Carla didn't know whether to be shocked or curious when he parked at the cemetery. She'd pulled into a different part of the carpark.

Now he waited near David's grave, shuffling from foot to foot. The cemetery was deserted—as it should be at night. She'd stopped a distance back, not wishing to intrude on his private visit to his friend's grave.

'There you are boss.'

The sound of a man's voice startled Carla and she ducked behind a tree trunk, heart racing. After a second, she peered around. No wonder Brad had said on the phone he didn't want his wife to know who he was meeting with. The awful Abel Farrelly was with another man... she couldn't make out who. Careful not to be seen, Carla darted from tree to tree until she found a better aspect. Was that the lawyer? The one on television with the escaped killer?

The other two men stopped between David and Susie's head-stones, and Abel leaned against the former.

So disrespectful.

'Why the cemetery?' Brad asked.

Abel smirked. 'I like it here, reminds me why following orders is important.'

Roscoe—that was his name—was quiet, his eyes darting from the headstones to Bradley then Abel. He looked nervous.

'You two had better not have been followed,' Brad said.

'Never happen. Not to me. How about you, Richard?' That Abel was too cocky for Carla's liking. Always had been one to push buttons.

'Let's do this quickly then,' Brad said. 'First off, Hardy is safe. Within two days he'll be starting his new life in a tropical paradise. It took a bit of messing around to make it happen but with the credibility Duncan Chandler brings and the freight company under control, we know this new enterprise of ours works. Law enforcement are hardly going to suspect toy transports.'

'Not relaxing until Malcolm is there. Let's not count our chickens too early.' Roscoe glanced over his shoulder. 'What if the truck gets stopped for some reason?'

'There's no risk,' Abel said. 'That container is impenetrable unless someone knows where to look. All the driver has to do is deliver the shipment and my contact will take care of everything else.'

Hardy? Malcolm Hardy the killer?

Carla could barely breathe. She felt sick to her stomach that her husband would know anything about that evil person.

Roscoe cleared his throat. 'I have two more shipments ready to be booked in. One in a week and the other in three. But I'm getting a lot of heat from the police and most of that is thanks to Jerry's death.' He stared at Abel. 'He was doing what we wanted. He always did.'

'He finally outlived his usefulness. Everyone is expendable.' Abel's laugh was like chalk on a blackboard.

Brad glanced around. Carla shrank as close to the tree as she could.

'We need to talk about Vince Carter.'

'Didn't you show him the photographs and letter?' Abel crossed his arms. 'There should be nothing further to do but welcome the kid into your home.'

'Except he threw it back in my face. He's not the pushover everyone thinks, and he'll protect Melanie to his dying breath.'

'There's your answer then.'

Before a gasp could escape, Carla covered her mouth with both hands.

'I'm not sure about it, Abel. There's still some legal channels-.'

'You're really prepared to risk him coming after you? He has the ear of cops. He is a man without a soul who won't stop until he finds a way to grind you into the ground and stop that kid seeing you and wifey again,' Abel said.

'Melanie has to be kept out of it.'

'Can't always help collateral damage.'

Brad lurched at Abel and grabbed the front of his jacket. Roscoe whipped his arm around Brad's neck.

Abel's smirk was back. 'Oh, I'd be real careful.'

Brad released him but Roscoe kept the hold on his neck. 'Just remember, Brad, you couldn't handle David. He was leaving you and taking his knowledge of our operation with him,' he hissed.

Roscoe removed his arm and pushed Brad away. He doubled over, sucking in oxygen.

'I never wanted him dead, let alone poor Susie,' Brad gasped.

Abel shrugged. 'Well, it worked in your favour.' He turned to Roscoe. 'Don't ever step in like that again. Your only purpose to me is providing criminals as cargo for a lot of money. If that dries up I will end you.'

Roscoe shrank back and Abel's laughter cut into the night.

At last they left.

She counted to one hundred to make sure the three men were well and truly gone before stumbling out from behind the trunk of a tree which had somehow kept her upright for the past few minutes when her legs wanted to buckle.

My husband...

Using all her willpower, Carla made it to place the men had stood.

Susie died because you are a criminal?

Had Vince been right for all those years? He told Susie to watch Brad. Warned her David was getting in too deep with a dangerous situation. But to be involved in killing a man who wanted no part of something criminal?

'But I never wanted him dead, let alone poor Susie.' Bradley had said those words.

Did you know? Did you make it happen?

The world was spinning, and Carla fell to her knees, and then, as sobs racked her body, she crawled to Susie's grave and lay beside it.

FORTY-FIVE

Vince's phone rang when his hands were in a sink of soapy water.

'Shall I answer for you?' Melanie was drying up.

'Um, yes, okay. I'll be there in a sec.'

She shot out to the living room while he dried his hands. Dinner was done and his next job was to talk to Melanie before Liz arrived.

Melanie was smiling as she reappeared, chatting to the caller. 'That will be nice to do. Grandad is here now. Bye, Liz.' She held the phone out with a solemn 'Liz the detective is on the phone for you.'

'Well, thank you. Do you mind finishing the dishes and I'll be right back?'

'I will have them *all* done.'

She probably would. Vince waited until he was in the living room to speak. 'Sorry, had my hands in water.'

'Melanie is so sweet. She asked when I am coming over for dinner.'

'She did?'

'I suggested next time you both come to my house.'

He couldn't recall the last time he visited her at home. Must be years.

She continued. 'I rang to let you know I'm caught up at work tonight. I'm really sorry because I know this is a big deal for you...'

It was relief he felt. Not disappointment.

Call me selfish.

'What's happened?'

There was a pause. In the background was shouting. A vaguely familiar voice. 'Are you at Spironi's again?'

Liz sighed. 'Yeah. We found Marco. Just not alive.'

'Shit. Not an accident?'

'Not unless he accidentally wrapped his apron strings around his neck and then accidentally moved his body ten metres. Mike is blaming you.'

He checked his watch. 'When was he killed?'

'Couple of hours ago. Got an alibi?' There was a touch of humour in her voice.

'Probably was walking the pony up to Lyndall's house about then.'

'Cool. I'll get Apple's statement tomorrow.'

Somebody called her name. McNamara.

'I have to go, but Vince? Not to alarm you but I have a feeling this wasn't Hardy. Pete disagrees but something is off. Really off. We're waiting on a warrant to search Pickering's warehouse so will you take extra care?'

'Always. You too. But why the warehouse?'

'Gotta go.'

'Lizzie... damn.'

She'd hung up.

Why would they seek a warrant? What was at the warehouse

which had anything to do with Hardy... or was he misunderstanding?

This is about David.

Vince sat on the sofa, turning the phone in his fingers. According to Susie, her husband wanted to move further out to a new house. Unbeknown to her, he'd also planned a career move, a big one. Did Pickering know any of this? Was that why they were arguing that night?

And the message on the answering machine. The threat.

I'm done with you ignoring me. Time's up, Weaver.

Not Pickering—it would be redundant seeing as they were about to have dinner. But Pickering had a stake in something important enough to fight about in a restaurant. In front of a little girl.

'Grandad? Are you alright?' Melanie moved her beanbag so she could see him when she flopped into it. She carried one of her art books and some pencils.

'Sure am. I was just thinking.'

She tilted her head, curious.

'Nothing important. Did you enjoy your day with Lyndall?'

Her smile answered. 'She's so fun. Did you know she used to be a famous artist? Some of her paintings are in big art galleries around the world. But she used a different name and now I've forgotten it.'

Is that right? Who is my neighbour?

'I didn't know. Well, I know she paints and is very good. But not the rest of it. Did she tell you the name of any of the paintings?'

'One is called *The Alone*.'

'*The Alone*? That's kind of a strange name.'

Melanie frowned. 'She painted it after her family died. All of them did. At least I have you, Grandad.'

Her hand reached out for his and he held it, forcing a smile even as his heart thudded. 'I'm not going anywhere, Melly-belly. You mean the world to me, and I'll protect you and be there for you always.'

She seemed satisfied with his answer and withdrew her hand to open the art book. 'I drew Lyndall, would you like to see?'

'Sit up here and show me.'

There were so many drawings. Lyndall must be helping Melanie with technique as the quality got better on the last few pages.

'Here is the one I did of Lyndall while she was drawing me. Isn't that the funniest idea?'

'It is very clever. And you have a lot of talent.'

'Oh! Lyndall said that. She said if I keep practicing then in a couple of years I should find a school which spesh... um, speshal...'

'Specialises?'

'Specialises, yes. Thank you. In art.'

'Hm. That sounds expensive.'

Melanie gave him a slightly impatient look. 'She says I could get a scholarship.'

'I see. And what is this? Did you draw a donkey?'

She giggled. 'They are kinda cute from a long way away. I might draw Apple next.'

'What about Robbie? Actually, where is Robbie?'

Jumping to her feet, Melanie ran out of the room. Vince picked up the art book and went back to the beginning. Page after page, the images were sad. Random drawings of tears and hearts that were broken in two. She really was talented. One of her mother, smiling, but with angel wings. A small groan left his lips.

One of Vince. The cottage—much nicer than it was in reality.

Then a series of faces. Carla, smiling. Pickering, angry. And another man… a lean face was all he could make out because she'd scribbled over it and all that was left was his eyes.

'He's angry.'

Vince shut the book.

'You found Robbie.'

'He was playing with the spinning toy.' She gently deposited him on the bean bag, and he meowed at Vince. 'It's okay to look at the pictures.'

'Who is the angry man? Only if you want to tell me.'

'I don't know his name. I might draw for a while. Robbie, will you sit on my lap?'

Vince handed over the art book and tickled Robbie's head. 'Do you mind if I go do some more boring paperwork? You sit here near the fire and stay warm, and I might pop that apple pie into the oven to warm up.'

She grinned. 'Hurry up!'

'But what if it doesn't taste good?'

'Impossible. It was made with love.'

He bit his lip to steady himself. This little girl was his whole world. There wasn't a thing he wouldn't do for her and that included finding out who the 'angry man' was.

———

Carla wasn't at home.

After driving around for half an hour processing what happened at the cemetery, Bradley knew he had to make an appearance. She'd be worried.

He stopped at the local liquor shop, chatted to the assistant for a while in full view of the camera, then went home to a house in darkness.

'Baby? Where are you?'

When no answer came, he ran upstairs. Then back down again.

'Carla, I'm home.'

Hadn't she said she was having a shower then starting dinner? But the shower hadn't been used... she always left the extruder fan on for ages. And the kitchen showed no signs of any preparation.

Did she go shopping?

That must be it. All day, she'd been loving and thankful for his small gesture of helping with the furniture for Melanie's room and she must have decided to buy ingredients for a special dinner.

His stomach turned. What if that bedroom ended up as a memorial for a child caught in the middle of a war not of her making?

He shook the thought away and dialled Carla's number. It went to her voicemail. 'Hi baby, I'm home now. Did you go shopping? I can order in if you like. Anyway, give me a call.'

This was annoying. She never went out without leaving a note. He poured a gin and tonic and stared out through the living room window for her car, rubbing his neck.

Roscoe was a nutter, grabbing him like that.

And Abel's threat to the man, his so-called friend, who'd done nothing other than intervene? It showed a whole different side to his employee. Bradley had been under the impression the two were old school mates, leveraging off each other's positions for mutual benefit. But tonight painted a different picture. Roscoe acted as though he was afraid of Abel. He'd backed down more than once during the conversation.

A message arrived from Carla.

At shops. Got held up. Back soon.

'Hurry up, Carla, I'm hungry.'

Another message... but not his wife—signalled a deposit into his secret account for an eye-watering amount. Roscoe had come through with the up-front payment for their next client which meant they were in business.

Early retirement with his own yacht and European home was just around the corner.

————

The warehouse entry points offered little resistance to bolt cutters and a battering ram. Liz and Pete led a small group of uniformed officers who spread out to cover different parts of the property.

Pete collected the chain he'd cut. Anything that might lead to the theft of the van would go to FSD.

'You know it wasn't stolen, Liz?' Pete caught up with her inside the side door. 'The question is who drove it the night of the crash.'

'Agree. And much as they'll try to pin it on someone else, only Farrelly and Pickering had anything close to a motive.' She found the overhead lights. 'If Vince's information is correct and David wanted out because of criminal activity, then he was a liability.'

'So which one do we call to advise we're here?'

'Pickering. He's the owner.' Liz headed to the back of the warehouse. 'How many shipping containers were here the other day when you stuck your head in?'

'Four.'

'Three now. Let's take a look at his office. Find out where it went.'

A search of Pickering's desk came up with an answer of sorts. Pickering had signed a contract with Duncan Chandler to make space available to new destinations. In the same week, he had made an agreement with a local freight company to pick up regular containers from the warehouse.

'All looks legit,' Liz said. 'But there's an interesting receipt here.' She handed it to Pete. 'Three months payment as a deposit. Is that normal?'

'Doubt it. Either they weren't sure of his commitment or solvency, or he needed something done quickly. Do you have the specs on that container?' He took a photo of the receipt.

'Shit.'

'What?'

'According to this, the first shipment was due to leave the day before yesterday but was delayed until last night.' Liz felt sick. 'Terry and I passed a truck loaded with a container around the corner when we got back from Roscoe's place. Thought nothing of it as it was in the direction of the docks... but also the freeway.'

'You couldn't know. I'll help you find its number and chase up the freight company. I've left a message for Pickering.'

'Then give me a hand going through that filing cabinet before he gets under our feet.'

FORTY-SIX

Whoever was decent enough to move the livestock from this bottom paddock needs a thank you. If they're not here they won't get curious or noisy. And this lean-to is in the perfect position to watch from.

The rain won't last.

I've done two trips to the car and have everything.

Rifle. Just for emergencies.

Ammo.

Accelerant... can't believe I'm getting to use this kind again. Next to no trace for anyone to find.

The cottage has movement still. It isn't late.

I can wait.

The other house up on the hill is in darkness though. She's old. Probably has nanna naps as well as goes to bed early.

I settle on an upturned feed bucket. There's time now to eat and prepare my mind.

Goodbye, Carter.

FORTY-SEVEN

Melanie was asleep, the kitten tucked up in its bed again. Such a good little creature, thanks completely to Melanie's bonding and attention. Vince closed the door with a smile. He'd never have seen himself having a cat in the house but Robbie was already part of the family.

Now that she'd settled for the night, he returned to the kitchen where the laptop was open on the table. So was the yellow envelope. He slid out the phone which was charged and on but needed a password. He'd have to get some help with it and soon, because this phone might be the one that caller referred to. The caller who'd threatened David. No suspicious messages or calls were on either David or Susie's phones from the crash.

The first letter might be addressed to Mrs McCoy but could hold important information.

It was from David to the principal and filled with apologies.

When I told you the company I part own was in trouble I wasn't completely honest. It is in trouble but not financially. I hope I have handed you this letter but if not, please accept my deepest apology for misleading you and for taking advantage of your kindness.

Since learning about my business partner's plans to undertake future criminal activities I have had no choice other than to accumulate as much money as possible in order to buy my own business and begin a new life with my family, which you will understand, mean everything to me. All owed monies will be deposited into the school account prior to the start of the next term; however Melanie will not be returning as our new home will be too far away to commute.

And so on.

Vince stared at the paper without seeing the words.

Why hadn't David spoken to him about this? Surely he'd know an ex-copper would have contacts who could help?

Except I'd made it impossible for him.

The lump in his throat refused to budge. He'd pushed David away for years—ever since he'd become Pickering's partner while he should have been supportive. David must have felt so alone.

There was a thud outside and his head flew up, listening.

It wasn't repeated.

On his feet, he checked the back door was locked then opened the front door and stepped out.

For a few minutes he stood still in the dark, watching and listening. A passing rain shower was clearing, and the clouds scuttled away. In the distance, a donkey brayed and closer, a night bird carried on, disturbed perhaps by some small predator. Once the cold bit his fingers too hard he retreated to the warmth in the cottage, locking the door and rattling it to be certain. In the living room, he checked the windows and then extinguished the remains of the fire with water from a bucket. In the morning he'd clean the area out and start over.

He made a pot of tea, staring at the will folded on the table as the kettle heated.

That first or the letter which accompanied it?

Tea made, he settled at the table.

There was much he didn't understand about David's plan. Susie and Carla were best friends so presumably he'd not shared his concerns with his wife. Did he expect her to cut ties once they moved? Unless Susie knew the reason, she'd never turn her back on someone she loved. Or did Susie know about whatever activity Pickering was getting into?

It was a copy of a will prepared by a different lawyer than the one Vince had dealt with up to now and was for David. He was clear about leaving everything to Susie and in the event of her untimely death, to Melanie. There were instructions that if they both died before Melanie was of age that she should be in Vince's care and custody.

Around his chest, a band of pressure made it difficult to breath. It wasn't a heart attack but a different kind of grief. One for all the lost time and misunderstanding.

I might have saved them both.

The letter was handwritten from Susie and dated the day before the accident.

> *Dear Dad,*
> *Hopefully, we have caught up recently in person and talked about all of this but if not, I need you to know I never stopped loving you. Never.*

He blinked rapidly.

You are harder on yourself than anyone should ever be. Until you forgive yourself for Mum's death, I fear for your mental health. The reality is she had an illness and died. If you'd been there she would still have died, Dad. Ask yourself if she'd have wanted you to blame yourself after all this time?

Marion was the most forgiving person he knew.
The band around his chest loosened.

But I'm not here to tell you off for the millionth time about that. This is about Melanie. David is leaving PickerPack. I don't know all the details, but I get the feeling Brad doesn't know and that there is something going on which has soured their working relationship. Despite what you think, David is ethical, and I've always quietly agreed with you that Bradley is not. He takes advantage of Carla's need for a child by discouraging her from working again which means that although they are Mel's godparents, I would not want them having custody of Melanie.

A long sigh left Vince's lips.

David insisted I put this in writing so there can be no doubt. He's done a new will and you know me... hate the things so I haven't read it or changed mine yet. David wants to take Melanie and me somewhere on the weekend to see something. I think it is to do with buying land like I mentioned a while back.

Once we get back I'm coming to visit, whether you like it or not. I'd rather tell you face to face that nothing matters more than knowing Melanie will come and live with you should anything happen to us. There, I said the scary stuff!

Anyway, nothing bad is going to happen but I feel so much better with something written down. Melanie is our world, and she couldn't be in safer hands than yours.

Love you, Daddy,

Susie

'She couldn't be in safer... safer hands.' Vince held the letter against his chest. 'I will protect her with my life, Susie.'

———

'We've got the last location of the truck carrying the shipping container.' Liz hurried into Terry's office. 'Stopped for refuelling only an hour ago so local law in New South Wales are gearing up to pull it over. He will be just inside the border with Queensland.'

'Hardy had better be in that container.'

'Pickering's staff are turning on him. Third one in a row confirmed that container was off limits for everyone other than him and Farrelly. There's a big bin for cardboard at the very back of the driveway and right at the bottom was a box from a portable air filtration unit. No sign of it on the premises so unless it went home with someone, odds are it is keeping Hardy's air breathable.'

Any sense of exhaustion was replaced by low grade adrenaline. Liz could smell the chase.

Terry answered his phone and held up a hand for her to stay. After a minute or two he hung up, amusement on his face.

'Mrs Hardy apparently just took muffins out to the uniforms watching her and said that she heard from her son. He wanted her to know he was going somewhere safe, and that Roscoe had instructions about her future financial security.'

The image of the elderly woman, cane in one hand and muffins in the other waiting for a police officer to wind down their window was priceless. 'I really don't know what to say.'

Terry laughed. 'Then wait till you hear this. She told Malcolm she's accepted a better offer, one from a developer, and that she does not need his filthy money.'

'Good for her. Don't suppose she knew where he called from?'

'Not yet. It was to her mobile, so someone is chasing it up with her telco.'

Pete stuck his head in. 'Got warrants for Pickering and Farrelly's respective homes. Seeing as he didn't bother to show up at the warehouse, what's the odds Pickering has skipped town?'

'Have you tried calling again?' Liz asked.

'Just then. Phone's off.'

She headed to the door.

'I've also put Mike from Spironi's into room three. He's calmed down and wants to talk to you, Liz,' Pete said.

'Does he have anything left to say? Where are you going?'

'Farrelly's house.'

Terry followed them. 'Pete, I'll head up looking at Pickering's house. Liz, speak to Mike and then reset the whiteboard based on all our newest information. And call me if anything comes up.'

Some of the earlier adrenaline faded. 'Are you sure he asked for me, Pete?'

Both men laughed on their way out.

'Fine. Just leave me here with the waiter who blames Vince for everything.' She muttered. 'But if he yells at me...'

One of the other detectives grinned at her as she stalked past.

Mike didn't yell anymore. He was measured as he apologised for not being more forthcoming when she'd first come to Spironi's. 'Just protecting my customers, and my staff.'

'I get that. But if there's anything you know about that night then please don't hold anything back,' Liz said.

'Poor Marco. Bit stupid taking money but he wasn't a bad kid or anything.'

'Do you know who gave him money?'

'Someone was in the alley a few days ago and told him to keep his mouth shut about the argument. Gave him a grand and said there'd be more... but warned him the money would go toward his funeral if he said anything.'

'Did he describe this person?'

'Said he knew them.'

He knew Pickering.

'Too late now but I'm going to get security cameras out the back and everywhere I'm legally allowed.' His face was grim. 'Didn't take it seriously and Marco has paid.'

'Marco's death is not your fault. When I came to see you that first time, you mentioned you took the Weavers and Pickerings to their table. Do you recall anything, no matter how small a detail, which struck you as odd?'

He nodded. 'It's why I'm here now. Mr Pickering arrived a while after everyone else. Maybe twenty minutes later. And he left before they did.'

'By how much time?'

'At least half an hour. Mrs Pickering asked me to call a taxi, but Mr Weaver insisted they'd drop her home.'

David was on that road because it was the straightest route from the Pickering's house to theirs. Pickering would have known they wouldn't let Carla take a taxi. He wanted them on that stretch. This was cold, calculated murder.

'Mike, you've been very helpful. Is there anything else you want to tell me?'

He shook his head and she excused herself.

She'd spoken to Pickering. Vince had. Pete had. The man had never once said a word about Carla being dropped off. Why would anyone hide that? And where had he been?

FORTY-EIGHT

Vince had never considered himself a tech-savvy person but lately he was surprising himself with what he could work out. Finding his way around computer systems had been part of being a police officer, but more recent technology such as navigation on mobile phones wasn't around back then.

His maths was strong, and his father was a carpenter so he'd learned from a young age how to calculate measurements. What he was doing now was simply a mixture of several skills.

He had a map of the city laid out on the kitchen table, folded to show the western suburbs out as far as his home and back across to Lygon Street in Carlton. He'd downloaded his travel record to his computer and moved the data to a spreadsheet showing start and end points, distance, time. With a black marker and ruler he traced where he'd been.

Pickering's house to Susie's house.

Susie's to the police station.

Police station to Lygon Street.

Lygon St to warehouse.

Warehouse to Balwyn North.

Balwyn North to home.

He calculated the route from the Pickering's to Susie's and then worked out Lygon Street to Susie's. He knew what time the bill was paid at Spironi's, thanks to David's credit card statement arriving in the post at Susie's house this morning.

'And it doesn't add up.'

After checking his notes he sat back, unsettled. Unless David had stopped somewhere between the restaurant and home, the time of the accident made no sense. There was more than half an hour missing. Bradley had looked him in the eye when he'd asked about the moment his family left Spironi's. 'They drove off with a wave. Melanie was sleepy. Nothing out of the ordinary, Vince.'

Then why did it take so long and why would they take that road?

He messaged Liz's phone.

> Are you still working?

Within a minute his phone rang.

'I was going to message you the same question,' she began. 'I looked at the time and thought it might be a bit late.'

'Why?'

He got to his feet not wanting to disturb Melanie. The living room felt cold without the fire.

'A lot has happened this evening, Vince. For one, we think... we're pretty certain, that Malcolm Hardy is hidden inside a shipping container on its way to Far North Queensland. Him and a load of toys.'

'Pickering.'

David must have known something.

'Yes. Who we can't locate at the moment. The other thing is that we have new information about the night of the crash.'

Vince sank onto the armchair. 'Go on.'

'A waiter from Spironi's came forward. Pickering arrived late and left early that evening. From what he understood, Susie and David were going to drop Carla home.'

His eyes closed and his body slumped back. 'That's why.'

'That's why what?'

'There was half an hour missing that night. And why else would David take that road?'

'I'd wondered it myself but hadn't had a chance to do the calculations with all the crap around Hardy,' Liz said. 'I can't believe this is all connected.'

'He lied to me.' He rubbed his eyes with his spare hand then opened them. 'Little shit told me he'd waved goodbye as they drove off when they all left the restaurant. Lizzie, he would know what their route was.'

'You think he's behind the accident.'

'Don't you?'

There was a long silence then Liz spoke softly. 'I'm going to come to you. Is the cottage locked up?'

'Why? What aren't you telling me?'

'You told me Melanie said something about David arguing with Pickering.'

'Except he doesn't know that.'

'Yeah. I think he does.'

You told him somebody had overheard. He thought it was the waiter and killed him.

'Have you led a killer to my grandchild—'

'I haven't. As far as we know he loves her. He certainly loves his wife and wants Melanie to be in their care, so it is you I'm worried about because *you* are the obstacle to their perfect life. You told us he's tried to blackmail you, and somebody is doing the rounds getting rid of people in their way. If he imagines Melanie told you anything then of course you are in his sights.'

Vince went to check the windows. There was no sign of

movement outside, not even any traffic. Just a typical late evening. In the far distance, lightning streaked through the sky.

'Look, either bundle Melanie up and bring both of you here, or else I'll head up shortly.' There was an edge to Liz's voice. Worry.

'Rather not frighten her. Okay, if it makes you feel better, come up. I can show you what I've been working on.'

'See you soon.'

Nobody would get into the cottage. Not unless they made a hell of a lot of noise breaking windows and by that time, Vince would have Melanie out of here. He'd thought about escape plans a hundred times, not just for Mel but for Susie after he'd killed the Anzac Day shooter. For years he'd lived in fear of some relative or friend coming to get him.

Nothing and no-one would harm Melanie.

———

Liz was heading out when the watch officer called her. Somebody wanted to report a missing woman—Carla Pickering.

You have to be kidding.

Bradley Pickering waited where he'd been sent to sit.

Here, in the station, we couldn't identify a current wanted person when he rocks up?

As she passed the officer, he whispered, 'Thought it best to keep him unaware of his status.'

I take it back.

Pickering looked up when she neared, a scowl crossing an already angry face. 'You?'

'Do you want help finding Carla?'

He got to his feet and followed her. Until she got him into an interview room she wasn't about to spook him. Having dropped himself into her lap, as it were, he obviously had no idea there was a city-wide alert for his apprehension.

'Take a seat, Mr Pickering.'

She ran through the usual words about the interview and sat opposite.

Pete will be annoyed he missed this.

'When was the last time you saw Carla?'

'Um... before dinner. Well, she said she was going to shower and then begin dinner. I had a meeting to go to.'

'But what time?'

'Six? Bit later.'

'Was that the last time you spoke to her?'

He shot her an impatient glance.

'Mr Pickering, is Carla missing? Or just not at home?'

'Missing. She never just goes off. Ever. And she sent me a text message at seven forty-five saying she was shopping. Getting something nice for our dinner. We have a lot to celebrate.'

'Something special?'

'Yes. But she still hasn't come home, and I've dialled her dozens of times.'

Of course you have.

The man was certifiable.

'Where have you been for the past six hours or so?'

'Me? What does that matter?'

'Putting a picture together.'

'Fine. I had a brief meeting to attend, went home, waited for Carla, then went looking for her. Local shops, then a bit further afield to some she likes to go to when she's after special ingredients. There's a couple of places open late she likes.'

'Where was the meeting?'

Mouth open to answer, Pickering snapped it shut.

'General area?'

'Nothing to do with Carla being missing.'

'In that case, tell me about your arrangement with Richard Roscoe to transport Malcolm Hardy to Far North Queensland.'

And there it was.

If a person could have shrunk into the ground, it would have been Pickering. An expression of disbelief, then horror crossed his face. Liz was happy to wait. It didn't take long.

'I want to see my lawyer.'

'Why did you lie about leaving Spironi's early the night of the crash, and that your wife was driven home by David Weaver?'

'I said I want a lawyer.'

'I'm sure you do.'

As soon as she left the room, Liz texted Vince.

> We have Pickering in custody. Let me know if you'd still like me to come up.

————

The message from Liz helped. He'd been on high alert and now, he let himself breathe—Pickering's people would lay low until they heard from their boss.

In preparation for a quick exit, his laptop and important items were in a backpack along with chargers and bottled water. If he'd had to get them out of the cottage without time to pack, at least they'd have something to drink until they got to a safer place.

But now I can rest.

Or at least lay down until dawn.

He tapped a message back to let Liz know not to bother driving up and then turned off the kitchen light and went to his bedroom. Rain began to fall in a gentle staccato on the roof.

FORTY-NINE

I wake from the half-sleep I allowed myself. With nothing to do but watch and wait my brain grew weary.

The cottage is still.

He won't see me coming.

The increasing pattering on the metal roof above me comes as a curse to my plans. Or perhaps a gift. Rain will make my job harder but will offer protection.

And if anyone happens to leave the house then they won't have the skills to deal with the weather... and me.

When will people learn to stay out of my way?

When will they learn I will always win, no matter the price to them.

FIFTY

'What lawyer does a lawyer call?' Pete was ridiculously cheerful as he handed Liz a coffee. 'Thought you could use this.'

'I can. Thank you. What do you mean?'

'Oh. Richard Roscoe was picked up trying to board a plane to Perth. Says it was a business trip but apparently whined about being bullied and bleated about wanting legal representation ever since.'

'Another one down! We just need to make something stick. What did you find at Farrelly's?'

He rolled his chair over.

'The man has excellent taste in interior decorating. A lot of money is in that house of his from top end appliances to expensive artwork. We'll check if the art is stolen but my instinct is that he owns them legally. Someone's going through his home office so we'll see what comes of it. No sign of weapons. Nothing out of order.'

'Then why are you so happy?'

Perhaps I could go home soon. Sleep sounds nice.

Pete raised his eyebrows. 'You haven't heard? The false

ceiling in Pickering's office in the warehouse had several duffle bags tucked away at the back. One filled with cash. Another with weapons. Our friend is going down for a long time.'

She couldn't help herself. She laughed aloud, ending with a short 'whoop'.

When his phone beeped, Pete read the message and pushed his chair back. 'No rest for me. Terry's heading back to the warehouse and I'm taking over the search of Pickering's house. I might see you in the morning, or I might be asleep.'

'Me too. Watch out in that storm.'

'What storm?' He grinned as thunder rumbled around the building.

Liz finished the coffee, letting her body relax for a few minutes and staring at the whiteboard. Two bad guys in custody. The other one, who might not even be more than Pickering's hired help with the containers, wouldn't be too far from capture. Hardy would be found within hours.

So why do I feel something's wrong?

Tossing the cup away, she began rearranging the whiteboard.

Pickering was running a racket to move criminals. Was Malcolm Hardy the first? Or had there been a succession of containers? She thought the former. David Weaver had been trying to extricate himself from the business so possibly had an idea what was ahead and wanted no part of it. The change of plans at the warehouse for a pick up from one night to the next might explain why Roscoe was a decoy. The pressure from Hardy to get him out of the city had clearly been mounting with him being responsible for three deaths...

Two deaths.

She put Ginny's photo up and beneath it, Jerry Black's. Both had strong ties to Hardy. Ginny had most likely been the one to remove his handcuffs and possibly offer him sanctuary and Black was involved in misdirecting the police and giving the criminal breathing space.

Ginny was strangled.

Black's throat cut.

But then there was Marco.

His photo went next. Strangled.

'It couldn't have been Hardy.'

He was—until proven otherwise—in a shipping container in another state when Marco died. Pickering was also accounted for. Roscoe was a coward, not a killer capable of strangulation.

Liz phoned Pete.

'Don't tell me I need to turn around?'

'Nah. Can you remind me what your informant said about Ginny? About a boyfriend?' She put a photo of the bolt-cutters she'd found in the apartment next to Ginny.

'Not much to tell. He was something of a handyman. Oh that's right, Ginny said the boyfriend had fixed a kitchen drawer. New sliders or something. Even took her with him to the hardware store in the city where she'd never been.'

'Hardware store?'

'Lots of blokes go to hardware stores. Lots of women too.'

'But only some grew up working in one. Any idea how long ago he took her shopping?'

'Lizzie,' he sighed loudly. 'No. Let's deal with one problem at a time and if we can't get anything out of the searches and the idiots in custody, then we'll start looking for footage. Okay?'

'Yeah. I'm a bit worried about Vince.'

'He probably has a gun, and no self-respecting criminal would take him on. Seriously.'

He was right. Vince was resourceful and street smart. But still.

One of the detectives waved to get her attention.

'Gotta go.'

She hung up and followed the detective, jogging to catch him. 'Where are we going?

'Sarge says it's like Grand Central Station as far as one family is concerned.'

'Okay, I'll go. Can you ask Bradley Pickering, very nicely, if he remembers where Farrelly was on the day Hardy escaped? Take him a coffee and let him know we called his lawyer.'

Back down at the desk, the watch officer rolled his eyes at Liz. '*Mrs* Pickering for you.'

Oh lord, is she here to report her husband missing?

Exhaustion was playing with her mind.

'Carla? Would you like to come through?'

The woman was soaking wet, her hair dripping water as she got to her feet. Her clothes were filthy down one side with what looked like mud.

'Let's get you some coffee and a towel.'

————

The woman sitting opposite her was no friend. But Carla had no friends anyway now. No love in her life. No husband. Not after this terrible night. Only by coming forward might she salvage her relationship with Melanie because if Vince cut her out of the little girl's life, there'd be nothing left to live for.

'Carla? Why were you soaked through? And so muddy? Did you fall?'

The detective had brought her tracksuit pants and a long-sleeved top, along with towels and some wet wipes. Then, she'd left her in privacy for a few minutes to change, returning with hot coffee.

'Why are you being so kind, officer?'

'Liz. Just call me Liz, okay? Did someone attack you?'

'Oh. Not physically. No.' She touched her face which was dry but must look a sight. She'd tried to clean off the mud and streaked makeup. 'Will you arrest my husband, please?'

The other woman's face barely changed expression but her hand, holding a pen over a notebook, raised a little. 'Why?'

Why? Oh my god, he killed...

Panic gripped her. If she said the words aloud, they'd be real. No going back from it. No unsaying the truth. All the years she'd loved him so deeply that she'd changed her life for him. Turned herself, bit by bit, into the woman he always wanted.

Not the woman I wanted to be.

Her heart hurt.

'You asked why I came in so wet and muddy. I was lying next to Susie's grave for hours. Even when the rain began I couldn't move. I was frozen in place from what I'd overheard.'

'What did you overhear? What made you go to the cemetery at night?'

Carla's fingers were turning her wedding ring around and around until she noticed and abruptly stopped.

'Brad was talking to someone on his phone. At home. I was going to ask him if he preferred white or red wine with dinner and accidentally heard him telling this person that... well, that he needed to discuss what to do with Vince. It was the way he said it that frightened me so when he left, I followed. The last thing I expected was for him to go to the cemetery.'

'Go on.'

'He met with that lawyer, Richard Roscoe and Abel. I can't stand Abel. I couldn't hear at first, but I managed to get close enough hiding behind the trees.'

'That was brave to do. They didn't see you at all?'

'No they definitely thought they were free to speak. Abel said something about Brad showing some photographs to Vince—I think to blackmail him, and Brad said Vince threw them back at him. You're Vince's friend. Do you know what he meant?'

She did. Her eyes betrayed her. 'I can't say.'

Carla's heart raced so fast she thought she might faint. But Melanie's sweet face was always in her mind and was the only thing worth fighting for.

'I'm pretty sure Brad had something to do with the car accident. He even admitted he'd not wanted David to die, let alone... Susie.' It was getting harder to speak as her throat tightened. 'I think he made it happen. But didn't do it himself. I think Abel did. He grabbed Richard Roscoe and was very angry at him and worst of all, said that sometimes collateral damage couldn't be helped.'

Liz leaned across the table. 'Collateral damage? What did he mean, Carla?'

'I'm so sorry. I should have come here sooner but I couldn't... didn't know what to do. I think Abel is going to try and kill Vince.'

———

Liz burst into the interrogation room, startling Pickering whose head was on the table in his arms. As his eyes focussed on her, he drew back.

'Where's my lawyer?'

Caught between desperation and rules, she dropped both palms onto the table with a thump and leaned as close to him as she could reach without grabbing his scrawny neck.

'One chance, Bradley, so listen. Carla just walked into the station and told me Abel Farrelly plans to kill Vince Carter. She is willing to give a full statement based on what she overheard earlier tonight at the cemetery.'

His mouth dropped open.

'If anything happens to Vince or Melanie, I will make sure you go to jail for a very long time. This is your one chance to give me information which might — *might* — help you. Is she right? Is Abel Farrelly after Vince and Mel?'

He pulled back as far as the chair allowed.

'Carla's here?'

'I don't have time for this.' Liz turned to go.

'No, wait. Is she in trouble?'

She damned well should be.

Liz spun back. 'I will do my best to help her but if I leave without an answer—'

'Yes. Abel is probably there now. I've got information about him. About what he did to his parents. I can help—'

Liz slammed the door behind herself, dialling as she ran for the lift.

FIFTY-ONE

Rifle strapped over his shoulder, Abel Farrelly ran along the fence line of the driveway, climbing over onto the barren ground around the cottage after a dozen metres. In one hand he carried the can of accelerant.

The storm was overhead, and he used caution when crossing open areas to avoid the flashes of light.

Rain had already made the ground muddy in parts which worked to his advantage. Years of regular running in the mountains prepared his body for the unexpected. If they escaped the house he'd hunt them down in seconds.

His mind was clear of everything other than the job at hand.

Elation buoyed his spirits.

These moments made his life bearable.

FIFTY-TWO

'Grandad?'

Vince jolted awake, half off the bed before seeing Melanie near the door. He was on top of the covers and still dressed, apart from his boots.

I fell asleep.

A flash of lightning lit the room. Melanie was wrapped in her dressing gown and held Robbie against her chest with the two teddy bears tucked down her front. When thunder rolled over the cottage, she ran to him.

'Come here, sweetie.' He lifted her onto his lap. 'Just a noisy storm. What if we go into the kitchen and make some hot chocolate?'

She nodded and he put her back onto her feet, which were bare.

'First, go and pop your slippers on. The floor is too cold. Maybe socks as well.'

'Can you take Raymond Bear and Topsy Bear?' She dropped them into his hands. 'There's not enough space for poor Robbie.'

'Um, sure. Are you okay to manage?'

'I'll hurry and think about the hot chocolate.' She jumped a bit with more lightning. 'Hot chocolate. Hot chocolate.' Her voice faded as she ran to her room.

Good girl.

He put on his boots and grabbed the teddies. 'Come on, you two.'

In the kitchen, he put them on the table and filled the kettle. That on, he collected mugs and teaspoons, glancing through the window as lightning turned the blackness outside into day for an instant.

Something moved near the clothes line.

He moved closer to the window, waiting.

A flash.

Nothing.

His gut churned.

There had been something out there. Someone.

In the living room he carefully moved a curtain just enough to see out. Through the hammering rain, a figure approached. There was no car. It wasn't Liz nor anyone else from the force. They carried a petrol can and a rifle.

Dragging on his heavy coat from near the door, Vince ran to the kitchen. Melanie was at the table, an art book open to draw in.

'Do you have Robbie?'

'Yes. What's wrong?'

'Slippers?'

He opened the backpack and shoved the teddies inside.

'Shoes. Why are you doing that?' She was on her feet, fear filling her face.

'I need to you listen carefully, sweetie. We need to leave the cottage right now. We're going out the back door and straight up to Lyndall's house, okay?'

Her words were almost impossible to hear over the rain. 'Is it the angry man?'

'I think so. But we're going to be safe. You, me, and Robbie.' He slid her art book into the backpack and zipped it up. His phone was on the table and that went into his coat pocket. 'Can you promise to do everything I say?'

Melanie nodded, tears glistening in her eyes.

'Are you right with the kitten?'

She lifted her head and moved her broken arm, so her hand covered the top of her dressing gown. He must be inside it like he often was.

Vince shrugged the backpack on. He wanted to carry Melanie, but they might be faster if she stayed beside him.

'Come on, then. Back door it is.'

FIFTY-THREE

Abel climbed the steps to the front door. He stopped, savouring the moment.

This was bliss.

Not at all comparable to the ugly act of murder using strangulation. Ginny died because he lost control. That was a mistake. Never kill with emotion. There was too much risk of making errors.

Like the bolt cutters he'd used to liberate Hardy's wrists from the handcuffs.

Not that his prints were on them.

Cops would be on his doorstep if they'd connected him.

Or maybe they were. His phone would remain off until he returned to his car.

No, there was no reason for the police to look closely at him, nor Bradley.

It had all fallen into place.

Only one obstacle remained.

Melanie Weaver.

She'd seen him at the restaurant.

How she'd survived the crash was a miracle. She should have died with her parents.

Inside the cottage, a phone rang.

He swung the rifle to his hands and kicked the door open.

The fireplace was dead. Soaking wet. Abel swore and worked his way through the cottage to Vince's bedroom.

Empty.

The back door slammed shut in the wind.

Rifle away again, he opened the can and poured accelerant over the bed.

FIFTY-FOUR

'Pick up, pick up.' Siren blaring, lights on, Liz sped through the outer suburbs. The phone was on redial to the cottage. Vince's mobile hadn't picked up either.

She slowed to go around traffic and the redial dropped out.

When her phone rang she stabbed the button. 'Vince?'

'Just Pete. Have you reached him?'

'No, god dammit.'

'I'll get there before you. Terry is on his way. Half the force is on its way.'

Abel Farrelly killed his own parents. That's what Pickering began to tell her.

'Can you get fire trucks out there? It'll be CFA where he lives.'

'And ambos. Will cover the lot.'

'CIRT won't get there before us. Just don't bloody get shot, Pete.'

He chuckled. 'Love you too.' He hung up.

She couldn't muster a smile. Too many hours had passed since Carla overheard the plan to kill Vince. All she could hope was Farrelly had waited until the conditions were optimum to attack.

I'm coming, Vince. Please be out of there.

She hit redial.

FIFTY-FIVE

Within seconds of exiting the cottage, Vince and Melanie's hair was plastered to their skulls. If he'd had another minute he'd have got her into a thick jacket. All they could do was run toward Apple's paddock.

Get to the driveway.

Reach Lyndall's house.

Borrow the rifle he knew Lyndall kept locked away.

Leave Melanie safe with her.

Find whoever was after them.

Stop them.

He'd left both the gates open after taking Apple to Lyndall's and collecting Melanie. They sprinted through the first gate into the paddock, Melanie's hand slipping from the rain. He had to hold tightly so she didn't fall at the pace he'd set. She didn't complain or look back or react to the storm which was directly above, thunder booming.

They came to a sudden halt at the second gate. Between the paddock and driveway, it was locked. A chain and padlock he'd never seen circled the post and gate.

'I'll boost you over. Hold onto the kitten.'

She gripped the front of the dressing gown as he lifted her up and over, setting her down with a groan. She was light but the angle was difficult.

'Come on, Grandad. Climb.'

'I will. But you go. Go now, run as fast as you can. Tell Lyndall I'm coming and need her rifle.'

'But I'm scared—'

'You are the bravest person I've ever met. Run, sweetie. *Run*.'

He would never forget the terror on her face as she staggered to the driveway. She wanted to wait; he could see it. She knew the angry man was coming and didn't want to leave Vince alone. Then she turned and was racing away into the night.

He stepped onto the lowest railing of the fence and pulled himself up. It was too hard and he slid back. Dragging the backpack off, he dropped it over the fence and started over. This time he got to the top and as he swung over onto the other side the sky lit up.

Not the sky.

That wasn't lightning.

'No, no, no!'

The cottage was on fire.

————

Abel tossed the can onto the bed and backed out as the flames made another whoosh.

It was beautiful... the power of the fire, the billowing smoke.

Things might not have gone the way he intended but that was why he had the rifle.

One old, unfit man and a little kid weren't getting far.

Probably still trying to unlock the gate.

The flames caught the flimsy curtains and that was his signal to leave. The weatherboards would take no time to follow suit and then this pile of shit would be ashes.

He couldn't help himself. He stepped into the kid's bedroom.

On her bedside table was a framed photograph of her with David and Susie. He took the photo out and slid it into a pocket. Nice to keep as a memory.

Outside he let the rain wash away the smell of the smoke from his skin as he scanned the property, waiting for lightning to show him where his prey were hiding. So many options.

Did they make a dash for the road? Unlikely with an ex-cop. He'd not want to risk running into his hunter and there was almost no cover between the front of the cottage and the road.

Were they hiding inside one of the sheds or under the lean-to? If they'd got to the gate he'd locked they might have sought cover. The old man was too fat to climb fences.

Even as he made his way to the pony's stall to check, a cry cut through the thunder.

'No. No. No!'

And there he was. Vince Carter, struggling his way up the driveway.

Excellent.

FIFTY-SIX

Move, Vince. Get to Lyndall. Get the gun.

His legs were lead.

His heart was stone.

A lifetime of memories was burning into nothing.

Vince stumbled, his heart jumping as he barely managed to keep on his feet. The ground was soggy and slippery. He moved to the very edge of the driveway where it was grass and just a bit firmer underfoot.

He sucked in air and forced himself to go faster, his muscles screaming abuse at their treatment. Visibility was low in the dark and the rain except those seconds of lightning. He had to avoid being seen yet try and pinpoint this madman.

Think it through.

Almost at the path leading to Susie's little orchard, Vince came to a halt, hard against a thick bush almost his height. From here the view of the driveway was unencumbered. He made himself to keep his attention on it but in his peripheral vision red and orange flames grew taller.

Melanie must be at Lyndall's, if not then very close. She'd

need to find a way to wake her from outside and with all the thunder what if Lyndall didn't hear her? This wasn't helpful. He slid off the backpack. It could be left here behind bushes. His phone vibrated. It was the first time he'd noticed. If he could call for help...

Zig-zagging across the sky, lightning hit something not far away with a loud crack. Just as fast, darkness fell again but Vince had seen the man jogging up the middle of the driveway, rifle in hand. Pickering's right-hand man.

Glancing at Lyndall's house, he estimated his chances of getting there before Farrelly caught him. He was almost within easy shooting range already.

I'd be leading him to Melanie and Lyndall.

If he stayed here out of sight, he might have the element of surprise. A quick look around offered no potential weapons. No loose branches or heavy rocks. The backpack might knock the man down if Vince swung hard enough but was unlikely to keep him down. Nevertheless, Vince picked it up.

Surely Lyndall would call the police immediately. Help would come. All he had to do was keep Farrelly away from the house until then.

I'll protect her Susie. I'll protect her with my life.

Vince ran to the path and when he reached it he waited.

With the next strike, Farrelly had closed the gap by half. Aware he was visible, Vince screamed in the direction of the orchard.

'Melanie! Come back.'

And with that, he tossed the backpack down and ran for his life.

———

'Hush, little one. We have to find Lyndall.'

Melanie was at the house, on the back deck. She had no idea how to find Lyndall and pounding on the front door only hurt her hand. Robbie was restless. Tears poured down her face and sobs caught in her throat, but she wasn't going to give up.

Grandad needed her to wake up Lyndall and ask for the rifle. He'd be here soon.

She tucked Robbie in a bit more. He was almost as wet as she was but it didn't matter. She had to keep him safe from the angry man.

The back door was a big sliding glass window. She'd been in and out of it a few times during the day, following Lyndall as far as the steps then retreating to the railing to watch her tend to the donkeys.

She tried to slide it open but there was a lock. She banged on the door. 'Lyndall! Lyndall, open the door!'

On the brickwork beside the lock was a button and she pushed it. A loud bell sounded, and she shrieked and jumped. Robbie clawed at her skin, and she began to cry in earnest. Her good hand went to his head to stroke him and he calmed down but she hurt and she was so very frightened.

The light came on above her and the door slid open.

'My poor little child...'

All of a sudden Melanie was lifted up into Lyndall's arms. The world spun around a bit and the door closed and clicked. They were inside.

'Melanie, what's happened?'

'Grandad...'

Now she was on a chair and Lyndall was kneeling in front of her, undoing her dressing gown. Robbie leapt out and tore away.

'Robbie.'

'He's fine. He'll go find his mamma so let's get you out of this wet thing.'

Melanie stood and helped.

'Darlin' you are soaked through. Where is Vince?'

'He was behind me. The angry man came. The angry man is after us.'

'I'm going to call the police. Come with me.' Lyndall took Melanie's hand and they ran to the kitchen. Melanie liked it in here with its big benches and windows looking down on the cottage but now, she screamed and pointed at the fire.

'Oh, my sweet lord, don't look there, Melly. Come here while I phone.'

Held against Lyndall's dressing gown which smelled of roses, Melanie tried to remember what Grandad needed. She was shivering and the tears didn't want to stop but Lyndall was talking to someone and saying their address and asking for police and fire trucks and ambulances.

'Listen to me, Melanie, everything will be fine. I'm going to take you to a special room I have where nobody, and I mean nobody will be able to find you. You will be able to see out and when you feel safe, there's a button I'll show you and you can press it to let the right people in.'

Again they were moving. Melanie looked everywhere but couldn't see Robbie.

'He'll be okay, I promise.'

'Lyndall, Grandad needs to borrow your rifle.'

They stopped outside a door. 'Is that right? Well, little miss, I'd better get you settled and make sure he gets what he needs.'

The door slid open and Melanie peeked in. There was a bed and a table and chairs and a sink and another door to a bathroom. A bookshelf was against one wall next to a refrigerator and there were three televisions on another wall.

'Let's quickly run through this and turn on the monitors then I'll go find your grandad.'

A moment later Lyndall kissed her and as she stepped out, Robbie and his mother and sibling bounded in. Scooping him up in relief, Melanie looked at the first screen. Lyndall was unlocking a high cupboard built into the wall across from this room. She pulled something long out. A rifle. And a small box. And then she was moving through the house. The next monitor showed her at the back door, throwing on her big coat and hat.

Once she went outside, Melanie couldn't find her on the last monitor, which showed some of the garden. She hugged Robbie. 'Let's find a towel for you.'

FIFTY-SEVEN

He'd not been along this path in years but his feet remembered the way. A narrow dirt track, almost overgrown with the soft, long grass which favoured this part of the property, followed a ridge for a hundred metres or so before veering away from the drop. There was a dip where trees began to offer some shelter, and then a rise.

For good measure, he called again, 'Melanie! Wait for me.'

If Farrelly wasn't on his heels he had no backup plan.

Vince's head spun from exertion and his legs were buckling. Every breath was gasped and painful. But he found the copse of a dozen grown trees—a far cry from the tiny saplings he'd planted with Susie so long ago.

Staggering to the closest one, he threw himself behind it, sucking in air. He had nothing left in the tank. Farrelly would find him and kill him, but he'd bought time for Melanie to get to safety. It was all that mattered. He'd kept her safe.

His hand pressed against the tree.

Susie planted this.

They'd spent endless hours up here, preparing the ground, planting, hauling water all the way.

'Look what we did, Daddy.'

Startled, he glanced around the trunk but there was nothing other than the other trees.

'One day these will feed and shelter us. Isn't that cool?'

I've lost the plot.

Sunlight streamed through the half-grown trees as fifteen-year-old Susie danced around them.

'Come and see this one. Look at the branch on the ground here. And where it fell from. Come on, Dad. Use your eyes.'

He followed her to the tree but when he reached out to touch her arm there was only the dark air.

At his feet, about the length of a baseball bat was a thick branch. And at his shoulder height, its jagged remains made a hook on the tree.

Vince ripped his jacket off and hung it.

He grabbed the branch and retreated into the night.

FIFTY-EIGHT

The storm was passing and the rain eased enough for other sounds to penetrate the night. Crackling and popping from the poor cottage. A distant siren. A snap as a twig was broken beneath a foot.

Vince held his breath and tightened his grip.

A shadow moved past his hiding place and stopped.

The ominous click-clack as the rifle was readied and then Farrelly raised it and fired at Vince's coat on the tree.

Branch in both hands, Vince swung with all his strength, hitting the back of Farrelly's head with a satisfying thwack. The man collapsed face down and the rifle flew from his grasp.

Are you dead?

He searched for the rifle in the grass where he thought it had fallen. Not there. He doubled back, eyes on the ground. Leaving it here wasn't an option.

'Now I have another reason to kill you.'

Vince spun. Farrelly was on his knees, rifle pointed, blood pouring down the sides of his head.

'And then I'll find the kid. And the neighbour for good measure.'

Sirens drew closer. Farrelly glanced in the direction for an instant and Vince threw himself toward the closest tree.

BANG.

Piercing pain.

His right leg wouldn't work, and he dropped to the ground, crying out in agony and despair. It was over. Farrelly was on his feet, walking toward Vince as he reloaded. It wasn't meant to end this way. Here, in Susie's orchard.

Police were close. He'd seen the cars hurtling up the driveway. Melanie would be safe.

I protected her, Susie.

Farrelly raised the rifle and aimed directly at Vince.

BANG.

BANG.

Mouth open in shock, Farrelly sank to the ground clutching his chest.

It didn't make sense. *He* was shot, not the killer. But there was no life in the other man's eyes.

The world went silent.

FIFTY-NINE

Dark... cold... death...

His eyelids were too heavy to open.

'Where's the ambulance? Can't you get them here faster?'

'It's Lyndall, right? Look, he's a tough old bastard. Probably not even really hurt and just lying there looking for attention.'

'Why did I have to do your job for you, officer?'

'You didn't. We both did my job. And call me Pete.'

A gentle hand touched Vince's face. 'Give me your jacket, Pete.'

'He really doesn't need it... okay, okay.'

The jacket smelled like junk food. But its warmth seeped into Vince's body. The voices were a dream. Some afterlife joke where McNamara would haunt him forever.

'Vince! Oh my god, Vince...'

Why is Liz here too?

More importantly, why was she crying?

This time his eyes opened, straight into hers. 'Hey, Lizzie. Don't cry for me.'

'Thank God. And I'm not crying.' She wiped her eyes with the back of her hand. 'Where are you hurt?'

'He was shot in the right leg, Liz. Think it went through.' Now Lyndall's face loomed beside Liz's. 'Bit of patching up and he'll be right as rain.'

'I will.' He pushed himself up onto an elbow and pain coursed up his leg, more an intense throb than the sharpness of the bullet. 'Farrelly dead?'

'Sure is.' Pete wandered into his line of sight carrying three rifles. 'Two big holes in his chest. And a whack on the back of his head. Was a dead man walking, I reckon.'

'Two holes?'

Lyndall shrugged.

'Where's Melanie. Did she find you? Is she—'

'Quite safe. She's a brave young lady who is probably drying herself off as well as that kitten of hers. I'm going back to her now. We'll meet you at the hospital a bit later once you look presentable and don't scare the poor child.'

Paramedics approached and Liz stood. 'Will you be alright without me for a bit?'

'Why are you leaving me alone with McNamara?'

'Nice.' McNamara scoffed.

'I need to get a statement from Lyndall, and I think it will reassure Melanie to have another familiar face. And before you ask any more questions, I'm going to have to sprint to catch up with Lyndall.'

I know that feeling.

It was just him and McNamara and the body. Smoke settled around them.

'Fireys are working hard to save what they can. Wouldn't mind my jacket back, Vince. Getting cold.'

'Help yourself. It smells disgusting.'

'Ta. You can thank me later.' For the first time in years,

McNamara's face showed no mockery or hatred toward Vince. He squatted nearby, careful with the rifles. 'You saved Melanie's life. No doubt about it.'

Taking the jacket with him, he straightened with a broad smile. 'And I was one of the two people who saved your sorry ass. Gonna regret it for a long time.'

SIXTY

Vince was asleep when Liz visited. He'd had surgery within hours of arriving at hospital and had been resting comfortably, according to the person she'd managed to speak to. She'd slept for half the day herself, exhausted on a level she rarely reached. After a couple of hours at the station, she'd had to come to see for herself he was alright. She'd made the right decision, going to Melanie first that night. Hadn't she?

'Why so worried, Lizzie?'

His eyes were on her, and she smiled and sat beside the bed. 'How are you doing?'

'Better than you. Did someone die? I have some pleasant painkillers and am alive.'

'And you wonder why I worry?' She took his hand. 'I thought we'd get there too late and when I arrived and saw the cottage... and I am so sorry about it. And then you lying there...'

He squeezed her fingers. 'But you must have seen Lyndall and the shithead and neither of them were crying. Surely you could tell I was fixable.'

'That shithead saved your life. Him and Lyndall.'

'Yeah... well Pete and I made our peace. For now.'

'Thank God for that.'

'What happened, Liz?'

She released his hand and leaned back. 'Short version? Farrelly had you lined up with a kill shot. You were already down from the shot in the leg and unable to find cover. There was no time to negotiate with the creep, so he got a couple of bullet holes into his chest.'

'Yeah. I get that bit. But Pete had three rifles. Farrelly's and his I recognised but the other one... oh. Lyndall?'

'Got it in one. Pete says she shot first but he won't put that in a statement in case it comes back to bite her. And he reckons she was a long way from Farrelly, up the hill. She shot, unloaded the rifle, and handed it to him without a word.'

There's a story there with Lyndall. People don't become expert marksmen without some special training.

'Is Melanie alright?' Vince grunted as he pushed himself into a more upright position. 'She was unbelievable, Lizzie. Did everything I said and more despite being terrified.'

She couldn't help the small smile. 'I got a lot of hugs, that's for sure. But once she knew you were going to be okay all she cared about was the cottage. Not for her own things she'd just lost but for you. For your photographs and carved birds and because it was Susie's home.'

Vince looked away, blinking rapidly.

'We recovered your backpack and everything is dry inside. Nothing broken. Would you like me to bring it to you?'

He nodded, still not meeting her eyes.

She glanced around and spotted a jug of water. 'You need to stay hydrated. Any idea how long you'll be here?' She poured him a glass and took it to him.

'Um, thanks. Not long.'

'You and Melanie are welcome to stay with me if it helps.'

Now, he grinned. 'Unless you have moved recently, I am not sure where we would fit.'

True. Her flat had one bedroom and one bathroom and was up three flights of stairs.

'Actually, scrap that. The elevator hasn't worked in weeks, and I doubt you feel up to climbing those stairs with crutches.'

'You need to report the landlord. In fact, you need to move to something nicer.'

They'd had that conversation before and he was right, but she didn't have time to look for another home. And had her own reasons to stay there.

'Did you know Lyndall has a panic room?'

His eyes widened. 'I did not.'

'Melanie told me all about it. Bed, bathroom, lots of food and water. Monitors which let her see who was outside the room. She thought it was, quote, very cool. So, at some stage, I'd love to have a chat about your neighbour.'

'Maybe.' He looked at Liz and his face brightened. 'They're here!'

Liz kissed his cheek. 'Behave yourself and phone if you need me. I'll get the backpack to you a bit later.'

'Grandad!' A blur of child rushed past.

Liz passed Lyndall near the door. The other woman gripped her hands and although she said nothing, there was warmth and gratitude in her eyes.

'He'll be pleased you're here.'

With a nod, Lyndall released her hands and stepped inside.

When her phone buzzed a message, Liz stopped outside the window to read it. When she glanced into the room, all she could see was love and relief from all three of them.

SIXTY-ONE

Vince was getting good with the crutches and had no trouble navigating his way to Terry's office.

A few heads rose from their work as he passed and there were murmurs of 'Hey Vince' and 'Good to see you.' Big difference from the day he'd burst into the office a few weeks ago.

Terry got to his feet and pulled out a chair for Vince. 'Coffee?'

'First someone tries to shoot me, now you offer me poison?'

'Fair call.' Terry laughed and returned to his seat 'Heard you and Melanie are staying with your neighbour.'

'Yeah. Just for a bit while I work out the insurance and crap for the cottage. We could go to Susie's house but the steps will defeat me until I'm off these. No idea yet whether I use this as a chance to move, you know, closer to Melanie's old life.'

'What does Melanie say?'

'She has drawn me a series of pictures of what our new cottage should be like once we build it.'

'I see.'

Liz stuck her head in. 'Well, look at you!'

'Join us, Liz.' Terry nodded to another chair. 'Do you want to update Vince on our investigation?'

'Love to. We've established that Farrelly was responsible for the deaths of Ginny and of Marco. Roscoe has been helpful, once he knew his career was gone and his only chance of avoiding a long jail term was co-operation. Farrelly bullied Roscoe from the time he moved into the Roscoe home at fifteen, to the point of getting him to do his own dirty work. He tracked Roscoe down a few years ago and began a long-term plan to build his wealth.'

'Using PickerPak to move criminals?' Vince asked.

'That was the latest thing. Pickering still won't admit to much, but we've pieced together—thanks to what you also provided—that David got wind of this new direction and when he tried to sell his share, was threatened by Farrelly to the point where he feared for his family.'

If only I'd been there for him.

'He was trying to get out without drawing attention to his plans. When it came down to signing that freight contract he dug his heels in.' Liz shook her head. 'I guess Farrelly saw him as an obstacle.'

'Do you have evidence Farrelly drove the van. Or was it Pickering?' Gut churning, Vince's hands curled into fists. 'Easy to lie now with Farrelly dead.'

Liz reached across, dropping her hand over one of his for a moment.

'It was Farrelly. Forensic evidence puts him at the scene of the accident thanks to his filthy habit of tossing half-smoked cigarettes away. Pickering knew but I can't prove it yet.'

The churning stopped. It was over. Truly over.

'Carla?'

Terry grinned. 'She can't stop talking. She's gutted by his actions, and she had access to all of Pickering's accounts and hidden data, just didn't know it existed but the moron only used one password which she guessed.'

'She won't be charged with anything,' Liz said. 'I believe she is innocent of any part of Pickering's activities, and she blames herself for the crash. We don't know where Pickering kept disappearing off to, but we'll find out. But Vince? She wants to see you. To ask if Melanie can still be in her life.'

'That's for Melanie to decide. Later. Once the dust settles. Melanie has a lot more to deal with now and all I can say is thank goodness for Doctor Raju.' He straightened the crutches. 'Now, if you will excuse me, I have a dinner date with my grandchild.'

———

'Can you find that grandchild of yours and let her know dinner is almost ready?' Lyndall called from the kitchen. Whatever she had cooking in there had Vince's stomach rumbling. He rubbed his gut. Too many more of Lyndall's meals, not to mention the treats she and Melanie made, and he'd need to take up running.

Once this leg works again.

Last seen, Melanie was on the back deck, playing with Robbie in the late afternoon sun. But neither of them were here and she hadn't come past him inside.

He carefully went down the few steps to the garden. She loved the expansive vegetable garden near the paddocks but wasn't in there either.

'Mel?'

Where else would she be? His heart thudded as he headed back toward the house, veering onto the path to go faster with the crutches. It wasn't like her to go any distance from the house without him or Lyndall.

There wasn't a lot of light left.

I need to get Lyndall and some torches.

A welcoming whinny from Apple came from the nearest paddock.

There was no chance she was greeting Melanie, who still refused to get within metres of her. Unless Robbie had run down there. He moved onto the grass and made his way past the garden beds, struggling with the crutches on the soft ground.

He was ready to call out again but then he saw Apple at the fence, and he stopped.

Melanie was only a couple of feet from the fence, Robbie perched on her plastered arm, peeking out from the sling. Typically friendly, Apple shoved her head over the gate, lips flapping as she investigated, but Melanie was just out of reach.

Apple's head went up and down a few times and then she settled, dropping her neck a bit to lower her head. Melanie extended her hand... and stroked Apple's forelock.

'Oooh...' Vince covered his mouth as the hairs on his arms stood up.

With a happy nicker, Apple pushed against the fence to give herself more of a chance to reach Melanie's pant pockets.

Mel giggled. 'No, I don't have any treats.'

I'm not going to cry. I'm not.

Everything got blurry when Melanie lifted the kitten up to show Apple. Robbie batted the pony's muzzle and Apple snorted, giving Melanie a fit of giggles.

Vince lifted his face to the sky and mouthed 'thank you.'

———

The washing up was done. Melanie had collected her new art book and pencils and with Robbie close by, sat at her favourite spot in the kitchen

Lyndall poured two glasses of whiskey and joined Vince in the living room, which let him keep half an eye on Melanie but from a more comfortable seat. 'Thanks,' he said. 'And for another lovely dinner.'

'My pleasure. I like the company. Didn't think I would after so long.' Lyndall took a small sip from her glass, her eyes on Melanie. 'She breathes new life into me.'

'And me.'

'Sure does.' Now, Lyndall was watching him with a small smile. 'Get the feeling some of the burden is gone. Never understood why you carried all that blame but we all have our baggage.'

Melanie giggled at something she'd drawn, showing it to the kitten before turning to a fresh page.

'I have no way to repay what you did for her. Keeping her safe that night.' Vince looked at Lyndall. 'And saving my life.'

'She was easy to protect. Perfect excuse to try out that room I had built. You? Thought I was too late. But we got there in the end.' Lyndall's eyes narrowed. 'What do you want to ask? I can see it on your face. Is it my world-class shooting or my panic room?'

'Both. We've lived side by side for decades but I have to wonder if you are a retired assassin or the like.'

She laughed shortly. 'Nothing so exciting. I'll tell you the whole story one day but for now, let's just say I understand about evil people with agendas. I know what losing your loved ones is like and having to leave your real life behind.'

Vince followed her gaze to one of the original paintings on the wall. He'd known she was talented and remembered Melanie talking about Lyndall being a famous artist. Did Marion know her story? There was so much he suddenly wanted to ask.

But her expression said otherwise, and she held the glass tightly.

He wouldn't press her for answers.

'Can we visit Mummy and Daddy soon, please?' Melanie

plonked herself onto the seat beside Lyndall, who dropped an arm over the little girl's shoulders.

'Let me get this leg sorted—'

'No need to wait,' Lyndall said. 'Happy to drive you both. Wouldn't mind visiting the place myself.'

———

Brilliant sunshine warmed Vince's face and for the first time in so long, he felt really alive. It was odd to be here, at his daughter's grave, and have hope in his heart. But she'd have been happy for him. Proud of him.

Melanie was chatting away to the headstone, telling Susie about Robbie and how much she liked her bedroom in Lyndall's house where she could see the donkeys and Apple in their paddocks. Then she talked about her new school, where she'd just started the term.

'I miss my old school, Mummy, but I've already made two friends who live just up the road from Grandad's. And they have bikes, so I need to learn to ride but Grandad says your old bike is a bit rusty so I'm getting a bike soon as well...' She glanced up at Vince with a wide smile. 'May I get one?'

'You have a birthday soon, so let's put one on your wish list.'

She gave a small squeal and then went back to her conversation.

He laid flowers on Susie's grave and then more on David's. He touched David's headstone. 'They've been stopped. I'm just sorry it took so long.'

After a while he and Melanie wandered further to another, much older grave.

'Oh, hi Grandma!'

'Mel?'

'Mummy and I came here all the time to talk to Grandma. I'll be right back.' She dashed off in the direction they'd come from.

'Of course you both did.' He didn't know what to say to Marion's resting place. She'd never left his heart in all these years but now he'd let go of the guilt. In its place was a calmness which brought colour back into his life. That and Melanie.

'Here we go!'

She returned with one of the lilies from Susie's grave and ever so gently rested it near the headstone. She whispered something then came and took Vince's hand.

'Thank you, sweetie. For the flower.'

'Mummy doesn't mind sharing. And I told Grandma that I'm going to take care of you because you take such good care of me.'

'We'll take care of each other, Melly-belly. Always.'

You've taught me how to breathe again, little one. I will live up to your trust and love every single day.

They'd lost so much.

In the distance, Lyndall straightened after placing flowers on a grave.

She'd once told him she didn't go to funerals yet here she was. Perhaps Melanie had given her hope as well.

'Come on, Grandad. I think Lyndall is ready to go home. And Robbie will be happy to see us. Even Apple. Maybe. And I want to draw some more because I'm going to be a famous artist one day.'

'You can be anything you choose.'

The smile Melanie gave him filled Vince's heart with warmth. 'So can you, Grandad. Grandma wants you to have joy in your life.'

As Lyndall approached, their eyes met. Each with their own deep-seated sorrow. And just possibly, a touch of new-found hope.

NEXT IN THE SERIES

A little girl is missing.
Is a serial kidnapper responsible?

Homicide Detective Sergeant Liz Moorland has seen this before. Another child, ten years ago. Same colour hair and eyes. Same sweet smile. And the same park. They never found her.

Liz has a connection to both disappearances and is convinced they are linked. But if she's to find *this* child she has to keep her head. And with the chance of being removed from what is the most important case of her life, Liz can't make a mistake.

Even if it means risking her career. And her life.

ABOUT THE AUTHOR

Phillipa lives just outside a beautiful town in country Victoria, Australia. She also lives in the many worlds of her imagination and stockpiles stories beside her laptop.

She writes from the heart about love, dreams, secrets, discovery, the sea, the world as she knows it... or wishes it could be. She loves happy endings, heart-pounding suspense, and characters who stay with you long after the final page.

With a passion for music, the ocean, animals, nature, reading, and writing, she is often found in the vegetable garden pondering a new story.

Phillipa's website is www.phillipaclark.com

Free short book when you join Phillipa's monthly newsletter (book chat, pets, gardens, puzzles, first-looks and competitions).

ALSO BY PHILLIPA NEFRI CLARK

Detective Liz Moorland - Melbourne Major Crimes

Rivers End Mystery Romances

Charlotte Dean Mysteries

Daphne Jones Mysteries

Bindarra Creek Rural Fiction

Maple Gardens Matchmakers

Doctor Grok's Peculiar Shop

Simple Words for Troubled Times
(Short non-fiction happiness and comfort book)

Prefer Audiobooks?

The Stationmaster's Cottage

Jasmine Sea

The Secrets of Palmerston House

Last Known Contact

Simple Words for Troubled Times

Till Daph Do Us Part

Lest We Forgive

ACKNOWLEDGMENTS

All books are far more than the author's imagination, research, and story. Lest We Forgive began life as a screenplay many years ago and needed a lot of work to rewrite as a novel.

Brilliant editor and bestselling author Louise Guy was my mentor, coach, and editor all rolled into one. I am deeply grateful for her belief in me and this story.

The stunning cover is again one from Steam Power Studios who have created so many for me.

I must acknowledge the one and only John Wood who took a chance on me to narrate the audiobook at the amazing Square-Sound Studios in Melbourne.

To my superstar ARC team - thank you! What a fantastic group of readers and I am so lucky to have you all. And to every person who contributed, encouraged, and cheered from the sidelines, my sincere appreciation.

Printed in Great Britain
by Amazon